Jan Butlin ... and television, including successful series such as *Life Begins at Forty*, *No Strings*, *That Beryl Marston* and *Third Time Lucky*, but *Grace* was her first novel and was warmly praised:

'The ingredients for turning her novel into a runaway bestseller are all there: passion, tragedy and sex wrapped up in a gritty rags to riches saga' *Sunday Express*.

Jan is married to broadcaster Martin King. They now live in Covent Garden but Jan knows and loves the beautiful East Anglian countryside in which this novel is set.

Also by Jan Butlin

Grace

The Legacy

Jan Butlin

HEADLINE

First published in 1993
by HEADLINE BOOK PUBLISHING PLC

First published in paperback in 1993
by HEADLINE BOOK PUBLISHING PLC

10 9 8 7 6 5 4 3 2 1

ISBN 0 7472 4145 7

Typeset by
Letterpart Limited, Reigate, Surrey

Printed and bound in Great Britain by
HarperCollins Manufacturing, Glasgow

HEADLINE BOOK PUBLISHING PLC
Headline House
79 Great Titchfield Street
London W1P 7FN

For my friend and sister, Peggy,
with love and gratitude.
For Martin, as always.
And for the 'Mysterious ones and proud'.
They know who they are.

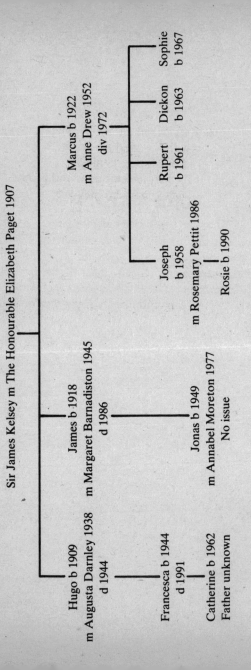

Sir James Kelsey m The Honourable Elizabeth Paget 1907

Hugo b 1909
m Augusta Darnley 1938
d 1944

Francesca b 1944
d 1991

Catherine b 1962
Father unknown

James b 1918
m Margaret Barnadiston 1945
d 1986

Jonas b 1949
m Annabel Moreton 1977
No issue

Marcus b 1922
m Anne Drew 1952
div 1972

Joseph
b 1958
m Rosemary Pettit 1986

Rosie b 1990

Rupert
b 1961

Dickon
b 1963

Sophie
b 1967

PREFACE

"Thou are the Great Cat, the avenger of the Gods, and the judge of words and the president of the sovereign chiefs and the governor of the holy circle. Thou art indeed . . . the Great Cat."

Inscription on a royal tomb at Thebes

← TO BUILDON AND COLCHESTER

ALL SAINTS AND SAINT NICHOLAS

THE OLD RECTORY — HOME TO
JONAS AND ANNABEL KELSEY.

THE GREEN
SOMERTON MAGNA

KNIGHTS CROFT — HOME TO HARRIET
1620 - 1674.

NOW TO MARCUS KELSEY, SOPHIE
RUPERT AND DICKON.

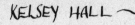

KELSEY HALL ~ HOME TO JESSLYN,
LADY KELSEY
1666-1682

NOW TO CATHERINE KELSEY.

TO THE GLASS MUSEUM AND THE SEA.

GIFFORDS.
HOME TO SIR EDWARD GIFFORD
AND JESSLYN
1650-1658
TO JOHN PIERRE 1662-1682
NOW TO BRETT FITZGERALD.

Artist: Martin King

CHAPTER ONE

THE CAT

'Friend of my toil, companion of my ease
Thine is the lore of Ra and Rameses;
That men forgot thou dost remember well'
                                    – Graham R. Tomson

CATHERINE: 1991

'What beckoning ghost along the moonlight shade
Invites my steps, and points to yonder glade?'
                                        – Alexander Pope

Terror holds me. I am being pursued. Hunted. A stone strikes my brow. Another splits the skin on my cheek. They are gaining on me now. But still I run.

I can see the dark, austere figure of Parson Hodge standing quietly on the edge of the green. For a brief desperate moment I think of begging his protection but his God is a God of Vengeance, not of Pity or Love.

Then a new cry is taken up: 'Brand her! Brand the sinner.' I can smell my flesh burning. I can feel the pain as they hold me down and the letter 'S' is seared into my forehead.

I try to scream but have no breath. My eyes are bleared by sweat and tears. My chest bursts with the effort of keeping ahead of the pack at my heels. I am young and healthy but my body is burdened by my unborn child. The cause of my shame.

Hoof beats are behind me now. I am lost. I am being ridden down. I cry out for my mother . . . but my mother is dead. Nothing can save us now. My child and I will . . . I can run no more . . . But I will have my revenge.

A paw gently touched my face and I opened my eyes.

Cat was sitting on the edge of my bed, regarding me gravely. I reached out and stroked his jet black, silky head.

'Oh, Cat,' I whispered, 'it was a dream. I was caught up in a terrible dream.' Cat's amber eyes searched mine. 'Why revenge, Cat? Why were my thoughts of revenge as I woke?'

I, of all people, had no cause for vengeance. But the feeling had been so real, so intense, that it had seemed part of me. I felt disturbed. Frightened even. The terror I'd felt in my dream held me still. Why? It had been a dream. Only a dream.

I shivered, then reached out and rubbed the black cat behind his ears. 'A goose walked over my grave, Cat!' He stretched out and rubbed his head against my cheek. The gesture was comforting and I started to relax. To push the dream from my mind. The cat circled as they do before settling down, then curled up against my body. Somewhere in the garden an owl hooted. Then silence. A gentle purr from Cat was now the only sound on the cool night air. I closed my eyes. Cat was with me and I was safe. I slowly drifted into a calm and mercifully dreamless sleep. As my eyelids closed Cat turned his head and a shaft of moonlight fell across him. I had the strangest sensation that he was watching over me . . .

I am Egypt. I am Mystery. I am Cat. I have lived many times. I have been worshipped. I have been outcast. Look into my eyes and know the wisdom of the ancient world. Humans have loved me. Humans have betrayed me. Since Egypt I have only cared for two mortals. Once was more than three hundred years ago.

Her name was Jesslyn. The second time is Catherine and I look over her because she is in danger. Grave danger.

'Jessyln! Jessyln!' I awoke with a start. Someone was calling my name . . . No, not my name. My name is Catherine.

Jesslyn . . . I had heard it so clearly but knew no one called Jesslyn. I was suddenly fearful. Had somebody broken into the old house? Common sense prevailed. An intruder was hardly likely to draw attention to his presence by running through the house calling out a name.

I glanced at my watch: 6.30 am. Old habits die hard. Until my mother's death three months ago I'd always risen at this time. To give her the drugs she needed to kill the pain. To help her wash. To make her comfortable and to help her apply the make up which she still insisted on putting on her poor wasted face. And what broke my heart throughout this daily routine, what made me love that foolish, delightful woman, was that she was so relentlessly cheerful. I forgave her everything in those last months. The selfishness. The occasional flashes of spite. The bitchiness.

We both played out the grand lie that she would get better. That her agent would send her a script with a part that was just right for her. That, yet again, she would make another come-back. Francesca Kelsey, cocaine addict, drunk, great beauty and former star, had been my mother. And I'd loved her desperately.

After propping her up against pillows encased in pure Irish linen slips trimmed with Brussels lace, a legacy from palmier days, I'd get our breakfast. Fish for Cat – for a stray he has very fastidious ideas about his diet – tea and a piece of toast for me, black coffee and freshly squeezed orange juice strongly laced with vodka for my mother. What in God's name had been the point of trying to change her then?

Until my mother became totally bedridden I'd worked for a firm of commodity brokers in the City as a filing clerk. Not the most distinguished of jobs, but then what other occupations are open to a twenty-nine-year-old spinster who can only fill in an application form – 'Previous Experience: My Mother's Keeper'?

I'd tried to break away, to make a life of my own. But whatever I did, wherever I went, the phone calls followed me. A harassed agent would call to say that my mother couldn't learn her lines without me. An anxious dresser would phone to say that the stage management had called the half – thirty-five minutes to curtain up – and my mother was very emotional (a euphemism for dead drunk) and calling for me. Always I'd go back. And it wasn't so much of a sacrifice. In a grey world, how many people can say they have been touched by magic? I've stood in the wings and watched my mother hold a thousand people spellbound. You could be burnt by the fire of my mother's charm but you could never regret knowing her.

I pulled back the bedclothes and virtually jumped from the bed to the floor. I'd slept that night in my grandfather's heavily carved oak four-poster and the mattress was a good two foot higher than any I'd known before.

Cat stretched and yawned. I stroked him and said, 'Come on, Sleepy! You're a country cat now!' His response was to curl himself into a tight little ball, one paw over his nose.

'Cat' might seem a cold name for a delightful animal. He had come into our lives one freezing November night when I had been thoroughly wet and disgruntled, the District Line from the City to Richmond having been plagued with more than the usual number of cancellations. My mother and I had a small apartment in a dingy building backing on to the railway sidings at Richmond. Not for us the magnificent green, the Theatre Royal, the wide walks beside the Thames. But my mother was adamant: 'It might stink, but at least it's a good address!'

I was just fumbling with my keys when I felt something brush against my legs. By the time I'd got the front door open, Cat was inside and streaking ahead of me to the gas fire in the sitting room.

The extraordinary thing about him was that he never fell under my mother's spell. He was always *my* cat. My mother, who was used to all creatures great and small being drawn to her, was amused and intrigued by his aloofness. And, although I enquired in the neighbourhood if anyone had lost a cat, the stray had obviously adopted us, and my mother started to call him, half affectionately, half mockingly 'That Cat'. In time this was abbreviated simply to 'Cat'. As I got to know him better, I felt it would have been presumptuous to call him 'Tiddles' or 'Blacky' or, Heaven forbid, 'Puss'. Because of his coal black coat, his pointed face and his handsome ears I'd once been tempted to call him 'Ra' after the Ancient Egyptian sun god who turned himself into a cat, but it was just a passing fancy.

The oak floorboards I crossed to reach my dressing gown had a patina on them that was beyond time. I stooped and stroked them with my hand. I'd never known such a sense of belonging . . . never known the richness of family possessions and tradition.

As I reached for my dressing gown I caught sight of myself in a cheval mirror. I turned and confronted my image. I was tall and raw-boned. My hair was thick and glossy but dangerously near that damning description 'mouse'. To me, my eyes looked too large in my thin, high cheek-boned face. My hands and feet were slender but large. Next to my exquisite, delicately boned mother I'd always felt like an elephant. I bowed to my image in the mirror.

'Catherine Kelsey, Lady of the Manor of Somerton Magna in the ancient Hundred of Dengie . . . Part of the Kingdom of the Angles . . . Bastard heiress to all you survey . . . You have come home!'

I bathed in the vast, chilly bathroom which was next to my grandfather's room . . . I'd have to stop thinking of everything as my grandfather's. The house was mine now. I'd gathered from Mr Pritchard, the solicitor, that my inheritance was considerable.

The sun streaming through the windows held promise of a beautiful day but still I shivered as I clambered into the large Victorian bath with its mahogany-panelled surround. I vowed that as soon as I was in full charge of my estate, extra radiators would be installed. If the room was like this in summer, what would it be like in winter when the cold winds blew across the low-lying meadows from the North Sea?

I lay back in the piping hot water – clearly there were

some modern conveniences at Kelsey Hall – and reflected on the incredible change in my fortunes that had brought me here.

When my mother was mortally ill I'd tried to persuade her to a reconciliation with my grandfather, but she would have none of it. 'That old bastard threw me out when he found out I was pregnant. We said terrible things to each other. There's no going back.'

I'd even taken it upon myself to write to my grandfather to tell him of my mother's illness but had received no reply. Eight weeks after I'd buried my mother I'd happened to pick up a copy of *The Times* that someone had left on the underground and had read my grandfather's obituary. From it I learnt that he had been born in 1909. His wife had died giving birth to his only child, Francesca, in 1944. She, a popular screen and stage actress in the sixties and seventies, had predeceased him. He had a granddaughter, Catherine. I read of his distinguished war record. The international reputation of the Kelsey Glassworks, which specialized in the manufacture of exceptionally fine lead crystal. And that his younger brother, James, had inherited the title.

I had thought no more about it. I was too busy trying to find a job. Trying to face building a new life out of my mother's shadow. It wasn't easy because I missed her desperately and our small, miserable apartment was still so full of memories.

In the evenings Cat and I would huddle by the gas fire, turned down as low as possible to save money, and I would go through all the old programmes, the press cuttings, the publicity hand-outs. Her star had shone so brightly when I was younger. Then we lived in plush hotel suites, expensive rented houses in London, New York and Los Angeles. But it couldn't last. The tantrums, the drink and drugs, the cures, the unsuitable lovers, the missed performances in the theatre and the lateness on set at the studios, all took their toll. By the beginning of the eighties my mother's career was on a downward spiral.

Then a miracle: Duncan Weldon of Triumph Productions asked her to join the cast of an all-star revival of Wilde's *Lady Windermere's Fan*. A decade earlier she would have been asked to play Mrs Erlynne. Now she was offered the smaller part of the Duchess of Berwick, but set London alight with her performance. She timed Wilde's lines to perfection. She wore the elegant Edwardian clothes exquisitely. She enchanted. She shone. And, once again, the world was at her feet. Then the cruellest blow of all. After a routine check-up for insurance for a film role, she was diagnosed as having terminal cancer.

I'd never loved her so much nor admired her so greatly as the evening she told me. In spite of the mountain of unpaid debts she'd insisted on renting an apartment in Mayfair for the run of the play at the Haymarket and, although that had just finished, we still lived there, the move to the dingy rooms in Richmond a few weeks away. I had a temporary job in an Oxford Street department store during the Sales. I came home exhausted, with aching feet and a mind numbed by the clamour of women searching for a bargain. As I entered the apartment I was assailed by wondrous smells coming from the kitchen – this in itself was astonishing as my mother rarely cooked – and the sound of Sondheim's marvellous song from *Follies*, that anthem to survivors 'I'm Still Here', playing on the music centre. My mother's delightful, husky voice joined Nancy Walker who was singing on the tape.

I laughed, hung up my coat in the hall and went into the small, elegant drawing room with its pretty dining alcove. I stopped as I entered the room. It was totally lit by candles and somehow my mother had cajoled the porter into finding fuel to light a fire in the Georgian grate. The dining table was set and a bottle of champagne was cooling in a bucket.

'Fran!' I said, delighted. 'Don't tell me! Spielberg called!'

She laughed and moved quickly over to me, taking my hands. 'Something like that, darling. Oh, Catherine, you look exhausted. Come and sit down and I'll pour you a glass of champagne.'

I sank gratefully into the armchair by the fire. I knew all would be revealed in time. I was used to my mother's swings of mood but I'd never known her go to so much trouble to entertain just me. So I relaxed and let her make a fuss of me. It felt good.

We sat either side of the fire and sipped an exquisite Pol Roger. After a moment I asked, 'Well, are you going to tell me what this is all about?'

'After supper, my pet. I've raided Fortnum's and Harrod's Food Halls. I want this to be something for you to remember.'

And so it was! We dined on a salad of warm quail's eggs on a bed of endive. Then grilled guinea fowl with limes served with tiny new potatoes and watercress purée. And, as if that wasn't enough, a wild strawberry soufflé to follow.

Afterwards I started to clear away but my mother would have none of it. 'Let's take a leaf from Scarlett O'Hara's book and think about the washing up tomorrow. Come and sit by the fire again and we'll have a brandy.'

She crossed to the music centre and within moments the room was filled with the wistful music of Erik Satie. He was one of my favourite composers and I was touched that my mother should have remembered that. As she poured us our brandy I glanced across at the bottle. 'A Napoleon cognac? Fran, something *has* happened. We can't possibly afford all this!'

'Shh! Tomorrow. We'll think about it tomorrow.'

We sipped our brandy in companionable silence. Then my mother crossed and knelt by me. She took my hand.

'Poor Catherine. I've been a cow of a mother, haven't I?' She raised her free hand. 'No. Don't answer that. Because knowing you, dear girl, you'll deny it. But it's true. I've kept you with me instead of allowing you to make your own life. Finding someone to love and perhaps marry. I just wish I had the time to make it up to you . . . because I would, my darling, I would! I know how much I've hurt you. By neglect. By selfishness. By simply not being there when you needed me. And now, when I've looked into my heart and recognized that you're the only damn thing in my life that's any good . . . the only person I've ever truly loved . . . it's too late. Oh, damn. I'm not going to cry. I'm not!'

I put down my brandy and hugged her to me. '*Fran!*

Fran, dear, there's no need for tears between you and me. And no more nonsense about not being a good mother. You're the only mother I've got and I love you!' I laughed suddenly. 'Okay, so you missed most of my Sports Days. And you dropped your hip-flask at the Bishop's feet during my Confirmation. But you should've seen some of the mothers who *did* turn up at school.'

I took her face in my hands. 'None of them wore shocking pink. None of them had the guts to do what you did: to bring up a child by themselves. You were only eighteen when I was born. You could've had me aborted . . . adopted . . . but you didn't! It hasn't been a conventional life, it hasn't been an easy life, but it's been rich and I wouldn't change it for the world. So come on. Let's raise our glasses and drink to the Two Musketeers. To our future – yours and mine!'

My mother raised her glass and said, 'To *your* future, Catherine.'

She rose and crossed to the mantelpiece, she stood for a moment staring into the flames then turned to me. 'I don't know how to say this except baldly. Quite simply, I don't have a future, Catherine. Six to nine months at the most.'

A scratching at the bathroom door brought me back to the present. 'All right, Cat,' I called out. 'Breakfast is on its way. If I can ever find the kitchen again, that is!'

Cat and I had driven down to Kelsey Hall late afternoon the previous day in chauffeured splendour, Mr Pritchard having arranged for the hired Rolls. I'd brought with me my mother's press cuttings and photographs, a battered old suitcase containing the most presentable of my clothes, Cat's litter tray and a packet of frozen cod from the supermarket. It says much for the chauffeur's training that he didn't bat an eyelid at the motley collection.

At the present there were no live-in staff at the Hall. The elderly couple who'd looked after my grandfather had retired on the handsome legacy he'd left them. Arrangements had been made for a cook, a housekeeper and a number of cleaners to come in daily until I'd decided what I wanted to do about staffing the beautiful old house.

Kelsey Hall was by no means a stately home, but even so it was large enough for me to get lost in. Its history was well chronicled and Mr Pritchard had lent me a number of books so that I could familiarize myself with my inheritance. A Sir Geoffreye Kelsey had grown rich through the wool trade and had pulled down the old fortified manor house which had formerly stood there early in the reign of Henry VIII and overseen the building of the present building. All that remained of the old manor was the gatehouse which still stood, although nowadays the moat was bridged by a structure rather more practical than the drawbridge shown in old illustrations.

The house that Sir Geoffreye built is timber-framed with brick infilling. As Cat and I were driven through the gatehouse, late-afternoon sunlight was reflected from the mullioned windows and the beauty of the Hall took my breath away. It had seemed to me then incomprehensible that my grandfather should have made me his heir. There had been no contact between my mother and myself and the rest of her family for twenty-nine years. And now, after all that time, although my great-uncle had inherited the baronetcy, as the estate was not entailed, everything my grandfather had possessed was mine.

'Why?' I had asked Mr Pritchard. 'Why? It doesn't make any sense!'

He handed me a thick file from his briefcase. As I looked through it the stubbornness of that hard, lonely old man nearly broke my heart. The file was full of reviews and press cuttings concerning my mother's career and highly newsworthy private life. There were a number of photographs of me taken without my knowledge. Reports from private detectives who, over the years, had charted my progress at school, my turbulent life with my mother, even a statement from my last employers where I'd worked as a filing clerk.

As I read I was unaware of the tears running down my face. Mr Pritchard, quietly and tactfully, handed me a beautifully laundered handkerchief.

'He never stopped loving your mother, Miss Kelsey, and yet he wouldn't have her name mentioned in his house. Then, gradually, he started to love you too.' He shook his head. 'He was a hard man.'

I brushed aside my tears and rose angrily. I crossed to the window and looked out across the Inner Temple. 'He was a stupid man! You don't know how I've longed to have a family, Mr Pritchard. My mother would never tell me who my father was. It would have meant so much to me to have met my grandfather . . . been loved by him. And, whatever my inheritance now, nothing can make up for those years of rejection.'

Well, now I had come into my own. I owned the Hall, tenanted farms, the Home Farm, and, most importantly, I was the majority shareholder in the Kelsey Glassworks. I had all that but, apart from Cat, I was totally alone in the world.

I quickly dried myself and pulled on a pair of old jeans and a loose-fitting jumper. At lunchtime I was to meet my family, my great-uncles and my cousins, but there was plenty of time still for me to make myself presentable and first I wanted to explore.

The evening before, a cold meal with a thermos of home-made soup and a bottle of wine had been left for me in the panelled dining hall, but I'd had to find the kitchen to cook Cat his fish. After my meal, quite unable to play the Lady of the Manor, I'd taken my tray through and washed up.

I hesitated for a moment at the foot of the intricately carved staircase. To my surprise Cat streaked ahead of me for all the world as if he had lived here for years. I followed him across the huge entrance hall with its massive fireplace above which was carved the Kelsey coat of arms. Cat led the way through the dining hall, past the Grand Parlour and Little Parlour then could go no further. The heavy oak door which opened into the buttery and beyond that the kitchen was closed.

I laughed, bent down and touched his head. 'You greedy little thing! You remember where your fish is, don't you?'

I opened the door and Cat now walked sedately before me, his long black tail swaying as he went. It was as if his dignity had been affronted by my accusation of greed.

17

I fed Cat and then made myself a cup of tea, rummaging in unfamiliar cupboards to find what I needed. The day was fine and sunny but the sunlight streaming in through the windows had not yet warmed the huge kitchen with its well-scrubbed stone-flagged floor. An Aga was set into the kitchen fireplace. It was warm so I leant against the rail on the front of it to sip my tea. Cat, having finished his breakfast, neatly washed himself then touched my leg with his paw.

'Want to go out, Cat? So do I. Come on, let's explore.'

We retraced our steps to the entrance hall and I pulled back the heavy iron bolts on the door which led to the porch. Then Cat and I stepped out into the courtyard. Because Kelsey Hall was moated the gardens surrounding the house were a little under an acre, with orchards and woods to the rear of the house on the other side of the moat. In front was a cobbled courtyard. I walked across this to the gatehouse. Cat was leaping about like a kitten, chasing a piece of thistledown, pouncing on imaginary mice, stalking nonexistent prey. I watched him for a moment, happy in his freedom. 'Perhaps you haven't always been a London stray, eh, Cat?' I said softly.

I left him to the chase and walked out on to the bridge over the moat. I suppose the village had grown up around the walls of the ancient manor of which now only the gatehouse remained and, because of the moat, my ancestor had had no choice but to build his beautiful new house on the site of the old. But Kelsey Hall was situated strangely close to the village green and church. The road at the top of the green led to

Colchester in one direction and to absolutely nowhere in the other. The houses that clustered around it were in a number of styles, shapes and sizes but none of them more recent than late-Georgian.

To the west of the Hall was the church of All Saints and St Nicholas with its surrounding graveyard. A Georgian rectory stood beyond. To the east was a long row of terraced, clapboarded cottages. They were roofed with ancient clay peg-tiles, their colour rich in the early morning sun.

Ducks swam on the moat and I wished I'd brought them some bread. I leant back against the wooden parapet which edged the bridge and turned my face up to the sun. I closed my eyes and relaxed. I stayed like that for a few moments, basking in peacefulness, the quietness of my surroundings.

Then suddenly I jerked upright. I opened my eyes, startled. I'd heard hoof beats, someone screaming . . . I looked around but the green was totally empty. Some early riser on the far side of the green was working in the garden. Otherwise Cat and I were the only living souls. I shook my head, smiling. The old house, the even more ancient gatehouse, the moat . . . the whole atmosphere was so romantic and yet Gothic I was letting imagination play tricks on me. At that moment Cat rubbed himself against my ankles.

Come with me, Catherine. Come with me. Come meet my Lady.

I bent down to stroke him but he dashed off across the bridge then turned towards the churchyard. I hurried after him, calling out, concerned, 'Cat! Cat, don't stray too far! You'll get lost!'

He leapt up on to the gate which led into the churchyard and for a brief moment seemed to look back at me, to check that I was following. Then he sprang down and disappeared among the gravestones and long grass.

I spent at least half an hour looking for him, calling to him. Perhaps it was ridiculous to be so worried but Cat was all I had to love now and he meant so much to me. Then I thought of the life he must have led on the streets of London and decided he was well able to take care of himself if he came up against a farm cat or a dog taking an early morning walk.

On impulse I walked to the church porch then tried the door to see if it was unlocked. It was. I slipped into the still interior of the Norman church. After the brightness of the day outside it took a moment for me to adjust my eyes. I knelt for a moment in silent prayer then started to walk up the nave. Everywhere I turned I saw the name Kelsey. Kelseys among the war dead. Kelsey tombs, the brass effigy of a Kelsey crusader, the Kelsey family pew, magnificent stained-glass windows donated to the church by the Kelseys. But I only bore the name of Kelsey because my mother had never married my father.

On the left, just before the chancel, was a small Lady Chapel. The entrance to it was through an exquisitely carved Jacobean screen. A single tomb stood in the centre. It was gloriously sculptured with an alabaster effigy of a woman on top of the marble monument. I moved towards the tomb. I looked down at the woman and saw that she had been incredibly beautiful. I was touched and amused to see that instead of the usual hound at her feet, her companion in eternity was the curled figure of a cat.

You are meeting her, Catherine. You are meeting my Lady.

I knelt and read the inscription.

Jesslyn, Ladye Kelsey.
Dyde ye XXVII of June 1682.
And her infant sonne deceased Hugh.
Dyde ye XXVII of June 1682.
Beloved of Guy de Burgh, Earl of Colne.
Truth was her loade starre, heaven was her desier.
Christ was her hope and in his Fayth shee dyde.

Hmm, I thought. I wonder how my Kelsey ancestor, the Lady's husband, took to that inscription? Then I took note of her Christian name. Jesslyn . . . the name I had heard on the edge of my dream.

A cloud must have passed over the sun because the interior of the church was suddenly dark. I found it difficult to catch my breath and was aware of my quickening heart beat. I clutched at the edge of the tomb to stop myself falling. Jesslyn . . . Jesslyn . . .

CHAPTER TWO

THE CAT

'I, born of a race of strange things,
Of deserts, great temples, great kings,
In the hot sands where the nightingale never sings!'
— Ford Madox Ford

JESSLYN: 1658

'What reinforcements we may gain from hope
If not, what resolution from despair'
                                    – John Milton

I screamed as the horse bore down on me. Then I was being lifted from the ground by strong arms. 'Hold on to me, Jess! Hold on! I've got you, little lovey.'

Mathew Vickerstaff held me to him and urged his horse forward out of the village along the road which led to Colchester. The shrieks of abuse gradually died away as Mathew's sturdy hunter took us from that hateful place.

When we were well over the parish boundary Mathew turned his horse from the road and on to a bridlepath which led through an ancient wood of oak and elm and beyond that to the fast-flowing estuary. At the edge of the wood Mathew reined in his horse, dismounted, then silently lifted me down. He pulled the kerchief from his neck and walked down to the edge of the river. He moistened the cloth with the salty water of the estuary then crossed back to me, gently starting to clean the bloody wounds on my face where the stones had hit me.

'Thank you, Mat. Thank you,' I whispered. I had escaped but I felt suddenly tired, drained. It was only my hatred of what the villagers had tried to do to me that sustained me.

'And they call themselves God-fearing! May those women rot in hell for this. Because it was the women, Jess. I came in from the fields at noon and the young dairymaid, Nell, told me what my dear mother –' he practically spat the word '– and the other goodwives of the village were planning.'

Tears were on my cheeks now. I clasped my hands over my swollen belly. 'This isn't a love child, Mat, they must know that. How . . . how can they be so cruel?'

'Oh, Jess, Jess! If only I could take care of you. I can't wish my father dead but when I come into my own . . .' He paused for a moment to contain his anger. 'When I come into my own, that bitch my mother will have no place at my hearth!'

'Why, Mat? Why do they hate me?'

There was silence between us for a moment. The trees suddenly rustled in a breeze from the estuary. I knew and loved these woods, the salt marshes and deep ditches of reeds. The turning of the tide always made itself known to the people of the Hundred.

Mat reached out and gently touched my face. 'You're too beautiful, Jesslyn. Your family are gentry and yet you and your father came to the village as poor as church mice. If you'd given yourself airs and graces they'd have been frightened of you and touched their forelock the way they do to the Kelseys. But you became one of us and yet still you stood apart. The one thing they cannot bear, it seems, is for someone to be different!'

Dear Mat. He looked so fierce and yet so young. We were the same age, sixteen, and had been friends since my father and I had come to Somerton after the execution of the King. I had come across some village boys tormenting an old cat. I was a skinny eight year old, small for my age, but I'd pushed one boy, the ring-leader, into the moat and had started kicking and punching the others. The cat had escaped and they had turned on me in a fury. Mat, the son of a prosperous yeoman farmer, had been riding by on his pony. He'd laid about the boys with his crop and had driven them off. Then a dignified, sturdy boy, he'd escorted me back to our cottage and the comforting arms of my father.

'What will you do, Jess? Where will you go?'

'I've had very little time to think. Until this morning, when the women came to the cottage, I'd planned to stay at Somerton . . . at least until the baby was born . . . then try to find work somewhere. But I have an aunt, my father's younger sister. I don't ever remember meeting her. Her husband is a master silversmith in London and very strong for Parliament. As you know, my father fought for the King but she wrote secretly to him and sometimes sent us money. She must have a good heart. I will try to make my way to her and hope she'll take pity on me. She's the only relative I have.'

'When you're safe, write to Miss Harriet. She'll get a message to me and read to me what you've written.' He flushed, embarrassed. 'I can read but a few words although I can write my name. Father reckoned 'twas all a farmer needed, but now I'm sorry for it.'

I reached out and touched his hand. 'You could still learn, Mat. Harriet would teach you, I know she would.'

But he shook his head. 'When I come into my own, Jess . . . then a lot of things will change.' There was a terrible longing in his eyes as he looked at me. He repeated, 'When I come into my own.'

Suddenly his mood changed and he turned from me, slamming his fist into his hand. 'If I could lay my hands on that . . . that animal who did this to you, I'd kill him!'

I caught hold of his arm and turned him to me. 'And be hanged for his murder? Promise me, Mat, *promise me*, when Luke comes back to the manor you'll not go near him?'

'I hate him so, Jess.'

'And you think I don't?' I cried out. 'But now that Father is dead, you and Harriet are the only people in the world who are dear to me. How could I live with the fact if I was the cause of your death? Because even if Luke is not Sir Thomas's legitimate son, he's still a Kelsey and the Kelseys would see you paid with your life if you harmed him.'

Mat shook his head angrily. 'The bastard should be in jail, not skulking on Sir Thomas's estates in Devon until the scandal dies down. There's no bloody justice in that!'

'What's done is done, Mat. My father always used to say that God pays debts without money.' I shrugged. 'Who knows? Perhaps one day Luke Kelsey will answer for what he has done to me.'

I turned away from dear Mat and walked down to the water's edge. The terrible memory of my rape suddenly overwhelmed me. I found I was shaking but tried to control myself for Mat's sake. I couldn't bear the thought of his putting himself in danger because of me.

It had been dusk when I'd slipped out of the cottage to the churchyard to sit by my father's grave. It had become a ritual for us to be together on either side of the hearth before I prepared our evening meal. In spite of the disease that was rotting his lungs – the result of his long imprisonment after the Battle of Naseby when King Charles and Prince Rupert had not only lost the battle but all hopes for the Royalist cause, my father would smoke his clay pipe and sip a goblet of Canary wine. Our old black cat always joined us then, sitting on either my father's lap or my own. More often mine. He was a stray who had adopted us when we came to the village. My father, rather fancifully, had named him Ra – after, he told me, an Egyptian god who had turned himself into a cat to fight evil. After Father died, however busy I tried to keep myself, at that time of day I was still drawn to the empty hearth.

That evening I had been unable to bear the loneliness any longer. Even Ra no longer kept our twilight appointment. If only I had gone to Harriet's handsome Tudor house on the green . . . But there is a limit to how much one can ask of a friend. Especially one who had already offered me so much comfort in my bereavement.

I picked some rosemary for remembrance, to place on my father's grave, then walked across the green to the church. It was dusk. A few men were coming home from the fields and the sound of hammering still came from the blacksmith's. But once inside the churchyard I was totally alone and was glad of it.

We had buried my father in a quiet corner of the

churchyard beneath an ancient elm. There were very few of us at the funeral. Harriet, myself, Mat – and, because even though he had fought for the King and was disgraced, with his land sequestered and his estate fined beyond redemption, my father had borne an ancient name and was a knight so the Kelseys also had attended.

Sir Thomas Kelsey was a tall, handsome man in his late-thirties at that time. His wife Dame Alice was a year or two younger but looked like an old woman. Sir Thomas's quest for an heir had taken a terrible toll on her. There were twelve small coffins in the Kelsey mausoleum. Even as we stood by my father's grave, I felt pity for Sir Thomas's wife. Her frail, thin body seemed misshapen by the bulk of yet another pregnancy, but Sir Thomas was neither kind nor caring to her. She had failed him and he would never forgive her that.

I had had no money to raise a headstone on my father's grave and at first had refused Harriet's offer to pay a stonemason. Finally she lost her temper with me.

'Do you think I did not love him too? Look at me, Jesslyn! I am near to forty years old, an old maid. Short, dumpy, anathema to most men because I am not only well tutored, but have a mind as sharp as any of theirs. Your father never held that mind against me. He treated me as an equal. How often have we sat by your fireside late into the night . . . debating, arguing, testing our intellect? Have you any idea what that meant to me?'

'I know what it meant to *him*. He . . . admired you, Harriet.'

'He admired me, yes, but I *loved* him!' She had been sitting on the oak settle that had been my father's favourite seat. Now she rose abruptly and crossed to the casement window. Angrily she pulled back the shutters, letting the late spring sunshine pour into the room. 'Let's not have any more of this, Jesslyn. The last thing your father would have wanted was for you to turn your face from the day. To deny yourself the continuance of life.'

She stared out into the orchard for a moment, then turned to me. 'I'm a wealthy woman, Jesslyn, but very few men have come seeking my fortune. Perhaps my father did a terrible thing in seeing that I was well educated and in taking pride in my scholarship. But he was forty when I was born and remembered well the old Queen. He would spur me on with tales of how the Lady Elizabeth had mastered both Latin and Greek by the time she was eight. Of her understanding of philosophy. That she dared to let men know she was an academic. Well, by God, those are the principles I have lived by, and your father was the only man who honoured me for it. Please, Jesslyn, do not let his grave go unmarked.'

Against such pleading I had set aside my pride and agreed that Harriet should pay for my father's headstone. Now I knelt by his grave and softly touched the stone. It read simply:

Sir Edward Gifford Kt.
Bereaft us with untymely death.
Memoria justi benedictionbus.

After a prayer for his soul, I sat by his grave and chatted to him as I had done on countless occasions in those twilight hours when the sun was setting. I didn't tell him how much I missed him, how I longed to be with him again, because I wanted him to be happy. That may sound foolish but I knew that although he had hated to leave me, had feared for me, his death was a release from constant pain and, in spite of his dangerous debates with Harriet about atheism, he truly believed that he would meet with my mother again.

There is a lowly ale-house about a half mile from the village on the road to Colchester. The slattern who runs it is rumoured to be Luke Kelsey's mother. Whether that is true or not I cannot say. What is certain is that, in spite of the terrible hurt it must have caused Dame Alice, who must surely have yearned for a living child as much as her husband did, Sir Thomas's natural son was taken into his home as a baby and thereafter his father pampered, spoilt and indulged the boy he must have longed to have had as his legitimate heir. The road that leads to Colchester curves around the edge of the churchyard and therefore many of the youths and men on their way to The Three Tuns made a short cut through the hallowed ground of the church.

I had not noticed the passage of time as I talked to the spirit of my father and dusk had given way to darkness. But I felt no fear as I rose and turned to walk back to the cottage, to Ra and our fireside. A watery moon edged its way from behind broken cloud and I saw three young men, boys really, walking towards me, cutting through the churchyard. Slightly ahead of the other two strode Luke Kelsey. He was the boy I had pushed into the moat all those years before when I had come to the rescue of the 'cat. It seemed to me a childish squabble that could easily have been put behind us but, from that day, Luke had been my enemy. I'd tried to overlook his churlish, bullying ways. His position in life was near intolerable. The English countryside was thronged with the unwanted by-blows of the gentry. Sir Thomas had at least acknowledged him his son; forced Dame Alice to let Luke be brought up in the Kelsey household. But he could never inherit. Was not accepted by Sir Thomas's peers. Was loathed by Dame Alice's family. The boy had only the village to turn to and so used his money and position, however dubious, to gather around him a group of boys who, if they had not been running as part of Luke's pack, would have been ashamed of their ways.

He swept off his hat and mockingly bowed to me. 'Well met, Mistress Gifford! What are you doing out after dark? Looking for sport? Taking over from Peg Jessop as the village whore, are we?'

'I don't know why you wish to insult me, Master Kelsey. You have no reason to be ill mannered towards me.' I turned to the other two boys. 'Neither have you, Samuel or Nat. Please let me pass.'

Luke edged nearer to me and I could smell from his breath that he had already been drinking. 'You know the penalty for whoring, Mistress Gifford, don't you? First the Constable slits your nostrils so that for the rest of your life all men who look on you will know of your shame. Then they strip you to the waist and tie you to a cart tail. After that the Constable whips you around the streets. All the village will be there to gawp. To look on your pretty, naked breasts and bleeding back.'

He suddenly took hold of me and grabbed one of my breasts. 'I bet you have pretty tits, Mistress Gifford!'

I pulled away from him angrily. 'Luke, stop this! You know very well I am no whore. Look at me. I wear black in mourning for my father. And I tell you this, Luke Kelsey, I am the daughter of a Knight, and if you dare lay hands on me again you'll pay dearly for it!'

He sneered at me. 'You may be the daughter of a Knight but you are also the daughter of a traitor . . . an enemy of Parliament and therefore of the people. That for Sir Edward Gifford!' And he spat on my father's grave. I sprang at him then, scratching and punching. It was a foolish thing for me to do because he was in a dangerous mood. But my grief for my dearly loved father was still so intense, so raw, that to see that drunken oaf defile his grave was more than I could endure.

Luke hit me savagely across the face and I staggered back. 'Right, you little bitch, you asked for this . . . Sam, Nat, hold her down!'

'Luke! There's no need for this. Let her be, man.' This from Nat, tugging at his arm.

'If you've no stomach for it, get out of here . . . but never think to be a friend of mine again!'

Nat hesitated for a moment, then shook his head and stumbled off into the darkness. 'Nat, help me!' I cried out. Luke clasped a hand across my mouth and I bit it savagely. He yelled with pain and let me go for an instant. I turned to run but Samuel caught hold of me. 'Please, Sam, let me go,' I sobbed.

'Hold her, Sam! Hold her! You can have her after me!'

I tried to scream but Sam's hand was over my mouth now, his grip so tight I was unable to open my jaws to bite. I heard my jaw bone crack as I struggled to free myself.

Sam was pulling me down on to the grass whilst Luke unbuttoned his breeches. Still I fought: kicking out, scratching, tearing at Luke's flesh with my nails. Then he punched me and I briefly lost consciousness. I was brought to by the terrible pain between my legs as he forced himself into me. As he thrust himself deeper and deeper into my body he tore at my clothes. My breasts were exposed and he reached for my nipples, kneading them cruelly, then tearing at them with his teeth. He not only wanted to rape me, he wanted to defile, to inflict as much pain as he could. Finally, with a savage cry of exultation, he spilled his seed into me.

He lay on top of me for a moment, panting, then pulled himself from me. 'Well, daughter of a Knight . . . *legitimate* daughter of a Knight . . . not so grand now, are we? Come on, Sam, I'll hold her. You can have your turn now.'

But Sam was trying to cover me. His tears fell on me as I lay stunned and bleeding. 'Oh, Miss Jess! Miss Jess! Forgive me. I don't know how this happened. Forgive me.'

'Do you want her or not, Sam? If not I'm off to The Three Tuns. If you want to stay here and snivel, so be it. But don't call yourself friend of mine if you do.'

Poor, weak Sam sprang to his feet at that. 'Friend of yours? I've never been a friend of yours! I've been your crony, your lickspittle, your bumsucker. But not any more! Not after tonight. Now I see you for what you are and I hate you for it. I hate myself even more!' He shook his head, crying, 'Oh, Miss Jess! Miss Jess!' He turned away and leant against a tombstone, sobbing.

'What a mewling, puking little peasant you are, Sam. If you can't have your fun like a gentleman, don't hang around me any more!' Luke swaggered off down the path towards the ale-house. Sam turned and shouted after him angrily: 'Gentleman? I may not be a *gentleman*, Luke Kelsey, but at least I know who my mother is. At least I know my ma and pa were married in this very church. At least I'm not a bastard!'

I lay on the grass, damp now with dew and with my blood, and listened to Sam. Still sobbing, he blundered off, trying to blot from his mind what had happened that night. Perhaps I was light-headed from pain and from shock but I felt a great sorrow for Luke Kelsey. Those taunts of Sam's had dogged him all his life, spoken or unspoken. He couldn't see how fortunate he was to be loved by Sir Thomas, cared for by him, instead of spending his childhood in some filthy hovel. He could only see that he was a bastard, and felt that he must punish the whole world for his illegitimacy.

I drifted into semi-consciousness for I don't really know how long. I was brought back to my senses by a rough scraping sensation against my face. My eyes were nearly closed by my tears and from Luke's blows but I could make out a black shape against the moon. It was Ra.

You must get up, Jesslyn. You must get up. Your destiny is not to die here.

I closed my eyes for a moment and when I opened them again he was gone. Had I imagined Ra had been there? But something or someone seemed to be urging me to move and I realized the wisdom of that. In my shocked state I could well have lain bleeding on the cold ground throughout the night. I moaned with pain as I tried to rise, turned myself over on to my knees and crawled for a few yards before collapsing. A sense of peace came over me as I lay on the damp grass, almost of euphoria. It seemed it would be so pleasant to sleep here. Just let myself drift away . . .

I am Egypt. I am Mystery. I am Cat. Your destiny is not to die here. I will not let you sleep. You will get up.

Harriet! If I could only get myself to Harriet. She would bathe my wounds. Care for me. I crawled a few more feet. The pain between my legs was excruciating now but still I crawled on. I was nearly at the lych-gate but could feel my strength ebbing from me.

Then I heard soft footsteps on the path behind me. I started to pray then. Dear God, let it not be Luke returning to attack me again. I heard someone quietly calling my name. 'Miss Jess . . . Mistress Jesslyn . . . are you all right?'

It was Nat. I tried to call to him but my mouth was so swollen I could only moan. Then he was by my side. 'Dear God! What have they done to you?' He was only about fourteen. His face was horror-stricken by what he saw.

I reached up and clasped his arm. 'Harriet . . .' I tried to say, and then: 'Help me.'

Somehow Nat understood. He placed his arms around me and gently eased me to my feet. I fell against him, gasping with pain. 'Miss Harriet? You want me to take you to Miss Harriet?' I nodded but in truth was practically beyond caring where anyone took me or what they did with me.

Mercifully I can barely remember the slow, aching walk across the green. It seemed that my soul and my body were no longer one. Someone was stumbling, broken and bleeding, across the green towards Harriet's house. But was that someone really me? And if indeed that poor creature was Jesslyn Gifford, why was she screaming within while no sound escaped her lips?

I came to my full senses a week later, Harriet and her elderly maid servant having cared for me, as kindly and lovingly as if I'd been a daughter of that house.

My body and face, although still badly bruised, were beginning to heal. But my mind was another matter. I felt unclean, utterly without a sense of myself. I had not only lost my virginity in that dark churchyard, I had lost my pride, my dignity. I felt like a thing instead of a woman. I was the victim and yet I was overwhelmed by a feeling of shame.

Harriet told me that at first light after my rape she had gone to the Hall to inform Sir Thomas of his son's crime. But he already knew and had taken speedy action. Luke had come home drunk and boasting of what he had done to me. Even such a doting parent as Sir Thomas could not help but be horrified. At dawn Luke had been packed off with Sir Thomas's steward to a small manor his father owned in Devon, part of Dame Alice's dowry.

'You could, of course, go to the Constable and lay

charges to be brought before the Justice of the Peace. But as that Justice is Sir Thomas, I cannot see you achieving very much by that. Even if Luke was brought to trial, he would be judged by a man before a jury of men. I can imagine what his defence would be: you asked for it. Oh, yes, it went a little too far but you had enticed him then refused your favours.'

'It's a man's world, Jesslyn, damn it! And with very little justice for women in that world.'

'Sam knows the truth! – He knows what was done to me, through no fault of mine.'

Harriet gave a harsh laugh. 'Sam's parents are Sir Thomas's tenants! You would either find that Master Samuel had had an acute case of memory loss or that he had run away to sea.' She took my hand. 'Jesslyn, you've your whole life before you. You're young and very beautiful. You mustn't let this terrible, terrible thing that has happened to you spoil your bright promise.'

'I thought you of anyone I know would want Luke punished. Would see things fairly.'

'But life isn't fair, my dear girl. It's one law for the rich, another for the poor. One law for men, another – quite literally – for women. I am my father's eldest child. If a son had been born after me, who do you think would have inherited? I would not be living as mistress of this fine house. No! I'd be some wretched man's wife who would only have taken me for my dowry – or else a semi-servant in my brother's house, with a roof over my head because of his charity. And if he took a wife and she didn't like me, then God help me! No, Jesslyn, life is not fair.'

40

'Then I'll make it fair. You say I have beauty? Well, that shall be my weapon. That will be my strength. I shall punish all men for what Luke has done to me,' I said bitterly.

'All men are not Luke Kelsey, Jesslyn. Was your father a Luke Kelsey? Is Mat Vickerstaffe not a good, kind, honest boy? Did Nat Dobson not come back for you and bring you to me? No, my dear, in trying to destroy others, you will destroy yourself.'

I did not reply but in my heart I already felt destroyed. And inwardly I vowed that by some means I would make Luke pay dearly one day. Very dearly.

Another week and I felt I could no longer impose on Harriet. She was kindness itself and begged me to stay on, but I knew that she hungered to get back to her quietly ordered routine with her books, her writing and her study into the medicinal use of herbs.

I tried to rebuild my life as best I could but it was a painful process and what made it all the harder was that instead of helping me, commiserating with me, the villagers avoided me. They curtly nodded to me when I greeted them as I went about the village but their eyes slid away from my face. It was a cruel way to treat me, but the cruellest blow of all was the realization that I was to have Luke's child . . .

Now I heard Mat stir behind me. I looked down into the fast-flowing waters and thought that if he were not here I would be tempted to slip beneath them. My plight was desperate. I had only the clothes I stood up in, no money, and just the faint hope that over eighty miles away in the City of London my aunt would give shelter to a niece who was about to give birth to an illegitimate child.

I turned and saw that Mat was walking down the bank towards me.

'Jess, I have decided. I am coming with you. Someone must care for you. Let it be me.'

'I have never heard such foolishness! If you were not your father's son you would be in the pillory or worse for helping me today. If you run away with me, do you not think your father would come after you? And when they found us, you would be dragged back and I with you!' I took his hand. 'You have an inheritance, Mat, and that brings its responsibilities. I must go alone. And I must go now. You know I'm right.'

He paused for a moment then said reluctantly, 'Yes. In my heart I know you are. But I am so fearful for you.' He took his cloak from his shoulders and wrapped it around me. 'I wish I had a ring to give you, Jess. You could pose as a widowwoman. As it is you must stay clear of the villages between here and Colchester. Somerton is not the only parish with a rabid Puritan for a parson. And here, I have a little money.' He handed me a purse. 'Only a few groats but it will buy you some food.'

'Mat, how can I ever repay you for your kindness? Somehow I will, that I promise.'

'I don't need repayment,' he said gruffly. 'I just need word that you are safe. I . . . I love you Jess. I couldn't bear it if I was never to see you again. Please say you will come back to Somerton one day?'

I hesitated. Why should I wish to return to a place that had used me so cruelly? And yet I knew that

Somerton was not out of my life forever. At that moment I felt a blinding hatred for the Kelseys, for the narrow-minded, vicious behaviour of the villagers. But then, perhaps hatred drives people even more than love? I would return, but whether to settle old scores or simply to see again Mat and Harriet, who were so dear to me, I knew not.

'I will come back, Mat. Neither of us can know when, but I will come back. Can I ask one more favour of you?'

'Anything, you know that.'

'There is nothing of any value in my cottage except for my father's books. Will you take them to Harriet, please? She will use them and love them. And would you find Ra and ask Harriet to care for him for me? He is an old cat now and I cannot bear the thought of him returning to the life he must have known as a stray.'

'I shall do both things this very day.'

'And now I must go, Mat. Don't let's say goodbye for I fear I might cry . . . I will just kiss you then walk away.' My voice was already breaking as I spoke. He hugged me to him then kissed me. Not as a boy but as a man. Then he gently let me go.

'God be with you, Jesslyn.'

'And with you, Mat.'

We walked silently back up the bridlepath to the road, then I turned towards Colchester and Mat towards the village. We said nothing to each other but when I reached the bend in the road I looked back and saw that he had stopped and was watching me until the very last moment. I waved briefly then hurried on. There was no way for me except forward.

★ ★ ★

I walked until nightfall and saw no one other than a few men in the distance working the fields. Except on market days the road to Somerton was rarely used. I saw in the distance the lights of a house. As I drew near I saw the bush hanging outside which indicated that it was an alehouse. So many things had been banished by the Puritans – the maypole, the performance of plays, morris dancing, festivities at Christmas – but the taverns were still open. Perhaps Parliament had known in its wisdom that to keep an Englishman from his ale would surely bring about revolt.

I was very hungry but, as I drew near to the tavern, I heard the sound of raucous laughter and raised voices and dared not risk an encounter with a group of drunken men. I was suddenly aware that I was desperately tired and knew I could go no further that night. I looked around to see if there was anywhere I could shelter unobserved.

To the rear of the tavern was a yard and stables. Beyond, a barn. I decided to make for this. I could hear the sound of the horses moving in their stalls as I crept past the stables but there was no sign of an ostler or stable-lad.

The inside of the barn was strangely empty but the loft piled high with hay. With the last of my strength I pulled myself up the ladder and then crawled deep into the hay. I lay for a moment panting, my heart pounding. Perhaps I had nothing to fear from the people hereabouts, but after what had happened at Somerton today I dared not take any chances.

After a moment I inched myself even deeper into the

soft, sweet-smelling hay, then drew Mat's cloak tightly around me and settled down to sleep. But I was too tired for the longed for rest to come. Instead I lay in the darkness and finally gave way to despair. I cried for my lost father. I cried in fear for what was to become of me and my baby. I longed to be once again with Harriet, helping her in her stillroom as she made her herbal remedies – or reading quietly with her. I wished I had been weaker with Mat and let him come with me. Then was ashamed that I should consider, even for a moment, exploiting his love.

Finally, exhausted by my tears, I started to drift into sleep. The moon which had lit my way into the barn had passed behind a cloud. I felt terribly alone within the walls of that vast, timber-framed almost cathedral-like barn as total darkness closed in on me. I pretended to myself that I was safe in my truckle bed at our cottage and that my father was downstairs reading late into the night. I pretended that soon Ra would leap from the apple tree into my room and curl up at my feet. And then I realized, with infinite sadness, that I would never see him again. Fresh tears spilt on to the hay as I slept.

I will return to you, Jesslyn. You have only to wait for me.

CHAPTER THREE

THE CAT

'Now from the dark, a deeper dark,
The cat slides,
Furtive and aware'

– Elizabeth Coatsworth

CATHERINE: 1991

'I have been here before,
But when or how I cannot tell.
I know the grass beyond the door
The sweet keen smell,
The sighing sound, the lights around the shore'
                              – Dante Gabriel Rossetti

I sat on the nearest pew with my head between my knees for a few moments. Could this really be me? Practical, prosaic, steady Catherine, half fainting because of a name on a tombstone? But how strange to dream of that name and then to see it so shortly afterwards.

I straightened up and laughed at myself. This seventeenth-century Jesslyn had been a Kelsey. She most probably had been mentioned in one of the books Mr Pritchard had given me. Even so, I thought, smiling, I must bear in mind that the Dengie Hundred is supposed to be the most haunted area in England. I laughed aloud then.

'From Ghoulies and ghosties and long-legged beasties, And things that go bump in the night – Good Lord deliver us!'

I rose and turned to walk down the aisle just as the porch door swung open. A truly beautiful girl stood framed in the doorway. There was no artifice about her beauty. Her long, rich, auburn hair was caught back in what seemed to be an elastic band, but the curls were so vigorous they refused to be constrained and so framed her face and tumbled on to her shoulders in a haphazard fashion. Her clothes were what I suppose might be called ethnic: an embroidered Indian blouse worn loosely over a hand printed cotton skirt. Both garments had been faded by much washing. Her feet were bare and in her arms she carried a huge bunch of cottage garden flowers.

We both started as we saw each other. 'Oh! I'm sorry if I startled you.' Her voice was light and breathless, almost child-like.

'And I'm sorry if I gave *you* a fright! I just slipped into the church on an impulse. It's very beautiful.'

'Yes, it is, isn't it?' Her face seem to light up as she looked around. 'I like coming to do the flowers early in the morning, then I can have them all to myself.'

'Er, all who?'

She laughed softly, as if I was a little dim-witted. 'Why, the Kelseys, of course! They're all here, waiting for us.'

'Well, I hope they're not too impatient! I'd like to live to a ripe old age before I join my ancestors.'

'Ancestors? Oh, how stupid of me! You must be cousin Catherine!' She threw down the flowers on a pew and hugged me. 'Welcome home, cousin! I'm Sophie. Oh, Catherine, I'm so thrilled to meet you.'

I was a little taken aback by the warmth of her greeting but then smiled inwardly to myself. This generosity of spirit was so like my mother. In that way, at least, Sophie certainly resembled Francesca. 'Thank you.'

I hadn't been expecting to meet any of my family until lunchtime and desperately wished that I wasn't so damned shy. That I could fully respond to her open friendliness. But Sophie didn't seem to notice my apparent diffidence. She put her arm through mine. 'I've always wanted a sister but I've been cursed with brothers. Oh, I don't really mean that, I love them all dearly, but you can't have secrets with a brother. You can't . . . Oh, I don't know.' She pouted prettily. 'I mean, men are all right in bed but I find them pretty boring when they're not between the sheets. Don't you agree?'

How to tell this outwardly waif-like but clearly sexually experienced girl that, apart from one fumbling, miserable encounter when I was seventeen, I had no knowledge of men between the sheets or anywhere else for that matter? 'I've met some men that I've become quite fond of,' I murmured.

'Oh, yes,' she replied impatiently. 'But you can't be *friends* with a man. That's why I've always wanted a sister. Someone to be really close with. Now I've got you!' Her mood suddenly changed and she looked dismayed. 'But perhaps you won't like me? Some people don't, you know.'

'I find that hard to believe and I'm sure we'll be friends. I'd . . . I'd like that very much. I was very close to my mother, you see, and I suppose she was more like a friend than a parent. I've never really had a girl friend my own age. Although,' I added hastily, 'I'm sure I'm somewhat older than you.'

'I'm twenty-four. How old are you?' Sophie asked directly.

'Five years older, I'm afraid.'

'Nothing to be afraid of. You don't look it anyway, and that's what counts.' She turned and picked up the discarded flowers. 'I'd better get these in water. Stay and chat to me if you like.'

'Thanks but I must find my cat. We only arrived yesterday and I'm worried he might get lost.'

You cannot lose me, Catherine. I have come to guide you.

'Oh, cats always turn up when they're hungry,' she said breezily. But Cat didn't seem to me to be that kind of animal.

'Well, I want to look for him. I'll see you at lunch. By the way, where do you live?'

'On the green. A rambling old Tudor house called Knight's Croft. You can't mistake it. It badly needs a coat of paint and looks as if it's falling down, which it probably is. You see, my father is the black sheep of the family. Not a nice, hard-working Kelsey at all! He's an artist. Happy as Larry but as poor as a church mouse.' She suddenly laughed. 'Spend an afternoon with cousin Annabel – she'll love dishing all the dirt about the family! She's an absolute cow but very well informed.

'I must see to the flowers . . . See you later, cousin Catherine.' And with that she turned and ran lightly up the nave towards the vestry.

I looked after her for a moment and then realized who she reminded me of. She was very like the beautiful alabaster effigy on the tomb in the Lady Chapel. I thought of my mother's beauty and wished wryly that the Kelsey good looks had been passed on to me.

I pulled open the heavy oak door which led to the porch and, as I walked out into the sunlight, practically stumbled over Cat. The early morning sun had crept into the church porch and he was stretched out in it, nonchalantly washing himself. I laughed and bent down to stroke him. 'Well, St Francis might have approved but the vicar probably won't! Black cats are supposed to be witch's familiars, you know.'

Cat's reaction to this was to yawn and then roll over on to his back. I bent down and picked him up. He immediately scrambled up on to my shoulder, leaning his soft, warm body against the side of my head. For some reason this was a favoured position with him. And so I walked back to my family's ancient home, looking rather like Long John Silver if he'd replaced his parrot with a cat.

Once again, as I walked through the gatehouse, the beauty of Kelsey Hall took my breath away. The rich red Tudor bricks which infilled the huge old timber frame practically glowed in the morning sunshine. From the entrance to the courtyard I could clearly see the three massive chimney-stacks, each topped with tall ornamental shafts above a diamond-patterned frieze. There was a richly carved bressumer above the opening to the porch and a date: 1521.

Time past and time present seemed to me to be reaching out and touching each other as I pushed open the studded front door and walked into the Hall. This illusion was immediately shattered by the sound of very loud pop music blaring out from a portable radio which had been left a few steps up on the staircase.

Cat took one look at the apparition dancing to the music then added to the cacophony of sound by letting out a blood-curdling yowl, leaping from my shoulder and disappearing in the general direction of the kitchen.

He had a point. I found myself looking at what I can only describe as a human version of a cockatoo. The dancer was very young and very thin. She wore skin-tight white trousers which were tucked into high-heeled cowboy boots. A multi-coloured tunic barely covered her buttocks and was belted by a heavily studded piece of leather. But it was her hair that was totally riveting. At the side of her head it was cut so short it was virtually shaven. The hair on the top of her head was much longer and apparently glued to stand upright as if its owner had had a severe electric shock. The exception to the shock effect was one lankly hanging quiff coloured a brilliant orange. I didn't know whether to burst out laughing or to applaud the dancer's originality.

As she gyrated to the music she waved aloft a can of polish in one hand and a duster in the other. The motion of her dance spun her round so that she came face to face with me. She let out a squawk then dashed over to the radio and turned it off. Then she turned back to me.

'Oh, flipping heck, I bet you're Miss Kelsey? My mum'll 'ave my guts for garters!'

'Hello. Yes, I'm Catherine Kelsey.' I held out my hand to her. She looked astonished at this for a moment then hastily transferred the duster to the hand which held the polish and shook my hand.

'You're ever so like the old man . . . Sir Hugo, that is. Spitting image. Well, except you're not old and you're not a man. But apart from that . . . spitting image. Oh, I'm Celeste by the way.'

'Celeste? That's a pretty name,' I said, trying to to come to terms with this exotic creature. I assumed she was a cleaner but, until meeting Celeste, had had visions of cleaners being motherly women in nylon overalls.

'Yeah, it is, in't it? Mum 'ad me christened Doris but I don't answer to that no more . . . Mum's in the kitchen if you want to say hello. Won't tell 'er I 'ad me ghetto blaster on, will you?'

'No.' I smiled at her. 'But I think she might have heard.'

'Huh!' she snorted. 'She'd 'ave been through like a dose of salts if she 'ad. Used to drive the old man mad, my radio did. "Jungle music" he called it. Place needs livening up, I think. I mean, look at it.'

Her scornful glance took in the heavy Jacobean oak furniture, the panelled walls, the family portraits. 'Like a bleeding museum, in't it?' Her hand instantly went to her mouth. 'Cor, sorry! I forgot you're one of them!'

'I forget it myself most of the time,' I laughed. 'And do please play your radio if you want to, if you could just turn it down a bit?'

'Really? Thanks! But . . .' she added, '. . . you will tell Mum you said it was okay, won't you?'

'Of course. But . . . er . . . who exactly is Mum?'

'Mavis Jessop. She does the cooking and that . . . She's in the kitchen now getting ready for your "do" at lunchtime. 'Ere.' She moved a couple of steps nearer and lowered her voice conspiratorially. 'Is it true that Mr James *and* Mr Marcus are coming?'

'Mr Pritchard, my solicitor, said all the family were

coming to meet me. Why do you ask?'

She glanced around to check that we were still totally alone then tapped the side of her nose with her finger. 'Tell me no secrets, I'll tell you no lies!' I wondered where on earth this was heading. 'But everyone knows that Mr James and Mr Marcus "'ate each other's guts". Something to do with selling shares when Mr Marcus got divorced. Before my time, of course, but the village don't 'alf like a bit of spicy gossip . . .'

'Doris! Doris!' a voice yelled from the direction of the kitchen.

'Oh, heck! Tell 'er I'm doing the library!' She grabbed her radio and dashed off across the hall. She turned for a brief moment in the library doorway. 'And tell 'er I don't answer to nothing but Celeste!'

'Doris, I told you I needed you to . . .' Mavis Jessop entered the hall from the corridor that led to the buttery and kitchen. She stopped short when she saw me.

'Miss Kelsey?'

'Yes. How do you do? You must be Mrs Jessop.' I moved towards her to shake hands.

'Oh, Miss!' For one awful moment I thought she was going to bob a curtsey. 'I am pleased to meet you . . . Spitting image of the old man, you are! . . . I am sorry I wasn't 'ere to do your breakfast. What must you 'ave thought of me?'

'It didn't occur to me that anyone would be here to cook my breakfast. In any case, I only wanted something light . . . By the way, if you're looking for Doris she's cleaning the library . . . Oh, and I don't think she likes being called Doris!'

Mavis Jessop snorted at this. 'I don't know where she gets her ideas from. She was Titania before she was Celeste. Her dad and me are plain, ordinary village people. But look at her! Take one look at that 'air-do and you want to say "Pretty Polly" to 'er. Excuse me, Miss.'

She hurried across to the library door and called, 'Doris, don't give me no lip! Just get into the kitchen and start on them vegetables like I told you!'

She turned back to me. 'I hope the menu for your lunch is all right? Mr Pritchard wrote and told me when you was arriving and just to go ahead and prepare lunch for the family. Good, wholesome English food it'll be. I've got no time for this new fad of covering a plate with five different kinds of lettuce but only giving a body 'alf a shrimp to actually eat!'

I was about to assure Mrs Jessop that I was certain that the meal she cooked would be splendid when the front door from the porch swung open and a very good-looking young man in his late-twenties entered. I knew immediately that he must be one of Sophie's despised brothers. He had the same fine good looks and unruly auburn hair. He carried a bouquet of roses and bowed when he saw me.

'Lady of the Manor, a true and humble knight comes hither . . . possibly even thither . . . to greet thee. Fair lady, would that I could be your swain! Accept this as a token of my love!' He held out the roses to me.

I was a little nonplussed by the eccentricity of my cousin's greeting. Not so Mavis Jessop. She cuffed him lightly around the ear. 'Rupert Kelsey, you are a daft bugger!'

Rupert laughed and gave her a hug. 'You know me through and through! How about a couple of cups of coffee and some of your fruit cake for me and the object of my desire . . . my beautiful new cousin Catherine.' He turned to me. 'You *are* cousin Catherine, I suppose? I haven't wasted my roses on an imposter?'

'Yes, I'm Catherine Kelsey. How do you do?' I said, cursing yet again my shyness. I should have loved to have been able to reply in kind. To have joined in with his nonsense. I thought how quickly and wittily my mother would have replied and hated my own inadequacy.

'How do you do?' he mocked, laughing. 'If we're cousins we must surely be kissing cousins.' And so saying he took me into his arms and kissed me thoroughly and, I imagine, expertly, full on my lips. I wasn't sure that I wanted to take being 'kissing cousins' to quite such lengths but Mrs Jessop was there before me. As Rupert let me go he got another cuff from her.

'That's enough of that!' she admonished, but with a twinkle in her eye. I could tell that she was fond of him. 'Men!' she said to me. 'Give 'em an inch and they take a mile. And if you give 'em a mile, you don't see them for dust.'

Rupert laughed then said, 'Now, Mavis, that's not the sort of information a good woman should have.'

'Oh, get on with you. Take Miss Catherine into the Little Parlour, it's nice and sunny this time of the morning there, and then I'll get you some coffee.' She forestalled Rupert just as he was opening his mouth. 'Yes, yes, *and* some fruit cake! . . . Give me the flowers, Miss, and I'll put them in water . . . Oh, and Mrs Garner will be here in about half an hour. She'll want to go through the linen with you.'

'What on earth for?' I asked, bemused.

'Well, she's the housekeeper. Got to do things right, 'aven't we? And when you've got a minute, Fred Watson would like to go through the accounts of the Home Farm.'

'They won't mean a thing to me.'

'Never mind.' Rupert took my arm. 'You've got to do things right.' He started to walk me out of the hall towards the Little Parlour. As we walked away we could hear Mrs Jessop at the library door. 'Doris! Doris! You get yourself into the kitchen real smart . . . Look, if you're Celeste, I'm the bloody Queen of the May. Get cracking!'

Rupert and I both laughed at this. 'Apparently she was Titania before Celeste. I can't say I blame her. I wouldn't much like to have been christened Doris,' I whispered.

The door to the Little Parlour was ajar and I immediately knew that Mavis Jessop was right and this was the sunniest room because Cat was stretched out on the window seat, dozing in the warm sunlight. I crossed and stroked him.

'What a handsome fellow. Is he yours?' Cat rubbed his black head against my hand to get me to carry on stroking him.

'Mine?' I smiled as he started to purr. 'I rather think it's the other way round! He came into my life at a very difficult time. I don't know why he chose our front door, but he did.'

' "I live alone, preferring the company of my cat",' Rupert teased.

'*The Lady's Not For Burning*! I've always liked Christopher Fry. But I'm not sure that quotation really applies to me.'

'It won't for long anyway! A lovely young woman suddenly coming amongst us? Half the county will be beating a path to your door.'

I shook my head. 'I'd rather be honest with myself and I find I don't mind any more. When I was younger I really suffered because my mother was so blazingly beautiful and I didn't take after her. But I loved her too much to envy her, and once I realized that, being a Plain Jane didn't seem too bad . . . By the way, I'm pleased to meet you but does the fact that you're here now mean you won't be coming to lunch?'

'Good God, no! I wouldn't miss lunch for the world. I just wanted to be the advance party.' He suddenly chuckled. 'Best sport in the world . . . seeing our big loving family tear each other's throats out. They'll all be prowling around each other, then around you. The best laugh I've had in ages was when Pritchard said straight after the funeral: "Sir Hugo left everything to Miss Catherine Kelsey." You should've seen Jonas's face! Forty years of sucking up to the old man dashed in eight little words!'

'I don't think it's very kind of you to poison me against the family. I've . . . I've always wanted to be part of one and I'm certainly not going to prejudge anyone on your say so.'

'Good for you. By God, the girl's got spirit after all! No. Don't scold me again. Let's be friends. Not another word about the family, I promise. Say you forgive me?' He held out his hand to me and, after a moment's hesitation, I took it.

I dressed carefully for the meeting with my family. My mother and I had always joked that the lawn cotton Liberty print blouse and skirt was my 'Sunday best'. At noon I'd unpacked it from the tissue in which I'd carefully wrapped it and shaken out the folds. The simple but very pretty design reminded me of the country garden flowers that Sophie had carried into the church that morning.

I examined myself in the cheval mirror. 'Yes,' I said ruefully, 'you've scrubbed up well!' Then I remembered the pearls that Mr Pritchard and I had taken from the vault of the bank where my grandfather had an account in the City. 'They were your great-grandmother's and then your grandmother's. It was Sir Hugo's wish that you should not only inherit them, but should wear them,' the old solicitor told me.

I crossed to the dressing table and unlocked the small jewel case. The pearls lay on a bed of black velvet. They were beautifully matched and the colour of a milky white dove. I was aware of Cat regarding me solemnly as I lifted them reverently from their resting place. I crossed to the mirror and hung them around my neck. Their beauty was quite simply breathtaking.

They become you, Catherine. They became my Lady also.

I felt very nervous sitting alone in the, to my mind, over grand Great Parlour, awaiting the arrival of my relatives. A large silver tray had been set on a low Oak

Carolean dresser, carrying a selection of drinks. Mrs Garner had asked me what wines I wanted served with lunch and I had swiftly handed that responsibility over to her. She suggested a vintage champagne as an aperitif but that other drinks should be made available as: 'Some gentlemen don't like the bubbles.' Everything seemed in hand, all I had to do was wait.

Celeste, looking quite extraordinary in an ill-fitting but clean and well-pressed black dress worn with a small white apron, came in with a tray of mouthwatering hors d'oeuvres: rolled pieces of smoked salmon stuffed with cream cheese, tiny vol au vents filled with mushroom and creamed chicken, anchovies in aspic on brown bread topped with thin slices of olives, slivers of pastry on which were piled caviare and chopped egg . . . it all seemed unreal to me. In only twenty-four hours Cat and I had not only travelled from our miserable apartment in Richmond, we'd moved into a different world.

Celeste set down the tray on the dresser next to the drinks. She winked at me. 'Mum's really pushed the boat out for you.'

'I can see that. Did my grandfather entertain in such style?'

'High days and 'olidays he did. But like Mum says, this is real special, ain't it?'

'Yes, it's very special. I've always wanted to meet my family. I wish I'd known my grandfather. But now the time has come, I feel . . . well . . . rather as if I was about to do an audition.'

'You do look a bit peaky. Tell you what, have a quick one. I'll get it for you. Have a nip of brandy.

That'll put some colour in your cheeks and it won't fight the champers when it goes down.' I hesitated. 'Go on, dutch courage!'

'I will if you'll join me.'

'What, me? Mum and Mrs Garner would string me up if I 'ad a drink in 'ere with you.'

'They won't if they don't know.'

Celeste looked at me for a moment then giggled. 'Neither they will!' She poured two drinks and then we drank them quickly, rather like schoolgirls in a dormitory having a midnight feast. We were just finishing when the front door-pull clanged. Celeste grabbed my glass from me and dashed over to a lacquered cabinet in the corner of the room. She popped the glasses inside and closed the doors. 'I'll fish 'em out later. Good luck!'

She was just about to leave the room when Mrs Garner opened the door. 'Mr and Mrs Jonas Kelsey, Miss.'

I crossed to greet my cousin Jonas and his wife. As I looked into his stiff, unfriendly face I remembered what Rupert had said about Jonas's dismay at my inheritance. His wife Annabel echoed my cousin's lack of warmth.

'Welcome to Somerton Magna, Catherine.' His lips were cool as he pecked at my cheek.

'Thank you,' I replied. 'It's good to come home at last.'

'Home?' Annabel queried tartly. 'A place you've never seen can hardly be home, can it?'

'It's my family's home,' I said firmly. 'Now it's mine. I hope to be happy here. And, well, I hope the whole family will regard it as their home also.'

'How magnanimous of you!'

Jonas shot a warning glance at his wife at this remark but she was already walking towards the drinks tray. It occurred to me that she was not about to pour her first drink of the day.

'Mrs Garner is going to serve some champagne if you'd like that.'

'No, thanks. Can't stand the stuff.' Her hand reached for the whisky decanter.

'Then please let me get you a drink.'

'There's no need for you to bother.'

'There's every need.' I took the decanter away from her. 'You're a guest in my house and I wouldn't wish to be discourteous.' I had wanted to be liked, perhaps even in time loved, by my family, but I suddenly knew that if I allowed myself to be downtrodden by any of them I would never gain their respect. If I didn't have their love, so be it. But I was damned if I was going to be treated as a nobody in my own house!

'Water? Soda? Ice?'

'Neat, thanks.'

'And for you, Jonas?'

'The same, thank you.'

As I poured the drinks I glanced out of the corner of my eye at my cousin and his wife. Jonas was, I knew, forty. His wife a little younger. She was a thin, impeccably groomed woman but her make up was a little too heavy and there were lines of discontent around her brightly painted mouth.

Jonas was a tall, handsome man beginning to put on too much flesh. He was dressed for the Stock Exchange rather than a family lunch in the country. His dark navy-blue suit was almost too well tailored. His shirt was striped with a white collar and he wore some sort of club tie. If there was a message that Jonas wanted to send to the world in general it was that he was rich and successful and – I suspect most importantly to him – powerful.

I handed them their drinks in silence. It seemed so clear to me that they had both made up their minds to dislike me that small talk seemed inappropriate.

After a moment Jonas cleared his throat and said, 'I was sorry to hear about your mother.'

'Thank you.' At that moment to my intense relief the door-pull clanged again and Celeste came into the room with a silver salver on which were several glasses of champagne. I heard loud, excitable chatter in the hall and knew that my other cousins had arrived.

Rupert and Sophie and another brother, either Joseph or Dickon, came into the room, flushed and laughing. Sophie came over to me and hugged me.

'We've raced across the green. I won, I always do. Hello again, Catherine! You've already met Rupert. He sneaked across and met you before lunch, the rotten beast! This is Dickon. He's an actor. He should by rights be in London, starving in an attic and waiting for the telephone to ring, but he so wanted to meet you!'

This all came out in a breathless rush.

Dickon crossed to me and kissed my cheek. His eyes were laughing. 'Thank God Sophie has to pause for breath occasionally otherwise no one else would ever get a word in. Hello, Catherine. Welcome home.'

'Thank you. It's good to meet you, Dickon. Will you have some champagne or would you prefer something else?'

'Oh, champers every time. Thanks.' He took a glass from the salver which Celeste offered to him. ' "Ill met by moonlight, proud Titania!" ' he teased.

'Oh, you are behind the times. I've changed it to Celeste now . . . I didn't know Titania was a blooming fairy!'

'I understood that your name was Doris?' Annabel said tartly.

'She can change it if she wants to. In the dark recesses of your soul are you really an Annabel? Hello again, Catherine!' Rupert kissed me, rather more circumspectly this time. 'Yes, please. I'd love some champagne. And can we start tucking into those goodies?'

'I already have!' This from Sophie, her mouth full of smoked salmon. 'Here, Dickon. These are delicious and you're always starving. Shall I pass them around, Catherine?'

'Yes, please. Is your father coming?'

'Yes, but he forgot as usual. He's scrubbing paint off himself. He'll be here in a minute.'

Rupert had crossed to Jonas and Annabel. He shook hands with Jonas and pecked Annabel on the cheek. 'Hello, Annabel. You're looking quite perfect. I bet if you'd been on the *Titanic* you'd have ended up in the lifeboat without a hair out of place. Don't the Kelsey pearls look terrific on Catherine?' he added wickedly. If the estate had been entailed Annabel could have expected the pearls eventually to come to her. I could understand why she resented me.

'I really hadn't noticed she was wearing them. May I help myself to another whisky, Catherine? Or perhaps Jonas might play the gentleman for once and get one for me.'

'Yes, do please help yourself.' I'd made my point earlier when she'd reached for the whisky decanter so pointedly and rudely.

The door was thrown open and a large bear of a man came into the room. He wore paint-spattered cord trousers, an open necked Viyella shirt, clean but with a worn collar, and a baggy cardigan. This could only be Marcus. Within seconds both my hands were being warmly clasped in his. Close to he smelt of pipe tobacco, turps and oil paints.

'Hallo, Catherine. Sorry I'm late. What have I been missing? Any family squabbles yet?'

'No,' laughed Sophie. 'But there will be now that you're here.'

'Nonsense! I'm the most easygoing person I know. Is that champagne?' He took a glass. 'I was sorry to hear about Francesca, Catherine. She was a delightful creature. You must miss her very much.' He put his arm around me and suddenly I was fighting back the tears. This was what I had needed when Francesca was dying. Someone who cared. Someone who comforted. Fortunately Marcus was distracted by Jonas walking past with a drink for Annabel. 'Good God, Jonas! You look as if you've been to a taxidermist!'

'We can't all lead a Bohemian life, Uncle Marcus. Some of us have to work for a living.'

'You see. You've started a squabble, Pa. You've a genius for it,' Sophie said, crossing to him. 'Have one of Mrs Jessop's wondrous titbits. You won't get this sort of treatment when you come to us, Catherine. It'll be stew and a glass of plonk at the kitchen table.'

'I'd like that very much.'

I'd heard Mrs Garner opening the door a few moments previously. Now she ushered in my great-uncle James and Marcus's last son, my cousin Joseph and his wife Rosemary.

'Sir James and Mr and Mrs Joseph, Miss Catherine. Will you ring when you wish me to serve luncheon, please, Miss?'

'Yes, of course. Thank you.' I crossed to greet the remaining members of my family as Mrs Garner left the room. Sir James was a tall, distinguished-looking man in his early-seventies. He was well and expensively dressed in a tweed suit. I noticed that the joints of his hands were gnarled with arthritis and he leant heavily on a walking stick.

My cousin Joseph was a more sober version of his brothers Rupert and Dickon. His wife Rosemary was a pretty, plump girl in her late-twenties, sensibly dressed in a tweed skirt and tailored blouse with a cashmere cardigan slung loosely around her shoulders.

'My God, I'd have known you anywhere, Catherine. You're very like Hugo. It's good to meet you at last.' My great-uncle steadied himself on his walking stick and offered me his hand. 'This is Joseph and Rose-mary. Sorry if I've held up lunch but I gave Joseph a lift back from the factory and we stopped to pick up Rosemary.'

'Factory?' Jonas said sharply. 'What were you doing at the factory, Father?'

Sir James turned to him. 'I may no longer be managing director but I'm still a director and have every right to drop in to the factory whenever I wish!'

'Of course, of course. I was just surprised that's where you'd been.'

'Give Catherine her gift, Joseph. That's why I've been to the factory, my dear.'

Joseph and Rosemary greeted me then Joseph handed me a presentation box with the Kelsey coat of arms on its lid. 'I hope you like it. Whatever you do, don't drop it!'

I took the box carefully and opened the lid. Inside was the most exquisite hand-cut crystal goblet. My name and the day's date were engraved on it.

'It's quite, quite beautiful. Oh, I can't thank you enough!'

'Well, it's not often someone meets all their living relatives in one go. I thought you should have something to remember it by.'

Before I could thank him again, Rupert was clapping his hands. 'Uncle . . . cousins . . . in-laws . . . Pa – I wish to propose a toast. See that Sir James and Joe and Rosemary have a glass, Celeste, and take one yourself.' She quickly crossed with her tray to the newcomers.

'To our new cousin. Long may she live amongst us. Welcome home, Catherine.'

My family raised their glasses to me. 'Catherine!' As they toasted me I felt Cat wind himself around my ankles. He must have slipped in when Mrs Garner had opened the door for Sir James. I bent down to stroke him, partly in greeting, partly to hide my emotion from my family.

Beware, Catherine. Beware. Someone in this room intends to kill you.

CHAPTER FOUR

THE CAT

'Cats by means of their whiskers seem to
possess something like an additional sense'
— Rev. W. Bingley

JESSLYN: 1659

'A great while ago the world begun,
With hey, ho, the wind and the rain:
But that's all one, our play is done,
And we'll strive to please you every day'
                              – William Shakespeare

I was dreaming that I was a little girl again. I was being held in my father's arms, my mother by our side. We were in the Great Hall of my father's manor house. He looked very handsome dressed in satin breeches and doublet with a wide lace collar, the same lace trimming the tops of his boots.

We were celebrating the twelve days of Christmas and the hall was decked with holly and ivy and mistletoe. I was clapping my hands and laughing because the mummers had come to the house and the whole household was in the hall watching and enjoying their antics. The Fool was striking a tambourine and leaping higher and higher in a cod galliard.

I opened my eyes and reality was before me. I lay in the straw remembering the days when laughter and joy were not a sin. When decking the hall at Christmas was not a pagan ritual, simply a time-honoured custom. When we were allowed the joy of making music and dancing. Then I heard the sound that had dominated the last moments of my dream. I heard, briefly, a tambourine quickly followed by a human voice: 'Shh!'

It seemed so inconceivable that in a barn behind an ale-house in the depths of East Anglia, someone had a tambourine to play that for a moment I thought I must still be dreaming. Then I heard another voice. 'Oh, shh yourself! There's no military between here and the garrison at Colchester.'

I became aware that the barn was no longer in darkness and that there was light flickering in the main body. After a moment curiosity overcame my fear and I quietly pulled back the straw covering the floorboards by my head. As luck would have it the boards were old and warped and I had a good view of the lower part of the barn through a wide crack. What I saw totally astonished me.

There were a number of men and boys grouped around a cart. A plump, good-natured-looking woman was lacing a boy into a lady's gown whilst he held up a mirror and painted his face. The gown was of the kind worn by ladies before the Civil War. Its bodice was very low cut and trimmed with silk ribbons. The taffeta overskirt was gathered up, revealing a different-coloured petticoat. The gown looked well worn and rather grubby but it was so colourful compared with the drab clothes women had had to wear since the Puritans had held the country in their dour grip that it was a joy to see.

The woman had now finished the lacing. She took two pieces of linen from the cart and pushed them down the bodice of the dress to simulate breasts. Then, softly, I heard the sound of a lute. I pulled my heavy body quietly and very slowly over the floorboards, drawn by the plaintive sound of the strings. Then the player came into view. He sat apart from the others, leaning against a heavy timber post. He was not a particularly good-looking man but there was something totally arresting about him – a kind of magnetism that I could feel even at my distance.

His age was hard to tell but he was, I surmised, in his mid-thirties.His clothes, like the boy dressed as a woman, were well worn but rich: rust-coloured velvet doublet and breeches with a lace collar. More lace at his wrists and trimming his soft leather boots. His hair was worn long and loose like a Cavalier. Then, softly, he started to sing.

' "Come away, come away, death. And in sad cypress let me be laid," '

From my studies with my father I knew it to be a song the clown sang in *Twelfth Night*.

' "Fly away, fly away, breath: I am slain by a fair cruel maid." '

The singer brought such an intense feeling of melancholy to his performance that I felt my heart would break.

Then the spell was broken. A heavily built man of about forty crossed to the lute player, laughing. 'A fair cruel *maid*?' he asked sardonically.

The player's mood changed chameleon-like and he too laughed. 'To an actor all things are possible.'

'But only on the stage. There's the rub! But no sad songs tonight, Richard. We're playing to peasants and they like to laugh.'

'They like to be moved to tears also. It's the other side of the same coin.'

'What the poor buggers like to do is to forget their miserable lives.' The man's manner suddenly changed. ' "Suppose within the girdle of these walls, Are now confin'd two mighty monarchies." We can do it, Richard . . . we can do it! Take the audience to France or to Athens. Take them to the Forest of Arden or make them believe that Bottom has an ass's head that isn't some tired old prop!'

The heavily built actor lowered himself somewhat clumsily on to the ground so that he sat beside the man he had called Richard. 'You and I have to live to see the playhouses open again. This sorry company . . .' he gestured towards the group around the cart '. . . have only our word what it was like. First the King murdered, then eight weeks later the soldiers pulling down the last of the theatres: The Phoenix in Drury Lane . . . Salisbury Court . . . The Fortune in Golding Lane . . . all gone in one day! And what bloody harm were we doing?'

The lute player sprang nimbly to his feet. 'What harm? What harm, Thomas?' he said sarcastically. 'Open men's hearts and minds to Shakespeare and Jonson and Marlowe and you do them infinite harm! Think how wonderful it was when the Church forbade men to read the Bible in English! They had to believe all the priests told them. Deny the people books and plays and poetry and you keep them bovine. They will be so much happier if they do not actually have to *think*! And our rulers will sleep more soundly whilst they keep men's minds captive.

'I'm disappointed in you, Thomas. You who have moved men and women to tears or to laughter on the turn of a phrase . . . a note in your voice . . . you must know the harm you did!'

The lute player moved away and the other man sadly

shook his head. His voice was a whisper but the quality of its tone was such that I could hear every word, every syllable. ' "If once we loose this light, 'Tis with us perpetual night." '

It took me a few moments fully to grasp what I was seeing. I'd heard that there were still a few wandering players giving performances in secret, always in fear that the military would raid them. I'd never been to a playhouse, never seen a play. Until the Civil War ravaged our lives mummers had come to our house at Christmas. I'd listened avidly when my father had told me of his visits to the playhouse when he had been a Gentleman of the Bedchamber at the Court of King Charles. How he liked best Shakespeare's theatre, The Globe, and how sad he had been when he'd heard that, in the name of Parliament, Sir Mathew Brand had had it pulled down and tenements built in its place.

'Little one,' Father had said, holding me on his knee, 'I have sat in a box at the Old Globe, all around me people cracking hazel nuts or sucking on oranges. Sometimes even fighting in the pit . . . but when the actors came from behind the curtains at the back out on to the wooden stage, I could forget everything! The noise . . . the smell of unwashed bodies . . . often cries of "Pickpocket". I forgot all that. I was at one with the actors. One day, precious, when the King comes into his own again, you'll know it for yourself.'

Well, the King had not yet come into his own again. And even in his wildest dreams or greatest fears for me, my father could not have foreseen that I would at last see a play while lying, heavily pregnant and afraid, in the straw like an animal.

Do not be afraid, Jesslyn. All things pass. I still watch over you.

There was a brief knock on the barn doors and then a young, roughly dressed boy pushed them open and entered. He looked around for a moment then approached the actor named Richard, who seemed to be the leader. He was standing by the cart adjusting a player's costume. 'Good God, man. You're supposed to be the Duke Orsino not a Blackfriars pimp! Yes?' This on seeing the boy.

'The Guv'nor wants to know if you lot are ready? He's got a good crowd for you.'

Richard looked around at his company of players and sighed. 'As ready as we'll ever be. Let them in.' The boy turned to go. 'Oh! And have you a look-out posted on the road?' The boy nodded then scampered away.

As soon as he had left, Richard crossed to a burly young man who looked like a wrestler. 'See that the doors are kept closed at the end of the Drolls until we've passed the hat around. I've not travelled to this Godforsaken place for a couple of groats and a bone button!'

After a few minutes the barn doors opened again and about forty to fifty people entered the makeshift playhouse. The audience consisted almost entirely of men, all of them carrying jugs of ale in their hands. The few women who were there were heavily cloaked with their hoods pulled well over their faces.

The change in the actors as their audience entered fascinated me. Some had been chatting, some seemed to be holding themselves apart from the others, their manner surly. The older actor named Thomas appeared to me to be deep in melancholy. Richard's manner was waspish, stinging the actors into the semblance of a company. But the moment the barn doors opened the air became electric with their personalities. They were as one in their desire to please and their confidence that they could do so. It was like seeing a group of people pass through a hidden door and, at the moment of passing, leave their true selves behind.

As the audience seated themselves on the barn floor or on bales of hay, one of the boys dressed as a woman started to dance a jig with another young actor. They moved to the music of pipe and drum and tambourine.

Then Richard stepped forward. In a voice thrilling but not over dramatic he told the audience of the joys that awaited them. The company were to perform two Drolls: the first, *The Story of the Steward Malvolio*, the second *The Tale of the Knight Falstaff*. I was mystified by this. Firstly because I had never heard of a Droll. Secondly because I knew Malvolio and Falstaff to be characters from the plays of William Shakespeare.

But there was no time to puzzle over this because the performance started and I was transported into another world.

The actors whom I knew only as Richard and Thomas played the leading parts in both Drolls. Richard playing Malvolio to Thomas's Toby Belch. Then Thomas playing Falstaff whilst Richard played Prince Hal. At that time I did not know whether or not the supporting company could, one day, match the talent of the two leading players. I only knew that, in spite of my loneliness, my fear, terror even of what tomorrow would bring, I felt a sense of belonging with these travellers. With these makers of magic. With these spellbinders.

It is your Destiny, Jesslyn. It is not Chance you came to this barn tonight.

I had edged myself forward to watch, making sure that I was hidden in the shadows. It was all I could do to stop myself laughing and applauding with the rest of the audience. Finally it was at an end. Richard stepped forward after the last of the applause had died down. His presence was so commanding that a hush fell over everyone in the barn. He held the pause for what seemed a daring but, oh so right, length of time. Then slowly he stretched out his arms. His voice when he spoke was soft and caressing but with an underlying feeling of wry humour and world weariness.

'If we shadows have offended,
Think but this – and all is mended –
That you have but slumber'd here
While these visions did appear.
And this weak and idle theme,
No more yielding than a dream.'

A moment's pause, then the audience broke into more spontaneous applause. Richard bowed, basking in their adulation, but at the same time giving a covert signal for two actors to move amongst the crowd with a cap whilst the heavily built man he had spoken to earlier moved to bar the barn doors.

Sensibly I knew that the actors had to be paid, but I had felt held by a kind of sorcery that night and somehow wished that the dream need not be debased by money tossed into a cap.

The audience slipped away into the night and I pulled myself back into the straw. I had just dragged Mat's cloak around me when the first pain hit me. I was unprepared for the intensity of it and couldn't stop myself groaning aloud. I heard a voice call out – Thomas's I think it was – 'My God, there's someone in the hay loft!'

'Christ! Do you suppose it's a spy?' another cried.

I lay drenched in sweat. There was nowhere I could hide. Nowhere to run to. After a moment the wrestler appeared at the top of the ladder, a dagger in his hand. 'Please! Please don't hurt me!' I begged. 'I mean you no harm.' Then another pain seemed to tear my body apart and I cried out.

The player peered into the gloom of the loft. 'Bloody hell! What you doing here, lass?'

'Hiding . . . resting. Don't hurt me!'

'I won't hurt you, love, but you need help!' He turned from me and made his way back down the ladder. 'Moll, this is a rum do! There's a lass up here having a baby. She's by herself. She'll need your help.'

I could hear the actors exclaim in astonishment. Then a woman's voice:' She can't have a baby up there, you daft bugger! We'll have to get her to the tavern.'

I heard someone climbing the ladder. The actor named Richard appeared and crossed to me. 'Are you alone?' I nodded, unable to speak for the pain I was in. 'Well, we'll get you to the inn. This is no place to have your baby.'

'It wouldn't be safe for me,' I managed to gasp. 'I am unmarried.'

Richard knelt down by me. 'You poor litle devil. Well, you've fallen amongst rogues and vagabonds . . . which is perhaps just as well in the circumstances. Our cart is full of props. A wedding ring can be found for you and I'll tell the innkeeper you're my wife. We've never played here before so he's not to know the truth.' He suddenly grinned. 'Besides, I'm an actor. I could convince the poor man night was day if I had a mind to . . .'

'I . . . I . . . don't think . . . I can get down the ladder.'

He took my hand then.' I'll get you down. Trust me. Will you trust me?'

I nodded, unable to speak as another pain gripped me. Richard crossed to the edge of the loft and called down: 'Charlie, bring the cart over here. That's it! Get it beneath where I'm standing . . . I'll lower the lass down into your arms. We'll be able to manage it if you stand in the cart.' Then he turned back to me.

'I'll be as gentle with you as possible . . . I promise I won't let you fall, and Charlie is built like an ox. Come on, little one, I've got you!'

Then I was being lifted in his arms. He carried me to the edge of the loft. I was by then half fainting. He put me down on the straw and swung my legs over the edge. 'You're going to have to be a brave girl and not panic . . . I won't let you fall, I swear.'

He knelt behind me and placed his arms under my armpits. 'Here we go, you'll be in Charlie's arms in a trice!' He lowered me slowly over the edge. The actor named Charlie was standing on a wooden chest on the cart. He placed one arm behind my knees, his other arm steadying me as Richard drew his arms from me.

'You're safe, lovey. You're safe,' Charlie whispered to me kindly as some of the actors let out a cheer.

After that, perhaps mercifully, my memory is blurred. I vaguely remember a ring being slipped on to my left hand. Charlie carrying me gently out of the barn to the tavern. Moll fussing around me. Richard running ahead and playing the anxious husband to the innkeeper. Then I was in a warm room in a soft bed. I remember pain, crying out for my father to make it stop. Moll and the innkeeper's wife caring for me. I was told afterwards that I laboured for eighteen hours and there were fears for my life. But at last, as I lay exhausted and barely conscious, I heard a baby's cry.

'Well done, my girl,' Moll said, bending over me. 'You've had a hard time but look what God has given you . . . a healthy baby girl.' And she gently gave my daughter into my arms. A newborn baby is not really beautiful but to me she was. No need to remember how I hated her father. How brutal her conception had been. She was mine and I loved her.

Twenty-four hours later I was able to sit up in bed. I was young and healthy and the terrible fatigue I had felt after giving birth was beginning to leave me. I wore a nightgown Moll had taken from the players' costume box. 'Just as well Lady Macbeth's sleep-walking scene features in one of our Drolls!' she whispered to me, winking as she helped me put on the nightgown.

'You've been very good to me, Moll. Why? I don't understand.'

'It's a wicked old world, lovey. And a hard one for us women. If we didn't help each other then God knows how we'd get on,' said Moll, taking my hand.

'I don't know what I would have done without you and Richard and Charlie. I would surely have died alone in that loft . . . and my baby with me.'

'Yes. Someone was looking over you that night! For we've never played here before.'

When the wind rattles the casement windows, when flying clouds scud across the moon, when you are warm by the fire, you will remember me. But I am with you always. Watching.

There was a brief knock on the bedroom door and then Richard entered. 'Good evening, Wife,' he said loudly for the benefit of any listener. He closed the door and crossed to the bed. He looked very different from when I had last seen him. Gone were the flamboyant clothes of a Cavalier. Instead he was soberly dressed in Puritan style with his hair pulled back and tied with a leather thong. He stopped at the bottom of the bed. 'How are you?'

'I am mending and have a beautiful daughter.' I indicated the cradle which the innkeeper's wife had lent me. I had fed my daughter half an hour before and now she slept peacefully. 'I am going to call her Lucinda after my mother.'

Richard crossed to the cradle and looked down at the sleeping child. 'A pretty name.' He turned and smiled at me. 'And if she inherits her mother's looks, she'll grow to be a beauty. Moll, you must be exhausted. Go and get your supper. I'll sit with Jesslyn. A serving maid is bringing up a tray with a meal for us.'

'I must say I could do with a bite . . . but don't you go tiring her. I know you when you get to talking,' Moll scolded. 'I'll just be downstairs if you need me,' she said to me, then left me alone with my baby and Richard.

I shook my head in wonder. 'I have never known such kindness from strangers. Why? Why are you helping me? Why have you all been so kind?'

Richard shrugged then crossed to the fire to kick life into a smouldering log. 'Players are strange people. Argumentative . . . jealous . . . competitive. But we spend our time looking inward to find some truth in our souls that can illuminate great writing. Perhaps in seeking that truth we touch humanity. Having done that it is hard to turn away when someone is in distress. But what of you, Jesslyn? Have you no home? Have your family turned you out?'

'I have no family. My mother died when I was five, my father a year ago. I . . . I cannot go back to my village. The villagers would brand me a sinner.'

He snorted in disgust at this. 'My God, what a mad world! In the name of the Lord churches have been desecrated! There must be no joy, no laughter in our lives, and every sin, real or imagined, must be sought out and punished. I had little time for that stubborn, proud fool our late King but I hate with my very being these bigots who govern us now!'

I was shocked to hear Richard talk of His Majesty in such terms. 'The King was a martyr,' I said stiffly.

'I'm sorry, I meant no offence. I fought for the King. Most players did.' He smiled suddenly. 'But whether from conviction or because Parliament had closed the playhouses, I cannot tell. So, what now, Jesslyn? Will the baby's father not help you?'

I was silent for a moment. 'This is very painful for me to tell you but Lucinda is not a love child. Her father raped me. He . . . he was drunk and is a bully and I've tried hard to forgive him but I cannot! And if one day, I can do harm to him, I will!'

Richard crossed to the bed and took my hand. 'I'm sorry, little one.' I felt tears sting my eyes because my father had always gently called me 'little one', and now Richard's kindness was almost too much to bear. I took a deep breath and fought back tears. Crying would not help me and my daughter to survive, and now that I had her, I was determined somehow to provide for her.

'What are your plans?'

'I had thought to go to my aunt in London. I don't think I have ever met her but she is my only living relative. Unfortunately she is married to a Puritan.'

'If she will not give you shelter, what will you do? Where will you go?'

Suddenly it was all too much for me and I could no longer try to be brave. I put my head in my hands and sobbed. 'I don't know! I don't know! What is to become of us?'

Richard sat on the edge of the bed and put his arm around me. 'Hush, love! Hush! I didn't mean to distress you. But cry! Cry all you must.' He held me close to him until I was able to regain a little control.

'I'm sorry.'

'No need to be. You look little more than a child yourself and have gone through so much. Look, I'll see what has happened to our supper. You'll feel better after a little food and some wine. I'll go and chase it up. I'll only be a moment, sweeting.'

Within a few minutes a flustered-looking maid servant carried a tray of food and wine into the bedroom. ''Tis simple fare, Mistress, but good.' So saying she set the tray down on a table by the fire. Richard pressed a coin into her hand. 'We'll serve ourselves.'

'Thank you, sir.' She bobbed a curtsey and left the room. I realized at the sight of the tray how hungry I was. There was a dish of jellied calves' feet, potted venison, a steaming hare pie, fresh bread and a side dish of asparagus. There was also a spiced wine custard and a jug of sack.

'First a little wine to bring the colour back to your cheeks. Then some food. Let's enjoy ourselves and talk of this and that. After supper I have a proposition to put to you.'

'Before I eat . . . how much will this cost? I have a few groats but . . .'

'Eat, you silly chicken! I want to hear no talk of payment. Eat!'

And I did. It was fine food but I was so hungry I think stale cheese would have tasted delicious to me. Whilst we dined Richard chatted to me. Asked me about my father. Which regiment he had fought in.

'Under Sir Thomas Dallison in Prince Rupert's Regiment.'

'Then he was at Naseby?'

'Yes. And taken prisoner. He was held in Norwich Castle for three years after that. It broke his health but he told me that many Royalist soldiers had been sent to the West Indies as slaves. Can that be true?'

'Yes, it's true, the poor devils,' Richard replied grimly.

When at last I was replete, Richard pulled the curtains and lit the candles then settled by the fire, a glass of sack in his hand. 'What I am going to tell you may shock you, but think of me kindly . . .'

'How could I think in any other way?' I interrupted.

'Wait until you hear what I have to say! I am known as Richard Warwick. It is not my real name. My father was the third son of a nobleman and thus went into the Church. My family was well-connected and my father had a rich living. When I was fifteen the players came to my grandfather's house. I knew then what I wanted to do with my life. When they left, I went with them. My father sent men to find me and I was dragged back and soundly thrashed. But, you see, I had not only fallen in love with the theatre . . . I had fallen in love, passionately in love, with one of the players. Do you understand what I am saying?'

'I . . . I think so. You loved another man. But how can that be?'

'I won't go into details,' Richard said wryly. 'Just accept that I am being totally honest with you, even if I lose your regard. I love the company of women but have never wanted to bed one. I am not and have never been promiscuous, but when I take a lover . . . well . . . it has never been a woman.'

'Why are you telling me this?'

'Because we can help each other, you and I! To be as I am is a hanging offence.' He laughed shortly and bitterly. 'Although half the late King's Court would have been for the gallows, also the late King's father, had the law been vigorously applied . . . but now it is dangerous. It is equally dangerous for you to have borne an illegitimate child. So let us provide cover for each other! I swear I will care for you as best I can. I will never question who you take to your bed and will be discreet with my own lovers. I know a priest in Cheapside who will marry us and not ask questions about Lucinda.'

He rose from the fireside and crossed to me. He bent and kissed me lightly on the forehead. 'Think on it. Sleep on it, little one. Good night.'

He left my side swiftly and the bedroom door closed quietly behind him.

I lay in the soft, flickering candlelight, stunned. At first it seemed an incredible suggestion though I was no stranger to the idea of arranged marriages. What would my life be like if I threw in my lot with the players? I remembered they had befriended me in my worst moments. Richard seemed scholarly and gentle . . .

Lucinda whimpered and I rose from the bed and crossed to her. I lifted her gently from the cradle and put her to my breast. Richard was right. I must think about his offer. I would give him my answer in the morning.

CHAPTER FIVE

THE CAT

'Mysterious one and proud,
In the land where shadows reign'
                    – L.H. Sigourney

CATHERINE: 1991

'I see the Past, Present and Future existing all at once
Before me'

– William Blake

I knew that my enemy was near. I felt their hatred. I could feel them watching and waiting in the shadows. My every sense told me of the danger I was in and yet my enemy had no face, no form.

They were in the house . . . in my room now. In the dark recesses they were readying themselves. I could just hear them breathing. A floorboard creaked. Why didn't I scream? Call for help? But who was there to hear me?

Fear held me captive. I knew that I wasn't asleep and yet what was happening to me seemed dream-like. Was I drugged then? What a terrible way to die. Aware of your fate but unable to fight it.

Another sound, nearer my bed now. I tried to pray but the only words that formed in my mind were: 'I want to live! I want to live!' A dark shape was by my bed. Man or woman I could not tell but I could just make out their hands . . . and their hands held a pillow. If only I could move. Cry out. Do something to stop my death from suffocation.

Then a cat sprang. A black cat. Its fur raised in anger, ears flattened, claws unsheathed. Its face looked almost terrible with mouth drawn back to reveal teeth ready to strike. I heard a cry as the cat clawed at my attacker's face. I whispered one word: 'Luke!'

I awoke bathed in sweat and with my heart thumping so hard I felt as if my chest would explode. This was my second night at Kelsey Hall. I had felt no sense of fear at staying alone in the old house yet, on both nights my dreams had been haunted by an unrecognizable terror. Now I felt sure there was someone else in the room with me.

I wavered ridiculously between wanting to lie so still and quiet that whoever – or, it had to be faced, whatever – was in the room with me wouldn't notice me, and the need to steady myself by gulping deep breaths.

I tried to force myself to be rational. Either there was someone in the room or I'd simply had another bad dream. Lying in bed, rigid with fright, helped neither situation. Coward! Better to attack than to defend. I leapt from the bed and pulled at the heavy, old-fashioned light switch. The room was totally empty.

I sat on the edge of the bed and put my head in my hands. I knew I'd been under intolerable stress during Francesca's illness. Knew that I had not yet come to terms with her death. On top of that, because of my grandfather's bizarre bequest to me, I'd been plunged into a new and alien world. No wonder I had strange and terrifying dreams!

'Oh, Fran, Fran,' I said silently to my mother, 'this legacy is too much for me. You should have stayed to share it with me, Fran dear. We could have had such a good time.'

I struggled against the bitter well of self-pity. I felt so

desperately alone. Then slowly, painfully, I forced myself to face a truth I had known for a long time: I had always been alone.

Fran had loved me in her own way but I had only been a small part of her life. Important, yes, to give her the support and blind devotion that she needed from me but I had never been at the true centre of things. A new lover, an exciting script, someone who made her laugh constantly took her away from me. I had served my purpose.

Well, so be it. I had loved her but now must find the courage to be me. What did *I* want from life? What did I need? Was I, once again, to live my life as others dictated? This is how the owner of Kelsey Hall behaves! Fills her days! A new life was opening up for me and I determined that it would be of my choosing. I had been badly shaken by my dream but suddenly I smiled.

I resolved that I would no longer sleep in my grandfather's bedroom with its dark panelling and heavy, oppressive tapestry curtains around the ancient four-poster. On my first night at the Hall a note from Mrs Garner had directed me to 'the master's bedroom'. The bed had been turned down. The fire lit in the Tudor hearth. I'd accepted that. Why not? But tomorrow I'd find a room of *my* choosing and then have it decorated to *my* taste.

I climbed back into bed and pulled the covers tightly around me. After a moment I found the courage to switch off the light. I lay in the darkness, listening. The old house was totally silent. Then I heard a slight rustling in the mulberry tree outside one of the bedroom windows. I smiled. Cat was on his way to me.

A gentle thump as he landed on the floorboards and then I felt him leap on to the bed. I stretched out my hand to stroke his sleek, dark head.

'Do you believe in ghosts, Cat?' I whispered.

You have nothing to fear from the past, Catherine. But you can learn from my Lady.

Cat's reply was to curl up gently against my body. I finally fell asleep to the sound of his soft purring.

When I awoke again I was alone. Cat had obviously made his exit down the mulberry tree. I glanced at my watch. It was nine o'clock! I couldn't remember when I had last slept in so late. I sprang from the bed and dashed into the bathroom. It was only when the huge Victorian bath was half full of steaming water that I took stock of things. Where was I rushing to? I no longer had to present myself to tight-lipped employers, explaining that signal failure had caused a thirty-minute delay, or that I'd waited forty minutes for a bus only to find that three arrived in convoy. In fact, I no longer *had* to do anything! Except, that is, to move myself out of my grandfather's bedroom. Even that, with bright sunshine streaming through the windows, seemed rather self-indulgent. I'd never been fanciful before. What presence did I feel in that room?

Come on, Catherine, I chided myself, simply change rooms, put the dreams down to all the excitement and too much rich food.

And yet, though I might not be fanciful, I felt I wasn't insensitive. I truly had sensed evil in that room. Known somehow that someone hated me enough to kill me. I couldn't dismiss it as just a dream, it had seemed so tangible.

Was I in danger? I simply couldn't believe it. Some of the family, Jonas and Annabel in particular, clearly resented my grandfather's will but there was a giant gap between resentment and murder. No, I had just had two bad dreams which could not possibly have a bearing on my own life.

As I passed the Great Parlour I could hear the sound of a radio played at a lowish level but with the unmistakable beat of rock music. Clearly Celeste was flicking a duster over the despised museum pieces!

When I entered the kitchen Mrs Garner was sitting at the long oak refectory table drinking coffee. Mrs Jessop had a mug of coffee by her side and was chopping vegetables at the sink.

'Good morning. I feel disgraceful, having slept in so late.'

'Oh, I'm sure you needed your sleep, Miss. Yesterday being such a big day and all. I've set a table for breakfast in the Little Parlour . . . Your grandfather always liked the early morning light in there.'

Only two days into my inheritance and I wanted to cry out: 'Ask *me*.' I'd lived in the shadow of my incandescent mother, I was damned if I'd live my new life just as my grandfather had. Just as well, I thought wryly, I don't know who my father is otherwise no doubt there'd be another mould I'd be trying to break.

I simply said, 'Thank you.' I started to leave the kitchen then turned back. 'Have you seen my cat, I wonder? There's a tiny bit of fish left that I need to cook for him. If he's about I know he'll soon be demanding his breakfast.'

Mrs Jessop's lips tightened. 'I shouldn't worry about his breakfast if I was you, Miss. He's already helped himself to a nice bit of saddle of venison! I was preparing a casserole to leave for your supper. My back was only turned for a minute! A stray did you say he was? Well, wherever he came from, he's picked up some fancy tastes!'

'He certainly has.' I suddenly grinned. 'I only hope he enjoyed the venison raw as much as I'm sure I'd have enjoyed it casseroled tonight. But even so, I'm sorry my cat hasn't better manners. By the way, you have remembered that Rupert is taking me to see the glassworks today and that I'll be out to lunch?'

'Yes, of course. You'll enjoy the glassworks, Miss. I don't know what people around here would do for a living if it wasn't for them. Everyone used to work on the land, you see. Now it's just two men and a lot of hired-in machinery. Isn't that so, Mrs Garner?'

'Yes, that's so! We used to be a tight-knit community, but what with the way the farms are going and the townies buying up the cottages for weekend places . . .' She shrugged then smiled at me. 'At least at Kelsey Hall things go on.'

But not to the extent of my spending another night in my grandfather's bedroom, I thought.

'Mrs Garner, I don't want to put you to too much bother but I'd really prefer to have another bedroom.' I saw the women exchange glances. 'I'm sure that my grandfather's room was always used by the master of the house but . . . well, there's a mistress here now and

I find the room too . . . too . . .' How to explain my fears? '. . . too . . . uncongenial . . .' I finished lamely.

There was a slight pause and then Mrs Garner said, 'But the Kelseys have always . . .'

'I'm sorry, I don't wish to appear rude, but I have the feeling that this house died nearly thirty years ago when my mother left. Although I have great respect for family tradition, I don't want to live in the past. I'd like a breath of fresh air to blow through these hallowed halls.'

Mrs Jessop and Mrs Garner looked thoroughly taken aback and, in many ways, I didn't blame them. There was nothing about me to suggest a rebel. Mrs Garner recovered first.

'As you wish, Miss Kelsey. Would you like me to put you in your mother's old room? – It's . . .'

'No!' I interrupted sharply. 'Thank you, but no. If you'd be so kind, just put me in the most comfortable guest room until I've had a chance to sort myself out. I really am sorry if it causes you any inconvenience. Now, if I may, I'll make myself a coffee. Can I make either of you another cup?'

'I'll bring a pot through,' Mrs Jessop said stiffly. I was about to say that there really was no need but then I accepted the situation. The fact that I'd much rather make my own coffee and then sit with them in the kitchen and drink it was neither here nor there. They would be more comfortable if I had my breakfast in solitary isolation in the Little Parlour. After all, that was what my grandfather preferred!

I sat in splendid isolation in the Little Parlour and asked myself what was I going to do with my life? As I sipped my fruit juice I glanced at the morning's papers. *The Times* and *Telegraph*. My grandfather clearly only wanted to hear the ruling classes' view of the world.

Mrs Jessop came into the room with a fresh pot of coffee. I thanked her. We had nothing more to say to each other. I knew I was incredibly fortunate but I had no idea of how to cope. In the more affluent days with my mother I'd been used to hotel staff or temporary hired help but had never before experienced the feeling that people who frankly didn't know you might offer loyalty. A kind of caring that was beyond price. I benefitted from that loyalty while I wanted to reject it. I had done nothing to earn it, I felt. Had simply been thrust into my new role of heiress. I was the luckiest woman in the world but could not, must not, allow my inheritance to suffocate me. However tentatively, however hesitantly, I must cease endlessly waiting in the wings.

As I sipped my coffee I glanced out of the window across the courtyard to the gatehouse. It was the only part left of the fortifications that must once have guarded the original manor. Whereas the Hall was timber-framed, infilled with brick, the gatehouse was built of stone. I'd read in one of the books that Mr Pritchard had given me that it was supposed to date from the end of the twelfth century. On the lower floors there were no windows, simply unglazed slits for arrows to be shot through in the event of attack. But on the floors above, in the opening that had accommodated the original drawbridge, some ancestor of mine had had mullioned windows put in. Perhaps to create a sanctuary for themselves so that they could escape from the responsibility of being a Kelsey!

I suddenly had an idea. I jumped up and hurried through to the corridor that led to the saddle room in the west wing. I'd seen a number of ancient-looking keys hanging there, each with a faded label. Sure enough there it was, the key to the gatehouse. The label was crumpled with age and the ink on it had faded to a lightish brown but I could just make out the word. I took the heavy iron key down off the hook and then retraced my steps to the front of the house and went out into the courtyard.

The narrow oak door swung open on well-oiled hinges. I suppose I had expected to find the interior covered in cobwebs and the dust of ages but my grandfather had clearly believed in keeping every bit of Kelsey property in good repair.

Worn stone steps spiralled upwards and I started the long climb to the upper floors.

At the top of the stairs there was another door, fortunately unlocked. I pushed the door open and stepped into a truly lovely room. The walls had been plastered and then simply whitewashed. There was a huge stone fireplace taking up most of one side of the room, bigger and more impressive than any in the Hall even. But it was the windows that drew me. The view from them was simply breathtaking. One could see over the village green to the fields beyond and then the water of the estuary glinting in the morning sun.

The room was unfurnished apart from a heavily carved Jacobean table and a high-backed oak chair. The table and chair had been placed to take advantage of the view. I felt that I had been right and someone had used this room as a retreat. I sat in the chair and leant my arms on the table, looking out towards the estuary. I felt completely at home, as if the room had been waiting for me.

It has, Catherine. You are coming close to someone who would have loved you.

I started as Cat jumped on to the table by my side. 'Cat! – How did you get in here? – Squeezed through one of the stone slits, did you?' I rubbed behind his ears and he started to purr. 'And what's this I hear about venison? Mrs Jessop says you've got very fancy tastes for a stray. Come on, I'm going to explore some more.'

A door led from a corner of the room and, once again, I was climbing upwards, this time accompanied by Cat.

There were two more rooms. The one immediately above had the same mullioned windows with their view over the village to the waters of the estuary. There was a fireplace, smaller than in the room below but beautiful in its simplicity. The window sill was deeper than in the room below, as if it had once held a cushioned seat.

I sat on the sill and opened one of the windows. I was suddenly reminded of a time when I was about ten or eleven. Francesca had been filming on location in the Loire – a big international movie where, once again, with a minimum amount of help from the army and the Resistance, a major star won the war. We stayed in an old château. To my delight my room was in a turret. I had sat at the window looking out over the acres of vineyards and had imagined myself to be a princess in a fairy story, letting down my silken tresses so that a prince could climb up and rescue me. Somehow there was the same sense of romance about the gatehouse.

I closed the window then went on to explore the top floor. The ceiling was much lower in that room and the windows smaller but it was ideal for the plan that was forming in my mind. I was a wealthy woman, or at least would be after probate had been completed on my grandfather's estate. I felt at home in the gatehouse in a way I felt I never could be at the Hall. After all the years my grandfather had lived alone there, the old house cried out to have a family in it. For children's laughter. For people to come in from walks with muddy boots and equally muddy dogs. Perhaps one day I would marry and have a family, although I doubted it. Until then the gatehouse would be my retreat. I could easily afford to have it converted into a small apartment. The top floor could be made into a bathroom and kitchen where I could make myself breakfast or a snack. The floor below would be my bedroom and the room below that a sitting room. I'd still live at the Hall but this would be my bolt hole. My very own place. I'd talk to Mr Pritchard about funds then find out from Mrs Garner the name of a local builder.

The sound of a car horn brought me back from my excited reverie. I glanced at my watch. It was eleven and I should have been ready for Rupert and our visit to the glassworks. I scooped up Cat and dashed helter-skelter down the spiral staircase.

When I got to the courtyard my cousin was just climbing from an elderly but clearly well-loved MGB Roadster.

'Rupert, hello. Forgive me, I started to explore and

lost track of the time. Give me ten minutes to put on my posh frock and some lipstick. Chase up Mrs Jessop for some coffee. Sorry!' I ran towards the house followed by Rupert, who was laughing.

'What's come over you, cousin Catherine? You seem quite scatty this morning!'

'No,' I called back over my shoulder. 'Just happy. Cat and I have just found our very own ivory tower. Won't be long.'

Twenty minutes later we were driving under the gatehouse and turning on to the road to Colchester.

'You all right?' Rupert shouted above the noisy old engine. 'Seemed too nice a day to bundle you into a company car. Even though one goes with the job.'

'Job?'

'Oh, yes. It's only Pa and Dickon who have escaped the curse of the Kelseys. I've sold my soul to the glassworks. Public Relations. So, you see, although I'm enchanted to escort you today, I'm also buttering up our major shareholder!'

'Don't look like that, Catherine. I was making a rather poor joke. Forgive me.'

'There's nothing to forgive. I met you and the family for the first time yesterday. Why should any of you give a damn about me? I don't know you and you don't know me. Tell me about the glassworks,' I said, determinedly changing the subject.

'My dear girl, I could bore you to death about the blasted glassworks but what I care about at the moment is that you'll accept my apology for making such a crass remark. You can give me a forfeit if you like. I know, you can condemn me to have dinner with Jonas and

Annabel every night for the next fortnight. Now *that's* suffering!'

I laughed in spite of myself. 'Okay. Let's begin anew. But I honestly do want to know about the Kelsey Glassworks.'

'Fair enough. Where do I start? At the beginning, as Alice would say! The original glassworks are just outside the village on the estuary. A museum now, also selling reject glass and ye olde cream teas . . . A splendid combination. The tourists get rooked on both counts!'

'But why on earth build a glassworks in such a remote place?'

'Well, by all accounts the founder, Sir Thomas, was an absolute nut about glass. Determined that we could make glass that would rival the Venetians.

'Can you imagine how much wood you'd need to heat a glass-making furnace? Half a forest, I should think! Once they found a way to use coal instead, what better place than on this estuary? The barges could bring the coal down from the north, the finished glass could be shipped down the coast and up the Thames to London. And, in those days, the sand in the estuary was very pure. You need a lot of sand to make glass.

'Thanks to the local Water Boards the estuary's too polluted for us to use local sand any more. We ship it in from Belgium. And natural gas is a lot cleaner than coal for heating the furnaces. I think it's called progress!' he added ironically.

We were on the main London to Colchester road now and I was glad of my woollen jacket and silk scarf in the open car. But Rupert was right – it was a lovely day and this style of motoring was much more fun than a company car.

He slowed down as we approached a well-landscaped factory site.

'Here we are, sweet cos. Your inheritance.'

The security guard on the gate waved us through and Rupert parked the car near the main entrance.

'One of the perks of being a Kelsey. Security turns a blind eye to your car being parked on areas forbidden to mere mortals!'

'Is that quite fair?'

'Good Lord, no. But who the hell wants to be fair? The more of the lion's share I can get, the better!'

As Rupert took my arm and we walked across the forecourt to the main reception, I wondered just how ruthless my cousin really was. His bantering manner made it practically impossible to glimpse the real man and his charm was such that, so far, I had not seen any side of his character he had not wanted me to see.

More security at reception as I was given a visitor's pass.

'Why so much security? Surely you don't expect a smash and grab raid?' I asked smiling.

'We've got five furnaces here, all heated to at least one thousand two hundred Centigrade by gas. The factory's as safe as houses but can you imagine what would happen if there was an accident? We'd need to be able to account for everyone. Glass-making is known as "the art of fire". It would be foolish to forget that. Now come on, to brighter things. Let me take you into the show room.'

It was beautifully lit so that the lead crystal and cut

glass almost seemed to take on a life of their own. Central to the display were a number of pieces of glass of quite breathtaking beauty. A discreet sign named them as part of the Fitzgerald Collection. I crossed to admire them, then gasped when I saw the prices written on small cards next to each item.

'Do people actually pay this much for glass?'

'They do indeed! The Kelsey Fitzgerald Collection is highly sought after. Fitzgerald's quite brilliant.' Rupert suddenly laughed. 'He's worth his weight in gold to the company but Jonas doesn't know whether to love him or loathe him!'

'If he makes these exquisite pieces and they sell at these prices, I should have thought Jonas would worship the ground the man walks on.'

'Ah, but Brett Fitzgerald is a perfectionist. More cullet comes from his Chair than any other in the history of glass-making.' He took in my bemused expression. 'Sorry, sorry. We may have a spanking new factory but the jargon used is the same as in the Middle Ages. Cullet is discarded glass that's then crushed up and a small portion melted down again. A Chair is a team. It's headed by the master, and under him he has two blowers, one foot maker, a bit gatherer, two overwarmers and perhaps a couple of apprentices. Clear as mud?' he teased.

'It's a lot to take in on just one visit! By the way, did Fitzgerald make the beautiful goblet that Sir James gave me yesterday?'

Rupert looked a trifle embarrassed. 'I'm afraid not. You see, Uncle James wanted to give you something traditional so he wanted the crystal to be cut. Fitzgerald *never* cuts lead crystal. He . . . er . . . thinks it vulgar!'

I looked around at the cut glass decanters, sherry glasses, fruit bowls, then back at the beautiful simplicity of Fitzgerald's designs. He could have a point, I thought to myself.

Rupert took my arm. 'Come along. We'll go up on to the observation platform and you can see some of your glass actually being worked.'

As we walked from the show room Rupert asked, a little over casually I thought, 'None of my business really but I wondered . . . are you going to sit on the board?'

'Good lord, I haven't given it a thought. Why do you ask?'

'Oh . . .' Rupert shrugged '. . . it's just you could if you wanted to. As the majority shareholder you could vote the present board out and a new one in. After all, it's a private company.'

'Why on earth should I want to do that?'

'Well, I'd do it for devilment!' he said, grinning.

'Not a very sound approach to business, is it? Original, but not exactly sensible.'

'And you're a sensible girl, aren't you, cousin Catherine? Here we are.'

We'd climbed to the second floor and now went through two fire doors. As the second door opened on to the observation platform above the main body of the glassworks, I immediately felt the heat from the furnaces. I watched, fascinated, as the different groups of men worked with great concentration down below on the factory floor.

Rupert touched my arm. 'Look over there. They're

just about to open the fire clay slab to gather some glass to work. The pots the glass is melted in are all made by hand, you know. We get through quite a lot because they only last for about six weeks.'

That didn't surprise me when I saw the bubbling, molten glass inside the pot as one of the men opened the fire door. A second man stepped forward and thrust a long, iron instrument into the red hot glass. He called out to a man sitting in a low, long-armed chair, 'It's sweet-natured!'

He quickly rotated the iron in the melted glass then took it from the pot. The fire door was closed as the blob of glass on the end of the iron was carried over to a table.

'That's a marver . . . an iron table covered in bees-wax. The glass has to be rolled on that to cool the surface and harden it. Otherwise, when the master takes over, the glass could blow out at the thinnest place.'

We watched for a few minutes while the glass was rolled. Then the blowing iron was handed to the master-blower, the man seated on the strange wooden chair.

'Let's move along to the next Chair. You might see a later stage.'

The men at the next furnace were waiting by the closed pot and so we moved on yet again. This time I was in luck because a beautifully shaped jug was before the master and he was shaping the lip with his sensitive hands.

'This is absolutely fascinating, Rupert. Thank you so much for bringing me! Although how the men stand the heat down there . . .'

'Oh, they get used to it. Now, come on. We'll move along to the last furnace and you can see our resident genius at work.'

We walked along the platform and stopped above the last team, or Chair as Rupert termed it. He nodded towards a dark-haired, good-looking man in his early-thirties. 'Fitzgerald.'

Even if Rupert hadn't indicated him I would have guessed who the man was. There was an air of authority about him and the members of his team were treating him with great respect. He had strong Celtic features and yet there was a sensitivity about his expression as he handled the beautifully coloured glass. They were at the last stage of the glass-making process. The bowl that Fitzgerald held in his hands looked exquisite.

Suddenly, and shockingly, he threw it into a wooden box where it smashed against other broken, discarded glass. I must have gasped at seeing something so lovely destroyed by its maker because Fitzgerald looked up to the platform. I was aware of intensely blue eyes regarding me with amusement. Even from that distance I felt the strength of personality of this highly individual craftsman.

I smiled inwardly. Brett Fitzgerald was a very attractive man and, had I been a romantic, I could almost have believed in love at first sight.

You can believe, Catherine. Learn from my Lady.

CHAPTER SIX

THE CAT

'Remember me when I am gone away,
Gone far away into the silent land'
— *Christina Rossetti*

JESSLYN: 1659

'Love all alike, no season knows, nor clime,
Nor hours, days, months, which are the rags of time'
                                    – John Donne

Richard and I had been married eight weeks when I fell in love.

We were staying in London at his house in Maiden Lane. Built a little before the start of the war, it was nowhere near as grand as the magnificent houses built by Inigo Jones on the site of the old convent garden of St Peter's, but it was light and elegant as no other house I had seen. It was built of brick instead of the traditional timber in filled with lath and plaster. And whereas in the City the tall houses jutted out so that the top floors nearly touched those opposite, thus making the streets dark and dank and evil-smelling, here the air was sweet. Richard's house was on the south side of the lane and behind it were gardens and fields running down to the Strand where the great palaces of the noblest families in the land had been built along the banks of the Thames.

It was late-May and the air was soft and warm. Moll and I had carried Lucinda's cradle into the garden. She was sleeping now in the shade of a gnarled old walnut tree, Moll dozing by her side.

I carried a bowl of flowers from the garden up the curving marble staircase, another innovation, to the first-floor parlour. I had no idea that Richard had a visitor. As I entered the room I heard a voice that was strange to me.

'. . . Willys is most definitely spying for Parliament,' I heard as I entered. 'You must warn the other members of the Knot. Tonight I leave for Brussels to alert the King and . . .'

The speaker broke off as he saw me in the doorway. I knew without being told that the young man speaking in such a conspiratorial manner with my husband must be related to him. He was taller and broader than Richard but had the same arresting presence. The same dark good looks. But whereas Richard's manner was quizzical, almost mocking, the young man standing beside him bore himself as one born to command. I saw alarm flare briefly in his eyes at my intrusion but this was quickly replaced by a cold, harsh look as he started to move towards me.

Richard reached out and clasped the young man's arm, stopping him.

'The King has no more faithful subject than this lady. Her father fought under Sir Thomas Dallison in Prince Rupert's regiment.' He smiled, teasing. 'When I called the late King a stubborn fool, had she been armed, she would have run me through with a rapier. All in all, you can trust her, Guy. Most especially because she is my wife.'

He held his hand out to me. 'Come, little one, come meet my cousin . . . Guy de Burgh, Earl of Colne. Guy, I present my wife, Jesslyn.' Suddenly Richard laughed. 'I can see your lady-like upbringing struggling with confusion as to how to curtsey with a vase of flowers in your hands. Here! Let me resolve the matter.'

So saying Richard took the flowers from me and went to place them on the heavily carved oak chest which stood by the front window.

I swept into a low curtsey. 'My Lord.' Guy de Burgh crossed and bowed low over my hand. His lips briefly touched the tips of my fingers. 'Mistress . . . Cousin! Welcome to our family.'

As I rose from my curtsey I looked up into his eyes and was lost. I, who had sworn to take my revenge on all mankind for the cruelty that Luke had inflicted on me, could think of nothing but how I desired this man. There was momentarily a look of confusion in Guy de Burgh's eyes, then he pulled his hand from mine as if he had been burnt by my touch. As he had.

I assumed it was to cover his feelings that Guy crossed to the side table on which stood a jug of wine. My world reeled. I was suddenly aware of a beating of wings. A butterfly was battering itself against one of the windows. I felt a moment's irritation which was unlike me. I was country bred and loved all creatures. I quickly went to open the window to release the now frantic creature.

Time was suspended. Guy was busy with his wine, I with the trapped butterfly. The room was charged with our need for each other. I heard Richard start to hum softly to himself. I knew the tune instantly. It was Feste's song from *Twelfth Night*. 'Oh, stay and hear your true love . . .'

I walked back to Guy de Burgh, determined to mask what was happening to us with a show of normality.

'My Lord, it is past noon. Will you dine with us?'

'Mistress, I would rather not place myself in a position where your servants can study me too closely. It might not be safe . . . for any of us.'

'Then I shall bring food to this room and serve us myself.' I bobbed a brief curtsey and left them, affording myself a wry smile at the formality of the hospitality I was offering. I was more used to life in a humble cottage than to the niceties of entertaining an earl, and yet the lessons of childhood die hard and I could just remember the gracious style in which we lived before the war between the King and his Parliament set brother against brother and tore so many lives apart.

Richard had confided in me when I accepted his offer of marriage as to his real name and family connections. As soon as he brought me to the house in Maiden Lane it was obvious that his life style was not supported by his work as an actor. We lived informally but comfortably with a cook, two maid servants, and Harry – who had no specific duties but worked like a demon. Richard had rescued him from an angry mob when he had been caught pickpocketing. Richard, a superlative actor, had pretended to be a Justice of the Peace and had marched Harry away by the ear. As thieving was a hanging offence Harry had every reason to be grateful to him but I felt that, more importantly, Richard was the first person to show him a spark of human kindness in his young life. A child of the gutter, Harry was now fierce in his loyalty to Richard and I felt we could trust him with our lives. And, if my suspicions were correct and the Knot I had overheard Guy de Burgh refer to was the Royalist secret society, the Sealed Knot, we might well have to.

The household was completed by Moll. Dear Moll had become my friend, my confidante, almost the mother I could barely remember. She had told me unsentimentally and with simple courage about the death of her husband.

'Will was an actor . . . a dear fool who was at his best playing fools! What did he know of soldiering? My sister runs an inn in Shoreditch. We could've gone there and laid low until those Puritan prigs let us open the theatres again. But no, my Will must fight for the King. "What has the King ever done for you," I asked him? "At least he hasn't closed the theatres," he said. As if that was a reason to get killed!'

'I'm sorry, Moll. Where did he fall?'

'He didn't fall, he was murdered. After the Battle of Basing House his troop surrendered. The officers were dead or dying and Will was sergeant.' She shook her head. 'They must've been desperate to make my poor Will a sergeant. Perhaps he was the only one who could tell his right from his left? Even then the poor dear would've called left the Prompt Corner!'

'But if his troop surrendered, how could he have been murdered?'

'How indeed? I was told he knelt and offered his sword to the Ironside officer. The officer took the sword, then shot him clean through the temple. I'll give those bastards their due – they hanged the Ironside officer. But that won't bring my poor Will back! Ah, well, life has to go on, lovey.'

When I entered the kitchen Harry was just bringing

in wood for the huge fireplace that took up nearly the whole of one wall. The meat for the evening meal was already turning on the spit. Another, to me, amazing innovation in Richard's house was that the spit rotated without a spit-boy having to turn the handle. Instead there was a jack that was wound up with a key. Once wound, the spit turned in one direction for a full hour then, wound up again, turned in the other.

I glanced around the kitchen to make sure Harry and I were alone. 'I'm going to take some food up to the parlour. I'll serve Master Warwick's guest myself. Can you see that no one disturbs us?'

'All taken care of, Mistress.' He threw down the logs and lowered his voice. 'I sent the two girls out on errands and Cook's 'aving a bit of a lie down.' He winked. 'I encouraged 'er to 'ave a bit more of 'er tipple than usual . . . She'll be sleeping it off for at least a couple of hours.'

I laughed in spite of my anxiety about our guest. 'Harry, you're incorrigible! But I don't know what we'd do without you.'

'That's something you'll never 'ave to find out, Mistress. I owe my life to Master Warwick and I ain't never going to forget it. Cor! When we got round the corner and 'e let go of me ear and started to laugh, I thought 'e'd gone barmy. I really believed 'e was a Justice, see!' He grinned. 'So did those bleeders . . . begging your pardon . . . who wanted to see me dancing at Tyburn!'

'Yes,' I said. 'Richard's a good actor. Who knows, Harry, perhaps one day we'll see him in a proper theatre? It's what he longs for.'

I crossed into the larder and started to load a tray. Harry fetched pewter plates.

'Now Tumbledown Dick's gone, things might look up,' Harry said. Then added gloomily, 'Then again, they might not!'

'Tumbledown Dick?'

'Gawd love you, Lady! Ain't you 'eard that's what they're calling Richard Cromwell! Just 'cos he was 'is father's son didn't stop 'im being a right idiot. Taken 'imself off abroad, they're saying in the taverns. Good riddance!' he added fervently. 'Want me to carry that tray for you?'

It was now piled high with cold beef, venison pasties, salmon and currant pasties, brawn, and a delicious quince and apple pie. The Earl and Richard would dine simply but well.

'Thank you, Harry, I can manage. But I'd be grateful if you would keep an eye open and warn us if there are any callers.'

'Like soldiers, you mean, Lady?'

'Yes, Harry, I'm afraid I do.'

I sat apart from Richard and Guy de Burgh whilst they ate. My emotions were in turmoil. On the one hand I was desperately worried, frightened even, about the threat to the safety of our household. No mercy would be shown to us if it was discovered that we had given shelter to a Royalist spy. And worse – far worse – I suspected that Richard was somehow involved with the Sealed Knot.

But surmounting even my fear and worry was my attraction to the Earl of Colne. I had read of love at first sight in plays and in poems and, if I'd given it any thought at all, had dismissed it as pure invention.

Yet I had studiedly avoided touching Guy as I'd served him with wine and food and knew that he too must be feeling something of this mysterious emotion as he was equally careful not to let his hand brush against mine. And all the time I was aware of Richard's amused observation as we played out our roles.

When the men had finished their meal, I rose. 'Richard, my Lord, I should like to speak with you.'

Richard reached out and took my hand. 'You look very serious, little one.'

'I am serious! I feel I should explain something to you both. Although my father and I lived humbly our lives were rich in scholarship. He and our friend Harriet both believed that women have brains and should be educated. I therefore know rather more of Greek and Latin than of the still room.

'I was raised to believe that women are equal to men. A shocking thought to most men, I know, but I am as I am. I therefore ask you to take me into your confidence. I can be as loyal as any man. I simply ask you not to treat me as you would a child because I am female.'

There was a pause as the two men stared at me. Richard glanced at his cousin after a moment, allowing him to take the lead in this.

'Cousin Jesslyn, it is unsafe for you to have this knowledge.'

'It is unsafe for me to be in ignorance of something that could affect the welfare of my daughter and this household! Let me tell you what I surmise. My Lord, when I first entered this room I heard you refer to the

Knot. Even in Somerton my father had heard rumours of the Sealed Knot, a band of gentlemen joined together to restore His Majesty to the throne. I assume that you are one of those gentlemen? And you, Richard.' I turned to my husband. 'I know you to be truly an actor. It is your life's blood. But what better cover to gain information and carry messages than that of a humble travelling player? Richard, please.' I knelt by him and took his hand. 'I owe you so much . . . let me share this with you. If there is danger I wish to know of it and face it head on, not live in a half world of suspicion and fear.'

He leaned forward and kissed me on the forehead. 'Little one, I would trust you with my life. Guy, it is up to you whether or not you take Jesslyn into your confidence. For myself, I am going to tell her the truth.' He rose to pour himself more wine.

'You both know my feelings about the monarchy. I do not believe in the Divine Right of Kings, and no monarch can any longer impose unfair and unpopular taxes on the people when their representatives in Parliament have not approved them. When the late King died . . .'

'Was murdered!' I interrupted hotly.

'What you will, sweeting.' Richard smiled. 'Do not be fierce with me, Jesslyn. I fear I will not be equal to the challenge!' Then he became serious again. 'If we had had a Republic where men could be free to follow their hearts and their conscience in matters of religion and politics, I have no doubt that I should have supported it. But we exchanged a despotic King – hear me out, Jesslyn! – we exchanged a despotic

King for a dictator. And one who seemingly believed so little in the will of the people that on his death-bed he named his son his successor, like any royal dynasty. And so, yes, I am working to restore the House of Stuart. At worst His Majesty Charles II will elevate pragmatism to a fine art. At best he will be worldly wise and let the nation heal its wounds.' Richard laughed suddenly. 'And the danger will be worth it to see a maypole. Once again to deck the halls with boughs of holly. To see pretty women wear bright colours and bare their shoulders. And, yes . . .' his beautiful voice fell to a whisper '. . . to hold an audience in the palm of your hand, so that they will laugh or cry at your will.'

'Thank you, Richard,' I said simply. Then I turned to Guy de Burgh. 'My Lord?'

There was silence in the room as Richard's cousin stared searchingly at me. Then he smiled and bowed low. 'I follow where my cousin leads, Mistress.'

'I promise you can trust me.'

'Very well. As you have already guessed, I belong to the Sealed Knot. Although I was too young to fight in the war, as soon as I was of age I travelled to the French Court to offer my sword to our exiled King.' He shrugged. 'But with over two thousand English gentlemen who have had to follow His Majesty into exile, yet another retainer was not welcome. I inherited the earldom from my father when I was only three years old, therefore neither he nor I had fought against Parliament and so I was free to travel as I wished in this country. His Majesty and his Council asked me to use that privilege to gain information. I became part of the network of like-minded men who form the Sealed Knot.'

He started to pace the room and I felt his frustration.

'My God, I knew we should have risen when Lambert and Cromwell's son-in-law Fleetwood deposed Richard Cromwell! But Sir Richard Willys, one of our most influential members, advised against it and persuaded the King of his views. I couldn't understand it then, but by Christ, Lady, I understand it now!'

'This Willys is a traitor?'

'And were it not for a cat, I should this very moment be held prisoner in the Tower.'

'Cat?' I asked, bemused.

Guy laughed. 'It sounds absurd, I know. But I followed a cat and in so doing have kept my head on my shoulders.'

'I don't understand.'

'I slipped quietly into England a week ago, having been on a mission to His Majesty in Brussels.' He suddenly grinned and his face, sombre for his age, for a moment seemed almost boyish. 'The smugglers of the Romney Marshes carry more than contraband across the Channel! I carried secret papers from His Majesty to . . . I am not at liberty to tell you his name, Mistress. Let us simply say to a high-ranking officer in the Model Army who is becoming sympathetic to our cause. I lodged with a Roman Catholic doctor in Drury Lane. Only my cousin and Sir Richard Willys knew of my venture and where I lodged. This morning I left the house in Drury Lane and was immediately aware that I was being followed. I recognized the man following me as Willys's servant. I needed time to think. I was . . .

am to sail tonight to take the General's reply to His Majesty. If I am taken, our cause will be greatly harmed.'

'Could this man have followed you here?' I asked, trying to keep the fright from my voice.

Guy shook his head. 'There is a tavern on the corner of Drury Lane and Bow Street, The Magpie. I ducked into there and took a tankard of ale to a quiet corner where I could observe the doorway. After a moment Willys's man entered.

'He bought a drink then took up a position at the entrance to the tavern. I was trapped! I'd drunk at The Magpie on several occasions and, to the best of my knowledge, the door opening on to Bow Street was the only way in or, indeed, out! . . . Now, Lady . . . forgive me, for you will think me mad, but suddenly I became aware that someone was watching me intently. I felt a gaze like a physical presence. At first I was wary of turning in the direction of the eyes that were upon me in case I confronted another of Willys's men. I sat for a moment totally silent, my face in the shadows. Then slowly I turned.

'A few feet away from me sat a black cat. Its gaze was unblinking. Something rare in cats, I believe. After a moment the cat jumped down and walked unhurriedly away from me. The rear of the tavern is low-beamed and dark. On the edge of that darkness the cat stopped, looked back at me and sat again. For some reason I was fascinated by the creature. Perhaps a minute passed, then it walked deliberately back towards me. Again it sat and stared unblinkingly at me. Then rose and retraced its steps.'

Guy stopped his pacing and sat in a chair by the hearth. He put his head in his hands for a moment then straightened and looked at me. 'I am not a fanciful man, Mistress, and I have already said you will think me mad . . . but I had the strangest notion that the cat wanted me to follow it!'

I do not heed Time nor Place nor Death. And you Love him, Jesslyn.

'And did you follow, my Lord?'

Guy shook his head disbelievingly. 'It is illogical but I did. That cat made slow and stately progress through a warren of passages. All the time I followed. Finally we descended some old worn stone steps which led to a cellar. I could barely see but there was a glimmer of light high up in one wall. The cat walked towards that wall then leapt on to a barrel and sat. Its amber eyes were on my face for a moment, but only for a moment. To my astonishment it started to lick itself for all the world like a kitchen cat before the hearth!

'I crossed to the light. It came from a trap door. I imagine deliveries to the cellar are made through it. In a matter of moments I was through it and out into the stinking alleyways behind Drury Lane. I crept to where I could get a view of my lodgings. I knew what I would find. Soldiers!

'Cousin Jesslyn, forgive me if I have endangered your household but I had to warn Richard and, through him, the loyal members of the Knot!'

'Thank you for your confidence, my Lord.' I turned to Richard. 'Does this Willys know of your involvement with the Knot?'

'No, thank God! I have always reported only to Guy.

In any case, my dear, I doubt the gentlemen of the Sealed Knot would have accepted me. Whatever my family connections, I am after all a mere player and therefore a rogue – although not a vagabond! An anonymous letter goes to Lady Ormonde at Wild House. She will see that her husband and other members of the Knot return quickly to their country estates.'

'I do not think that Willys will betray the whole Knot. His aim is to stop me getting through to Brussels with my message for the King.'

'What are your plans, my Lord?'

Guy hesitated for a moment. Richard moved to him and touched him lightly on the arm.

'It would be ridiculous not to trust her further, Guy!'

'As soon as it is dark, Jesslyn, I shall slip through the gardens and fields down to the Strand. A lighterman will be waiting at the Essex Steps to row me across to Southwark. You are gently reared, Lady, so forgive me when I tell you that Southwark is infamous for its stews. Even the Puritans seem to feel the need for some . . . er . . . pleasure. One of the brothels is run by a brave woman true to our cause. A fresh, fast horse will be waiting for me in the stables of her house. Two changes of mount will be waiting at inns along the way. If I ride hard – and I will – I shall leave on the morning's tide.'

'The Knot is well organized, my Lord.'

'It has to be . . . if the King is ever to come into his own again.'

'God grant it so.' I turned to Richard. 'It seems we have only to wait for night to fall . . .'

I was interrupted by a loud banging on our front door. Richard crossed to the windows and, keeping out of sight as best he could, glanced down into the street. 'Soldiers!'

The parlour door was thrown open unceremoniously by Harry.

'Soldiers, guvnor, front and back!'

'Jesslyn, forgive me. I should never have . . .'

'No time for regrets, Guy. Follow me. We must hide you.'

'But Richard, where? This is not an old house with . . .'

'Secret hiding places? There you are wrong, Jesslyn,' he interrupted me. 'The old man who built this house was a Catholic. He had lived long enough to remember the Gunpowder Plot and how members of his faith were persecuted after that. Come quickly! He had a priest's hole hidden in his beautiful new home.'

Richard started to lead the way from the parlour. Guy and I followed. Then I turned back to Harry. 'Get rid of that tray! They will wonder why we dined here instead of the dining hall. Then answer the door. I shall come down.'

When I reached the landing Richard and Guy were already halfway up the stairs to the next floor. I hurried to catch up with them.

'It is in your bedchamber, Jesslyn. At the rear of the hanging closet.'

Now we were in my bedchamber, Richard quickly opened the door to the hanging closet inset in the oak wainscot.

'Jesslyn, remember this. The false panel is opened by twisting the carved Tudor rose in the bressumer over the fireplace. Now go! Play the meek goodwife for the soldiers!'

I ran down the stairs praying for all our sakes that Guy de Burgh's hiding place would not be discovered. Harry was waiting for me in the hall. More loud banging came from the front door. 'Open up, in the name of the Protectorate!'

'Shall I let them in, Mistress?'

'I don't think we have much choice,' I replied with some irony. 'I'll receive them in the library. Oh, Harry, would you please ask Moll to take Lucinda to her sister's in Shoreditch and keep her there until I send word? That's if she can get past the soldiers.'

'Huh!' he said scornfully. 'I'd bet Moll against a *regiment* of Ironsides any day.'

I entered the ground-floor library quickly and tried to appear composed, a hastily snatched volume of Milton's *Lycidas* in my hand. I had taken up that book by chance but thought wryly that my choice should find favour with the representatives of Parliament as Milton was fiercely anti-Royalist.

I heard the front door open and close then Harry knocked at the library door. It opened and a young officer entered. He stood in the doorway, his steel helmet under one arm. He was fresh-faced and had the look of the country about him. The younger son of a yeoman family, I surmised, trying to make his way in the army. He was about the same age as Guy de Burgh and my heart nearly broke to think that in better days the two might have been friends. Now this young officer could be the instrument of another country-man's death.

'Mistress Warwick?'

'Yes.' I rose and bobbed a curtsey. 'You are welcome in my house, sir. Although I cannot understand why men-at-arms should come banging at my door.'

'Please forgive the intrusion, Mistress, but we are searching for the traitor, the Earl of Colne . . . a cousin of your husband's.'

'A distant cousin, yes. But why search here? Surely the Earl would be at his estate in Wiltshire? And . . . why do you say traitor? Forgive me, I know little of politics but . . .'

'That is how it should be,' the young officer interrupted. 'I honour women, Mistress, but not for their minds.'

I was sorely tempted to hurl Milton's book straight at his head. Instead I asked meekly, 'Would you care to speak with my husband?'

'Thank you,' he replied curtly.

I led the way from the library into the hall. Two experienced-looking soldiers were stationed by the front door. Clearly escape was impossible. We climbed the marble staircase in silence. The only sound was the swish of my skirts on the stairs and the occasional clank as the officer's sword touched against the banisters.

We entered the parlour and I halted, astonished at what I saw. Richard was apparently blind drunk. His clothes were dishevelled and stained with wine. He held a goblet of wine unsteadily in his hand. At sight of me he looked furious, then staggered across the room to me to strike me heavily across the face.

'I told you I did not wish to be disturbed, wife!'

I had staggered back from the blow and the young officer instinctively put his arm around me to steady me.

'Sir, I cannot believe that such boorish behaviour is necessary.'

Richard threw himself drunkenly into a chair and looked the officer up and down.

'And since when has the army interfered between man and wife? She is mine. We are married. Short of murder I can treat her as I will. I have her money. I have her body. And if I wish to beat her, I shall! Now, who the hell are you? Disturbing a man's peace!'

The officer stood to attention. 'Captain Ovington from the Whitehall Garrison, sir. We are searching for the traitor, the Earl of Colne. I am informed that he is your cousin. It seems a natural assumption that he might have sought shelter here.'

Richard shouted with laughter. He rose and staggered across the room to replenish his goblet of wine.

'Natural to whom? Not to my very *un*natural so-called noble family! Look at me, sir. Behold the black sheep.' He attempted to bow, stumbled, then clung to a chair, toppling it over.

'Sir, you are not yourself!'

'Sadly,' I murmured, 'he is very much himself.'

Inwardly I applauded Richard's performance, in spite of my stinging face. It was a brilliant distraction and must make it difficult for the Captain to believe that a couple who lived in such violent disharmony would conspire to hide a Royalist spy.

Richard pulled himself to his feet and lurched towards me.

'I'm sick of your long face and mealy-mouthed disapproval, wife. I'm for the tavern!' He caught my arm. 'I shall expect to dine well when I return. Another tough piece of meat from the spit and you know what to expect, don't you?'

'Yes,' I said, my voice hardly a whisper.

'Well, what? What?' Richard shouted, apparently twisting my arm. Captain Ovington moved to the other side of the room, embarrassed.

'A beating.'

'Yes . . . a beating.' He glanced at the Captain whose back was to us, winked at me and mouthed: 'Good girl!' Then he made apparently drunken progress to the door. In the doorway he turned. 'Your servant, Captain. And if you catch my dear cousin . . . invite me to the execution!'

The door banged shut behind him. The room was in silence for a moment. Then Captain Ovington turned to me.

'Mistress, have you no family you can turn to? I shudder to think of such a gentle lady at the mercy of a man who does not honour her.'

I took a handkerchief from the sleeve of my gown and twisted it in my hands.

'I have no living family, sir.' I moved away, dabbing at my eyes with my handkerchief. The look of concern in the young officer's eyes was so genuine I felt a pang of remorse until I remembered what a deadly game we were playing.

'In any case, Captain, I have my duty . . . and you

have yours.' I turned to him and was surprised to find how easily my eyes filled with tears. I was actually *feeling* the role I was playing.

'You must, of course, search the house.'

'I am satisfied that Guy de Burgh would not find solace here.'

'You are correct but . . .'

'I am satisfied, Mistress,' the Captain interjected harshly. He walked briskly to the door then turned and bowed briefly. 'I shall pray for you in your unhappiness. God be with you.'

I was saddened by my deception. But one kind young man did not reflect the punishment that would have come upon us had the Earl been caught in our home.

I waited two long hours before I dared to release Guy from the priest's hole. Harry had reported to me that he and Moll had strolled past the soldiers at the rear of the house. Apparently they were no more than boys and could see no reason to stop the formidable Moll. Once at the Strand, Harry had stopped a passing carter and had paid him to take Moll and Lucinda to Shoreditch. I knew my baby would be safe with Moll.

At last I felt it was safe to open the priest's hole. I entered my bedchamber full of fears that there had not been enough air to the hiding place. That the panel would not open. That . . . And then the false panelling slid open and I was in Guy's arms. Perhaps our need for each other was heightened by the danger we had both experienced, but I believe that our love was a deeply felt force that simply could not be denied. Richard had told me he would never question who I took to my bed but, even so, in other circumstances I would have felt a sense of loyalty to my husband although he had never made love to me nor ever would.

And yet our passion for each other was so gentle, so caring. When I look back at that moment of, for me, true lovemaking, I remember it as a kind of beautiful dance.

Kissing, touching, caressing, we removed each other's clothes. There was passion, there was hunger, but it was not rapacious. Above all, there was love.

His lips and tongue sought my nipples and I felt them harden with desire. Then his lips found my secret place but it was secret no longer. It was his. His.

'Oh, my dearest, you are ready for me.' He was inside me. Loving me. I, who had only known the cruelty of a man's lust, now knew its beauty. My body arched, moved to his rhythm. There was pleasure, yes, but there was more, so much more than that. Guy cried out at the same moment that the ache of my desire gave way to pleasure so intense I felt I could die of it.

Afterwards I lay in his arms and he held me so close I knew he shared my anguish at our parting. We both knew we might never see each other again. And yet in my heart I could not believe that God would play so false as to take this man from me.

We stayed in each other's arms until dusk, so complete that we felt no need to do more than kiss and caress and whisper the things that lovers do.

We told each other everything . . . well, almost everything. I had no wish to spoil our idyll with talk of Luke. We talked of our childhood. Our dreams. Of our longing to live in an England no longer *fearful* . . . And, as I drifted into sleep in his arms, I told him – I don't know why – of Ra. Of my love for him and how I had received word from Harriet that he was dead. My eyes were moist with tears as I told how Harriet, at Mat's request, had gone to find my cat. She had found him sleeping beneath the apple tree by my window. At least, she had thought him sleeping. She had buried him there.

No need for tears, Jesslyn. Wait for me.

CHAPTER SEVEN

THE CAT

'And looks commercing with the skies
The rapt soul sitting in thine eyes'

— *Milton*

CATHERINE: 1991

'Now stir the fire and close the shutters fast'
– William Cowper

Sophie was right: supper was just stew and plonk. But the big, untidy kitchen at Knight's Croft had become a haven and a second home to me in the eight weeks since I'd come to Kelsey Hall.

Knight's Croft was a rambling timber-framed Tudor house on the opposite side of the green from Kelsey Hall. It was in considerable disrepair but nevertheless had a dignity and beauty all its own. But above all the house had a kind of warmth. It might seem fanciful of me but I had the feeling that the house liked people. For centuries it had been home to changing families. Some happy. Some sad. But the house had always been there to shelter and embrace them. Nonsensical or not, I felt that Knight's Croft had a heart.

Life there revolved around the kitchen and Marcus's studio. Sophie had briefly shown me the drawing room with its intricately carved oak wainscoat walls, and the formal dining room where a splendid walnut Jacobean dining table was surrounded by mismatched but beautiful antique chairs, all sorely in need of a good polishing. My cousins appeared to have no time for the formal rooms in their house or, perhaps, simply couldn't afford to heat them.

My visits to Knight's Croft always followed the same pattern. I was seldom asked to dine in advance. Instead Sophie or Rupert would telephone and say: 'Marcus has bagged a couple of rabbits . . . care to come over for a stew tonight?' Or: 'Old so and so has dropped off a brace of pheasant. You know Sophie, everything goes into the pot. Come and eat with us!'

As long as she stuck to stews Sophie was an inspired cook. Knight's Croft had an old established, although overgrown, herb garden and a vegetable garden that Sophie worked at diligently. Sometimes I'd wander across the green to offer my help in preparing a meal and was always amazed at how totally haphazard my cousin's cooking was.

'How many carrots shall I scrape?' I'd ask.

'Oh, I don't mind. As many as you like then we'll just bung them in!'

Swedes, potatoes, turnips, pearl barley, rosemary, tarragon, sage and purple sage would be thrown in with gay abandon and soon the kitchen would be filled with a marvellous rich aroma coming from the large enamel casserole which Sophie had plonked on the ancient and none too clean Aga.

Whilst we prepared the meal we'd sip wine from mismatched and often chipped tumblers. Always red wine in litre bottles, bought, it would appear, in bulk from the supermarket on the outskirts of Baildon, our nearest town.

At first I had brought wine with me from the cellar at Kelsey Hall. Marcus had taken one look at the bottle and had nearly had apoplexy.

'My dear girl! Are you mad? A Château Batailley . . .

Grand Cru Classe . . . to drink with one of Sophie's stews!'

I found myself blushing, more for Sophie than myself. But I need not have bothered. She threw back her lovely head and roared with laughter.

'Thanks, Pa. You say the sweetest things!'

Marcus put his arm lightly around my shoulders.

'Don't look so crestfallen, dear child. It's just that my palate is shot to pieces and the offspring have never had the chance to develop one! But tonight I'll remember times past and drink good wine. We'll save it for the cheese . . . a Grand Cru and some of the Post Office's mouse-trap. Wonderful!'

A few weeks ago this remark would have left me wondering but now I knew that the Post Office doubled as grocer's, hardware store, newsagent's and local gossip column.

It was late-September and the evenings were drawing in. By five o'clock in the afternoon I was longing for the phone to ring and a friendly voice to ask me across the green to my cousins' welcoming kitchen.

The truth was I was damnably lonely. Cat and I rattled around by ourselves in the evenings at Kelsey Hall. During the day I could keep myself relatively busy. But when Mrs Jessop, Mrs Garner and Celeste left for their own hearth and home – or in Celeste's case the back of her boyfriend's motorbike and a trip to a disco in Colchester or Ipswich – I longed for company.

Rupert was wrong, the county had not beaten a path to my door and it was entirely my own fault. Though one I could not regret. For a country dweller I had one glaring, overriding fault: I hated hunting.

I had been at the Hall for only a couple of weeks when I received a note from Sir Dennis Kemp. It simply and rather curtly welcomed me to my grandfather's home. Then stated, rather than proposed, that the Hunt would look forward to a continuation of the hospitality afforded by my grandfather. That the first Hunt of the season should meet at Kelsey Hall, and also on Boxing Day. Tradition must be adhered to.

On questioning Mrs Garner I gathered that tradition meant a stirrup cup of cherry brandy before the Hunt and an elaborate breakfast for the prominent members afterwards.

'Over my dead body!'

'I beg your pardon, Miss Kelsey?'

'I'm not having some poor living creature torn to pieces on any land that I own . . . and I'm damned if I'll feed the faces of people who call watching such a death "sport"!'

If I'd landed from a flying saucer Mrs Garner could not have looked more shattered.

'Miss Kelsey, I don't know what you're thinking of! Until the last few years your grandfather always hunted with the Dengie. He was Master for nearly twenty years.' She shook her head. 'You just can't imagine what a kettle of fish it will be if you . . . Oh, Miss, just stop and think!'

'Mrs Garner . . .' I suddenly stopped short. 'Look, I hope it won't offend you but do we have to be so formal? You must have a Christian name. I'd be so pleased if you'd let me use it?'

She surveyed me for a long moment then shook her head. 'You're a funny one, Miss Kelsey.'

I let the moment lie between us then said, 'Catherine.'

'Yes . . . yes,' she said slowly. 'I can see that's what you'd be happy with.'

An abyss opened at our feet for a few seconds. In it lay centuries of privilege, the British class system, old loyalties, a desire to hold on to values that gave her a sense of continuity and, through that, security. I saw the doubt in her eyes and thought I had lost. Then she smiled.

I held out my hand to her and said again, 'Catherine.'

'Margaret,' she said in response, then laughed. 'Sir Dennis will go bonkers, Miss . . . Catherine! And a bloody good job too!'

I'd written a polite note to him regretting that as I was opposed to blood sports, I could not continue the hospitality to the Hunt afforded by my grandfather.

Margaret was wrong. Sir Dennis did not go bonkers. My cousin's wife Annabel did.

I'd borrowed Rupert's goofy fat old Golden Retriever and we'd gone for a walk along the sea wall. As I left the Little Parlour – which was, in truth, virtually the only room I lived in at Kelsey Hall – I'd rubbed a sleeping Cat behind his ear and apologized for the fact that I was about to consort with a dog.

Rupert's dog Lottie was such a glorious fool. I knew that he had not trained her as a gun dog but, even if he had, I had an image of that honey-coloured idiot sitting behind the beaters with her paws over her ears.

I was casually and somewhat scruffily dressed in old jeans and a rugby shirt. Lottie had dashed in and out of the estuary, rolled in the soft sand, shaken herself in close proximity to me . . . surely dogs do this deliberately? In short, I was a muddy, happy mess with my arms full of driftwood when I returned to the Hall.

Annabel's immaculate Mercedes estate car with its to me faintly ridiculous mascot of a hunting dog with pheasant in its mouth was parked in the courtyard. Bristling with hostility, she was just climbing from the driver's seat. She took in my appearance at a glance and had one short, sharp devastating thing to say to me.

'Really, Catherine!'

Annabel was, of course, impeccably dressed, Sloane-style, for the country. Hermès headscarf knotted just on the chin, cashmere jumper, well-tailored skirt, navy blue tights and well-polished brogues. Over the beige jumper she wore a navy blue sleeveless padded Puffa jacket. She looked as if she was about to enter through French windows in an old-fashioned West End play and call out, 'Anyone for shooting!'

A few weeks ago her scorn at my appearance would have hurt me. I'd grown up a little since then . . . about time too at twenty-nine! Now I was merely amused.

'Hallo, Annabel. As you see I've been for a walk by the estuary with Lottie. We both enjoyed it but we're an awful mess. Sorry if it offends you!' I added with a grin.

Lottie, who had slumped down on my feet, chose that moment to stand up and shake herself vigorously. Wet sand scattered over Annabel's Dior tights and Jaeger skirt.

'Get that bloody dog away from me! If Rupert can't

train an animal properly he shouldn't own one. If she was mine I'd have her put down!'

I bent and patted Lottie's head. 'Just as well she's not then. I need to get her some water and rub her down. Would you care to come in, Annabel?'

'Thanks, I need to have a word with you. Sorry if I lost my temper but I'm going on to drinks at the Kemps' and I don't want to look a wreck.'

'Well, I can find you a clean pair of tights and the mud will brush off your skirt as soon as it's dry. No real problem,' I said as I led the way into the house.

'Do you mind if we have tea in the Little Parlour? A fire's laid in there and I can rub Lottie down in front of it?'

'Fine by me. But I'd rather have a Scotch than tea. There's a sharp wind off the estuary and it's cut right through me,' Annabel added rather lamely.

I suddenly felt sorry for her. For all her aggression and domineering manner, she seemed basically insecure. And the carefully applied make up couldn't hide the lines of discontent forming around her mouth, nor the strained look in her eyes. I wondered about her marriage to my cousin Jonas. He didn't seem to me to be an easy man to live with. They had no children and Jonas would one day inherit the title if not the estate. Was that perhaps the root cause of this woman's peevishness? That she was unable to give her husband a longed-for heir?

I knelt before the hearth in the Little Parlour and put a match to the well-laid fire. Lottie grunted and flopped down in front of it. Oh, well! I'd apologize to Mrs Jessop for the mess. Then inwardly smiled at my increasing acceptance that I had servants. I wouldn't apologize to Mrs Jessop, I'd clean up myself!

Cat was still stretched out on the window seat. He opened one eye as Lottie came into the room then closed it again, totally relaxed. This was his domain and dogs had better understand that!

I rose from the fire and crossed to the drinks tray.

'Would you like me to get some ice, Annabel?'

'No, thanks. Just straight.'

I poured her a generous Scotch in one of the cut-crystal glasses from the Kelsey Glassworks. The crystal was hand cut and, because of the lead content, the glass was very heavy.

'Won't you join me?' she said.

It was only about four-thirty, too early for me to want a drink. But I saw the need behind Annabel's eyes for someone to drink with her and, in doing so, make her need for alcohol seem normal. 'Yes, that's a nice idea. I'll have a sherry.'

The sherry decanter, although heavy, was uncut and deceptively simple in its lines. But its beauty was such that I wondered if it was the work of Brett Fitzgerald.

The kindling had caught the logs and the fire had sprung to life. Lottie was now sound asleep and snoring in front of it.

'Let's settle down by the fire, Annabel. I'll leave Lottie to steam for a bit. Cheers!' I raised my glass to her then sat in one of the comfortable, loose-covered armchairs by the fire.

She gulped at her Scotch, then started to pace the room. 'For God's sake, Catherine, whatever possessed you to send that letter to Dennis Kemp?'

'Conviction,' I replied, at ease with myself. 'And it's gone rather further than that, Annabel. Mr Pritchard has written to Fred Watson at the Home Farm and to the tenant farmers stating that although clearly hunting is a question of personal choice, I will not have the Hunt cross any Kelsey lands. As well as a personal – and very polite – letter from me, copies of that letter have gone to the secretary of the Hunt and to Sir Dennis. As you'll gather, it's something I feel very strongly about.' I suddenly smiled. 'Perhaps it's the *only* thing I feel very strongly about. But that's surely my privilege?'

'You bloody fool!' Annabel rounded on me. 'You can't imagine the harm you've done with your townie conscience. And you can't imagine the embarrassment you've caused Jonas and me.' She downed the last of her Scotch then crossed to the drinks tray to replenish her glass.

I was astonished. 'How can I possibly have embarrassed you and Jonas? If you both want to hunt that's none of my business. But I'm afraid it won't be over my land and I won't be giving you breakfast. Not such a hardship, surely?'

'It's not the bloody Hunt! It's Sir Dennis. Jonas has only his salary as income. All right, it's handsome as managing director of the Glassworks. But can you imagine what it costs to support our life style? The Old Rectory alone costs a fortune to heat and maintain.'

The Old Rectory, where Jonas and Annabel lived, was the splendid Georgian house set in large grounds next to the village church. I'd never been invited there but, unlike my other cousin's house, Knight's Croft, it appeared to be very well maintained: the drive free from weeds, the paintwork gleaming, the gardens immaculate. The Church of England, I'd gathered, had very sensibly built a modern, easily run bungalow for the Vicar on the outskirts of the village. I'd no idea what a Vicar's stipend was but I could guess. Our young Vicar and his wife, who cared for the souls of three parishes, looked permanently darned. The days had long gone when livings were in the gift of the local gentry and a priest was often the younger son of a noble family and could afford to live well and keep an impressive household.

'I sympathize, Annabel. But I really don't see what this has to do with me.'

'Look, Jonas has a standing in the county. The Kelseys have been here since God knows when. Dennis Kemp is a nobody. New money. But he's stinking rich.' She stopped pacing and took a deep breath. 'We've . . . we've helped him.'

I stared at her for a moment. 'For money?'

'Of course not for money. What do you take us for? For . . . for favours, I suppose. Quid pro quo. A shared box at Ascot but Dennis footed the bill. A dinner party at the Rectory. Dennis sends a case of vintage champagne as a "Thank you" present. Every New Year he rents one of the most expensive villas on Mustique. We're always invited to join the house party.' She suddenly smiled bitterly. 'We've also been able to tell him that Princess Margaret's favourite tipple of an evening is Famous Grouse. He had it flown in by the caseload!'

'I'm sorry, Annabel, but I'm still quite bewildered as

to what this has to do with me.'

'The first Meet and the Boxing Day Meet have been held at Kelsey Hall for over two hundred years. You can't imagine what it means to Dennis to be Master of the Dengie. Now one of the oldest families in the county – Jonas's family – seems to be turning its back on him. And he's hopping mad. So am I!'

'But I explained in my letter that it's a matter of principle. I couldn't give a damn about Sir Dennis Kemp or whether he made his money from toilet seats or inherited ill-gotten gains! And with all due respect, Annabel, if he's going to dump you because you can't use your influence with me over this, what kind of friend is he anyway?'

'Oh, for Christ's sake, don't be so naive! He's a fairweather friend and a bloody bad person to cross!'

'Well, I've crossed him. Perhaps we should both just wait and see and live to tell the tale?'

'You've no idea, have you? Hugo must've been gaga to leave all this to his daughter's bastard. Jonas always said Francesca was a slut. We just didn't expect the slut's by-blow to inherit!' She made to fill her drink yet again. I rose and took the glass from her hand. I was so angry that my own hand was shaking.

'Francesca may have been capricious . . . perhaps even feckless . . . but she was never a slut! When she was only eighteen she did an incredibly brave thing. She gave me the right to live. And, whatever her faults, she had in abundance what you and Jonas will never have or even understand – she had a generosity of spirit that made people love her. She died loved. Will you?'

It was a terribly harsh thing for me to say to Annabel but I still missed Fran desperately and no one was going to insult her in my presence.

For a moment I thought that Annabel was going to strike me. To my surprise Lottie pulled her arthritic old legs into a sitting position and growled softly.

Then, rather like the wicked witch in *The Wizard of Oz* who is reduced to just a tiny pile of clothes, Annabel sank into a chair and put her head in her hands. Sobs started to rack her thin body.

'I'm sorry! I'm sorry! That was an unforgivable thing for me to say. You can't know . . . Jonas . . . he's never *pleased* with me now. Oh, Christ! – And I'm drinking too much.' She raised a tear-stained face to me. 'I'm going to lose him, Catherine.'

I had no way of knowing whether that was true or false, I simply and instinctively sat by her and took her in my arms. This brittle, sophisticated woman needed to cry. She probably would never forgive me for this moment of vulnerability. Never forgive that her husband's over tall, plain cousin had been afforded a glimpse into the despair that haunted her life. Just now all that mattered was that Jonas had sent her on a mission and she had failed and needed comfort.

An hour later I walked a well-groomed Lottie across the green to Knight's Croft. I'd made coffee for Annabel, brushed her skirt, given her the use of my rather limited range of make up and generally helped to mop up as best I could.

I'd walked her to her car and, to my amazement, she'd rounded on me just as she was about to get into the driver's seat.

'You'll tell Jonas about this, I bet. I know you Kelseys. You all stick together!'

I reached out for her hand and squeezed it. 'I'm new at being a Kelsey, Annabel. I haven't a clue what their loyalties are. But I know what mine are. I promise you, what was discussed between us this afternoon is just that . . . between the two of us. No one shall hear of it from me.'

But her newly made up face was already setting into the harsh demeanour with which she usually faced the world. She looked at me steadily. 'It's just not bloody fair! Jonas always counted on Sir Hugo leaving him the estate. Now you've ruined everything.'

I shook my head sadly as the Mercedes was driven from the courtyard with much too much acceleration. A couple of pieces of gravel that were thrown up clipped my cheek and stung. Absurdly, I felt my eyes fill with tears.

Careful, Catherine. This family will break your heart if you let them. One of them would even take your life.

I brushed the back of my hand across my eyes then clicked my fingers to Lottie. The silly dog followed me across the green, wagging her tail and proudly carrying her lead in her mouth. Somewhere deep down she knew herself to be a Retriever.

I walked around to the kitchen door and knocked on it. No one ever used the front door at Knight's Croft. As I waited for a reply I heard a tapping on one of the windows of the old conservatory which Marcus used as a studio. I turned and saw him beckoning to me and holding up a glass of wine. I smiled, nodded, then went through the kitchen, along the flagstoned corridor that led to the Victorian glass double doors into the conservatory.

This ran the whole length of the back of the old house. It was both a studio and a den for Marcus. There was an assortment of battered armchairs and sofas all covered with throws that he had hand-printed. There were chests of drawers, tables and chairs all in various stages of being painted. As well as his work on canvas, Marcus sold a variety of hand-painted furniture to a number of craft shops throughout East Anglia. In fact, I suspected that was the more successful side of his work.

I knew I would have found his large, forceful paintings difficult to live with but his furniture delighted me. Chubby, naked ladies danced over the front of chests of drawers, their full pink nipples forming the knobs. Painted cats slept, curled up, on the seats of wooden chairs whilst a chorus line of top-hatted mice did high kicks on the top of the slatted back. A table top had Bacchus presiding over a Roman orgy. The fact that Bacchus was a Greek god did not deter the likes of Marcus.

The conservatory smelt of paint and turps and size. It was heated by a large old pither stove on top of which stood a tin of size that threatened to boil over. From the stains on the stove and on the floor around it, the size had often done more than just threaten.

It was here that my evenings at Knight's Croft usually began. Family and sometimes friends would flop down in battered chairs and sofas and drink copious amounts of red plonk. There would be arguments, laughter, music – anything from Bach to Bunk Johnson.

As I entered the conservatory a tall, dark-haired man rose from an armchair by the stove.

'Hello there, Catherine!' Marcus said, handing me a glass of wine. 'You know Brett, don't you?'

'Well, not exactly *know*,' I said, shaking hands. 'I watched him break an exquisite piece of glass. It really shocked me.'

'Ah, now,' Brett Fitzgerald said teasingly. 'Are you speaking as a shareholder or a connoisseur?'

'Mmm, well, the shareholder part hadn't occurred to me.'

'I wish your cousin Jonas was of a like mind!'

I smiled at him. 'I've only met Jonas a couple of times but I don't imagine myself a soulmate!'

Marcus turned to Brett and laughed. 'There's hope for the girl.'

'I saw your work in the show room and thought it was stunningly beautiful,' I said sincerely. 'And to see you smash something so lovely . . .' I shook my head. 'But then, I don't really know anything about glass.'

'Then you must be educated. Have you been to the museum yet?'

'No, I'm afraid not. Rupert says he'll take me. I could have gone by myself, of course, but I'd like to go with someone who knows about glass.'

'Then you shall go with me.'

Ridiculously, I felt myself blushing. 'There's no need. I mean, I wasn't fishing for you to . . .'

'I can assure you, an attractive young woman doesn't have to do any fishing for me to offer to take her out,'

Brett said, his intense blue eyes smiling into mine.

'There you are. He can't say better than that,' Marcus interrupted. 'Now, enough argy-bargy. Set a date to see the blasted museum and we'll all have another glass of wine! By the way, Sophie's off chasing some man and Rupert's wining and dining a few overseas buyers. But Brett here is a dab hand with an omelette so why don't you stay and join us?'

I was about to refuse but the thought of another lonely evening in the Little Parlour persuaded me. Also, I had to admit that I found Brett Fitzgerald a very fascinating man.

He called for me the following evening just before six. The museum closed then but Brett had arranged to pick up a key. 'We can't have the Kelsey heiress being trampled to death by tourists the first time she inspects her heritage!' he'd said, laughing.

I was a little surprised to discover that Brett drove a Jaguar XJS. But then, I supposed that no glassworks could keep such a brilliant craftsman without paying him handsomely. And, so far as I knew, he had no family to support.

He must have caught my expression as we crossed the courtyard to his car. He grinned at me. 'My one indulgence!'

Once through the gatehouse he turned the powerful car on to the road that led only to the original glass-works and the sea. The glassworks were about a mile from the village and I asked Brett why he thought they'd been built there.

'Possibility of a fire hazard to the village. The quality

of the sand in the estuary. But, I imagine, most importantly even at low tide the water there is deep enough for the barges to have docked at the landing stage. There's still a few barges under sail, you know. There's a yearly race from Baildon, down the river to the open sea, then on to the mouth of the Thames. It's a great sight, seeing them race. Mostly they have red or orange sails with their hulls tarred black. There's only one hill around here to speak of . . . at Latchingdon. That's the place to watch the race.'

'The top room of the gatehouse has a marvellous view over the estuary. I wonder how many Kelseys have watched from there?'

'Well, the race goes back to the seventeenth century. So do your sums. Quite a few!'

'When is this race?'

'Always the first weekend in May.'

'Then next year I'll give a party! My Knight's Croft cousins at least will come.'

To my surprise Brett took his hand from the steering wheel and briefly touched my hand. The gesture was sensitive and not remotely patronizing. 'You're finding it hard, aren't you, Catherine? Adjusting to your new life.'

How to cope with that moment of understanding? Last night he had called me an attractive woman but I had no illusions about myself. All my life I had only to look at my mother to know what true beauty was. As I'd explained to Rupert, I'd come to terms with this. I certainly didn't look upon myself as an ugly duckling, but how can you live in the shadow of a renowned enchantress and not find yourself wanting?

If I hadn't been so shy I could have been easy with this man. Instead I replied, stiffly, 'I'll learn to cope.'

To my surprise, Brett laughed. 'My God, you're like Hugo! Inside, a depth of feeling. Outside, ice. No, that's not fair. When he talked about glass there was fire in his belly.' Then he added softly, 'We were friends, you know. We had one great thing in common . . . the art of fire. Glass.'

'I wish I'd known him.' Then I suddenly blurted out: 'I wish I could hate him! Fran, my mother, was so unforgiving. He didn't reply to my letter telling him that she was dying . . . yet he made me his heir. Mr Pritchard, our lawyer, says he never stopped loving her. But why not build bridges? I sense it could have meant so much to them. Why did they both have to die without . . . without . . . I don't know, reaching out to each other? Sorry!' I added hastily. 'I must be boring you to hell.'

'If you're not careful, Miss Kelsey, you'll end up with me nicknaming you "Sorry!" '

'Oh, that really isn't fair!' I protested.

'Isn't it? I asked to show you the museum and you apologized. You told me something that you felt from the heart, then apologized. Do I seem like the kind of man who would seek someone's company, man or woman, other than if I wanted to? Or the kind of man who reaches out to another in sympathy without truly caring?'

'No, you don't,' I said slowly. Then I suddenly blurted out, 'I'm ridiculously, horribly, damnably shy! It's an absolute bloody curse. Shy is such a small word . . . like "nice"! But it's a blight. I wish to God you could go to Shy Anonymous. Like Alcoholics Anonymous or the Betty Ford Clinic! All my life it's made me say the wrong thing at the wrong time. Or else be unable to have as much fun or be as gracious as I'd like. When I'm with Sophie and Rupert I feel like a lumbering, tongue-tied idiot! There, I've told you. That's the root of my problem.' I suddenly threw back my head and laughed. 'And I'm buggered if I'm going to say "Sorry"!'

Brett was silent for a moment, then he smiled.

'I like you, Catherine Kelsey. I really like you.'

A few minutes later we pulled into the car park of the Kelsey Glass Museum. The building was like a long barn, built of flint. Through the middle was a massive double chimney. I pointed to this as we left Brett's car. 'The art of fire, indeed.'

'The original pots for melting the glass have long since gone but there are replicas around that chimney, which served the central furnace.'

He took a set of keys from his pocket. 'Hang on a minute while I turn off the alarm.'

'Alarm?' I queried.

'Well, it's linked to the local police station, so the village bobby could always come along and throw his bicycle in the path of the getaway car,' Brett said, smiling. 'It's for insurance, really. Apart from early Kelsey glass, your grandfather collected a superb variety of English glass. I wouldn't say it's priceless, but it's incredibly rare and quite irreplaceable.'

He unlocked the main door, then quickly punched in the code to an alarm control. Next he turned on the lights and I gasped at the beauty of the glass displayed.

Brett stood still for a moment, simply drinking in the exquisite glass. Then he said softly, 'It never ceases to fill me with awe. To inspire me. To make me feel very humble.'

We were both quiet for a moment, Brett because his very spirit seemed to be enthralled by the beauty of his own craft. For myself, I at last began to understand the richness of my inheritance.

Brett broke the spell. 'Rupert got a top theatrical lighting designer in to display this collection. Your cousin may seem over strong on charm and charisma but he's very good at his job. Look how the glass comes alive! It's lit by spots from above and below, from back lighting . . . just about every trick in the trade!'

He reached out and gently touched a heavy, ridged piece of glass. He could have been caressing a lover. 'All very fine for the tourists,' he said quietly. 'But this needs only a glint of sunlight to bring it to life and dazzle your eyes with clear glass that has a thousand colours in it!' He turned to me and said, as if that explained everything, 'It's Ravenscroft.'

'Ravenscroft? That doesn't mean a thing to me.'

'He was the father of English glass. This ewer is over three hundred years old. Up until Ravenscroft, domestic glass was made from imported Venetian glass pebbles and worked mainly by Italians or sometimes master glassblowers from Normandy or Lorraine.'

'What's so different about this glass?'

'It's crystal. Glass of lead, as it was called. The Venetian glass was much thinner. Although it could be worked into more complicated designs, it just didn't have the brilliance of lead crystal. Ravenscroft was a chemist first and foremost. He used silica from English flints and mixed it with potash instead of the Venetian soda . . .' He suddenly laughed. 'Now it's my turn to ask if I'm boring you?'

'No, I'm fascinated. You love glass, don't you?'

Brett shrugged. 'Not all glass. I was apprenticed in Ireland. At the end of five years the apprentices had to cut a blank crystal bowl on a carborundum wheel. They give you fourteen hours to do it in. One slight scratch and you're out! Well, I cut the bloody, pretentious thing. They patted me on the back, engraved my name on the rim and presented it to me. I smashed it there and then and went on my travels!'

'Why Kelsey Glassworks?'

'Because your grandfather understood what I wanted to achieve and gave me a free hand to do it. Simple as that. Fortunately, he also gave me a contract. Jonas can't do a damned thing about it.'

'Can I see some of the Kelsey glass?'

'Yes, of course. Over here . . . look. This is our earliest piece.' He pointed to a tall flute glass, beautifully engraved.

'It's to commemorate the Restoration of Charles II. See? "The daye of our Lorde 25 May 1660". The cluster of oak leaves is in memory of his escaping after the Battle of Worcester by hiding in an oak tree. Beautiful, isn't it?'

I reached out and took the glass in my hands. Time stopped for me.

'Catherine! What's the matter? You're shaking!'

I carefully put the glass back into its display cabinet and went to sit down. I shook my head.

'Too much imagination. The wind in the reeds as the tide turned . . . For a brief moment I thought I could hear . . . hear cheering . . . Horses . . . Just my imagination!'

You are getting close to her, Catherine. You are getting close to my Lady.

CHAPTER EIGHT

THE CAT

'. . . somewhere, beyond space and time . . .'
– Brooke

JESSLYN: 1660

'Christ, if my love were in my arms'
                    – 16th century Anon

It was late January and I'd heard no word from Guy. Neither Richard nor I had any way of knowing whether he had been taken, whether his ship had foundered, whether . . . My fears for the man I loved so deeply knew no bounds. I swore to myself that if only he lived I would find the strength to acknowledge that all I had meant to him was a moment's solace from fear. But my heart called me a liar because I knew that the man who had held me close, had loved me with such gentleness as well as passion, was neither a fairweather friend nor a false lover.

Richard and his troupe of actors had banded together again as the autumn nights grew darker. He had asked Moll if she would like to stay behind with me or join them in their travels? I was so relieved and grateful when Moll said, with no hesitation, that she had no intention of leaving Lucinda and myself to the care of a street urchin, two daft maids and a drunken cook!

We had seen Richard briefly at Christmas. Usually the roads were so clogged with mud during January and February that few travellers strayed far from home but, even before Twelfth Night, Richard and the actors had taken to the road again. I did not challenge him as to his motives but felt sure that the actors' travels through the country had more to do with the restoration of the King than with the performing of Drolls.

There was an air of excitement and hope running through London that you could almost reach out and touch. Harry told me that in the inns and taverns a toast to His Majesty was drunk openly – unthinkable a few months previously. Harry told us how many shops and taverns throughout London had broadsheet pictures of His Majesty nailed to their walls and that one poor fellow, who had stopped by a picture and said he had seen the King in Brussels and he was not as fine-looking as his picture, had been beaten by a mob. And yet there was no news. No news of His Majesty. No news of Guy. And I had heard nothing from Richard.

Moll and I were huddled by the fire in the first-floor parlour. A wild wind was rattling the windows and whirling in the chimney. Even Richard's splendid new house fell prey to the elements and the candles flickered and were sometimes suddenly snuffed out by the wind's wilfulness.

Both of us were stitching. I was doing my best to apply smocking to a new dress for Lucinda. Moll was hemming linen for our beds. I was frustrated by lack of news and, I must admit, by the fact that I was no needle woman. Suddenly I could bear it no longer. I threw down my work and cried out, 'So women must watch and wait?' I started to pace the room. 'I don't know about you, Moll, but I'm being driven mad by the waiting. By the questions I keep asking myself. Where

171

is Richard? Will the King really come into his own again? Where is . . .' I cut myself off, afraid to speak his name. I sat back abruptly in my seat by the fire and started to apply my needle savagely.

I was aware of Moll's gaze upon me and felt myself colouring. I kept my head down and stitched as if my life depended upon it. When she finally spoke her tone was amused, affectionate and kind.

'Oh, lovey, I love Richard, have come to love you like I was your mother. But do you really think your marriage could fool old Moll? We're a funny lot, humans! She reached out and took my hand. 'Richard loves you, really loves you, but he'll never want to bed you. That's how he is and I don't question that. But you're a young woman with a young woman's needs and you have a right to be loved. Oh, Jess! My Jesslyn! I've watched you fretting these last months.'

Before Moll could say more there was a tap at the parlour door and Harry entered. 'Begging you pardon, Mistress, there's a lady . . . er . . . woman, asking for you.'

'At this hour?' Before Harry could reply, Moll had intervened.

'A lad of your age should be able to tell whether you're talking to a woman or a lady. What's the matter with you, boy?'

'Well, Moll, me old love, you tell me. When a female talks like a lady but comes to an 'ouse after dark and is painted like a . . . sorry, ladies . . . painted like a whore . . . what am I to make of her?'

Moll opened her mouth to reply but I felt the time had come for me to take charge of the situation. 'Please show our guest in, Harry. And could you bring wine and sweetmeats?'

He gave a challenging look to Moll then briefly nodded to me. After a moment the door opened again and Harry ushered in a tall, heavily cloaked figure. As the woman entered she pulled back the hood of her cloak. I heard Moll gasp.

'My Lady, is it really you?'

The woman swayed and I thought might well faint.

'Harry, get wine, milk, spices. I must make a posset for this lady. Quickly!'

I plunged the poker into the heart of the fire. I needed it to be red hot to thrust into the posset. Whilst I was doing this, Moll half carried our guest to a seat by the fire.

She sat for a moment in silence, head thrown back, her breath laboured. Moll had her arm around her and was whispering comfort.

'There, my Lady. Just take your ease. You're amongst friends. Oh, my poor lovey . . . let old Moll rub your hands. Skin and bone, you are,' she chided. 'But you're safe here, my Lady . . . safe!'

Slowly our guest's breathing became easier. I looked upon a woman who must once have been very beautiful. Now she was ravaged. Her dry, dead-looking hair was tortured into limp curls. Her thin, drawn face was garishly painted and the clothes I could see beneath her dark cloak were of a like I had not seen since my childhood: glimpses of brightly coloured satin, exquisite lace, shoes with gaudily coloured ribbons adorning them.

'Mistress Warwick, forgive me. These days I am not

myself,' our visitor said through laboured breaths. Then she clasped Moll's hand.

'Moll? Moll Hardwick? Is it truly you?'

'It's me all right, your Ladyship. Just rest now. We'll soon have something hot for you to drink.'

Our guest leant back in her chair and closed her eyes. 'Thank you!' It was almost a whisper. 'And, dear Moll, no more your Ladyships . . . just Alice will do.'

There was a tap at the door and Harry entered carrying a tray on which was wine, sweetmeats and a tankard of fresh milk and wine, highly spiced.

'I poured a drop of brandy in there as well, the poor lady looks as if she could do with it.'

'Thank you, Harry.' I took the tankard from him and crossed to the fire. The poker was by now red hot and I pulled it out and plunged it into the posset. With a hiss the contents of the tankard foamed and bubbled. The aromatic smell of cinnamon and nutmeg rose from the tankard. Moll took it from me and crossed to the lady I knew only as Alice. She put her arm around our guest and gently lifted the posset to her lips.

I turned to Harry. 'Harry, ask Cook to send up a dish of cold meats, will you, and to place some broth over the fire?'

As Harry made to move to the door Alice spoke. Her voice was now a little stronger. 'I thank you for your kindness, Mistress Warwick, but truly I could eat nothing.'

'As you wish. But, Harry, get Cook to heat up the broth in case our guest can manage something a little later.'

He nodded and left the room. I sat in my seat by the

fire and watched as, with Moll's help, the lady drank down the hot posset. I had no idea why she had come to the house and could only wonder at her dress and painted face. Both the richness and colour of her clothes and the paint on her face must surely lead to a day in the stocks at the very least.

'Thank you, Moll. I must pull myself together, I come with an important message.'

'Message?' It was all I could do to stop myself leaping to my feet and shaking her into life. But Moll frowned at me and I knew she was right to let this poor, sick woman recover a little more.

'You just rest a few more moments, my Lady. Let that posset warm you through.'

The woman nodded and closed her eyes but one could almost feel the return of her steely willpower as she tried to force herself to regain a little of her strength.

Moll crossed to me and said quietly, 'The Lady lost her husband and two of her sons on the same day. The day my Will was murdered. We met searching the battlefield . . . hoping all the time our loved ones would be only wounded, not dead. Her husband, Sir Ben, led the troop Will was in. We comforted each other and buried our dead together.' Moll shook her head. 'So many lives wasted. But men will never learn.'

We sat in silence for a few moments, the only sound the wind at the windows and a log falling in the grate. Then the Lady Alice opened her eyes and pulled herself upright.

'Forgive me, Mistress Warwick. I am not long for this world and the smallest effort seems to . . .' She shrugged. 'Enough of that! I bring a message for you, and a very important message for Richard Warwick. We dare not commit it to a letter because if it fell into the wrong hands it could be a disaster for our cause.' She stopped suddenly and pressed a hand to her thin chest. Her eyes closed in pain. 'This will pass. I am sorry.'

I rose and quickly poured a little wine and took it to her.

'Please, please, your Ladyship. Try to take a little wine.'

I helped her to a few sips then she opened her eyes and gave me the sweetest smile. Again I was aware of what a beauty this woman must once have been.

'I have already said, not "your Ladyship". The paint on my face tells you of my trade. A woman who runs a brothel is not a lady. So, please, just plain Alice.'

I heard Moll gasp behind me but, at the mention of the word 'brothel', I knew who this woman was. I remembered Guy saying that in Southwark there was a brave woman true to the cause. 'It was to your house that Guy de Burgh went on the day he escaped from Parliament's soldiers. Oh, please, Alice . . . tell me! Do you have word of him?'

Once again she smiled at me. 'I do, my dear. Word came today from one of the gentlemen of the Marshes.'

'A smuggler?'

'And a true friend. He came to my house ostensibly to use its services but in truth bringing messages from His Majesty's Court in Brussels.' She took my hand. Hers was dry and so thin it could have belonged to a child. 'Guy is safe. He sends you his love. His ship was engulfed by a terrible storm and blown off course. It foundered. Guy was one of only six who survived.'

The sailors drowned a cat to bring them luck on their voyage. It's an old superstition and could not go unpunished. But you love him, Jesslyn.

'And he's not injured? He's truly safe?'

'To the best of my knowledge, my dear. But you won't see him until His Majesty is restored to the throne. His life would be forfeit if he returned to England.'

I rose from Alice's side and said passionately, 'I don't care about seeing him. I don't care about anything so long as he's alive and well!' Then my voice steadied. 'That's . . . that's not true. I care about my daughter deeply. I love the new friends I have made.' I smiled at Moll. 'And I have come to love Richard, but . . .' My voice trailed off.

'But not as a husband. My dear, I have known Richard for some time and can guess at your relationship.' Then her voice lowered almost to a whisper. 'Now to my message for him. Moll, will you check that no one else is within earshot? My message is sensitive and highly secret.'

Moll crossed to the door and looked out. Then she turned back into the room, smiling. She closed the door. 'Well, he's not near enough to hear what is said but I guess that young devil Harry has the right idea. He's sitting halfway down the stairs, apparently whittling at a piece of wood – but that's a sharp knife he's using! You can speak in safety, my Lady!' Alice made to protest. 'I don't care what you say, I don't give a tinker's curse what you've done or are doing, you'll always be your Ladyship to me and that's that!'

Alice smiled at Moll and nodded, then turned to look at me.

'Richard is to make his way to Sir John Grenville.'

'Grenville?' I exclaimed involuntarily.

'Yes. The nephew to Sir Richard, the King's General in the West, but with a cooler head on his shoulders! The message he gives to Sir John comes directly from His Majesty. He is ready to discuss terms with General Monck. Sir John is to be the go between.'

Moll and I stared at Alice for a moment, practically open-mouthed. 'General Monck?' I managed to say. 'General Monck! The commander of Parliament's Army is for the King?'

'So it would seem. But we have yet to see whether he can be trusted. I have heard he is an honourable man, though.'

Moll interrupted. 'Huh! A man who started as a Royalist and ended as an Ironside?'

'A man who changes sides once can change again. I can condemn no man for following his convictions. There was right and wrong on both sides, Moll. But now I truly believe the people are tired of the Puritans. Tired of sombre clothes. Tired of never having any fun, any joy in their lives. God grant this May we will have the King restored, the old maypole set up in the Strand. And it is the people who will have their say. The late King did not understand that. From all I hear, His Majesty King Charles II will not make the same mistake.'

The effort of speaking for so long seemed suddenly to drain her and she slumped back in her chair. I hurried to her and put my arm around her to support her. 'Moll, quickly! A little more wine for the lady.'

Alice's voice was weak as she spoke but there was a slight smile on her lips. 'No more wine, thank you, I shall return home in my cups. If I can just rest a little, then I must be gone.'

'Will you not stay here with us, Alice? It could be dangerous trying to return to Southwark tonight. The curfew. Your . . .'

Alice interrupted me before I could finish. 'My style of dress? My dear, the garrison at Whitehall are well bribed and I have a coach outside. Besides, too many powerful men use the services of the Southwark stews for us to be victimized. And, after all, all the stews pay rent to the Bishop of Southwark. That surely gives us a little respectability?'

Moll went to her, clearly distressed. 'My Lady, it's none of my business but . . . why? Why?'

'Money! After Basing House my family – what was left of it – lost everything. The manor, the farms, all were taken from us. And the fines left us destitute. Literally destitute. I had only one son left.' Her expression softened with love as she spoke his name. 'James, my baby. He was only a boy of twelve when his father and brothers were killed. I sent him into exile to the French Court. I had been a Lady in Waiting to Queen Henrietta Maria and she had a fondness for me. She took him into her exiled household.' She closed her eyes for a moment. 'Perhaps a little wine after all, Mistress Warwick.'

'Of course. And, please, my name is Jesslyn.'

I poured wine and took it to her. She sipped at it and

after a moment continued, 'I feel certain that one day the English will rebel again and the King come into his own. When that happens my son will need money to find a place at Court. I knew how to run a household, how to manage a stillroom, how to blend herbs for medicine, how to honour and do duty to my husband, and how to embroider. Could I make money through those skills. Can any woman?'

I thought of my own plight when I became pregnant with Lucinda. If Richard had not rescued us I had little doubt that both my baby and I would be dead from starvation by now.

'There is now a considerable sum held by our family lawyer, a man I can truly trust. He is sworn to secrecy about my trade and my whereabouts. In fact, I have instructed him that when James returns he is to be told I am dead. My son will never know where his fortune came from.' Her eyes suddenly misted with tears. 'I should have liked to see him just once more before . . . but it cannot be.'

I gently took her hand. 'Guy was right. You truly are a brave woman.'

Alice rested for a while and then Moll and I helped her down the stairs and out into the deserted street to her coach. The coachman who had been holding the beautifully matched horses' heads opened the door for her and pulled down the steps into the coach. We supported her as she painfully climbed the three steps then fell back on to the velvet-covered seating. The coachman closed the door and moved to climb on to the box. Alice pulled herself to the window and lowered it.

'Jesslyn, I wish you love and luck. As for you, Moll, I pray you have found a kind of happiness. I shall never forget you on that battlefield. So sad but still caring for others. As for me . . .' She smiled and again I noted its sweetness. Her ravaged face lit up. 'Well, pray for me.'

With that the coach clattered off over the cobbled street into the darkness of the night. Moll and I watched the coach disappear along Maiden Lane and turn into the street that led to the Strand. From there it would make for London Bridge and then the teeming slums of Southwark.

'Poor lady! My poor, poor lady!'

I took Moll's arm and led her back into the house. 'I think not, Moll. What she has done she has done for love. With that motive I doubt one can ever feel unclean. And to come here with those messages when she is so ill! I just hope to God that Richard will return soon so that her bravery will have been worthwhile.'

We waited eight nail-biting days for his return. Then, as dusk was falling and I was lighting the candles in the parlour, I heard the front door slam to and his voice call out, 'Harry! Harry! Where are you, you young devil?'

Then Harry's voice, warm with welcome for the master he adored. 'Well, Guvnor, you're a sight for sore eyes! Thought you'd fallen for some country wench and deserted the Missus, I did!'

'You're a cheeky monkey, Harry, but it's good to see you. Be a good fellow and go along to the livery stables. See the lad gives Old Nick a good rub down and some oats. The boy's new there and seemed a bit thick, between you and me!'

'I'll sort him out, sir. He'll do the job right or feel the back of my hand.'

By then I was at the bottom of the stairs and running towards Richard. 'Oh, Richard, thank God you're home!'

He was instantly concerned. 'Is something wrong? Is it Lucinda?'

'No, No. Come up to the parlour, please. Quickly!'

'I hope there's a jug of wine there. I've had a long ride,' he said as he followed me up the stairs.

Once in the parlour I quickly poured wine for him. 'Come to the fire, Richard. You must be frozen through.' I drew him there and handed him wine. Then I dropped my voice to a whisper. 'Alice – Lady Ketton – came here eight nights ago.'

'Came here? Then something truly important has happened. The lady is dying and rarely moves from her bed. What is it?'

'A message from His Majesty. You are to go to Sir John Grenville. His Majesty is ready to negotiate with General Monck. Grenville is to be the go between.'

Richard sank into a chair by the fire and gave a long, low whistle. 'So, at last! The old fox must have showed his hand.'

'You knew about Monck?'

'Suspected. I doubted that he really marched his army south to London just to get their pay from Parliament. But until now we didn't know whether he was secretly for the King or seeking power for himself.' He reached out and took my hand. 'Oh, Jess, Jess! You know what this means?'

'Yes,' I replied happily. 'God willing, the King will come into his own.'

'The King? The King!' Richard threw back his head and laughed. 'To hell with the King. The theatres will be open again!'

Four months later, on the twenty-ninth day of May, four days after the King had landed at Dover, I walked into the parlour hardly knowing myself. Since I was a child I had only worn clothes of a drab colour, my shoulders covered by a plain white kerchief. Now I wore a gown of pale primrose taffeta, the front ruched to reveal a petticoat of silk a slightly deeper shade of primrose. Beneath that coat I wore six stiffly starched petticoats of finest linen, all trimmed with Brussels lace. My shoulders were bare and the neck of the dress cut daringly low, revealing the swell of my breasts, and more lace edged the neckline.

Instead of my unruly auburn hair being scraped back under an ugly linen bonnet, it hung loose about my shoulders. As if all this was not enough, I had on silk stockings dyed to exactly the same shade as my over-dress and heeled shoes with matching ribbons. On my head was an absurd but very flattering hat. Its huge brim, tilting slightly across the side of my face, was trimmed with ostrich plumes and ribbons. I felt incredibly excited and slightly nonsensical. Like a little girl who has been allowed to dress up in her mother's finery.

My finery was entirely due to Richard. Not simply the cost but the fact that the materials could be purchased at all and a tailor found to cut and sew them.

Since it had been declared in Parliament six weeks ago that the King was to come home, silk, satin, taffeta, lace and ribbons had become like gold in London. The world and his wife wanted fine clothes in which to greet their monarch. Tailors were working day and night and making fortunes. Those unable to bribe, cajole or pay an extortionately high price for their new clothes had opened long closed chests, had shaken dried lavender and rosemary from faded garments and were now wearing them with joy and pride.

I had tried to thank Richard and to ask him how he had achieved such privileged treatment. He had simply laughed and said, 'Some things are worth paying for, little love!'

As I entered the room he turned from the window. He was now the Richard I had first seen in the barn. A Cavalier. His clothes rich, his hair loose about his shoulders.

'Such a merry throng, I swear there are only peacocks out there. Man or woman, not a peahen amongst them.'

He stopped short as he saw me. 'Jess! Oh, my Jesslyn! I knew you for a beauty but nothing like this.' He crossed quickly to me and kissed my hand. His eyes smiled at me but his voice was tinged with regret. 'I love you, little one. If only . . .' Then, like quicksilver, his mood changed and he added grimly, 'If wishes were horses, beggars would be kings. Sweeting, you are such a baby still. I swear I would give my life to protect you but there are some cases where I can only stand by helpless. I have heard of Charles's reputation. He will be bringing the morals of the French Court to England.

Your beauty will mark you out. I pray God you will not fall victim to that lecher.'

I pulled away from him. 'You are speaking of His Majesty!'

'Grow up, Jesslyn. Grow up. When we lopped off the King's father's head, we English said goodbye forever to the Divine Right of Kings. Charles is just a *man*! A man born of the right father, in the right bed and on the right side of the blanket. Good God, girl, he already has an illegitimate son by Lucy Walter, another boy from Catherine Pegge and a daughter, Charlotte, by Betty Killigrew.'

I had moved from him and, after a moment, felt his hand on my arm. He gently turned me to him. 'Let's not quarrel, little love. It is simply that I care about your happiness. You, Lucinda, Moll and Harry are a family to me and I want nothing to hurt any of you.' He offered me his arm. 'Come, wife, we are to take wine with Sir John at his lodging in Bedford Street, then on to Whitehall to cheer His Majesty home!'

I stopped on the stairs and looked out into the garden where Moll was playing with Lucinda. Moll saw me and picked up my daughter to wave. I had felt it unfair that Moll should stay behind to care for my child and not join the celebrations in the street or at her sister's inn. But she said, 'If my Will was here to cheer with me, I'd go. We'll hear the bells and cannon from the garden as the King passes. I'll be happier here with Lucinda.'

The noise once out in the street was deafening. All the church bells were ringing. The streets were jammed with revellers all trying to make their way to the Strand to see the King and his retinue pass by on their way to Whitehall.

Traders and hawkers were calling out their wares. We had been told that throughout the City fountains would be running with wine. Flags flew from rooftops and many windows had tapestries hanging from them. Flowers had been strewn on the cobbles. It was impossible not to be caught up in the excitement. I felt such wonderful joy because not only was the King coming home, Guy would be amongst his courtiers.

Sir John Grenville's lodgings in Bedford Street were only a short walk from our house in Maiden Lane but we were going against the crowd and it took us nearly an hour to make our way through. But the jostling and and pushing was so good-natured it simply added to my sense of excitement. Richard bought a posy of country flowers from a young girl.

'The cornflowers will enhance the blue of your eyes, Jesslyn,' he said gallantly as he gave them to me.

At last we arrived at Sir John's lodgings, the bells of St Paul's drowning anything we could say to each other whilst we were on the street. A liveried footman opened the door to us and led the way up an imposing staircase to a very grand panelled first-floor parlour. A lute was being played, its sweet sound nearly muffled by the laughter and excited chatter. Clearly the celebrations had been going on for some time.

Immediately we were announced, a tall, rather sardonic-looking man came over to greet us.

'Richard, it's good to see you. And this must be Mistress Warwick.' Sir John kissed my hand and bowed low. I dropped him a curtsey, thankful that Richard had coached me in such courtly ways. 'By God, Richard, you're a lucky fellow. This little beauty rivals the lovely Barbara.'

We were served wine in beautiful fluted Venetian glasses and offered sweetmeats and little cakes. Sir John led me into the room and introduced me to so many people I found it hard to remember their names. He was courteous and charming but held my hand a little longer than was necessary when presenting me, and I knew from his eyes that he desired me.

There was an atmosphere in that elegant room that I had never encountered before and found hard to define. It wasn't simply that these ladies and gentlemen had at last cast off Puritan clothes and manners. There was a kind of wantonness in the air, a sexuality barely disguised by their courtly manners. Was this what Richard had warned me against? The morals of the French Court?

After a while I found myself by him again. 'Enjoying yourself, little one? You've already broken every man's heart!' he teased.

'It's a very fine company. In truth I feel a little overwhelmed. The change from drab clothes and curfews to all this in a few short weeks is hard to believe.' I sipped my wine for a moment then asked Richard, 'Who is this Barbara Sir John likened me to?'

'You're not going to like this, sweeting. She's cousin to the Duke of Buckingham, so well born, but from what I hear with the morals of an alley cat! Her poor fool of a husband took her with him when he carried money to the King in exile.' He laughed. 'Now he wears a cuckold's horns! His Majesty took not only

Palmer's money, but his wife as well. Have I shocked you?'

I thought for a moment. 'You told me to grow up, Richard. I think I am beginning to understand what you meant. From what you have told me one would be very naive not to realize what the new King's Court will be like.' I suddenly laughed. 'And if I'm going to be constantly shocked, I shall die of exhaustion!'

From then on I threw myself into enjoying the mood of the party. We drank the King's health and wished him a Happy Birthday, this day being not only the day of his arrival in his capital city but also his thirtieth birthday. I flirted and laughed, acknowledged compliments, declined to have a duel fought over me, and tried to present to the world a sophistication I did not really feel.

Sir John had arranged for us all to dine in private rooms at The Cock and Magpie, an inn nearby. An almost ludicrously obsequious landlord bowed us through the low-ceilinged, heavily beamed hall into rooms at the rear of the tavern. I had never been into such a place before. A gently reared woman may dine in a private room when travelling but would never dream of entering one of the public rooms.

The carnival atmosphere in the streets was even more marked within the walls of the ancient inn. As we passed along the hall the noise from the public rooms told its own tale. Laughter, whoops of joy, a rather drunken rendition of 'Here's a Health Unto His Majesty . . . *And he who will not drink his health, I wish him neither wit nor wealth.*' This was followed by shouted loyal toasts. London would awaken to many sore heads in the morning.

The room into which the inn-keeper led us was again heavily beamed and low-ceilinged, this being one of the oldest taverns in London. A refectory table had been laid with fine silver and a side table seemed almost to groan with food. There were pasties and pies, a huge ham, various custards and tartlets, cheeses and fruit from the traders in Covent Garden market. And, as I discovered, that was not even to be our main meal.

Immediately we were seated a serving girl poured wine then left jugs on the table for us to serve ourselves as we wished. This raffish company was already a little heady for me and I resolved to drink only a little wine.

The door to the dining room opened and dish after dish was brought to the table. There were soused oysters, a highly spiced salt fish pie, buttered whitings, roast calves' feet, a huge rib of piping hot beef served with an orange gravy, dishes of artichokes, split peas with saffron . . . I simply lost count of Sir John's largesse. But the food smelt delicious and I realized that I was very hungry.

I was seated between Sir John and a fresh-faced young nobleman, Peter, Lord Westland. Both men paid me marked attention, trying to replenish my goblet, offering tasty pieces from their plates. At one point I simply burst out laughing because both at the same time, casually and apparently accidentally, placed an arm along the back of my chair, ending up with arms entwined. But the atmosphere and their rivalry was good-humoured and they had the grace to laugh with me.

We finished our dinner at three o'clock and then coaches were waiting to take us to the Palace of Whitehall. Because of Richard's family connections and his work for the King we were privileged to be amongst the nobles and their ladies waiting to greet the King at Whitehall.

The journey to the Palace was madcap with the crowds waving and cheering as we passed by, the coachmen swearing and laughing as they tried to guide the coach and horses through the mob.

The King was expected to arrive at Whitehall a little after four o'clock and we quickly took our places in the Banqueting Hall. Whitehall was an extraordinary place, a jumble of buildings and courtyards which stretched for half a mile along the banks of the Thames. How anyone, King or courtier, could ever find their way around such a rabbit warren was beyond me.

The Banqueting Hall was crowded and stiflingly hot. By six o'clock there was still no news of the King's arrival.

'Richard,' I asked, 'could we not walk for a little in the park? We can see the King from there as easily as in here and without the risk of fainting. I swear, before long all you will see of me is a pile of my new finery and a puddle of water. Nothing else left!'

Richard laughed and took my arm. 'I agree. And who knows how much longer we may have to wait?'

We pushed our way through the crowds and out into the blessedly cool air of St James's Park. It was thronged with richly dressed lords and ladies all waiting to greet His Majesty. I looked around me, practically clapping my hands with excitement. 'Oh, Richard! I shall remember this day for as long as I live!'

We strolled for a while exchanging greetings with people whom Richard knew, meeting up with some of Sir John's party. Then, when it was nearing seven o'clock, we heard the noise of trumpets and drums. Of thousands of horses. Of cheering. This even above the noise of cannon and pealing bells.

I grasped Richard's hand and we ran across the grass to the Palace Yard. The cheering reached a crescendo and into the yard rode a tall man on a silver horse. I had seen broadsheet pictures of His Majesty and my immediate thought was of the poor man who had been beaten by the mob because he had said that King Charles was not as good-looking as his pictures. It was true, he was not. His lean face was nearly ugly. His complexion dark. But his jet black hair curled luxuriantly to his shoulders. He bore himself with pride. And, above all, even at the distance I was from him, I could feel the man's charm.

Into the yard and then on to the park came his entourage. His Majesty rode with his brothers, York and Gloucester. Behind them were about three hundred gentlemen, his Court in exile, all dressed in cloth of silver. Then the Lord Mayor of London and Aldermen, all in scarlet. Thousands upon thousands of soldiers paraded into the park, horse and foot. Their buff jackets, which could have been an unwelcome reminder of the Parliament they'd served until six weeks ago, were transformed by slashes of silver cloth on the sleeves.

The ladies curtsied deeply and the gentlemen bowed low as His Majesty reined in his horse. Then hats were thrown into the air and the loudest cheering broke out. King Charles smiled and waved in acknowledgement but, on a human level, I suddenly noted how tired he looked. But my eyes were no longer on the King. I looked for a dear face amongst the gentlemen attending him, and he was there! My love, my lover, Guy de Burgh.

Do not love too deeply, Jesslyn. It may break your heart. But I watch over you.

The King, his brothers and gentlemen dismounted, and grooms ran forward to lead away the horses. I longed to speak with Guy but the Earl of Manchester, as Leader of the House of Lords, addressed His Majesty at great length and I kept thinking, Richard is right; he is, after all, only a man, and one who desperately needs to sit down and rest.

Then the tedious speech ended and the King entered his palace. Within minutes Guy was by our side.

'Cousins!' He bowed low over my hand, his lips lightly brushing the tips of my fingers. I was desperately aware of other places his lips had kissed.

Richard hugged Guy to him. 'My God, you're a sight for sore eyes! But how did you see us in this crowd?'

'Oh, I was looking out for you,' Guy replied lightly. Then laughed. 'And who but Jesslyn and the Lady Barbara has hair of such a shade of auburn?'

Again I was being likened to Barbara Palmer. I prayed that Guy did not think me a woman of loose morals too.

Suddenly Richard started and waved across the yard. 'Excuse me, Jesslyn! Guy!' Then he was running across the grass like a madman and another man was running towards him.

'Killigrew! Killigrew!' I heard Richard shout.

'Killigrew?' I frowned, trying to place the name.

'A man of the theatre. He fought for the King and followed His Majesty into exile after Worcester. He's a Groom of the Bedchamber now and has the King's ear.' Guy smiled. 'I think Richard will not have to wait *too* long to play before an audience again.' Then his voice lowered. 'You cannot imagine how I have missed you. Longed for you. May I call upon you tomorrow?'

I was about to reply when a number of coaches rattled into the yard. Guy turned from me and smiled. 'Ah, the ladies! Come, Jesslyn!'

He took my arm and led me across the yard to where a richly liveried footman was pulling down the steps. A young woman, not particularly good-looking but with a haughty expression, accepted Guy's hand as she alighted from the coach.

'Cousin Jesslyn, allow me to present Marie-Louise. My new Countess.'

I hold faith.

CHAPTER NINE

THE CAT

*'The Egyptians have observed in the eyes of a cat
the increase of moonlight'*

– Edward Topsell

CATHERINE: 1990

'Cast your mind on other days'
                                    – W.B. Yeats

As I crossed the green towards the church, the last of autumn's chrysanthemums in my arms, the remains of the previous night's bonfire were still smouldering. It had always struck me as rather macabre to burn the effigy of a man every November the fifth but the English have been burning poor Guy Fawkes for nearly four hundred years so I doubt the custom will ever die. Certainly at Somerton Magna the celebrations were taken very seriously.

In early October the manager of the Home Farm, Fred Watson, had called on me. He was chairman of the Parish Council.

'Well, Miss Kelsey, it's about Bonfire Night. Always have a big "do" at Somerton. Er, the thing is, the village gets together the bonfire, makes the guy and all that. But, er, when it comes to the fireworks . . . er . . .'

'My grandfather provided them?' I asked, seeing that this could be a very long conversation if Fred didn't come to the point.

'He did that! Soon as they were back in the shops after the war. I was but a lad but, by ginger, I remember seeing my first Catherine Wheel!'

'I'll be happy to continue the tradition.'

'Thanks, Miss, the village will be right glad. Er, there's something else. Well, a Kelsey always lights the bonfire. You won't mind doing that, will you?'

'Of course not. I take it the village makes quite a party of it?'

'Always has done as far as I can gather.'

'How about refreshments? Do people come back to the Hall afterwards?'

'Good Lord, no, Miss!' Fred replied, quite shocked. 'Couldn't have Tom, Dick and Harry traipsing all over the place.'

'I don't see why not.'

'Apart from anything else, they wouldn't feel . . . comfortable like. The village knows its place. So should the Hall,' he added rather severely.

'In the latter half of the twentieth century?' I began, but from the set look on his face I knew I would be fighting a battle I could only lose.

'Now what your grandfather always did . . .'

I clenched my teeth to stop myself yelling at Fred. 'My grandfather was an old man, set in his ways. Don't try to make me live my life in his shadow!'

'What your grandfather always did was to provide a couple of kegs of beer, mulled cider and jacket potatoes with cheese and sausages and stuff to bung in them. We had it round the bonfire or in the village hall if wet. You ask old Peg Jessop. She's been running the show for the past twenty years or more.'

I bowed to tradition. A large barbecue was set up near the bonfire on which sausages sizzled, potatoes were kept hot, and a pretty heady brew of mulled cider bubbled. Strangely the village had no pub but there was a very old inn about half a mile away on the Colchester road. Fred went down there with his tractor and a trailer and hauled back two large kegs of beer and dozens of bottles of strong cider. Basically all I had to do was write out the cheques and enjoy myself.

And I did. My Knight's Croft cousins walked across the green to the party. Joseph and Rosemary brought their young daughter, Rosie, driving over from the rather upmarket close of houses built near the glassworks. My uncle, Sir James, telephoned to say that his arthritis couldn't take the night air but he'd be thinking of us. Only Jonas and Annabel remained aloof and, I thought rather ridiculously, gave a Bonfire Night party of their own at the old Rectory. Their action made me realize again how deeply Jonas resented my inheriting the estate.

The village women helping Mrs Jessop, who had been steadfast in her refusal to be on Christian name terms with me, were seeing that the undernourished-looking young vicar and his wife had their plates constantly replenished. I thought how kind these people were. Of course, there must be rogues among them – for all I knew, wife beaters and adulterers – but overall they were a community, secure in themselves. And, for the first time since coming into my inheritance, I felt a sense of peace and being part of something. Fran, if she had mentioned Somerton at all, had referred to it as 'That bloody, feudal dump', and I could see that the steadiness of the way of life here must have driven her mad. I, who during all my crazy life with her had longed for some stability, to have a proper home, to know my father, had been fighting against accepting the warmth of spirit that was being offered to me. That night, for the first time, I felt I belonged.

The flames leapt high around the guy and illuminated his face, a large turnip with nose, mouth and eyes carved into it. It looked so real that I involuntarily shuddered. A voice said softly, 'It's not really Guy we're burning! It's the fire of the pagan festival that marked the beginning of winter.'

I turned and saw Brett Fitzgerald by my side.

'Like mistletoe at Christmas being more to do with the Druids than Bethlehem?'

'Well, there's not a lot of mistletoe and holly in the Middle East, is there? And green has always been part of the old religion.' He caught my expression. 'No! Not the Roman Catholic church. A much older religion. How are you, Catherine? I haven't seen you since the opening of my exhibition last week.'

'Rupert says it's been a great success.'

'Mmm, yes. A gratifying number of red stickers.'

'Congratulations.'

'I suppose I should be immodest and say "Oh, not really!" or "I've been very lucky!" But to hell with that!' Then his face became serious. 'I feel very humble when I look upon a piece of Ravenscroft or a Façon de Venise wine goblet or . . . Oh, Catherine, have you ever seen the Breadalbane Amen glass? But I'd be a fool not to know I've got a God-given talent.' He smiled at me. 'Now that *is* lucky!'

I thought back to the previous week when the Kelseys had turned out en masse to support and honour the glassworks' master glass-blower.

A gallery in the small market town of Lavenham had approached Brett about mounting an exhibition.

The gallery, although situated in the depths of East Anglia, had an international reputation. To be invited to exhibit there was recognition of a major talent. To be given a one-man show was beyond price.

I drove my Knight's Croft cousins in my grandfather's elderly Rolls, Marcus having quite bluntly said: 'None of our lot will be sober enough to drive home!'

We were to meet Jonas, Annabel and my Uncle James there. Brett had been staying at The Swan for a couple of days to organize the lighting of his glass.

I'd never been to Lavenham before and was awestruck that such a place could still exist. Although I was now used to the Tudor beauty of Kelsey Hall, to see so many beautifully restored medieval timber-framed buildings, the plaster between the beams washed with colours that ranged from deep amber to Suffolk pink, was like a time slip.

We parked in the market square in front of the impressive and lovingly restored Guildhall. From the number of expensive cars parked there it seemed to me that the gallery really knew its business and was promoting Brett's work well.

The main gallery was approached through a covered courtyard which had some striking modern sculpture on display.

Entering from the courtyard, I nearly gasped at the beauty of Brett's glass. It had been splendidly lit, but the assurance and style that he brought to his work would have been striking in any circumstances.

I was about to talk to him about his work when Sophie came over with a plate of food for him and a tankard of beer. Soon they were laughing and flirting. It struck me how well suited they were, with their good looks and their ability to charm. I knew that Brett was a regular visitor to Knights Croft and I briefly wondered about their relationship. Whatever it was, at that moment, I was back to feeling an outsider.

I suddenly shivered in spite of being warmly dressed for the church, which was always freezing. I realized I'd been standing staring into the remains of the bonfire which last night had burnt so fiercely, for quite a few minutes. There was a slight frost still on the grass and my feet were becoming damp.

Then I had the strangest sensation that I was being watched intently. My back was to the Hall and I turned to see if a watcher was there. As I turned I thought I saw a face at the window of the gatehouse, in the beautiful panelled room where the table and chair were placed to see the estuary. Then the sun came from behind a cloud and my eyes were momentarily dazzled. When I could focus again there was no one there. I smiled. Now there was a face at the window. Cat had jumped on to the window seat and was staring down at me. Rather idiotically, I waved!

The room in the gatehouse had become a favourite place of ours throughout the summer. I was a long way from realizing my plans to make a snug retreat for myself there thanks to England's convoluted planning system, especially as the architect I'd engaged had to apply for Listed consent. But Cat and I had spent many an afternoon there, the window open to the soft wind from the estuary. I'd found that my grandfather had a comprehensive collection of books on glass in his library and was trying to learn as much as I could about the basis of my family's fortune.

I had made a habit of taking a book from the library and going over to the gatehouse to read and study. I would curl up on the window seat and within no time hear the soft tread of paws on the stairs. Cat would join me. He would doze by my side, sometimes gently purring to himself as if a sudden memory had pleased him. It was wonderfully companionable and I felt so happy and content at those times.

My Lady was happy here too, Catherine. For a while . . .

As I pushed open the heavy oak door of the ancient village church I knew that although I had made an early start, Sophie was there before me. She had been cleaning and dusting the church, arranging the flowers, setting out the hymn books virtually single-handed, and I had gradually slipped into the habit of helping her.

Since arriving at the Hall I had only been in Somerton for one major festival, the Harvest festival. That had been well attended, with the church piled high with produce, sheafs of barley, autumn fruit from local gardens and a wonderful selection of intricately woven corn dollies. Apparently attendance at Easter and Christmas was also high but for the rest of the time the congregation averaged about eight or nine worshippers. I suppose when it came to religion I myself did little more than travel hopefully. In truth I think I walked across the green to a Sunday service more out of pity for the vicar than from any strong conviction.

But I liked the beauty of the wording of King James's bible and Cranmer's prayer book and, of course, there was a Kelsey pew which traditionally could not be without a Kelsey on Sunday.

Nicholas, our new young vicar, fresh from a curacy in London's East End, had tried to – as he put it – reach out to the people of the village. As this seemed to mean playing a guitar in the pulpit and handing out a balloon to any small child dragged along to church, his congregation was very soon down to four: Sophie, myself and two elderly spinster sisters who gazed upon him with such rapt attention I think they came more because they had a crush on him than because they believed that he was their earthly link with God.

I gather Fred Watson, who was not only the Parish Council chairman but also Church Warden, quietly dropped the word to the vicar that he should give up the guitar and the balloons. Word went out and our congregation doubled again: Sophie, myself, the two sisters, a retired colonel who was nearly totally deaf and kept shouting out 'Eh?' during the sermon, an incredibly old woman supported by her unmarried son, and a solemn child who sat by herself at the back of the church and had clearly hated being given a balloon.

I called out a greeting to Sophie then went through to the vestry to put my flowers in water. My cousin had already thrown out the dying flowers we had arranged the week before and a selection of vases and bowls were set out by the sink ready for us.

Sophie had a bucket of hot water and was mopping the tiles in the Lady Chapel. Even early in the morning, wearing old jeans and one of her brother's rugger shirts, she looked incredibly beautiful. She had made an attempt at controlling her long, naturally curling auburn hair by pulling it back with what looked like a school tie but, as always, it defied any constraint and fell across her face and shoulders.

I marvelled, not for the first time, that such a stunning, charismatic creature could be content to spend her life in Somerton. To keep house for her father and brothers. To be seemingly without any artifice about her beauty. Add to that the fact that although she was totally at ease with the villagers, and they with her, she took her role as a Kelsey seriously, in particular her devoted care of the parish church, and yet did not seem to me to be a deeply religious person. It occurred to me that although Sophie and I had become very close and I counted her a true friend, I didn't truly know her.

She looked up and saw me standing in the chancel.

'Day dreaming? Or too much mulled cider last night?'

'A bit of both probably! I did enjoy it though. Even so, I find it strange that people can do exactly the same thing year after year and not want to change the slightest thing.'

'How odd. I find that wonderful! It gives me such a sense of belonging. All right, you might have a goose one year instead of a turkey, but even so every Christmas you sing the same carols, gather around the same table, set up the crib in the nave.'

'If you're fortunate. Some people . . .'

'Yes, yes!' Sophie interrupted impatiently. 'I'm not talking about the Salvation Army. I'm talking about here . . . Somerton. Tradition is very important to us here. The village and the Kelseys. The Kelseys and the village.' She suddenly laughed and sang to the tune of 'Love and Marriage', 'You can't have one without the other!'

I smiled at her. 'You truly love it, don't you, Sophie? The church. The village.'

'Don't forget the Hall! That's always been part of my life too. You do care about it, the Hall and everything, don't you, Catherine? You should! You must!'

I thought for a moment before I replied. 'It's all so new to me, Sophie. But, yes, last night I started to recognize how deep my feelings for this place could become. Are becoming.'

'Good!' she declared. She kissed me lightly on the cheek, then handed the mop to me. 'Just for being a devoted, true Kelsey, I give you the freedom of the mop! You carry on while I go and make a start on the flowers.'

I crossed into the Lady Chapel and stopped by Jesslyn, Lady Kelsey's tomb. 'She's very like you, you know, Sophie.'

'Oh, do you think so?' she exclaimed, pleased. 'She's always been my favourite. When I was a little girl and someone was angry with me I used to creep in here and tell her my woes . . . I like to think she listened.'

'Why a cat at her feet, do you think? It's surely very unusual. And why is she beloved of the Earl of Colne and not her husband? That must have caused quite a scandal!'

'Her husband was Sir Thomas Kelsey. He died quite a few years before 1682. I don't know any more than that. At least she died beloved. That's a blessing, isn't it?'

'Yes, I suppose so,' I said slowly. 'If it was a love she wanted. If she loved in return.'

Sophie tossed her lovely head. 'Oh, men are such pesky creatures! I'd settle just for being loved, then you can curl them around your little finger.'

'I doubt you have any problems doing that.'

To my surprise Sophie's face became suddenly sad and she blinked back tears. 'You'd be surprised, Catherine. Let's just say I should be lucky at cards.'

'Oh, Sophie, is there something really wrong? Can you tell me? Can I help?'

'No! I'm just being foolish. Look, I was telling you about Sir Thomas. You've no idea how many sad little coffins of his children are in the family crypt! I've just thought, Catherine, I bet you've never been in the crypt?'

'Well,' I replied dryly, 'it certainly hasn't been a high priority with me.'

'Then it should've been. Your very own family is laid to rest there.'

'Not my mother,' I said tersely.

Sophie looked at me for a moment and put her arm around me. She spoke softly. 'No, not your mother, Catherine . . . and we're all so sorry for that.'

'I don't think that "all" includes Jonas and Annabel. She has told me in no uncertain terms what they think of Fran . . . and my inheritance.' I suddenly laughed. 'In fact, I think the only thing that would bring a smile to their sour faces would be to see my coffin carried into this family crypt!'

'Not "this" family crypt . . . *our* family crypt. Come with me and see it, Catherine. It's part of our heritage. Please. It's important to me.'

I looked at her pleading face. I'd loved my mother but simply could not understand this obsession with the family, with the Kelseys. But I could see it was important to her and she was such an enchanting companion, such an amusing and increasingly loved friend, that I could not deny her.

On the opposite side of the nave from the Lady Chapel, and in front of the Kelsey pew, was an intricately carved and beautifully gilded screen. Behind was a small chapel dedicated to St Nicholas. The entrance to the crypt was in this chapel.

Sophie ran into the vestry and quickly returned with a candle and matches. I let her lead the way into the chapel. The entrance to the Kelsey crypt was heavily and, in my view sentimentally, carved with plump weeping angels and cherubs blowing trumpets. Sophie pointed to it scornfully.

'The bloody Victorians! Heaven alone knows what piece of exquisite medieval sculpture they destroyed when they put up that monstrosity!'

'So not all Kelseys are good Kelseys?' I teased.

Sophie laughed. 'Well, if the worst the black sheep can be accused of is bad taste, there's hope for the family!'

She laid the candle and matches on top of an angel's wing.

'Give me a hand with the door, will you? It's solid marble and weighs a ton.'

Actually I was surprised that the door swung back

quite easily. The early morning light streaming through the chapel's windows showed stone steps leading down into gaping darkness. I shivered. 'Must we really go down there, Sophie? Quite frankly, it gives me the creeps.'

She was lighting the candle. 'Oh, don't be such a baby. Come on.' With that she walked ahead of me into the body of the crypt. After a moment, I followed.

I'd never been into a crypt before, family or otherwise, and didn't really know what to expect. I suppose my imagination had been considerably heightened by watching late night horror movies and I found myself shaking as I stepped on to the floor of the crypt. The chamber was really quite small but from the floor to the low ceiling was shelf after shelf of coffins. There was no smell of corruption, just a musty feeling of damp. Some coffins were tiny and sadly pathetic-looking. Some had tattered folded flags on them, presumably Kelseys who had fallen fighting for King and Country. I found myself whispering.

'All right, Sophie. I've seen it. Can we go now?'

She looked at me, astonished. 'You really don't like it, do you?'

'I doubt many people would!'

'Rupert and Dickon and I used to have picnics down here.'

'What?'

'I suppose it was a kind of dare, really. Then we got to like it. It was our secret place. Joe would never come with us. He took being the eldest very seriously and he's . . . I don't know, sort of solemn compared with the rest of us. Perhaps he's a changeling!' she giggled.

'I'm going back into the church now, Sophie,' I said firmly. 'You should come too. You'll catch your death down here.'

We both looked at each other and laughed at what I had unthinkingly said. Sophie followed me out of the crypt and we swung the heavy door back into place.

'Rupert locked Dickon and me down there once. He thought it was a great joke. But when he came back we were barely conscious. It's airtight, you see.'

'My God, what a crazy thing to do! He might have killed you both.'

'He didn't know that, did he? It was just a prank. Rupert's quite mad, you know.'

'Mad's a bit strong, isn't it? He seems to me . . . feckless, I suppose. I imagine that if Rupert really wanted something, he'd blunder straight in in such a way that would make the Charge of the Light Brigade seem quite tame by comparison.'

'Yes, you're right. It's as if the part of our brain that makes the rest of us think before we leap has been left out with Rupert. He's very taken with you, you know.'

'Oh, don't talk nonsense. Come on, let's get back to work.'

I went back into the Lady Chapel and picked up the mop. Instead of going into the vestry to start arranging the flowers, Sophie followed me.

'Why is it nonsense? You're very attractive, you know, Catherine, and could be more so. Why shouldn't a man want you?'

'Because . . .' I started. 'Oh, Sophie, let's drop it. Please.'

'Okay. But you shouldn't underestimate yourself.'

With that she wandered off into the vestry. In my mind I finished the sentence. 'Because I'm plain. Because my mother was a great beauty and men were drawn to her like moths to a flame. Because, even though she's dead, I cannot shake off the habit of being in her shadow.'

By late-November the days were growing shorter and I spent more and more time by the fire studying my grandfather's books. I'd also been back to the glass-works several times to watch the glass-blowers at work as I began to understand and appreciate more and more about their ancient craft.

After one such visit I was just about to drive away in my grandfather's ancient Rolls when I saw Brett Fitz-gerald waving at me from the other side of the car park. He quickly crossed over to my car. Watching him stride across to me, I thought how handsome he looked. He was casually dressed in dark slacks and a Donegal tweed jacket but wore his clothes with effortless grace. No wonder he and Sophie made such a handsome pair, I thought ruefully. Then I wondered if it was Brett that Sophie was having trouble with. Before I could specu-late further he was by my car.

'Hello. You're becoming quite a regular visitor.'

'Yes. I find I'm fascinated by the glassworks. I wish I could come and work here.'

'Why not?'

'Jonas would have a fit. A Kelsey as a filing clerk! And I'm afraid that's all my work experience.'

'Why not in the board room? It's no secret that you're the majority shareholder in the works.'

I shook my head. 'I don't know enough yet. What would I have to offer?'

'Good taste and common sense – and that's more than Jonas has. Think about it. Promise me you'll think about it? You've got to stop being a chrysalis one day, you know.'

'What a funny thing to say!'

Brett smiled at me. 'But I think you know what I mean.'

I changed the subject. 'I've been reading about Ravenscroft glass. You remember you showed me that piece in the museum? I keep meaning to go back and look at it again but the museum's closed now, isn't it? Until the spring.'

'That's no problem. Why don't I get the keys and take you there again? We could have dinner afterwards.'

I hesitated. 'Well . . .'

'No "well", "ifs" or "buts". Yes or no? Do say you will!' Brett interrupted.

'Yes, thank you, I'd like that.'

'I can't manage tomorrow, but how about Friday? I'll pick you up about six, all right?'

As I drove to the Hall I asked myself if I was falling in love with Brett Fitzgerald? And what did it feel like to be in love? What did it mean? No bells had rung. My heart didn't pound when I saw him. And yet . . . and yet . . . I found myself hoping to be in his company. I admired the passion he felt for his craft. I recognized his brilliance and individuality as a glassmaker, but I could also make an educated guess that, if thwarted, he could be a very difficult man.

The next day Sophie telephoned and asked me over to Knight's Croft for supper. As always I accepted. No longer out of loneliness but because of genuine affection for my cousins. I had decided not to say anything about meeting Brett at the museum and then dining with him, in case Sophie had been involved with him. I counted without Rupert.

We were halfway through eating yet another of Sophie's stews, a delicious concoction of rabbit coated with honey and mustard and then simmered in cider, when Rupert started teasing me.

'So! A date with our resident genius? Glass is the art of fire, Catherine. Don't get burnt.'

'He's just opening up the museum for me and then we're having a meal. Hardly a date. Anyway, how did you know?'

'We're setting up a big promotion of Brett's new work, so he and I had lunch with Jonas today. He happened to mention he needed the keys to the museum.'

Dickon was home for a few days, and from the way he was wolfing his supper I think he had probably been starving in a garret. In between mouthfuls, he added to Rupert's teasing.

'Just think, if Brett and Catherine make it down the aisle, the one thing we *won't* have to give them is a set of crystal glasses!'

'Stop tormenting the poor girl,' Marcus growled over a glass of wine. 'You're boring me, children . . . And I'm a pain in the arse when I'm bored!'

The conversation, thankfully, veered away from my meeting with Brett to a lively discussion as to whether

Shakespeare's sonnets were written to a man or a woman. Rupert, as always, had the last word. 'Let's not worry about who he wrote the sonnets to, let's argue about who wrote Shakespeare!'

The next morning found me going through my very commonplace wardrobe trying to find something that would make me feel attractive when I met Brett that evening. I finally had to admit to myself that I found the man fascinating to be with and was looking forward very much to meeting him. Once having been honest with myself, I was also honest about the fact that there was really nothing in my wardrobe that I wanted to wear. The time had come to spend some money on myself.

My first instinct was to telephone Sophie and ask her to drive into Baildon with me. I really needed some advice. Then I hesitated; if she had had an unhappy affair with Brett it would be so unkind to ask her to come with me to choose clothes that were obviously being bought because of my having dinner with, perhaps, her former lover.

As I drove away from the Hall, by chance I saw Sophie taking Lottie for a walk, heading along the road that led to the museum and beyond that the sea wall where I often walked Rupert's dog. We waved to each other and I was once again struck by her stunning beauty. Surely there wasn't a man in the world who would treat such a creature badly? But then Fran had been beautiful too and had had her heart broken time and again by unfaithful lovers.

I went on a total spree. When I was old enough to take an interest in clothes, Fran's career was slipping and it was important that any spare money be spent on her. I'd never known the heady feeling before of saying 'I'll take that . . . and that . . .' and not bothering to ask the price!

I drove back to the Hall in the early afternoon with the car piled high with bags and boxes. There were shoes, silk underwear, new dresses, a very elegant suit and a new winter coat. Absolutely nothing was sensible or bought to last. I'd chosen some beautiful clothes in vibrant colours because another thing I'd realized about myself was that I'd always dressed to disappear into the background.

When I entered my bedroom, my arms full of shopping, Cat was asleep on the bed. He uncurled himself and stretched then came to investigate my purchases, rubbing the top of his head against them the way cats do, to mark everything in their home with their scent.

'I've gone raving mad, Cat, and it's made me very happy!'

Just then there was a tap at the door and Mrs Jessop entered.

'Oh, Miss Kelsey, I thought I heard you come in. There was a message for you while you were out. Mr Fitzgerald phoned, or it might have been his office.'

My heart immediately sank. He was going to cancel our meeting. I tried to sound casual.

'Oh, yes?'

'Would you mind meeting him earlier? Say about five o'clock. I gather he'd like to meet you there. No need to phone back if that's all right.'

'Perfectly, thank you.'

'Can I get you anything? Nice cup of tea?'

'No thanks, I'm going to unpack my shopping. I've been very extravagant.

'About time too, Miss! You're a young woman. Have a bit of fun while you're still fancy free, that's what I always say. Just give me a call if you change your mind about the tea.'

I was relieved that I was still going to meet Brett but it did cross my mind that it was a little strange that he wouldn't be picking me up, because he had to drive past the Hall to get to the museum. Then I shrugged. Perhaps he wanted to study the beautiful collection by himself before showing it to me again.

I bathed then dressed myself in my new finery. When I looked into the long mirror on my wardrobe I was relatively pleased with what I saw. I wore a deceptively simple dress made of very soft fine wool. Its colour was a subtle coral. The sleeves were long and the bodice tight-fitting. Then, from a waist that was softly belted in the same material, the skirt was cut on the cross and swirled out as I turned. As I was conscious of my height I had bought black patent pumps with a low heel to wear with it, but they were made elegant by the thin band of gold set into the heel. At my neck I wore a simple gold chain. My hair was caught back in a small gold clip.

'Well, old girl,' I said to my reflection, 'you'll never be a great beauty but you've scrubbed up pretty well, I'd say.'

As I hated the idea of wearing real fur, I'd bought a fake fur coat in deep cream. It had a huge collar and wide sleeves with turnback cuffs. It was crazy but great fun, the kind of design you'd see in an old movie worn by a glamorous nineteen-thirties star. Only her coat would have been made of ermine or white fox. I shuddered at the thought.

Celeste and Mrs Jessop were just leaving when I came downstairs. They were practically speechless on seeing my new clothes. Celeste, naturally, recovered first.

'Cor! What you done to yourself? I was only saying to Mum the other day, "If Catherine did herself up a bit she wouldn't be 'alf bad-looking!"'

It was rather a backhanded compliment but I thanked Celeste for it, then said goodnight.

'See you tomorrow, then!' She winked at me. 'Don't do anything I wouldn't. That'll give yer plenty of scope!'

Mrs Jessop slapped her lightly, 'You're too cheeky by 'alf, young woman. 'Night, Miss.'

When I drove up to the museum I was surprised that there were no lights on and that Brett's car wasn't there. I climbed out of the ancient Rolls and went to the main door. It was locked. I wandered back to the car, puzzled. But perhaps Brett had simply been held up? There was nothing for it but to wait.

My car was parked on the seaward side of the museum and before getting back into it I looked out along the estuary. It was dusk and the tide was running high. To some the place might seem desolate but I found it incredibly beautiful.

As I looked I could just make out the outline of a sailing barge moored at the old landing stage. I remembered that Rupert had told us the previous evening that a young couple at Baildon had stripped out an old barge and converted it into a restaurant. Jonas and Annabel were giving a dinner party at the weekend for some important German customers and Annabel had struck on the idea of renting the barge. The young couple had sailed it down river from Baildon and moored it ready for the party.

Lights were on in the main body of the barge and so I decided to walk along and see if anyone was about. There was no sound of life as I walked up the gangplank but then the owners could well be working in the galley.

'Hello?' My voice echoed across the racing water. 'Hello! May I come aboard?'

Still no reply, but by then I was curious to see the inside of the barge. I walked around the deck. A door was open and I could see steps leading down into the main body of the barge. It was dimly lit but although steep the steps looked quite safe. I started to climb down them. I thought I heard footsteps on the deck behind me. I called out, 'Brett? Is that you?' Then the door slammed shut behind me.

I stood quite still for a moment, for the first time a little afraid. Was someone out there? Then I heard the water. Not gurgling or seeping into the barge but rushing in. In the poor light I could just make out a door at the far end of the cabin. It was slightly ajar and water was gushing through it. I knew I had to get off the barge, and fast. I ran up the steps and pulled at the door. It was jammed tight. I was trapped. I pulled at the door. Pushed at it. Impossible to open it. Was there another way to get off? I had to find out or drown. I jumped down on to the floor of the cabin. The water was well above my ankles and rising fast. I slipped and slithered my way to the partly open door. A sign above said 'Cloakrooms'. I tried to push the door shut but it was impossible against the pressure of the water. I think I started to cry. Then I pulled myself together, forced myself to look around the cabin. Panicking wouldn't help me. And if I was going to die, it wouldn't be without a fight.

I started to call for help in the hope that Brett had arrived but there was no way I'd be able to hear a car above the rushing water. I didn't imagine it would be long before the barge started to sink.

The portholes were hinged but much too small to climb through. The windows that had been set into the hull were sealed and double glazed. The water was nearly to my knees now. I desperately looked around for something to smash through those windows but the seating was banquette and fixed to the walls and the tables screwed down.

I think it was then that I wondered if I should just give myself up to the water? Have a peaceful death, not one where I was hopelessly clawing at life, dying choking in the muddy water of the estuary with no time to compose my thoughts as I faced death.

I will not allow you to die here, Catherine. Fight. Think.

The galley! I suddenly thought of it. This was a restaurant. Perhaps there would be something in the galley? The barge by now was tilting in a way that terrified me. It was incredibly difficult to stay on my feet. By grasping on to anything I could, I dragged myself to the galley. Nothing! Nothing I could use. Then I saw it. A Calor gas cylinder. That's how the oven was powered. I had no idea if I was going to blow the barge up if I just pulled the cap off it, but it was either that or drown.

The cylinder was very heavy but I had the strength of desperation. I pulled and dragged the damned thing back into the main cabin. I have only a vague memory of rolling the cylinder on to some seating then smashing it into one of the windows. At my third attempt the glass shattered. As I climbed through the window I could feel myself being cut by the jagged edges of the glass, but the important thing was to escape.

The water of the estuary was freezing and I could feel my sodden clothes pulling me down. I knew I had to swim as far as I could from that barge or when it went down I would be sucked down with it. It would have been so easy to slip beneath the water into the tall reeds. I was tired. Incredibly tired. I wanted to sleep. Then I found an inner strength. I wasn't a strong swimmer but I swum, quite literally, for my life.

Somehow I got myself to the bank of the estuary and pulled myself ashore. I simply lay where I was, totally shocked and exhausted. I knew the cold could kill me but I could do no more. I was vaguely conscious of the lights of a car. Of Brett's voice. 'Catherine! Christ, dear girl! What's happened?'

I couldn't find the strength to answer. I felt myself being wrapped in something – Brett's coat? – then lifted in strong arms.

By the time we got back to the Hall I was shaking uncontrollably. My memories of the rest of that night are blurred. As if I'd partly dreamt them. As if I was watching and seeing the events happening to someone else.

I remember Brett pulling off my clothes then lowering me into a warm bath. He rubbed me vigorously with a towel, desperate to keep my circulation going. To raise my body temperature. And all the time there was but one thought in my head: Someone tried to kill me.

Yes, but I watch over you, as I did my Lady.

CHAPTER TEN

THE CAT

'I shall remember while the light lives yet,
And in the night time I shall not forget'
— A.C. Swinburne

JESSLYN: 1661

'. . . "Is there no more?"
She cries. "All this to love and rapture's due:
Must we not pay a debt to pleasure too?" '
                    – John Wilmot, Earl of Rochester

For months after Guy had introduced me to his bride I behaved like a mad woman. I know Richard and Moll were desperately worried about my behaviour but I cared for nothing except the pursuit of pleasure.

Every gift, every letter, every posy of flowers was returned to Guy's London mansion in Kings Street. When we met at Court I declined to dance with him, even to speak to him. I knew my behaviour was irrational. That he had to marry and have an heir. But the knowledge that all the time I had fretted for his safety, had longed to be in his arms, he had been marrying and bedding another woman, drove me to distraction. To despair.

I set out to show him that if he did not want me, other men did! I flaunted my conquests before his eyes. And when the King's trusted secretary, Will Chiffinch, handed me a note inviting me to dine privately with His Majesty, I was tempted. It was well known that a staircase from Chiffinch's rooms led to the river where two or three boats were always waiting to take His Majesty to some rendezvous. I assumed that somewhere along the river, perhaps in the village of Chelsea, the King kept a house where he could be a man and not our Sovereign Lord. Certainly for him to have any secrets in the teeming Palace of Whitehall was an impossibility.

That would have been the ultimate action to throw in Guy's face: to be the mistress of the King. The only thing that stopped me was Lucinda. She had grown into a beautiful, sweet-natured, little girl and I loved her dearly.

It was one thing for me to be one of the hedonistic crowd who thronged the Palace. For me to be seen dancing pavans and galliards, each dance with a different gentleman. For me to play cards and throw dice as rakishly as any man. Even, on occasions, to play Pall Mall with the King himself. But, if I became the King's mistress, I would be notorious and Lucinda's future life would be placed in jeopardy. I had no illusions, but knew that my darling girl must make a good marriage to have a place in Society. Very few women were as fortunate as Harriet, living comfortably at Knight's Croft in Somerton with her fortune and her books and her beloved herb garden. Whether humble serving wench or a Duke's daughter there was no escaping the fact that a woman's life would be dominated by men, be they husband or father.

My face softened as I thought of this. No one could have been gentler with me than my father. And for all the sham of our marriage of convenience, no one could have been kinder to me than Richard. I felt ashamed when I saw the hurt and concern in his eyes when he looked at me nowadays but I was driven by devils I must exorcize.

I was careful never to meet with a lover at Whitehall.

The Palace was a maze of rooms and apartments. At Whitehall there was much secrecy but no privacy. Courtiers and government officials vied with each other for the most splendid rooms and apartments.

His Majesty's suite of rooms overlooked the Thames: The Presence Chamber, Withdrawing Room, Privy Chamber and Bedchamber. But by far the grandest rooms, many times larger than the King's, were those set aside for Barbara Palmer, the King's principal, but not only, mistress. And, since February, a nursery had been added to those rooms as Barbara had borne the King a daughter, christened Anne.

Although the King was not faithful to her, Barbara Palmer was virtually the uncrowned Queen of his Court. Every day at noon he would dine publicly in the Banqueting Hall and, until the last stages of her pregnancy, Barbara was always by his side, her unfortunate husband having wisely taken himself off to his country estates.

These were heady days. Yes, the Court was lascivious and the country took its cue from Whitehall. But they were also days of a new enlightenment. The King encouraged the composition of music whose sole purpose was to entertain and not to enrich the soul. He was accessible, walking in St James's every morning with his beloved spaniels. At that time, any of his subjects could approach him. It was fashionable to follow the King on these early morning walks and to share the syllabub that he had made by the dairymaids from cows which grazed in St James's Park, being milked directly into jugs of white wine.

He was also passionately interested in science and

mechanics. I think everyone at the Palace was driven mad by the constantly chiming clocks which His Majesty collected avidly. He founded the Royal Society of Science and, when they were not trying to discover whether or not a spider would walk from a ring of powdered unicorn horn, encouraged them to push their minds towards a new age. In the Privy Gardens a herb garden was planted and the King took great interest in experiments upon their medicinal use. But, above all, for Richard and Moll and fellow actors, the King was going to license the opening of two theatres.

I can look back now and marvel at the changes that were taking place but at the time I was preoccupied with my own private hell. Nothing I did, no man I took, not even the admiration of the King, could kill my love for Guy. And yet my hurt was such that I took pleasure in denying him even a touch of my hand, a murmured greeting.

The King's Coronation was to be held on the twenty-third day of April, St George's Day. By tradition he would spend the night before his Coronation in the Royal Apartments at the Tower. But, on the night before that, a great ball was to be held at Whitehall. On this occasion I attended with Richard.

Guy had been right: Thomas Killigrew did have the ear of the King who had, apparently, during his exile formed a passion for the theatre. As a very young man, before the Civil War, Richard had been a member of Killigrew's company. And, from the attention and friendship offered to him now, I can only assume an incredibly talented member.

The dreadful night in the barn before I had given

birth to Lucinda was the only time I had seen actors perform. I had no way of judging what was good or bad. What I did know was that Richard had held that raggedy audience spellbound. Looking back, I could not see that he had pandered to them or betrayed his integrity in any way. In fact, I think he had made daring demands on them. But he had always kept them enthralled. I felt no surprise that Killigrew was not only a good friend but wanted Richard for his new company. It was he who had invited us to the ball.

As one of the young maids, Kitty, helped me dress, I again wondered at the changes that had taken place in so short a time. A year ago dancing had been forbidden. Drab clothes were the order of the day. Adulterers could be hanged.

Now the King openly kept his married mistress by his side. I was dressing to dance until dawn in a sensuously cut but deceptively simple gown. And, in readiness for May Day, the maypole had again been erected in the Strand. And it was the old maypole. When Parliament had ordered its removal a butcher from Cheapside had bribed the soldiers to sell it to him. It had remained hidden in his storehouse all those years.

I had chosen my gown for such an important occasion very deliberately. I was tired of having my looks likened to Barbara Palmer's although, I must admit, greatly flattered as she was held to be a great beauty. But the lady favoured vibrant colours and clothes that bordered on vulgarity. Her father had died of his wounds fighting for the late King and she had had a penniless upbringing. This, said her friends, excused and explained her later avariciousness. And the King, though perhaps no longer quite so besotted by her, was still of a nature to give in to her endless tantrums. She was always bedecked with the jewels he had lavished on her.

I therefore had made a gown of oyster-coloured taffeta, the neck cut very low, exposing not only my breasts almost to my nipples but also my shoulders. The sleeves were ruched and the gathers caught by tiny pearls. The neckline was edged with delicate lace. It fell into points, each having the same seed pearls stitched into it. The overmantle of my shirt was gathered up to reveal a petticoat, again made of oyster taffeta, the only decoration being that the hem of the petticoat was also edged with seed pearls. I had never seen a gown before where the petticoat was not in contrast to the overmantle and, although the tailor had protested long and loudly that I was ruining his reputation, was pleased with the innovation I had wrought. I was determined that tonight no one would liken me to Barbara Palmer.

A choker necklace of pearls was at my neck and drop pearls hung from my ears. I wore my hair loose about my shoulders but with the hair around my forehead caught up in a simple pearl slide. There were only two colours on show that night, my auburn hair and my blue eyes.

I knew I was taking a tremendous risk. At a Court where flamboyance was all, to dress so starkly could bring ridicule. Or success.

As I entered the Banqueting Hall, that night transformed to a ballroom, I felt nervous. Was I making a fool of myself by dressing so? For I could not pretend that by wearing only one colour, and that so pale, I had not boldly set out to attract attention. Richard sensed my apprehension and squeezed my hand to reassure me.

'You're beautiful, sweeting! And you have spirit. Never let anyone tell you otherwise.'

I noticed Barbara Palmer across the hall on the arm of her cousin, the Duke of Buckingham. So! As close as this to his Coronation, King Charles was showing some propriety in his relationship with his mistress.

As I had imagined, although looking incredibly beautiful with her heavy-lidded, slanting eyes and sensuous, full bottom lip, she was gaudily dressed in brightly coloured silks and satins. Her wrists, neck and ears were adorned with dazzling jewels. The whole effect I found fulsome but tasteless. But the lady, if no longer fully holding the King's heart, certainly had a sexual attraction which kept the King regularly in her bed.

Suddenly, in the distance, there was the sound of trumpet and drum, drawing nearer and nearer. The musicians in the gallery stopped playing. Then two of the richly dressed guard threw open the doors to the hall which led to the King's Privy Apartments. Even on an occasion such as this the yapping of His Majesty's spaniels could be heard through the music that attended his approach.

Then he entered: a tall, world weary man whose lean face simultaneously expressed cynicism about the way of the world but also a love of life and of people.

He was exquisitely and richly dressed as one would expect. But how to marry the character of a prince who attends his own Coronation Ball dressed in velvet and cloth of gold but is unable to leave behind his beloved dogs?

The company bowed and curtsied deeply as His Majesty entered. The spaniels, about ten of them, showed no such respect, dashing about the hall excitedly, one of them cocking his leg happily against a powerful nobleman.

The King nodded and the musicians started to play again. The music was for a graceful pavan. The company waited for the King to take the floor with Barbara Palmer. I think I was the most amazed and shocked when His Majesty crossed the hall and bowed before me, offering his hand.

'Richard, you lucky fellow, you will not deny your Sovereign a chance to dance with this ice maiden?'

Richard bowed low as His Majesty led me into the dance.

'Mistress Warwick,' the King chuckled, 'how daring of you to stand out as a dove amongst peacocks. I congratulate you. I also wish to know the name of your tailor.'

'Your Majesty is too kind,' I said as we met and parted, dancing the intricate steps.

'But you are not, Mistress!'

The steps of the dance took us apart and our hands touched other partners. Then I was by the King's side again.

'I could command, Jesslyn.'

'Oh, Your Majesty, why command when you have only to beckon? And they say all cats are grey in the dark.'

'But in candlelight, Mistress, you are anything but grey,' he said, smiling.

Again we parted. Then were together again.

'Your Majesty, who dares say no to a King. But . . .'

The shout of laughter that came from him turned all heads. 'You do, Jesslyn. You do. I think no ill of you for it. I shall simply seek out grey cats.'

After that one dance His Majesty paid ceaseless attention to his mistress, but the whole Court as well as that lady had been made aware that no one, certainly not a woman, dare predict the mind of the King.

What a triumph! The whole Court – and Guy, especially Guy – had seen the King seek me out. Had seen him kiss my hand as if in fond farewell at the end of the pavan. Would recognize that there was no sexual tension between us, only amusement and, yes – dare I say it? – a sense of friendship. I thought that, for all his womanizing, His Majesty was not really a rake but genuinely enjoyed the company of women. Loved them for their wit as well as the comfort they offered in bed.

I danced with Richard and so many different men. Some to whom I had given my body but never my heart. I was partnered by the King's brother, the Duke of York, in a galliard. As he lifted me and swung me high in his arms I came to rest opposite Guy. The look of anguish mixed almost with disdain made me want to throw myself into his arms and beg his forgiveness. Then I thought of that moment when he had said 'My new Countess'.

I was being partnered by Richard in an old country dance, the Sir Roger de Coverly. Dancers formed a line of eight and changed partners with every stance of music. I had not noticed who the other dancers were and so was surprised, but pleasantly so, to find myself in the arms of Peter, Lord Westland.

'Mistress Warwick! I hope you may remember we met on the day of His Majesty's entry into London? At Sir John Grenville's and . . .'

But the dance carried us away from each other. When our arms were entwined again he whispered to me, 'Mistress, every man here tonight, including the King, desires you. All I ask is that you will let me be your gallant!'

And I thought, Why not?

All through that summer Peter danced attendance on me. We were part of a group of 'merry' friends who surrounded the Monarch. We were all younger than the King but he laughed with us and enjoyed our diversions. As if to ward off a deep-seated melancholy, His Majesty pursued gaiety. The only exception was on a Sunday evening when the whole Court knew he chose to spend his time alone in his apartments writing to his much loved young sister, Henrietta-Anne, whom he called Minette. She was now in France and married to the Duc d'Orleans, brother to the French King and, it was rumoured, a vicious homosexual.

For the men in our group the day began early for, however late to bed, His Majesty rose at five o'clock. He loved to swim in the Thames and his younger courtiers joined him. Then they would boat or fish until the King felt inclined to take breakfast.

Peter and several men friends would then come to

the house in Maiden Lane to take chocolate, a new fashion. Sometimes, but rarely, Richard and Killigrew would join us.

I always enjoyed, perhaps childishly, the preparation of the chocolate. Our cook would crush and boil the cocoa nibs for several hours with sugar, cinnamon, cloves, orange-flower water and vanilla straws. This mixture would be brought to the parlour warm from the kitchen fire and I would beat in milk and eggs, then serve it to my guests.

The young men would leave by ten and I would finish my toilet. At half-past eleven Peter would call again to escort me to Whitehall. Sometimes we would simply watch the King dine at noon; on other occasions we were invited to join him.

The afternoons were given over to many pleasures. Gaming, dicing, picnics, riding, and frequently making love. Beyond a passionate kiss and, on the rare moments we were alone, a hand slipped into the low-cut neck of my dress to fondle my breasts, Peter had remained true to his word. He asked only to be my gallant. And, if he suspected that I had the odd, brief dalliance with some of the young noblemen in our circle, he made no show of it. Or perhaps he simply did not care. Perhaps, like me, his heart had been broken and all he wanted was to live life so fully that the pain was briefly numbed.

By late summer, whilst not remotely in love with him, I had grown fond of Peter. The summer had been hot but we had been fortunate in London, there having been only a brief outbreak of the Plague in the most scurvy areas of the old City. The deadly disease had not reached the wide squares and new streets of Covent Garden nor the Palace of Whitehall. I went to St Paul's in the Piazza and prayed for the poor souls in the old City.

Peter's family owned one of the great mansions on the banks of the Thames to the south of the Strand, but he had recently taken lodgings in Henrietta Street in Covent Garden – a street named in honour of the Queen Dowager. It was not difficult for me to guess at his purpose in taking rooms there. The gardens of the houses in Henrietta Street ran down to Maiden Lane. It would be so easy to slip from a house there, through those gardens and into the back entrance of a house in the street that ran parallel. It amused me to see how long it would be before Peter suggested that I did just that.

I had not long to wait. We were on one of ten barges which sailed down the river, following the King to Hampton Court for a daylong rout. It was a ridiculous, delightful day. Couples quite deliberately got lost in the Maze. There was boating and fishing on the river.

It being a beautiful day, trestle tables were set out on the lawns. In a courtyard beside the kitchens a bullock was roasted. The gardens at Hampton Court produced a huge range of salad herbs, also radishes and lettuce, tasty young onions, baby cucumbers, freshly dug potatoes, all served with a delicious range of sauces. Set all along the tables were jugs of Rhenish wine and bowls of Quiddonay made from plums or apples or apricots but all a delicious relish.

In the late-afternoon we set back for Whitehall. Now

the tide was against us and the wind had dropped and so each barge was rowed by sixteen brawny young oarsmen.

I looked out across the river at the fields we passed, at the cottages and farmhouses. Were there happy people there? I asked myself. And if they were not happy, were they not, at least content? I longed to end the nightmare of my own recklessness, my uncaring taking and discarding of lovers. I could no longer recognize the person I had become. Inside I was still surely the girl my father had loved. What would he think of me now?

Peter lightly and discreetly touched my hand. I knew that the moment had come.

'Jesslyn,' he whispered, 'as you know I have lodgings in Henrietta Street. Would you consider coming to sup with me tomorrow evening?'

My dear Peter, I said to myself, I feel I have supped with the Devil himself, why not you?

'At what time?'

'Shall we say seven of the clock? If a cold supper would be agreeable, I shall see that there are no servants in the house.'

'That seems wise,' I said wryly. 'And, yes, a cold supper will suffice. After all, tomorrow at noon we dine with the King.'

The following evening I let myself quietly out of the house in Maiden Lane. I wore a hooded cloak over my gown although I doubted that anyone would recognize me as I hurried across the few feet that separated Maiden Lane from the gardens of the houses in Henrietta Street.

I was almost at the door when it was opened by Peter.

'I have been watching for you,' he said, then swept me into his arms. 'Oh, my love! How I've longed for this.'

He took my cloak and draped it over a heavily carved chest in the hall. I was about to enter the door he held open to the parlour when I became aware that I was being watched. I looked along the hallway and, at first, in the flickering candlelight, could see nothing. Then the candles illuminated golden eyes in a black face. Hunched on a chair was a little black cat. I crossed to stroke him.

'You have a cat.'

'Not really. My manservant feeds him scraps. He comes and goes as he pleases.'

'That is the nature of cats. But has he no home? Where has he come from?'

Peter shrugged. 'Who knows? The streets are teeming with cats. Watkins says he thinks this one comes from the tavern on the corner of Bow Street and Drury Lane but . . . well, a black cat is, after all, just a black cat.'

A tavern on the corner of Bow Street and Drury Lane . . . A brief memory of Guy's encounter with a black cat crossed my mind. But this was not a night to think of Guy.

I stroked the cat's silky fur. 'A black cat is not *just* a black cat to me! I once had a cat . . .'

I turned away and fought back tears. Not only for Ra who was long gone from me, but for remembrance of innocent days spent with my father and Harriet and our much loved cat before the fire at the cottage at Somerton.

Trust me, Jesslyn. I will not fail you.

Peter ushered me into a large, beautifully proportioned room. It served both as bedchamber and living room. A settle stood at an angle to the fireplace where a fire had been laid but not lit, in anticipation of the chill which came with evening now that the summer was nearly at an end.

A table had been placed by the settle and on it was a selection of pies and pasties and cold meats with side dishes of artichokes and asparagus.

As soon as the door was closed Peter took me into his arms again. His kiss was passionate and I opened my mouth to it.

'Oh, Jesslyn, I want you! Let me love you now. Take off your clothes, my darling, and stand before me naked. I long for that.'

I laughed. 'I'll take off my clothes with pleasure but you must be my maid servant. There is a great deal of unlacing to do!'

My bodice was laced at the back and Peter untied the silken strings, kissing my shoulders and the nape of my neck as he did so. Finally corsets, petticoats, my under and overmantle, lay on the floor in a heap and I stood before him.

He stood and stared at me for a moment.

'Jesslyn,' he said huskily, 'I have dreamt of this moment, but even dreaming did not truly appreciate your beauty. I've waited so long. I wanted you to . . . no, not love me but like me a little. I wanted to be unlike all the others. A moment's passing pleasure but with no true feeling. Please say you like me, Jesslyn. Please!'

I moved to him and put my arms around his neck. 'Peter, dear Peter, enough of this foolishness. Take me to bed.'

For all his youth and boyishness he was a good and thoughtful lover, giving pleasure as well as taking it. His lips and tongue caressed each breast. Then he was sucking at them, gently nibbling. I felt myself growing moist. He lips were between my legs now, his tongue seeking, finding. I fondled him, stroked him and then he was inside me.

'Oh, Jesslyn, Jesslyn, I love you!'

Afterwards we lay in each other's arms exhausted. I drifted into sleep.

I don't know how long I slept but was awakened by a hand stroking my buttocks.

'Jesslyn, you will enjoy this,' Peter whispered. 'It is the best, the very best way to make love.'

I opened my eyes as I became aware of a cord being tied around my wrist.

'Peter!' I cried out fearfully. 'What are you doing?'

The face that met mine was no longer that of the fresh-faced young man who had courted me all summer long. His eyes were staring and he was breathing heavily. On the table by the bedside was a riding crop.

'Struggle if you like, Jesslyn. It makes it more exciting,' he said, pulling the end of the cord now tied tightly around my wrist towards the bedpost.

Before I could pull my arm away he had tied the cord around the post. I struggled, scratched at him and fought as he tied another piece of cord around my other wrist, but he was too strong for me. I was helpless, face down on the bed, my arms stretched wide. I was literally sobbing with fear. 'Peter, please! Please, don't do this! Don't hurt me!'

'Hurt you, Jesslyn? I am going to give us both joy. This will excite you.'

I screamed as he brought the crop down on my buttocks. 'Yes! Scream, Jesslyn! There is no one to hear you but I like it when they scream!'

Even through the pain of the crop mercilessly being brought down on me, I bit my lip until it bled to stop my cries giving the pleasure he desired.

But as the crop landed time and time again and I moaned into the pillows with pain, I knew it was no longer pleasure he sought. He wanted to humiliate me. To punish me. But why? What harm had I done him?

From the sound of his breathing I knew he was becoming excited by beating me. I heard the crop being thrown to the floor. Then he was on the bed, pushing open my legs, lifting them. Then taking me from behind as a dog does a bitch.

He lay for a few minutes upon me after he was satisfied, then rolled off me. After a moment I felt his hand in my hair and he cruelly pulled my head up.

'That's how I treat whores, Jesslyn! And, along with all the so-called ladies of the Court, you're a whore. Oh, yes. I ran your errands. Paid court to you. Played my role of dutiful admirer. But all the time I waited. Waited for this!'

He let go of my hair and my head dropped back on to the bed. He is mad! I thought. Quite mad. God knows what harm he will do me. I must pacify him. Escape.

'Peter,' I said, as calmly as I could, 'I am truly sorry if I have offended you in any way. You are right about the morals of the Court. But I never meant you harm. Please will you not untie me and let me go free? You clearly have so little regard for me, what is the point of keeping me here? Please, Peter. Be kind.'

'Let you go free? Oh, I think not, Jesslyn! I have not finished with you yet!'

For three or four hours I lay tied to that bed. My body ached from the beating I had been given and, where I had struggled, the cords that bound me cut cruelly into my wrists. The ache in my shoulders because of the unnatural position I had been forced into was becoming more and more intolerable.

I started to cry. Silently, not sobbing. I cried for the fool I had been. Richard had warned me against the debauchery of the new Court. If my heart had been broken by Guy, I still had people to turn to who loved me and whom I loved. That I was young was surely no excuse. That my head had been turned by the attention of the King was no excuse either. I had been caught up in a madness which, seemingly, I had been unable to control. But I knew I was not a whore. And I knew I did not deserve this cruel punishment of my body and, yes, my soul.

All the hours I lay there I feigned sleep. In truth the emotional turmoil I felt and the pain I was suffering made even dozing impossible. But I was terrified to provoke Westland. I could no longer think of him as Peter.

From time to time I heard him moving about, refilling his glass. I was fearful of him now, knowing him for a pervert and a madman, but would drunken-ness induce sleep or more excesses?

Just before dawn I heard his slurred voice. 'Time for more enjoyment, Jesslyn. Time for me to love you again. Then you must be punished.'

I lay still as he untied the cords which bound my wrists to the bedposts. I thought, this man is truly mad. He thinks I will allow him to make love to me then submit myself to another beating.

I surmised that he was, by now, quite drunk. If I could use surprise I might still escape. Thankfully, mercifully, the cords were released and my arms no longer spreadeagled.

'Wake up, whore! I need you again. I'm going to take you . . .'

I let him roll me over on to my back and groaned as he did so, partly pretending that I was asleep but also because of the pain from the cruel cuts made by the riding crop.

I waited until he was lying against me, then sprang from the bed. I was on the side nearest the door and as I ran through and slammed it shut behind me, I heard him stumble from his side of the bed and lumber after me.

My body was stiff and unwieldy but terror motivated my movements. I grabbed at my cloak left on the chest in the entrance hall, then struggled to pull back the bolts on the door which led to the garden.

I heard Westland wrench open the door from the bedroom just as I had the bolts free.

'Bitch! Bitch! I haven't finished with you yet!'

He was going to catch me, I was heartbreakingly

sure. I had no idea what further excesses his crazed mind had in store for me, but now I feared even for my life.

As I tugged open the door I heard a curse and then a crashing sound behind me. The black cat I had seen the previous evening – Oh, God, it seemed a lifetime away – streaked past me and ran into the gardens. I realized in that moment that Westland must have tripped over the animal which had been waiting to escape the house.

As I passed through the doorway into the garden I briefly glanced back. Then I stopped and turned, horrified at what I saw.

Westland had fallen on to the sharp edge of the intricately carved chest. There was a terrible gash in his temple and, as I watched, a trickle of blood ran from his gaping mouth. His eyes were glazed and were clouding over. I had no doubt that he was dead.

Who touches you, – touches me, Jesslyn. I am Egypt. I am Mystery. I am Cat.

I forced myself to walk slowly back down the hall to where his body lay sprawled. He had used me cruelly but even so if a physician could save his life I could not leave him to bleed to death. And yet I knew he was dead. I bent down and reluctantly reached for his wrist. There was no sign of a pulse. He would ill-treat no more women.

Then a new horror: supposing I was accused of his murder? I was fearful for my own life, my own safety, but in that moment my thoughts were mainly for Lucinda. To have a mother accused of murdering her lover! To grow up and know that her mother had been hanged at Tyburn!

Think, think! No one knew that I was coming to Westland's lodgings that night. I edged past his body and re-entered the bedroom. I had eaten nothing, drunk nothing, whereas Westland had drunk a great deal. The near empty jug of wine and the one used glass would tell their own story. A young nobleman expecting a lady he desires to visit him. She does not keep the assignation. He drowns his sorrows and tragically, drunkenly, falls and fatally injures himself. And that was mainly the truth of it. Who could have foreseen that the black cat would run under his feet at that moment?

I quickly remade the bed, then pulled on those of my clothes I could manage. The garments that needed lacing I bundled under my cloak.

Once in the cool air of the garden, the dawn light just a hint in the sky, I felt such shame. But I knew also that it was over. I knew I would try to build a life where I could respect myself again. Perhaps, one day, even grow to like myself again. There were no more devils.

CHAPTER ELEVEN

THE CAT

'Darkling I listen'

— *John Keats*

CATHERINE: 1991

'And life is colour and warmth and light
And a striving evermore for these'
                              – Julian Grenfell

Someone tried to kill me. Someone tried to kill me. Was it true or merely the imagining of my feverish mind? As I slipped in and out of consciousness I had no answers, only questions.

It was eight weeks before the doctor allowed me to come downstairs. I sat by the fire in the Little Parlour, a rug over my knees and Cat curled up by my side. The trays of food Mrs Jessop brought in to me remained almost untouched. I had no appetite. I felt removed from my life. As if I was watching someone else playing my role. I, who had fought so hard to live that terrible evening in the sinking barge, now lacked the will to go on.

I had been ill, very ill but my life had never been in danger. Except from the person who had tried to murder me.

I had spent a week in the cottage hospital in Baildon. Some of the cuts from the broken glass in the window I had smashed were deep and had glass embedded in them. I developed a fever and then pneumonia. Once the cuts were healing and I was over the worst of the fever I could be nursed at home. To my surprise Jonas organized everything: a private ambulance to take me back to Kelsey Hall and a rota of nurses to care for me. Christmas came and went. I was in a fitful sleep when the old year gave way to the new. My cousins visited and brought gifts, as did Brett. But the only companion I really sought was Cat. For some strange reason when I was with him I felt safe and all through my illness, he rarely left my side.

I struggled to regain my health, to shake off the terrible lethargy I felt. The sudden, inexplicable bouts of crying. In my heart I knew that this was not only to do with my near drowning, it was a reaction to the long weeks when I had nursed my mother and seen her die. Only someone who has cared for a person they love in the last stages of a terminal illness can understand the strain. The constant battle to stay cheerful. Never to give way to the healing benefit of tears. When I could think rationally enough to be honest with myself, I realized that I must have been having some kind of breakdown.

And I was fearful. Over and over again I asked myself: Who? Jonas, Rupert, Dickon, Marcus, Sophie . . . they had all known that I was going to go to the museum with Brett that evening. But why should any of them wish to kill me? I had to acknowledge that Jonas had strong motives, both envy and the fact that under the terms of my grandfather's will, if I died without issue, then the estate would go to my uncle, Sir James. Jonas was his only son. But it's one thing to have a strong motive, quite another actually to try to take another's life. I simply didn't believe that Jonas would go to such lengths.

But Annabel might, a small voice in my head told

me. When she had visited me about the Hunt I had seen beneath the veneer she presented to the world. I knew her to be a deeply unhappy woman. But even if she was lacking in all morality to the extent that she would try to kill her husband's cousin, was she the type of woman to risk life imprisonment if she was caught? I thought not.

Then I remembered her saying that she was going to lose Jonas. What had she meant by that? That their relationship had broken down beyond repair? Or had he a mistress? If he had, that mistress had as strong a motive as Annabel if Jonas was going to leave his wife for her. Even in my distress, I had to recognize that this line of thought was getting too fanciful.

My mind turned to my Knight's Croft cousins, but they simply had no motive. They would gain nothing if I died. And they had shown me such warmth and affection that I felt they would never try to harm me.

Perhaps, after all, the police's explanation was the correct one. When I'd been well enough to be questioned the local policeman had taken a statement. Soon after his visit a Detective Inspector from Baildon called.

'Detective Inspector Ringwood, Miss Kelsey,' he said as Mrs Jessop ushered him into my bedroom. He showed me his warrant card. 'Just to let you know I'm not really a double glazing salesman! May I?' He indicated a chair by the window.

'Of course.'

He picked up the chair and carried it to the side of my bed. 'Do you feel well enough to answer a few more questions? I got permission from your doctor to call but he said it was up to you as to whether or not you felt strong enough.'

'Inspector Ringwood, I believe someone tried to kill me. I certainly want to give you all the help I can.'

He looked slightly embarrassed by what I had said. 'Have you any reason to believe that someone would wish to kill you, Miss Kelsey?'

'No . . . no, I haven't,' I replied reluctantly. 'But I know what happened that night. What other possible explanation can there be?'

'Believe me, Miss, if we thought you were in danger we'd take the matter very seriously. We sent down police divers and now the barge has been raised by the salvagers. The evidence is very positive. There was a fault in the jubilee clips. Those are clips which are on the pipes to the sea toilet. Naturally they're below water level. If the clips don't hold, then instead of the sea toilet pumping out, the water simply rushes in. I think you said to Constable Watts that the water was rushing in through the door that led to the cloak-rooms?'

'Yes . . . yes, I did. But how do you explain the footsteps? How do you explain that the door to the deck was jammed? How do you explain . . .' I stopped and tried to regain my composure. I knew that I must sound a little hysterical and perhaps I was. Perhaps I had reason to be.

We sat in silence for a moment, then I turned and looked into Inspector Ringwood's kindly and concerned countryman's face. 'Believe me, Inspector, I don't want to think that anyone wishes me harm but . . .' I took a deep breath. 'But I had a truly terrifying experience that night. And if there is an innocent explanation . . . if my fears are groundless . . . why did someone telephone and change the arrangements I'd made with Brett Fitzgerald?'

'Let's take one thing at a time shall we, Miss? We know why the barge flooded – the jubilee clips. Now as to the door being jammed. Is it likely, do you think, that you saw the water rushing into the barge and panicked? Forgive me, but I've been talking to your family and they're very concerned about you. Yes, about what has happened and your ill health but . . .' He hesitated for a moment. 'I gather that the last year has been very stressful for you. Am I right?'

Ridiculously I felt my eyes start to blur with tears. 'Yes. Yes, it has,' I whispered.

'Now let's come to the message which Mrs Jessop took. It was a bad line, she said. Well, that's not new around here. Back of beyond, isn't it? We know that Mr Fitzgerald neither made the call nor instigated it but is that evidence of attempted murder? Could it have been a prank? Cast your mind over the possibility that someone resented your friendship with Mr Fitzgerald. Or that a member of the staff at the glassworks thought it would be a hell of a joke to mess up a meeting between the major shareholder and the star glassblower.'

I lay back against the pillows and closed my eyes. Yes, it was a possibility. Brett and Sophie seemed so right with each other. Was Brett an ex-lover? Was he the man who was now making her unhappy? Even if he was I had to dismiss from my thoughts any idea that Sophie would ever do anything to hurt me. We had become so close, such good friends and there was a simplicity about her that was surely guileless. No, not Sophie, I was sure.

But how about Rupert? Sophie had said that he was attracted to me. Or, I thought wryly, attracted to the Kelsey fortune. I thought of the prank he had played on Sophie and Dickon which had nearly ended in tragedy when he'd shut them in the family vault. Yes, Rupert could think it funny to have me hanging about the museum for an hour before Brett came. After all, he had no way of knowing about the barge. I felt that Rupert liked to be a puppet master, pulling the strings of other people's lives. I knew he wouldn't do anything from wickedness, but did I know that he couldn't be motivated by a deep sense of mischief?

'Miss Kelsey, I'm sorry. I've tired you. Would you like me to leave now? We'll continue our investigations, I promise.'

Perhaps, I thought. But it was all so pat. A newly converted barge that had fallen victim to some shoddy workmanship. A prank telephone call. A neurotic young woman who was deeply distressed by the loss of her mother . . . But I wasn't neurotic, I knew I wasn't! I was just tired. So very tired.

'Yes, I'm sorry. I am tired. But . . . supposing someone who knew about barges – or, I suppose, any boat that has a sea toilet – simply loosened the jubilee clips? Supposing that person already knew I was going to meet Brett at the museum and changed the time and place of our meeting? It's very likely, isn't it, that instead of just hanging around waiting for Brett to turn up, I'd be curious about the old sailing barge? After all, it had lights on and . . . Yes! That's it! It had lights on. Why did it have lights on when no one was on board? Answer me that!'

There was a pause and then the Inspector shook his head. 'Miss Kelsey, there are two points here. Firstly, a barge moored on a river such as the Blackwater would, by law, have to show lights after dusk. Mr and Mrs Morley hadn't intended to be away from the barge for long, they were going through the menu for the dinner party with Mrs Kelsey . . .'

I felt my heart lurch. 'Annabel? They were with Annabel?'

I turned to look at him and in so doing realized that for all his appearance of a bluff countryman, he was a perceptive and shrewd policeman.

'So that's who you suspect! Why, Miss Kelsey? Why would Mrs Jonas Kelsey want to kill you?'

I was silent for a moment, my thoughts racing. I had no evidence, no reasonable grounds to suspect Annabel. It would be irresponsible to let the police suspect my cousin's wife. In any case, she was with the young couple who owned the barge at the time, and I'd heard footsteps. Or had I? It had been high tide, the waters racing into the mouth of the estuary. Perhaps after all . . .

'There is no reason, Inspector,' I said at last. 'And I wouldn't want to make that kind of accusation against a member of my family. Perhaps I've just had a tremendous fright and am being foolish?'

Again I was aware of his shrewd gaze. 'And perhaps not,' he replied. 'May I ask who benefits from your death? Have you made a will?'

'It's not really necessary at the moment. Under the terms of my grandfather's will, if I marry and have children, my eldest child, boy or girl, will inherit the Hall and the estate, with a trust to be set up for any other children. If I die childless then my uncle inherits.'

'And who is your uncle's heir?'

'I can't know for certain but Jonas is his only son. I can think of no reason why Sir James would disinherit him. But I truly can't think . . . don't think . . .'

'Miss Kelsey,' the Inspector interrupted. 'I've known people killed for twenty quid! What's your inheritance worth? The Hall and estate alone must be well over a million. Then there's the Kelsey Glassworks and whatever you've got in the bank.' He suddenly shook his head. 'But there's no evidence to suspect foul play. None at all.'

'Where were all my family when the . . . accident happened?'

'Annabel Kelsey is the only one with an alibi. Mr Rupert Kelsey and Mr Jonas Kelsey were both, so they say, driving home from the glassworks. Dickon Kelsey was driving back to London. Mr Marcus Kelsey was alone in his studio. Sir James was at home by himself, it being his housekeeper's day off. Mr Joseph Kelsey was driving to a trade fair in Birmingham. The most bizarre, in my opinion, Miss, is Miss Sophie's whereabouts. She says she was in church talking to Jesslyn, Lady Kelsey.'

So, I thought, Sophie is deeply troubled about something. I remembered her telling me that day in the church how she had always gone to the Lady Chapel and Jesslyn's tomb when she was unhappy.

An idea suddenly came to me. 'Could it have been the Morleys? Could a trap have been set for them but I came along? Have they any enemies?'

Inspector Ringwood nodded. 'It's a line we've been investigating. Young Morley and his wife seem pretty clean, but his family! This is strictly off the record, Miss Kelsey, because as yet we've no way of nailing his dad and his uncle. But give us time . . . give us time! East End villains who moved into Essex. On the face of it they're hoteliers. Four nicely appointed country hotels and a very popular restaurant just outside Braintree. But I'll tell you this . . . when young Morley's mum was murdered, a hit job if ever I saw one, his dad charged the Bill for every cup of coffee the investigating officers drank! How's that for a grieving husband?'

'Did they find the murderer?'

A pause and then Inspector Ringwood sadly shook his head. 'A gangland killing. The contract is handed along four or five times before it happens. That way the person who actually makes the hit has no idea who ordered it or paid for it. No, they never got the bastard. Excuse my language, Miss.'

I smiled at him. 'In the circumstances I think I'd use worse! So, my fears could be groundless?'

Oh, Catherine, my Catherine . . . Beware.

'I didn't say that. I promise you we'll keep the file open.'

That, I thought to myself, is a police euphemism for: 'The case is closed' or 'We have neither the time nor the manpower to pursue this further'.

In the days that followed I tried desperately to put what had happened behind me. But still I felt a listlessness, a sense of unreality. And, yes, I had to admit it, fear.

These were my thoughts as I sat by the fire in the Little Parlour one day in late-January. There was a brief knock at the door and then Mrs Jessop came into the room. She immediately looked at the tray of food I had set aside. 'Oh, Miss! There wasn't much on you before. Now you're just skin and bone, and you've eaten nothing. Nothing!'

'But she will.'

Brett Fitzgerald's tall frame virtually filled the Tudor doorway into the Little Parlour. 'The door to the Hall was open and so I let myself in. Mrs Jessop, be kind enough to heat up that delicious-looking soup. If I have to hold her nose and pour it down her throat, Miss Kelsey will eat it. She'll also eat what looks to me to be homemade custard tart. And if she doesn't,' he said with mock solemnity, 'she'll have to stay behind and be punished by the dinner monitor!'

For the first time in I don't know how many weeks, I laughed. Brett smiled at me.

'That's better! The soup, please, Mrs Jessop. I think our patient is on the mend. Oh, and a bottle of Sir Hugo's fine Burgundy wouldn't go amiss. One more request: is there enough of that soup for me to have some too? Nor would I say no to the custard tart.'

Mrs Jessop looked at me and winked. 'Nice to have a man about the house!'

Fifteen minutes later Brett and I were seated at a small table which he'd placed in front of the fire. Bowls of steaming chicken soup were before us and a basket of home baked rolls. A bottle of Chassagne-

Montrachet was on the hearth breathing. I suddenly realized that at last I was hungry. I had two bowls of soup and two helpings of Mrs Jessop's delicious custard tart. After that she carried in a round of Stilton cheese into which port had been poured. It was so ripe the only way to serve it was with the silver scoop set out on the cheeseboard.

We sipped the rich, dark wine with our cheese and chatted about nothing in particular. I felt wonderfully easy in Brett's company and once again asked myself if I was a little in love with him.

'Well, I'm glad I decided to walk across the green from my cottage to see how you were. Apart from the pleasure of your company, I've fared rather better than the supper I'd planned for myself! I've been worried about you, Catherine, we all have. It's time to rejoin the human race, my girl. You've got three weeks to feed yourself up on Mrs Jessop's cooking and get back to looking like you used to.'

'Three weeks? What on earth are you talking about?'

'Because in three weeks' time I'm taking you to the St Valentine's Ball at Hindlesham House!'

'You're what? I don't understand!'

'Of course, if you don't want to come with me . . .' He shrugged.

'It's not that! It's just that I would have thought you'd be taking Sophie,' I blurted out.

Brett looked at me keenly for a moment. 'Why would you think that?'

'Well, she's so beautiful and . . . well, I don't know. I thought perhaps you and she . . .' I trailed off lamely.

Brett didn't reply. He sipped his wine for a moment

then reached out and gently touched my hand.

'I'm asking *you*, Catherine. I'd be honoured if you'd say yes.'

'Yes,' I said slowly, 'I'd like that very much. I warn you, though, I'm not a very good dancer.'

Brett slapped the table in mock anger. 'Good God, girl. You're apologizing again. I'm not exactly Fred Astaire and certainly don't expect you to be Ginger. Just wear a lovely dress and look beautiful.'

It was on the tip of my tongue to say that I could buy a lovely dress but that wouldn't make me beautiful. But Brett was right. I apologized too much. If only I'd had a Fairy Godmother stand by my cradle and say: 'This child will never know what it is to be shy.'

We were seated in the big, chintz-covered armchairs by the fire, sipping our wine, when Mrs Jessop tapped on the door and came in.

'Anything more I can get you? By heck, Miss Kelsey, I'm glad to see you feeding your face again!'

'I couldn't manage another thing, thank you. How about you, Brett?'

'Not another morsel. But if I'd known what an angel you had in the kitchen I'd have walked across from Gifford's more often.'

Mrs Jessop laughed then turned to me. 'Never trust the Irish, Miss, they're all born with blarney in their blood! If it's all right with you I'll clear up in the morning? I'm pretty sure we'll have snow tonight and I'd like to get off home.'

'Of course. I'm sorry to have kept you so late. And I can easily clear away . . . I'm not to the Manor born, you know.'

Brett laughed. 'Well, that makes three of us. Off you go, Mrs Jessop. I'll check that she washes up. You can see she's decided to stop being an invalid.'

'Washes up? You're behind the times, Mr Fitzgerald. I told Sir Hugo years ago, either a dishwasher comes into the house or I go out of it. Goodnight. I'll see you in the morning, miss.'

Brett insisted on helping me clear the table and take things through to the kitchen.

'You know, I was one of nine children, all boys. My mother washed, cleaned, scrubbed for us all *and* went daily to the Big House to skivvy, and yet my father never lifted a hand to help in the home. And she wouldn't hear of us boys helping either. She was forty when I left Ireland and she looked sixty.' He shook his head. 'I don't understand how a man can do that to a woman.'

He suddenly looked so sad that I realized beneath the confident exterior he presented to the world he was a caring and sensitive man. It was that side of him that showed through in his art.

'Do you keep in touch with your family?'

Brett shook his head. 'Hardly at all since my mother died. My brothers, like so many other Irish, are scattered all over the world.'

'And your father?'

'He was a bully and a drunk and I think I grew up hating him. But I send him beer money. I just don't want to have to be in the same room as him!'

'I'm sorry, Brett.'

He smiled at me. 'You're a nice girl, Catherine. Don't be taken over by this whole Kelsey thing, will you?'

'I've tried not to,' I replied. 'But every way I turn I hear "your grandfather always did this or that". The Kelseys are expected to light the bonfire on Guy Fawkes night. Play host to the blasted Hunt. Well, that was one bit of tradition that went out of the window!' I added crisply.

'So I heard. Good for you. Well, I've got an early start in the morning.' He stood up and stretched, then offered me his hand. 'It's been a grand evening, Catherine. I'm glad you're my friend.'

Friend, yes, I thought. But is Sophie your lover?

Slowly, gradually, I started to regain my strength. When I looked in the mirror I no longer saw a gaunt stranger. And I started to look forward to going to the St Valentine's Ball with Brett. Was that why he'd asked me? I wondered. To buck me up, to give me a goal. A means to pull myself out of the lethargy – no, more than that – the despair I was feeling?

Mrs Jessop had been right. It snowed and snowed and for two days Somerton was completely cut off. Fred Watson had told me how my grandfather had refused to cut down the hedgerows when the Government was offering grants to do so.

'Not often I heard Sir Hugo swear, Miss, but by God he did then. "Silly buggers," he yelled. "Don't they know what they're destroying? A thousand years of intricately balanced nature! No windbreaks and they'll lose their top soil. Silly buggers!" '

But other farmers had not had my grandfather's wisdom and as quickly as the snow ploughs went through, the wind, with nothing to stop it, swirled the snow into drifts again.

Even before the snow there was a strong sense of community, of caring, about the village. But now it was marked. People called on elderly neighbours to bring in fuel and see that they had hot food. A farmer got through on his tractor and brought churns of fresh milk to the Post Office. 'It's not pasteurized but sod that!' Celeste told me he'd said. 'Who the bloody hell is going to tell the Ministry?'

Brett and Marcus used their combined talent to make a huge snowman on the green, then Marcus held open house to anyone who'd like a glass of his red plonk now heated up into a fearsome mull.

The children, freed from getting on the school bus that took them to Baildon, threw snowballs and rolled in the snow. I felt so much better but not strong enough to join in, so Cat and I sat on the window seat in the Little Parlour and watched the flurries of snow coming down. And I picked up my grandfather's books and started to educate myself about glass again.

Hindlesham House was a magnificent Palladian mansion set in two hundred and fifty acres about twenty miles from Somerton. As we drove the twenty miles in Brett's elegant Jaguar, he told me a little of the house's history.

Our hosts, Sir Michael and his wife, Alice, had bought the Grade I Listed mansion as a total wreck. During the Second World War, apparently, the house had been requisitioned by the War Office. At the end of the war there were no Hindleshams left, Lord and Lady Hindlesham having been killed in a bombing raid on London. They had gone up to the War Office to try to find news of their youngest son who had been posted missing after the fall of Singapore. He died in Changi jail.

The eldest son, the new Lord Hindlesham, fell during the assault on Monte Cassino, whilst the only daughter, who had married a Frenchman, was taken by the Gestapo after the French Resistance leader, Jean Moulin, and other Resistance workers were betrayed at Caluire. She and her husband were shot.

'That one family should suffer all that!' I said with a shudder.

'I'm sorry. Perhaps I shouldn't have told you? But the house belonged to the Hindlesham family for over two hundred years. I like to think that what Mike and Alice have done to it would please them.'

'How did you get to know them?'

'Oh, they're filthy rich and have a passion for glass. They've bought quite a few of my pieces. We got to know each other, became friends. He's a publisher and has made a fortune out of those magazines you see advertised on the television. Collect twelve issues of *The Deadliest Weapons in the World* . . . or twelve of *The History of Werewolves and Other Creatures of the Night*. I always wonder who buys them but somebody does . . . Mike's worth a mint!'

He certainly was. The magnificent house was ablaze with light, the gardens subtly and beautifully lit. As soon as we stopped by the stone steps which led to the graceful entrance to the house, a young man was there to park the car for us. Brett came around to the passenger door and held it open for me.

'You're a sight for sore eyes, young Cathy, my girl,' he said, putting on a broad Irish accent. And then he offered me his arm to lead me up past the delicately beautiful statues that graced the wide balustrade which edged the sweeping steps.

For once in my life I thought that, yes, perhaps I was a sight for sore eyes. Mainly because of my stunning ball gown. When the roads were passable I had driven into Baildon to the little boutique where I'd shopped the day I was to dine with Brett and had so nearly drowned. I'd felt that the clothes on display there had been chosen with style and flair and excellent taste. Also I'd liked the owner, an elegant widow in her late-fifties.

I parked the car and walked through Baildon's slushy streets to the old part of the town where Mrs Blake had her shop. It was a delightful early-Georgian building still with the original bow windows.

Mrs Blake was bringing some frocks through from the rear of the shop to hang on the display rails. She was simply but exquisitely dressed in a Ralph Lauren mid-calf warm brown skirt and beige cashmere sweater with a light woollen Liberty shawl tied loosely around her shoulders.

She smiled as she recognized me. 'Miss Kelsey! How delightful to see you again. I'd heard you'd been ill, I'm so sorry.'

'News certainly travels in the Dengie Hundred,' I said with a grin.

'It certainly does, but there's a simpler explanation.

Your cousin's wife, Mrs Jonas Kelsey, shops here regularly.'

No wonder Annabel is worried about money! I thought to myself. Mrs Blake's prices, although fair, were pretty high.

'I hope you're feeling better now?'

'Yes, thank you. So much better that I'm going to a St Valentine's Ball. I'd hoped to find a beautiful dress to wear.'

Mrs Blake's face fell. 'Oh, I'm so sorry, Miss Kelsey. I have evening wear but most of the entertaining around here is fairly informal. I simply can't afford to carry a range of ball gowns. You really need to go to London for that.'

How to explain that, as yet, London was the last place I wanted to go to? Too many memories of Fran. Her glittering success at the Haymarket Theatre. The lovely little house in Mayfair. The dingy flat in Richmond.

'I'd really prefer to shop nearer home. Is there anywhere in Colchester you can suggest?'

'Not really. Not for the kind of gown you're talking about. Look, may I make a suggestion? Although it will be a race against time . . . A young woman, Cherry Holmes, who lives locally brought in some of her designs and samples of her work. She's just finishing a course at the Art School in Ipswich and has won a place at the Royal College of Art to study Fashion and Design. I've commissioned quite a few things from her. Look.'

She took down from a rack a long dress. It was swathed in polythene which she carefully removed. I practically gasped. It was a wedding dress made in heavy ivory satin. It was stunning with its square neck and long tapering sleeves, its narrow, pointed waist then a billowing skirt reminding me of portraits I'd seen of Anne Boleyn. The front of the skirt was shorter than the back which fell away into a train. The underskirt at the front was the only part of the dress that was decorated. Again the material was ivory satin but it was richly embroidered with dark golden thread. The theme was lover's knots.

'I'm practically speechless. It's one of the loveliest things I've ever seen. Do you think she would make something for me? I'd be so grateful.'

'I'll phone her tonight and then, if she can take on the commission, I could drive her over to the Hall.'

'No, I can't put you to that bother.'

'It'll be no bother.' Then she smiled. 'Cherry would enjoy it. Poor girl! Her family live in a tied cottage on a farm labourer's wage. There's four children still at home and her mother's an absolute slut. I think Cherry would enjoy a trip to Kelsey Hall. If that's all right with you, Miss Kelsey?'

'More than all right! I'd enjoy the company. Are her brothers and sisters talented?'

'Good Lord, no! Heaven knows where Cherry's gift sprang from. It's strange, isn't it, but you get that in a family sometimes? Just one bright, shining star.'

Mrs Blake telephoned the next day to say that Cherry was more than willing to make my ball gown. But, because of the time factor, we'd have to move quickly. I invited them both over that evening and arranged with Mrs Jessop to leave a casserole in the oven for me to serve them.

'Just something simple,' I'd said. But I'd reckoned without Mrs Jessop's love of cooking and sense of occasion. When I went into the kitchen at about five o'clock, just before she was leaving, she amazed me with what she'd prepared.

'All you have to do, Miss, is take it out of the fridge and the Aga. There's a smoked salmon pâté for starters and a couple of cock pheasants braising in the Aga. It was a favourite recipe of your grandfather's. Cooked on a bed of apples with Calvados. Then there's a casserole of diced swede with sage and duchesse potatoes. And plenty of that Stilton left. Will that be all right?'

'All right?' I replied, stunned. 'You really shouldn't have gone to all this bother. I just asked them to supper.'

'Don't want to let the side down, do we, Miss?' she said briskly. 'Well, I'll be off now.'

Her coat and hat were laid out ready on the high-backed wooden chair set by the Aga. She smiled at me kindly. 'You should do this more often. Get to know some people, invite them round. Do you the world of good.'

'Thanks. And thank you for preparing such a lovely meal.'

'Well, you know me. Never does anything by halves, my old man says. Good night. Enjoy yourself.'

I had been going to suggest that we eat in the kitchen but remembered what Mrs Blake had said about Cherry Holmes' home life. It would have been ridiculous for the three of us to rattle around in the Dining Hall but I set the breakfast table in the Little Parlour for dinner, setting out the best silver and cut glass goblets from the Kelsey Glassworks.

Although the room was called the Little Parlour it was really a very large and beautiful room. Old panelling, a magnificent fireplace, comfortable armchairs mixed with some beautiful antique furniture, and some fine paintings. I looked around me and once again was astonished at what my grandfather had left me.

Mrs Blake and Cherry arrived just after seven. I showed them into the Little Parlour and offered them drinks. Within no time it seemed we were sitting around the fire and chatting as if we'd known each other for years.

Cherry was an extremely striking girl of about twenty-one. She was small and delicately boned. Her heavy dark hair was cut very short but with a fringe which helped to emphasize her large brown eyes. She wore jeans and a baggy cotton jumper with a wonderful design on it. She told me she'd painted it on herself.

'But what will you do when you want to wash it? Surely all those wonderful colours will run?'

'Oh, no! You'd be amazed at the range of artist's colours you can get now. This has been in and out of the launderette heaven knows how many times.'

'Would you design one for me? I'd love it.'

'Of course. But I think your ball gown had better come first,' she laughed.

After dinner we sat by the fire again with our coffee and, as I threw on some more logs, Cherry took out her sketch book.

'I'm going to be very positive about what I want to design for you, Catherine.' As she talked her pencil flew over the heavy paper. 'Have you ever seen *Gone With the Wind*? I caught up with it on television last Christmas.'

Whilst I'd been ill I'd had a small portable television in my bedroom. I had seen the classic film.

'Yes. I saw it at Christmas too.'

'Do you remember the scene where Scarlett pulls down the heavy velvet curtains and then makes a jacket and a skirt which went over a crinoline hoop? Well, people don't often think of using velvet for a full skirt but with plenty of petticoats it could look marvellous, sweeping out as you're dancing . . .

'And that's something else I want to think about. The petticoats. Because they show when you're dancing a reel or a waltz. I don't want them to be boring old white cotton trimmed with broderie anglaise. And I want you to look dramatic. You're tall and you can carry that off. And no flat pumps, please, be proud of being tall. There! What do you think?' And she showed me her sketch.

Two weeks later, on the evening of St Valentine's Day, Cherry and Suzie Blake helped me dress. I tried to protest about them driving over to Somerton but they'd insisted.

'I want plenty of orders from the women who see you tonight,' Cherry had teased at the final fitting. 'So nothing is stopping me from seeing that everything is just right.'

I was amazed at what they had achieved when I stood before my mirror. The dress Cherry had made and designed was made of dark green velvet. The neckline was low and cut straight across, with the tiniest sleeves on my upper arm. The waist was tightly cut and from it the skirt billowed out, tied with a taffeta cummerbund dyed exactly the same green as the velvet. Beneath the dress was layer after layer of jet black net petticoats, each edged with green taffeta to match the cummerbund. Cherry and Suzie had made me swirl in front of the long mirror and the effect of the black and green petticoats was simply stunning.

'Any family jewels?' Cherry had asked wistfully at one of the fittings.

I told them about the Kelsey pearls. 'No, not pearls!' she had said as if I could conjure up heirlooms at the drop of a hat. 'I want you to look dramatic. Amethysts or perhaps sapphires.'

I'd telephoned Mr Pritchard to ask if there were, indeed, any family jewels. He was upset and very apologetic.

'Dear me, Miss Kelsey. How thoughtless of me not to have sent you an inventory of the jewels in the safe deposit in your grandfather's . . . er . . . *your* bank.'

The change in my fortunes was such that I could hardly stop myself from laughing when I said, 'Either sapphires or amethysts would do nicely.'

On the afternoon of the Ball a security van delivered a boxed set of jewels to the Hall and would take them back to the bank the next day. They left, having given me endless instructions to be sure I locked them in the safe in the library overnight.

I gasped when I opened the box. They were exactly what the dress needed. I knew little about jewellery but these stones seemed perfectly matched and appeared to be in their original wrought gold setting.

They were given with love . . . to my Lady.

When I showed them to Cherry, she laughed delightedly.

'I knew you wouldn't let me down!'

The grandeur of the entrance hall of Hindlesham was almost overwhelming. Soft Chinese yellow walls set off the elegant biscuit-toned plasterwork. I was incredibly impressed but at the same time couldn't imagine anyone wanting actually to live here. But once Brett had introduced me to Sir Michael and Lady Brownjohn, I was so caught up by the pleasure they felt in their good fortune that I could understand that the house was exactly right for them.

As we waited in line to be welcomed I had a chance to study our hosts. Sir Michael was a short, chunky man in, I guessed, his early-sixties. He had the ruddy complexion of a countryman, but the intelligence in his eyes and expression indicated a man who was nobody's fool. And if, as Brett had told me, he was a self-made man who could now afford to own one of the last great Palladian houses in the country, he was not only intelligent, he was brilliant.

Alice was a few years younger than her husband. Her well-cut evening dress couldn't disguise the dumpiness of her figure but she had a beautiful complexion and luxuriant silver hair framing a pretty face.

'So, you're Catherine Kelsey,' Sir Michael said in a hearty voice with strong traces of a North Country accent. 'Heard about the stand you took against those daft buggers who dress up in a red coat and dash about the countryside after some poor fox. Good for you, lass! When are you going to ask us over to Kelsey Hall?' he added bluntly. 'I hear it's a Tudor gem.'

'Nothing to compare with this but I'd be delighted if you and Lady Alice would dine with me, Sir Michael.'

'Bugger Sir Michael. I'm Mike and my wife is plain Allie! Have fun, the pair of you!'

First there was a buffet supper served in the vast dining room. Then at ten o'clock the sound of a small string orchestra could be heard. Sir Michael banged on the table with a silver bucket which had been holding champagne.

'Ladies and gentlemen . . . boys and girls . . . there is now dancing in the Long Gallery. Breakfast will be at dawn, and heaven help any of you who want to slip away before that because the kedgeree is Allie's mum's very own recipe and you'll never have tasted another like it!'

Brett and I sipped our champagne for a few moments and then he took my arm and led me towards the Long Gallery. It was an incredible room decorated in rococo style with oyster moiré wallpaper and exquisite plaster-work. The Doric-style columns were picked out in gilt leaf. Hanging from the centre of the delicately painted ceiling was a huge and exquisite glass chandelier.

Brett nodded towards it and said, 'Beautiful, isn't it? It's an Osler.'

'F. and C.' I added. 'A Birmingham firm who specialized in large-scale glass fabrications. In fact, the centre-piece of the 1851 Exhibition was a three-tiered glass fountain made by them. Did you know that?' I finished cheekily, with laughter in my voice.

Brett laughed out aloud. 'By God! You're a chip off the old block, Catherine. And you're getting to know glass.'

'And to love it,' I said, softly and sincerely.

'That's my girl!' Brett said as he took me into his arms and swept me on to the dance floor.

It was at that moment that I knew for sure that I was in love with him.

Do not let him break your heart, Catherine. As my Lady's heart was broken.

CHAPTER TWELVE

THE CAT

'She waits for me'

— *Thomas Hardy*

JESSLYN: 1663

'The play's the thing'
                    – William Shakespeare

The smell of a hundred candles . . . of the paint on our faces . . . and, yes, of human sweat – all mingled with the pungent aroma of oranges – this was what my senses were aware of as Richard led me forward to deafening applause.

I was an actress.

We bowed and bowed. It was the first performance at the Theatre Royal, Drury Lane, and not only did Killigrew's fortunes rest upon this moment, I gathered that Richard too had also been a major investor. Not to secure his place as the leading actor in the company – Thomas Killigrew's respect for Richard's talent had easily placed him in that role. No, it was his own enthusiasm and joy at the re-establishment of the theatre in London that led to his involvement in every aspect of the new Theatre Royal.

I had lived through my own private hell and survived. At least I hoped I had survived. For many months after Peter Westland's death the dream – no, the nightmare – returned to haunt me.

I was always pursued by him, as I had been before the black cat ran before him and he fell. But in my dream he caught me. He did bestial things to my body and then his hands were around my throat. I fought, I clawed at his hands, but I could not free myself. I had no breath. My eyes were bulging. I was dying. At my last moment of life, I screamed.

'Hush, little one, hush!' Richard's arms were around me. His hands were stroking my sweating forehead. 'You're safe, sweeting. You're safe. Oh, dearest girl, let me help you come back to us! We've missed you.'

'You make it sound as if I've been on a journey.'

'You have. A journey to find yourself. But instead of finding the true Jesslyn, you set out to mask your feelings with gaudiness. You weren't born to be a butterfly. I know your worth. Your strength and determination. Put the last year behind you. It never happened.'

'But it did, Richard. It did! And I'm so ashamed. So ashamed,' I added in a whisper.

'Sleep, little love, sleep.' He gently took me in his arms. 'I'm here for you. Always here.'

And I slept, a gentle, untroubled sleep, until noon the following day.

When I awoke Moll was sitting by my bed. Her hands, as always, were busy with exquisite embroidery.

'Moll, there's no need to sit with me.'

'There's every need, young lady,' she replied stoutly. 'You've worried us all more than something.' Then she took my hand and squeezed it. 'But Richard reckons you're coming back to us. And so do I.'

Tears of weakness ran down my face. 'I don't deserve you. I don't deserve your . . . your care.'

'You were going to say "love", my girl. That's about the right of it. We love you. We've seen your hurt, your unhappiness. Oh, my dear girl.' I could see that Moll's eyes were moist now. 'I've loved you like a daughter but this last year I haven't known how to reach you. To help you. The madness, if I can call it that, is over now, isn't it?'

'Yes,' I said slowly. 'It's over. All I want now is to live quietly here among the people I love. To care for Lucinda and . . .'

'God help us!' Moll said through a shout of laughter. 'If that isn't the best performance I've seen of Mistress Goodwife in many a long year.'

Her arms were around me and she hugged me to her. 'Yes, you love Lucinda and your strange, new family.' Her hands stroked the hair from my forehead as if I was a little girl. 'But never forget that your looks set you apart. The night Lucinda was born you asked me why I cared for you? I answered that the world is a harsh place for women and we have to help each other. But more than that, dear child, we have to grasp our destiny.' She kissed my face tenderly. 'I somehow cannot believe that yours is to spend your life between babies and the still-room!'

'That's what I long for now, Moll, but . . .'

'There will be no babies. Not while you're married to Richard.'

I paused for a long while. 'How to explain, Moll? I love him. I truly love him. Whatever happens in his bed or mine cannot change that. And perhaps I have already brought shame to this house . . . to Lucinda? I pray not. But at last I know the difference between being truly admired and being a plaything.'

'Well, at least there's some sense in that pretty head,'

Moll said briskly. 'Sleep a little while longer, Jesslyn. Sleep and heal.'

My eyelids were heavy. So easy to deliver myself to sleep. 'Lucinda?' I murmured. 'Where is she?'

'With Richard. Do you think I'd let her out of my sight if she wasn't in safe hands? Thomas Killigrew arranged for her to see His Majesty's new puppies. Not those by my Lady Castlemaine, or Moll Davis, or God knows who else!' She chuckled. 'No, by one of his prize bitches.'

I could not resist. 'And you said *not* by my Lady Castlemaine?'

I had expected Moll to laugh even though what I had said was not particularly witty. Instead she took my hand.

'Have a care, child. The lady reigns supreme. Oh, no, His Majesty is not faithful. But then,' she added wryly, 'few men are. But Castlemaine, from what I hear, has him in her thrall, and in spite of the King's having a new bride poor lady! – he publicly acknowledged Castlemaine's new child, a boy, and attended the christening. Until her star wanes – as it will, evil-tempered harlot that she is – have a care what you say.'

'She is very beautiful.'

'Huh!' snorted Moll. 'Beauty is as beauty does. And as for the wretched woman insisting that she's to be one of the new Queen's Ladies in Waiting . . . the insensitive cheek of it! Then what must the Queen's chaplain do but tell Her Majesty exactly how close to the King this proposed Lady was! Killigrew said all hell broke loose after that. The little, dark Queen sobbing and jabbering away in Portuguese, Castlemaine shrieking and demanding, and the King sulking in his apartments as if *he* was the one who had been badly done by! I tell you, lovey, if we women couldn't laugh at men, they'd drive us mad.'

I laughed then, probably my first genuine laughter since that terrible night in Henrietta Street. I hoped with all my heart that Richard was right and I was at last returning to the real world.

'By the way . . .' Moll said over casually '. . . Thomas Killigrew says His Majesty has been asking after you. Your absence from Whitehall has been noted. Obviously the King,' she struggled to choose her words carefully, 'has . . . er . . . cast his eyes in your direction.'

'Yes, Moll, he has. But even I am not so much of a fool! You know, I was brought up to look upon a monarch as if he was almost God. I'm a Royalist through and through. But in the time since King Charles came into his own again I've grown up. I look at the King and see the man. And, in spite of his womanizing, I see a good man. A charming, intelligent man who seems for all his elegance to be forever touched with sadness. If that man were not also the King I would have been tempted to take him as a lover. But to become embroiled in the intrigues and politics that surround His Majesty . . .' I shook my head. 'As I said, even I who these last months have danced through life like a poor butterfly which can only live for one day . . . even I would not be such a fool! That I promise, Moll.'

She sighed with relief, then chuckled. 'There'd have been a title in it. When Castlemaine's husband was made an earl no one thought it was for *his* services to the Crown.'

I laughed again. 'The tale at Whitehall was that it was the first time a man had joined the nobility because of his talent for turning a blind eye.'

At that moment my bedchamber door was thrown open and Lucinda came running in, followed by Richard. In her arms she hugged two wriggling puppies.

She was flushed with excitement and looked almost heartbreakingly pretty. I thanked God again for the gift of my daughter.

'Mama, look! Look! They're mine . . . although you can play with them too.'

She dropped the two puppies on to my bed. They ran around excitedly, wagging their tails and yapping. I caressed their silky little heads. 'They're beautiful. But how are they yours, dearest?' I glanced anxiously across at Richard. 'Surely His Majesty *didn't* . . .'

Richard laughed. 'Don't worry, we shall not be sent to the Tower. The King gave them to her. He was going to give her just the one but madam here –' he ruffled Lucinda's hair affectionately '– pointed out that the puppy would be lonely by itself . . . His Majesty solemnly agreed and so we now have brother and sister spaniels!'

'What can we call them, Mama?' Lucinda asked, crawling up on to the bed to join the puppies.

'They're your puppies. You choose.'

'I don't know! I don't know!' She turned her head to Richard. 'Papa?'

'Now let's see . . . The naming of a puppy is a very serious business. Don't you agree, Moll?'

'Very!'

'I have it. What do you say to this, Lucinda? This being a theatrical household, how about Beau and Fletch after the playwrights Beaumont and Fletcher?' Richard turned his attention to me and smiled. 'Killigrew has acquired the rights to all their plays. Davenant is hopping mad and as jealous as hell. I've asked them both to sup with us later today to try to get them to make up so please join us and be at your most charming, little one.'

He sat on the bed and put his arm around Lucinda. 'So, does Beau and Fletch please you?'

'Oh, yes!' She was trying to catch both puppies who were now chasing each other all over my bed. 'But which is Beau and which is Fletch?'

'Well, the girl puppy will have to be Fletch, otherwise we should call her Belle.'

'How do we tell which is the boy and which is the girl?'

'Ah!' replied Richard. But before he could say further Moll took matters into her capable hands. 'The little boy has a larger brown patch over his eye. See? Now, come along, young lady. That's enough excitement for one day. Some bread and milk for you and then your nap. Yes, the puppies can come too. If we can catch them!'

After Moll and Richard had caught the puppies and Moll had shepherded my flushed and laughing daughter from the room, I held out my hand to my husband.

'You're so kind to her, Richard. She loves you so! With your permission I never wish to tell her who her real father was and how she was conceived. I want her to be yours.'

'She *is* mine, Jesslyn.' He dropped my hand and turned from me. 'I . . . I can't tell you what it means to me to have her trust. Her uncomplicated love. Never think, will you, that my love for her is only assumed? That I would use her as a smoke screen to hide what I truly am.'

I climbed from the bed and crossed to him. I moved to look at his face and was distressed to see a hint of tears in his eyes.

'Richard, Lucinda and I owe you our lives. You will always have our love. I will never . . . can never . . . think ill of you. It is you who should think ill of me! I came so near to being just another well-born Palace whore! What of Lucinda then?'

'What of Jesslyn?' he said softly. 'What of her?'

I had wanted to organize the supper that so clearly meant much to Richard but he would hear none of it.

'Sweeting, I want you to rest and then be at your most beautiful. Would you, as a favour, wear your dark green velvet and taffeta gown?'

'Of course, yes. But why?'

'Oh!' Richard shrugged then added enigmatically, 'It goes so well with blue.'

We were to sup at six o'clock in the evening. In spite of their differences and rivalry, Davenant and Killigrew would be at the Cockpit Theatre for the day's performance.

To my shame I had at first paid little attention to Richard's passionate involvement in the restoration of the country's theatres. After the dreadful events in Henrietta Street, however, we had evenings together when I wanted so desperately to cling to some kind of normality that I would sit and listen carefully as he poured out his heart and his plans.

Richard was an advocate of Killigrew's but as he told me the manoeuvrings surrounding the re-opening of the theatre, I privately thought that Master Killigrew must be a shrewd and cunning diplomat.

'Little one,' Richard cried, pacing the parlour, a goblet of Jerez sack in his hand, 'there are quite simply no plays, no playwrights and no theatres left!'

I knew little of such matters but dimly remembered a stray remark from one of the travelling players when first I met up with them.

'I thought the Red Bull . . .'

'That's not a theatre! It's a tavern where the landlord was sometimes able to bribe the garrison at Whitehall to keep to their beds of an evening when a play was performed. And what else have we got? Thomas and Davenant squabbling over some brokendown, dirty, rat-ridden relic, where the audience have to suck on oranges to stop themselves choking on the dust that rises every time the actors move!'

He crossed to the fire and kicked savagely at the glowing logs.

'But the audience flock to the Cockpit,' I said reasonably.

'Of course they do. They want to see a play! To dream a little. To laugh. To cry. In short, they wish to be transported to another world. A land of . . . oh! A land of rough magic.'

He threw himself down on the settle by the chimney-piece, then reached out to the side-table and poured more sack.

We sat in silence for a little while. Then I spoke. 'Join them, Richard. Join them. It's breaking your heart this . . . this waiting.' I shrugged. 'And waiting for what? Killigrew has already offered you . . .'

He rose and started his pacing again.' I will *not* be part of some shoddy charade to please . . .' He stopped himself and sighed. 'I was going to say, to please the rabble. But the truth is, to please myself. I *know* how it must be! Oh, Jesslyn, when you meet Thomas, listen to what he has to tell of the French theatres. They have scenery. Can you imagine that? Painted scenery that backs differing scenes.

'And the King and His Court and the gentry go to the theatre there. There are row upon row of boxes for them but the common folk are not excluded because there is a pit in the body of the house. In the past the actors always took their plays to the nobles. On the continent, so Thomas tells me, all the classes join together to experience one common thing: theatre. Oh, my dear, this is a revolution beyond belief and I have lived to see it. One more thing . . .' He suddenly shouted with laughter. '. . . and we must tell Moll this, because she has spent years on the road stuffing old rags down the front of young boys to make it appear they have a bosom. The King has decreed that in future all women's parts shall be played by women!'

'I wonder why?' I said dryly. But Richard could see only his vision of a new theatre. He came and took my hand, then kissed it gallantly.

'And you, sweeting, will be one of the most beautiful and talented of . . . we must have a new word. Yes! . . . our actresses.'

At the time, I laughed.

Moll and I helped each other dress. She was, of course, included in the theatrical supper party. I thought she looked handsome in her best gown of plum-coloured taffeta. Her hair, although sprinkled with grey, was still luscious and rich and I thought, not for the first time, what a handsome woman she was.

'Moll,' I asked tentatively as she laced my stays, 'have you ever thought of marrying again?'

'God bless you, no!' she replied as she tightened the cords that pulled together the boned corset. 'Only one man ever for me, poor fool that he was.' Then her expression softened. 'I keep saying he was a fool, lovey, it helps me in some silly way. He just could not see that what he thought was his duty was less important than me living the rest of my life without him! We were so happy, my Jess.' Her voice was almost a whisper. Then she rallied, 'And if there is an afterlife as the Archbishop assures us there is, well then, my Will will be waiting for me and I'll give him what-for for leaving me alone all these years.'

I hugged her to me. 'Please, Moll, not alone. Never alone.'

She held me at arm's length. 'In the sense that counts,' she said with dignity.

After Moll had left the bedchamber I sat silent for a while. I knew she was not denying the warmth of affection, love even, that Richard, Lucinda and I felt for her and she for us. For Moll there had only ever been one man. I prayed that the same was not also true of me. At that moment I faced but refused to give in to the fact that I longed only for Guy.

I crossed to the fire and took my curling tongs from it, holding the handles in a padded cloth. My mind was on Moll but my hands followed the ritual of testing the heat of the tongs on a piece of parchment, then twisting my hair into ringlets at the side of my face.

After a few moments there was a brief knock at my bedchamber door and then Richard entered. He looked elegant in satin breeches, fine silk stockings, a linen shirt edged with Brussels lace and a richly embroidered doublet. The doublet's sleeves were slashed to reveal the fine linen sleeves of his shirt. Richard's hair curled naturally and he wore it loose to his shoulders.

I turned from the mirror and smiled. 'I have a handsome husband.'

He crossed to me and kissed my hand. 'And I a beautiful wife. And I bring her a gift!'

I noticed then that he carried a velvet bag which he laid on my dressing table.

'These are for you, Jesslyn.'

Richard drew from the velvet bag the most exquisite sapphire necklace. I was speechless as he placed the jewels around my neck.

'This is why I wanted you to wear the dark green velvet gown.'

I gradually found my voice. 'Richard . . . I cannot . . . I do not deserve . . .'

'They were my grandmother's and she would have liked you,' he said simply. 'She was the only member of my family who understood. Her will said: "To my beloved grandson, Richard, sell or keep these jewels known as the Gloriana necklace as you need. Or give them with love." '

'Gloriana necklace? I don't understand.'

'How much is legend, how much is truth?' he said, smiling. 'My grandmother was a Lady in Waiting to Queen Bess in the last years of her life. Family legend has it that the sapphires were part of plunder taken by Her Majesty's unofficial pirates from Spanish treasure ships and given to my grandmother as a wedding gift.'

I touched the beautiful jewels at my neck. 'It's a vivid story.'

'Yes. Until you remember that Good Queen Bess was renowned for her meanness and parsimony. That even after the Armada was defeated she somehow forgot to pay her victorious sailors. No, I choose to think that my self-willed, strong-minded grandmother made quite clear the price of silence when the young Essex crept into the Virgin Queen's bedchamber!' Then his mood changed. With no intention of hurting me, his hands gripped my shoulders. 'Wear them in all your young beauty, Jesslyn. What matter a jewel's history? The moment is now!'

I touched the sapphire necklace with awe. The stones were exquisitely cut and matched and set in finely wrought gold. From the centre of the necklace fell a short chain of gold. The largest and most magnificent stone hung as a pendant from this.

'I ask only one thing,' Richard said, meeting my eyes in the mirror. 'Please keep it always. My grandmother's love meant a great deal to me. However hard the times I have never even been tempted to sell her necklace, although she gave me leave.'

'I swear to you, Richard, that come what may I will keep the necklace and try to wear it with honour.'

A little later I joined Moll and Richard in the first-floor parlour for a glass of Rhenish before our guests arrived. I had checked that all was ready in the dining room. The table had been beautifully set with pewter plates and fine Venetian glass. The candles in their silver holders had been lit and the serving table was ready.

To save our none too sober cook too much work, Richard had arranged for many dishes to be sent in from The Cock and Magpie and an excellent pie shop on the corner of Vere Street. The cook was providing a duck and onion soup, a tart filled with the meat from pig's trotters and spinach and marigold leaves, rolled fish fillets and buttered whitings. But our main meal would be sent in as soon as Harry alerted the pie shop and the tavern that we were ready.

I glanced around the handsome room and wondered about Richard's finances. 'However hard the times', he had said about the beautiful necklace I wore. And yet he was so generous to his friends and entertained, if not lavishly, handsomely. I was suddenly overwhelmed by the kindness Richard had shown to me and to Lucinda. If only . . . if only . . .

'Tell me about Sir William,' I said as I sipped my goblet of Rhenish. I had met Thomas Killigrew on a number of occasions but, until that evening, had known Sir William Davenant only by reputation.

'Well,' Richard began, 'he was Shakespeare's godson.'

'My, my! Aren't we discreet?' Moll interrupted, hooting with laughter. 'Take away the first three letters of godson and you've got a more fitting tale!'

Richard joined in the laughter. 'Moll, you're an incorrigible gossip. Just as well the Puritans no longer hold sway. They'd have had a gossip's bridle on your head and put you in the stocks for a day.'

'But what is the truth?' I asked, exasperated.

'I'd say only his mother knows that for sure,' Moll replied briskly. 'She was the hostess of the Crown Inn at Oxford and from . . . Yes, Richard, gossip! . . . I hear tell he didn't get his talent from *that* lady!'

'It's a long way from a tavern in Oxford to being a Knight. How on earth . . .?'

'Oh, the man has talent,' Richard replied. 'He devised Masques and Operas at the Court of the King's father. The late, not greatly lamented King Charles appointed him Poet Laureate . . . and thanked him prettily with a Knighthood.'

Before I could ask more about Sir William, Harry ushered in Thomas Killigrew. Richard rose to greet him and both Moll and I dropped a curtsey. Then Killigrew hugged Moll to him. 'Good to see you again, Moll. I swear you get younger with every passing year.'

She slapped him, laughing. 'And I swear you've got a tongue that would flatter Satan himself.'

Killigrew bowed low over my hand. 'Mistress Warwick. As beautiful as ever. We have all missed you at Court.'

I felt the colour rise to my cheeks. 'I have a young

daughter, Master Killigrew. A good deal of my time is spent with her,' I replied rather stiffly.

'Of course, of course,' Killigrew said smoothly. He turned to Richard. 'We'll have to wait on Davenant. The Duke of York was at the play this afternoon. Davenant will be fawning on him for a while yet.'

Richard laughed. 'Now, Thomas, if it had been His Majesty, Davenant would be here saying the same of you! What will you drink? Rhenish? Sack? Canary?'

'A tankard of good English ale, if you have such a thing. The dust at that damned Cockpit is enough to choke a man.'

Richard crossed to a side table where there was set a tray with tankards and a flagon of ale. He poured the ale and handed it to Killigrew.

'Your health, ladies,' he said, and then set about his ale with relish. I sipped my wine and studied him as he drank. He was of medium height and stockily built but with no spare flesh on his frame. He wore the handsome gold and red livery that marked him as a servant of the King, as did all the actors in his company.

It was Killigrew who had persuaded the King to license only two theatre companies. Killigrew headed the King's Company of Comedians, while Davenant formed the Duke's Players under the patronage of the King's brother, the Duke of York. At present both companies shared one venue, but it was clear that because of the rivalry between them, that state of affairs would not last long!

Richard took the flagon to replenish Killigrew's tankard. 'Is there any news, Thomas, about the riding stable?'

'There is, Richard. There is,' Killigrew said solemnly. Then suddenly his face broke into a huge grin. 'No, I cannot tease you, my old friend. Bedford has leased it to me! It is to become London's first Theatre Royal!'

'Oh, Thomas! Thomas!' Richard put aside the flagon of ale and shook Killigrew warmly by the hand. 'By Heavens, we'll have something to celebrate when we sup tonight!'

'Riding stable?' I asked, bemused. 'And you intend to perform plays there?'

'I intend, Mistress, to build a theatre inside the shell of the covered stables.' Killigrew turned enthusiastically to Richard. 'It will be as I told you. Like those I saw in France. With rows of boxes for the Court, a thrust stage for the actors to perform upon, but with room for elaborate scenery behind them. Below and in front of the stage will be a place for the musicians. The world and his wife will go mad for it!'

'And the Duke's Players? Are they to share this new theatre?' Richard asked.

'They are not!' Killigrew replied stoutly. 'Thank God Davenant has found a real tennis court in Lincoln's Inn Fields. Now, the race is on to see who can open first!' He slapped his fist into his palm with relish and there was no doubt in my mind who would be the victor.

'And what of the women to play the parts that once boys took? Where will you find them?' Moll asked.

Killigrew was silent for a moment then shook his head. 'I know not. But where did we find boy actors? We didn't look, they came to us.'

'Yes, but they were following a tradition. This is totally new.'

'I've wondered about the orange girls. They're lively young lasses and give as good as they get.'

'Huh!' Moll said hotly. 'From what I hear they most probably give rather more than that. As long as coins are exchanged for their favours!'

Killigrew grinned into his ale. 'Well, Moll, at least a prostitute should know how to act.'

Richard came and took my hand. 'I nominate Jesslyn! We had trouble with some of Parliament's soldiers when my cousin Guy was hiding in the house. I created a little diversion and my good wife joined in as if she had been treading the boards all her life.'

It was Moll who finally persuaded me to join the new venture. The weather at the turn of the year was particularly foul and we rarely braved the slush and slime on the cobbled streets. Lucinda played happily with Beau and Fletch. Moll was busy about the house or with her needle. Richard was endlessly busy with the building of the new theatre. Only I did not seem to have a true role in life.

I was sitting one dark afternoon watching the rivulets of rain running down the window panes. I had curled up on the window seat in the parlour trying to read a book of verses by John Donne. But his poems were as melancholy as me . . . ' "I long to talk with some old lover's ghost, Who died before the god of love was born." ' I sighed and pressed my forehead against the freezing glass.

I heard the door open and the rustle of skirts on the

highly polished floorboards.

'Do it!' Moll said briskly.

I turned and looked at her in astonishment. 'Do what?'

'Join Richard and Killigrew. Be in the play that opens the Theatre Royal. I mean it! I want you out of the house and doing something with your life.' I opened my mouth to protest but Moll did not give me a chance. 'I can take care of Lucinda and this household. Besides the play's only performed of an afternoon. You'll still have plenty of time for your daughter. I mean it, my girl. First thing tomorrow we'll hire a dancing master. And I know an old actor long retired who'll come in and teach you a few tricks of the trade. It'll give him something to do with his days and some coin to get drunk on of an evening.'

And so my days were taken over with learning this strange new skill. At last I felt ready to perform before Richard. I wanted no favours to get me into the King's Company and knew him well enough to realize that, although he was the kindest of men, he was uncompromising about his beloved theatre.

Moll had simply said to him, 'Will you stay a while in the parlour after we have dined? Jesslyn and I have a surprise for you.'

Richard was lolling by the fire smoking a clay pipe when I entered. I wore my dark green velvet and taffeta gown and his grandmother's sapphires.

'Jesslyn, why are you . . .?'

I put my lips to my fingers. 'Shhh! – Simply watch and listen then tell me the truth.'

I had learnt Viola's speech from *Twelfth Night*,

beginning: 'Make me a willow cabin at your gate. And call upon my soul within the house'.

When I had finished Moll and Richard were totally silent for a moment. Then Richard rose and came to me. I feared the worst. That I had little or no talent. Then he bent low and kissed my hand. 'Welcome, little one! Welcome!'

On the seventh of May the Theatre Royal, Drury Lane, opened. His Majesty was in the Royal Box as was the Duke of York. My Lady Castlemaine sat between them, beautiful as always, but gaudily dressed. Her neck, ears and wrists were strung about with precious stones. No wonder the common people had grown to loathe her.

But that afternoon I cared for nothing except the play. Before it started I had been literally sick with nerves, but once I stepped out on to the stage I entered a different world. I was no longer Jesslyn Warwick, I was totally and completely the character I played. So much so that, as the first act ended, I could scarcely remember where I was.

Finally there was the excitement of the audience's reception of the play which, appropriately, was by Beaumont and Fletcher, a fact that Lucinda kept telling her spaniels. Afterwards in the tiring-room His Majesty came to congratulate the cast and Killigrew.

The King bowed over my hand then whispered to me, 'If only it had been mere play-acting when you said "No" to a King!'

He passed on to offer more congratulations. I turned and found Guy beside me. I had not seen him for two years but I looked into his eyes and knew beyond doubt that I could no longer deny my love.

Remember, Jesslyn. Remember . . .

CHAPTER
THIRTEEN

THE CAT

'Ah! Cats are a mysterious kind of folk. There is more passing in their minds than we are aware of'
— Sir Walter Scott

CATHERINE: 1992

'To strive, to seek, to find, and not to yield'
                                    – Alfred, Lord Tennyson

'Don't be ridiculous!' Jonas said, then pressed a discreetly positioned bell on his mahogany desk. 'My secretary will show you out. Thank you for calling in, cousin Catherine.'

The door to Jonas's office opened and his secretary entered, her footsteps hushed by the thick, fitted carpet. In fact, I thought, everything surrounding Jonas was hushed as if he considered it ill-bred to make any noise. The telephone on his desk made only a low key bleep. All callers, of course, having first to run the gauntlet of his mousy-looking but determined secretary.

'Miss Kelsey . . .' Jonas began. But I interrupted.

'Will be a few moments more with Mr Kelsey, thank you, Miss Myers.'

Jonas's face flushed angrily. I could see him struggling to keep his temper. But a show of family unity won the day.

'That will be all for now, thank you,' he said curtly to his secretary. Evidently she was more than used to his bad manners. She simply turned and left the room as silently as she had entered.

'I want you to hear me out, Jonas. Hear why I want

to find some kind of work here. Even before my . . . my accident . . .' I still found it hard to accept that someone hadn't tried to kill me. I *knew* I'd heard footsteps. I *knew* that the door on the barge had been jammed. But why? That was what I kept coming back to. And when I could find no reason I tried to thrust my fears to the back of my mind. 'Even before that I was studying my grandfather's books, trying to learn about glass. Day after day I've been to the glassworks – watching, absorbing. I've sat in with Joe in Marketing and Rupert in Public Relations . . .'

'Why wasn't I told of this?' Jonas said angrily.

'Why should you have been? Where was the harm? Jonas, please try to understand.'

'I understand that I should be informed about everything that concerns my company!'

I stared at him across the desk. Somehow I'd got to find the guts to see this through. It was important to me. Brett had been so right when he'd said I couldn't be a chrysalis all my life. I'd lived too long in the shadows. I desperately wanted to be Catherine. Not Francesca's daughter. Not Sir Hugo's granddaughter. Me, Catherine.

'*Your* company, Jonas? I rather thought the company belonged to the shareholders!'

Even he had the grace to look a little shamefaced but he quickly recovered and said pompously, 'Mine in the sense that as managing director I am responsible for the day to day running of the business. For its success . . .'

'Or failure?' I replied tartly. I could have bitten my tongue. I wanted him for an ally not an enemy. A hopeless aim perhaps but if I was to achieve my ambition of finding work at the glassworks, I had to try to win him around.

'I'm sorry, Jonas. I didn't mean that as it sounded. I simply meant that as managing director I suppose one has to take the rough with the smooth?

'Look, Jonas,' I continued. 'You've turned me down without giving me a chance.'

'It simply isn't appropriate for . . .'

'You haven't asked me what I've learnt! Ask me what temperature the furnaces must be kept at? Where we import our sand from? The percentage of lead in our crystal glass? Where the first English glassworks were? How our founder, Sir Thomas Kelsey, brought craftsmen glass-blowers over from Normandy to work and teach. Do we use potash or soda for our alkaline flux? *Ask* me, Jonas!' But his face was set against me.

I took a deep breath and tried again. 'I have to do something with my life. I can't simply rattle around in that huge house, day after day.'

'You have only yourself to blame for that. If you hadn't made that ridiculous fuss about the Hunt you'd have a full and varied life in the county. Instead I gather all you're left with is the company of our resident genius and that common as muck couple, the Brownjohns!'

'I find them delightful company. They're dining at the Hall this weekend. I telephoned Annabel and invited you both but I gather you have a previous appointment. That's the polite euphemism for no, I take it?'

'They're simply not our sort,' he replied stiffly.

'Oh, I see. You only mix with the nouveau riche if

they ride to hounds and send you cases of champagne as a bribe for seating them at your table, is that it?'

'I don't think we have anything more to say to each other, do we, cousin Catherine?'

I sat for a few moments more twisting a button on my jacket around and around in my hand. I *had* to be in control of this situation. I had to be in control of my own life. People in control, I thought ironically, do not do battle nervously fiddling with a button! I forced my hand to the arm of the chair.

'Jonas, I want us to be friends. All I ask is for you to consider, with an open mind, whether there is something I can do to involve myself more closely in the family business? I am, after all, the majority shareholder.'

He leant across the desk. 'A majority shareholder who seems to have had a nervous breakdown. Are you sure you're capable of handling your inheritance with good judgement?'

I stood up and walked to the door. Then I turned back. 'I gather you make much of the fact that I'm a bastard, Jonas? Well, so I am. That is an accident of birth. What is so pathetic about you is that you've made yourself into one!'

Fine words but afterwards I sat in my grandfather's old Rolls in the car park literally shaking with distress. Did Jonas have a valid point? It was true that I'd had some kind of breakdown after the incident on the barge. Everyone seemed to believe that the loose jubilee clips had been an accident. I'm sure the police were convinced that if it wasn't an accident, the intended victims had been the Morleys.

Was I unbalanced? And if I was, how might it affect my business affairs? I had always thought of myself as eminently sensible, almost to the point of dullness. But since that night on the barge I had this terrible feeling that someone was waiting for me, watching me, wanting to do me terrible harm . . .

I sat for about ten minutes until my hands were steady and breathing controlled. I must be practical, think this through.

I realized that I had no way of knowing if Jonas's none too subtle threat about my mental competence had any substance in company law. One could perhaps be nutty as a fruit cake and still control a company. How was I to know? I couldn't remember Fran and I ever holding a ticket for a lottery let alone shares.

The first thing I had to do was to find out more about the legal position. But from where? I could buy a book, of course, but would it give me the answers I sought? I couldn't involve Joe or Rupert and Mr Pritchard was the family solicitor. I really couldn't place him in a compromising situation. Then who? Brett, I was sure, neither knew nor cared about such matters. I needed a good businessman. Then a thought struck. Or woman.

Two days later Suzie Blake had lunch with me at a small fish restaurant on the Hythe at Baildon. At first glance Briggs, as it was called, looked little more than a fish and chip shop. Or perhaps even a public lavatory. The walls were covered in white tiles. The tables had formica tops covered with paper cloths. The cutlery was of the cheapest Taiwan stainless steel. But the fish!

Briggs had their own smokery so there was a wonderful selection of smoked salmon, mackerel, trout, cod's roe and even eel which, rather childishly, I couldn't bring myself to try. There were oysters from Colchester, cockles from Leigh-on-Sea. Cod, haddock and Dover sole had been landed on the Hythe that morning. You brought your own wine and the only pudding they offered was Spotted Dick, a suet pudding filled with mixed dried fruits, which they served with real home made egg custard. Not surprisingly they did a brisk trade.

I waited until Suzie and I were tucking into the Spotted Dick rather guiltily. It was, after all, simply laden with calories, but to miss it would have been an even greater crime. During the meal we'd chatted about this and that. Suzie expressed her gratitude to Cherry Holmes and her talent.

'I don't mind telling you, with the recession I've sometimes wondered how I can keep going. Then along comes an order for one of Cherry's designs. I only take a small commission but it keeps the business alive.'

I reached across the table and touched her hand lightly. 'If things are ever . . . well, if you need help, come to me, won't you? Please promise. I've been left rather a ridiculous amount of money! I hope I haven't spoken out of turn?'

'Oh, Catherine. Out of turn? I may well take you up on your offer! But I hope not. At present I'm just keeping my head above water. May I say something to you? Don't apologize for your generosity of heart.'

I thought immediately of Brett. How many times had he told me not to apologize? I smiled inwardly. Too many times.

'Whenever the need, Suzie, just ask. Please. Now I

have something to ask of you. I want to find out in the most simplistic terms all about company law. I honestly don't know who else to ask.'

She poured us a little more wine then smiled.

'I do!'

A week later I was waiting for Visiting Hour at Colchester jail to commence.

We were a strange mixture of young mothers with crying children, who would be cared for by accompanying grans when the doors opened; strained, chainsmoking, hard-faced women who looked as if they'd made this trip for too many years; elderly women who could no longer believe themselves when they said, 'My son is a good boy,' but had such a heartrending combination of despair and stoicism in their workworn faces.

Then a door opened. A warder entered and simply nodded. We surged forward. Inside stood a row of tables with seats either side. On the wall a large notice read: IT IS FORBIDDEN TO TOUCH THE PRISONERS. My heart lurched at that. Not for the men who presumably had committed some crime and were paying for it. No, for their womenfolk who were trying to carry on with their lives, look after children, keep a home together, but were denied so much as the human comfort of a clasped hand.

'Miss Kelsey?' A hard-faced warden approached me. 'The Governor asked me to . . .' He nearly sneered '. . . make the introductions.'

'Thank you.'

The warder nodded down the row of tables. A good-looking young man in his late-twenties was just taking his seat. In spite of the prison denims his whole bearing said 'public school'. He was slightly built with fine, almost sharp, features. His hair was very fair and, as I watched him, he pushed it back from his face a couple of times but it was so fine it immediately flopped back over his forehead.

'Yes, there he is. There's Gentleman Jim. Off to an open prison in a couple of days' time. There's class equality for you, eh?' the warder said bitterly as he walked away.

I walked swiftly down the row of tables, my heart nearly breaking as I heard snatches of the day-to-day trials that these women were pouring out to their men. 'And all the time the little bugger was playing truant!' 'Gran can't stay on her own any longer.' 'I told her to keep her trap shut when they come round from the Welfare.' 'Had to get rid of her dog. Won't allow 'em on the new estate.'

Archie Paget rose politely as I approached the table at which he sat.

'Miss Kelsey, how delightful,' he said. For all the world as if we'd just met in the Royal Enclosure.

'I'm . . . I'm sorry we're meeting in these circumstances,' I said awkwardly as I sat.

'Think nothing of it!' Archie replied expansively. 'Anyone who's been to an English public school would find this jammy. You still have to watch your bum but at least they don't whack you across it! Now, we only have half an hour, Miss Kelsey. Can I be assured that you've . . .?'

'Oh, yes. A thousand pounds was paid into your bank account three days ago. It would be ridiculous for me to talk about some good friend seeking advice . . . *I* need advice. No, not so much advice as a simple understanding of things.'

'I am at your service, Miss Kelsey.'

'I am a majority shareholder in the Kelsey Glass-works.'

Archie Paget gave a low whistle. Then, 'When you say majority . . .?'

'My uncle, Sir James, owns twenty per cent. Another uncle, Marcus, ten per cent. I therefore own . . .'

'Yes, yes, I'm good at arithmetic.' He smiled ruefully. 'Perhaps a little too talented for my own good! You're sitting pretty, old girl. What's the problem?'

I took a moment before I answered. 'I was ill following an accident last year. I don't know for sure but I may have had a breakdown. You see, I . . . well . . . I'd had rather a difficult time before that,' I said lamely.

I glanced across at the prisoner and was surprised and a little moved by the compassion in his eyes.

'I think you'd better tell me, Miss Kelsey. I might be able to help. And in here I do have time to think.'

And so I told him, this stranger. This thief. I told him about Fran. About her last illness and about my grandfather's totally unexpected bequest.

I sat in embarrassed silence as Archie Paget looked at me once I'd finished my story.

'Bad luck, old love. Bad luck. But to practical matters . . . probably company articles have clauses about directors going potty. Not to hold office over the age of seventy, etc, etc. But a shareholder can be as mad as a hatter and get away with it! Your dear cousin

Jonas is bluffing. First he'd have to get you certified, and that's not likely,' he smiled, 'having met you! Secondly, all you have to do is give a proxy vote to someone. Can't be your solicitor – not allowed. Could be your accountant. My advice would be to give an undated letter to someone you trust. If it's ever needed they can vote in your absence and in your best interest. So, who's on the board? Who do you want to kick off?'

I looked at him for a moment, not understanding what he was saying.

'I'm sorry, I . . .'

Archie gave a hoot of laughter. 'You don't get it, do you? And your friend Jonas is banking on that! My dear lady, yours is a private company. With seventy per cent of the shares you can call an extraordinary share-holders' meeting. You can vote every board member off, including the managing director, Twinkle-toes Jonas. With your voting power you can appoint any damned director you like. Wait another twelve months and you can appoint me!' he added, grinning.

I smiled and was about to ask another question when a whistle blew.

'Ah. The animals are to be returned to their cages!'

'Please, let me ask you this quickly. Are you saying that as a majority shareholder I can vote on or *off* members of the board?'

Archie nodded.

'And if I give my proxy votes to someone else . . . even if certain people try to make out I'm ill . . . I will still control the company. Yes?'

'Right! Let's 'ave you! Everyone out!' the warder in charge was shouting.

'Yes, by George, she's got it!' Archie's languid face was suddenly serious. His mouth twisted into a sad smile. 'Come and see me again, would you? No charge next time!'

He rose from the table and walked back to where I assumed were the cells.

'Archie!' I called out. 'I'm sorry. Suzie Blake asked me to send you her love. I never did find out how she knew you . . .'

He turned in the entrance to the cell-block. His expression was amused but I could see the pain in his eyes.

'Knew me? Well, Miss Kelsey, let's just say I'm her longlost black sheep!'

When I got back to the Hall I lost no time in going through the local telephone directory to find a firm of solicitors. I planned to tell Mr Pritchard what I had done but not to embarrass him by getting him to arrange things for me.

The next morning I drove into Baildon. On the corner of the High Street was a handsome double-fronted Georgian house. 'Fortescue, Fortescue and Brown' was painted discreetly in thin gold lettering on one window.

I was ushered into young Mr Fortescue's office. If he was young Mr Fortescue, I thought, old Mr Fortescue must be about ninety-five! I saw before me a well-dressed, elderly man of about seventy. He had a thin face and a long nose on which were perched old-fashioned pince-nez. He bustled forward to shake my hand.

'This is a great pleasure, Miss Kelsey. I, of course,

knew your grandfather although we were not so fortunate as to do business for him. Please sit down. Coffee and biscuits are on their way.'

He indicated an upholstered chair by his desk then had to stoop down and pick up a large, sleeping ginger tom cat from it.

'That's not your chair,' he admonished the cat and carried it carefully to a cushioned basket by the coal fire. 'I live alone now,' he explained to me. 'I feel Ginger would get lonely if I left him by himself all day. Now! To business. Forgive my mentioning this, Miss Kelsey, but I shouldn't like to feel that we were . . . er . . . poaching a client from another firm. Especially a firm as old established as the one Mr Pritchard represents.'

'There's no question of that, Mr Fortescue. It's simply that I don't want to place Mr Pritchard in a position where he might have to take sides. Between members of my family, that is.'

'I see!' We were interrupted by a slight knock on the door and a grey-haired, neatly dressed woman in her mid-sixties entered, carrying a tray.

'Ah, coffee and biscuits! I hope you remembered the custard creams, May?'

The woman smiled. 'Mr Fortescue, you've been asking me that every weekday for the past thirty-eight years. When did I ever forget your custard creams?'

'Once, May! Once!'

'I didn't forget them, Mr Fortescue. It just was such a blizzard I couldn't get up the High Street to the shop.' She turned to me, smiling. 'That was eighteen years ago and he's still going on about it! Men!' she added shaking her head.

'Can I pour you coffee, Miss Kelsey?' she then asked.

'Thank you.'

The tray was silver and had been set with a hand-embroidered cloth on which stood a silver coffee pot with a matching milk jug and sugar bowl. The silver practically shone it was so well polished. A fine china plate carried an assortment of biscuits.

May deftly poured out coffee and offered biscuits then went to the door.

'Oh, and Mr Fortescue . . . don't forget to take your tablets in half an hour – the green ones. The blue ones you have after lunch. Don't forget now.'

As the door closed behind her, Mr Fortescue smiled and shook his head. 'As you see, Miss Jenkins seems to think the world would stop turning if she didn't take care of me.'

And it probably would, I thought. We sipped our coffee and made polite conversation. Then settled down to business.

'It's quite simple, Mr Fortescue. I hold seventy per cent of the shares in the Kelsey Glassworks which, as I expect you know, is a private company.' The elderly solicitor nodded. 'I was involved in an accident towards the end of last year . . .'

'Yes, Miss Kelsey, I read about it in our local paper. Terrible! Quite terrible! You could so easily have drowned.'

'I nearly did. Afterwards, well, I was ill for some time. I'm quite recovered now but if . . . if I should become incapacitated through ill health again, I would wish someone I trust to keep the best interests of the glassworks at heart, to have the power to use my shares if necessary.'

'You wish to give this person proxy voting power? I see. It will be a simple matter for me to draw up the papers but I do ask you to think very carefully before you sign. You're sure you can trust this person?'

I smiled across the desk at the kindly old man.

'With my life.'

I was dining with Brett that evening and I'd tell him then . . . ask him rather . . . to use my voting power should the occasion ever arise.

As I drove slowly back along the winding roads to Somerton, I allowed myself to examine my feelings for Brett. That night of the St Valentine's Day Ball at Hindlesham, I was so sure that I was in love with him. He was the only man I'd ever met in whose company I felt truly relaxed. Shyness and the conviction that I was too large and too plain had always made me uneasy before when I met attractive men. Although I had felt like that at first with Brett, now I counted him a true friend.

Yes, I thought wryly, that's the problem. He's a friend, but only a friend. What was the point of being secretly in love with a man as charismatic as Brett? Especially when, in our small circle, there was a young woman as beautiful as Sophie.

As I turned the old car on to the road that led to the village, I thought about May Jenkins. She was so clearly in love with Mr Fortescue, I wondered why they'd never got together. Was he a widower? He'd said he lived alone now. I reflected that perhaps people were so often alone because they didn't reach out and take what they wanted. I sighed. Well, at least Mr Fortescue had his ginger tom and I had Cat!

For always, Catherine. For always.

That evening was the first time I'd been to Brett's cottage, Gifford's. I'd asked him about the name but he'd shrugged and said that perhaps once upon a time, someone called Gifford had lived there. It was basically a labourer's cottage and so the deeds gave little information beyond the fact that it had once belonged to the Kelsey estate.

Cat watched me from the window seat as I dressed for the evening. I had seen little of Brett since the St Valentine's Ball and had been surprised by his invitation to supper.

'I'll cook the only thing I know how,' he'd said, laughing, on the telephone. 'Irish stew as you'd never believe, mavourneen!'

I pulled on dark brown velvet trousers and a top that Cherry Holmes had made for me. She'd spent hours sketching Cat and now I had a sweater painted with multi-images of him. It was my most treasured piece of clothing.

I sat on the bed and rubbed Cat behind his ears. Within moments he started to purr.

'Oh, Cat! Cat! I think I've fallen in love with this man! I am not . . . for your ears only . . . a virgin. But my experience is so limited and not good!'

I stood up and crossed to the dressing table. I picked

up my hair brush and started vigorously to brush my hair.

'In any case, I . . . he . . .'

I put the brush down and looked at myself in the mirror.

'Oh, Cat!' I whispered. 'Why don't I look like Sophie?'

At seven-thirty I walked across the green to Gifford's. It was a small, detached cottage, probably about four hundred years old. It stood well back from the green surrounded by old established gardens. The cottage was two up and two down with a solid chimney-stack thrusting through the centre.

Inside was a revelation. I'd expected ye olde beams and an inglenook fireplace. Well, yes, the ceiling beams and the studwork in the walls were exposed and stained. There was also an impressive fireplace with a dog grate filled with flaming logs. But after that the latter half of the twentieth century took over. The two original rooms downstairs were now knocked through, the massive central chimney being the only divider. The plastered walls between the studwork were simply painted white. Flagstones had been cleaned and polished and there were hand-woven rugs strewn apparently haphazardly over them. In fact, they had been placed by a keen eye.

A sofa and two armchairs in the living area were upholstered in leather, their design simple but very sophisticated. There was also a strange-looking chair placed by the fire. Its tall back was red, the slatted arms black. I'd never seen anything like it. I sat on it and was surprised to discover how comfortable it was.

Brett smiled at me as he came into the room with two glasses of wine.

'Ah! You've discovered my pride and joy. It's an original Mackintosh chair.' He saw my puzzled expression. 'Charles Rennie. He designed the building and all the furnishings for the Glasgow School of Art. I love the boldness of his design and yet it's deceptively simple.'

'Yes. I can see why you'd be attracted to something like this. Your glass has the same quality.'

'Thank you, Catherine. I value that. You're growing to love glass, aren't you?'

'Yes, I am. I have a lot to learn but I feel . . . well, almost a passion for it. Is that crazy?'

'In my eyes it's eminently sane,' he said, smiling. We sipped our wine in comfortable companionship.

'I really like this wine. It reminds me of gooseberries. Or does that sound rude?'

'No. You've said exactly the right thing again. It's a New Zealand wine. A Montana Sauvignon. I'm not really a wine buff, just know what I like and all that.' He suddenly laughed. 'Or don't like! I mean, how much of Marcus's red plonk can you drink without taking the lining off your stomach?' He lifted his glass. I recognized it as Kelsey but not cut crystal. 'I'm told this can compete with a good Sancerre. But being a poor peasant from Ireland, I wouldn't know!'

'A poor peasant with a Godgiven gift, a Mackintosh chair and a Jaguar in the garage. Oh, yes. I can see you're very disadvantaged!' I teased.

'Underneath that cool exterior you're a saucy piece

of work, aren't you, Miss Kelsey?' He held out his hand
to me. 'Come and eat.'

He led me into a large kitchen which ran the length
of the cottage under a cat-slide roof.

'This would originally have been a roofed area for
carts, pigs, chickens . . . God knows what. The only
problem is that the nearer to the back door you get, the
more you have to stoop!'

I liked Brett's kitchen. Apart from the sink and a
couple of appliances nothing was fitted. I suppose if I'd
given any thought to what a kitchen in a cottage such as
Gifford's would be like I'd have imagined it to be all
stripped pine and copper pans. Instead there were
freestanding cupboards and chests made of limed oak,
their design almost Art Deco.

The kitchen had style but it was also a place to work, to
eat, to enjoy. Again I reflected what flair this man had.

'Mmm! Would you swop Gifford's for Kelsey Hall? I
feel comfortable here. All it needs is Cat curled up on
one of your chairs!'

My tone was light but Brett must have sensed my
inner feeling of isolation.

'No, I wouldn't swop,' he replied seriously. 'But
neither should you. You have a great inheritance. All
you need to do is make it your own.' Then his mood
changed. 'Now, come on. Let's eat. The soup's out of
a tin, I fear, but I've poached a wild sea trout and
mixed a good dressing for the salad. Then there's a
very decent blue Gloucester which I got from Collins
in Baildon. Eat! Enjoy!'

And I did enjoy myself. The food was simple but
delicious.

'This is all very well but I thought I was going to dine on Irish stew!'

'My dear girl, I ate nothing but Irish stew for the first fifteen years of my life! I'll only dine at Knight's Croft if Sophie promises *not* to cook it.'

Oh, how I longed to say: 'Have you had an affair with her? Are you still having one?' But it was none of my business. And yet I so wanted to know.

I waited until we were back in Brett's living room, drinking coffee and sipping a smoky, smooth Irish whiskey.

'Brett, I want to ask you an enormous favour . . .'

He looked surprised but said, 'Ask away!'

'Jonas implied that because I'd had some sort of a breakdown a few months ago, I might not be competent to use my votes as majority shareholder.'

'My God, I'd like to break that bastard's neck!'

'I suppose, to be fair, I must have come as a terrible shock to him. He'd expected the estate either to go to Sir James or to him. He must resent me very much.'

'Then he hasn't got the sense he was born with! I knew and liked your grandfather. In fact, I owe everything to him. He was a hard man but totally honest. And anyone who bothered to get close to him would know that his own flesh and blood meant everything! He never discussed his family with me but he was a shrewd old devil and I can't believe he was taken in by that load of slime, Jonas.'

'Well,' I replied slowly, 'I didn't have the privilege of knowing my grandfather. I'm still, I suppose, struggling to forgive him for that. But in any case, I'm not going to be pushed around by Jonas! I've taken some advice.'

I smiled. 'From a rather bizarre source! And I'm having papers drawn up so that if there is ever a crisis at the glassworks and I'm . . . unwell again, then someone I can trust has got my vote by proxy. That someone is you, Brett. Would you mind?'

He looked at me for a moment then came and kissed me on the cheek.

'You're a dear, good woman, Catherine. Of course I don't mind.'

I'm not sure quite how it happened but suddenly his lips were on mine. I returned his kiss passionately. I had no illusions that this man loved me but I had a great need for him.

But when I was in his bed I felt shy and clumsy. Brett was kind to me, caressed me, tried to get me to respond. And I tried. But how can you try at making love? I wanted him. I needed him. I gave of myself. But not enough of myself. I felt less than a woman.

That night in my own bed I hugged Cat to me and cried into his soft, black fur. I struggled not to give in to self-pity, but I felt so alone. I was close to Sophie; all my Knight's Croft cousins had shown warmth and friendship to me. I occasionally saw Sir James. But I lived alone and slept alone. Apart from Cat.

I watch, Catherine. I watch.

The next morning I awoke early to find that Cat was still by my side. This was surprising as he was usually out hunting at first light. It seemed ridiculous but it was as if he'd felt my need for his company.

I stroked his head. 'What say we take some books and retreat to the gatehouse today?'

As did my Lady.

I really didn't want to see anyone that day. I left a note for Mrs Jessop to say that I had taken some books that I planned to study and would be at the gatehouse. I didn't want to take any calls and had arranged my own lunch.

I took some fish for Cat from the fridge and made myself a sandwich. Then I went into the library and chose some books. Nothing to do with glass! I selected a Dorothy L. Sayers Lord Peter Wimsey novel, a collection of Swinburne's poems and, I don't quite know why, a book on the Restoration Theatre.

I'd dressed warmly, it was late March and the wind from the estuary was so cold it felt as if it could cut you in half. As soon as I was in the gatehouse I set about making a fire from the basket of logs set by the hearth. Within no time the logs were blazing and I curled up on the window seat. I closed my eyes and listened to the reassuring crackle of the wood as it caught and then leapt into flames.

I'd left the door to the gatehouse slightly ajar in the hope that Cat would join me. I was surprised and strangely touched when he leapt on to the window seat, walked the length of my body then curled up on my lap. He was the first cat I'd ever lived with and it always puzzled me the way he never took a direct route. On the bed he'd often walk over my shoulders before he settled down by my side. If I was sitting in a winged armchair, surely it was easier to leap on to the arm, not on to the back and then walk down my body to my lap? And yet it was this perverseness that I found so endearing.

I tried the Swinburne first.

> For winter's rains and ruins are over,
> And all the season of snows and sins;
> The days dividing lover and lover,
> The light that loses, the night that wins.
> And time remembered is grief forgotten
> And frosts are slain and flowers begotten,
> And in green underwood and cover
> Blossom by blossom the Spring begins.

'Time remembered is grief forgotten'. How I longed to reach that plateau. A time when I could look back and remember only the good times with Fran, never the bad, never her dying. A time when I could recall my friendship with Brett and forget how humiliated I'd felt the previous night.

I read for quite a few hours. Fed Cat his fish and ate my sandwiches. Made up the fire. Returned to the window seat. I started to read the Sayers novel but found Lord Peter something of a snob and rather irritating. I felt my head nodding. Finally I slept.

When I awoke the light was fading across the estuary. I could hear someone calling my name. It was Mrs Jessop.

'Miss Catherine! Miss Catherine!'

I rubbed my eyes and swung my feet stiffly to the floor. Cat, wisely, had abandoned my lap by the cold window for the rug in front of the fire.

'Yes! Yes, Mrs Jessop? I'll come down.'

I climbed down the stone steps to the gatehouse door, trying to force down my sense of irritation that

I'd been disturbed when I'd asked to be left alone.

'Miss, I'm sorry to bother you but you've got a gentleman asking to see you. Very grand he is!'

She nodded across the courtyard where a chauffeur-driven Bentley was parked.

'I didn't really like to take the responsibility of turning him away.'

'No. Of course not. Thank you.'

As I hurried across the courtyard I was totally mystified as to who my visitor could be. But the moment that I walked into the Great Parlour – Mrs Jessop had been impressed enough to give this gentleman the full Kelsey hospitality – and looked at the tall, raw-boned man who rose to meet me, I knew.

This man was my father.

CHAPTER
FOURTEEN

THE CAT

'For I see best without the light –
The everlasting cat!'

– William Bright Rands

JESSLYN: 1665

'Ring o' ring of roses'
— Nursery rhyme, Anon

All I could do for Richard was to keep his fevered body as clean as possible. Constantly change the sheets soaked with his sweat. Simply give what comfort I could.

He had the Plague, the Black Death that had brought the great city of London to its knees.

We had escaped for so long. I thanked God that when the first cases were reported in the old City, Richard and I had insisted that Moll and Lucinda go to Harriet at Somerton.

She and I had written to each other as time and messengers allowed. I had felt sure that she would give a roof to my daughter and friend. A protesting Harry had gone with them. The roads were dangerous and travellers so often the victims of footpads or highwaymen that Richard had persuaded him that an unprotected woman and child travelling alone was unthinkable.

'I 'ate the bleeding country!' Harry had said. 'It's so quiet, how do them folks know when they're dead?'

Richard had laughed. 'Harry, old son, when were you last in the country?'

But still he'd sulked. 'I heard tell,' he said gloomily.

I knew now that Richard would die. I had little doubt that I would join him in a Plague pit.

The enemy within had been so quick and yet so slow. No one knew or understood how the Plague spread so quickly but when the devastation in the old City was realized the theatres were closed down. That was in May. It had always seemed unthinkable that the newly laid out piazzas and well-appointed houses of Covent Garden could harbour the terrifying disease. But by early June three houses in Drury Lane bore on their front door a red cross and the words, 'Lord have mercy on us'.

It was the hottest summer within living memory. By July the air was not only hot and heavy, it was full of the putrid smell of decaying bodies. Most of the clergy and doctors had fled to the country. Burials were no longer private and after dark the carts went through the street accompanied by the cry of: 'Bring out your dead!'

Houses where the Plague had struck were sealed, the occupants left to die or to survive but not allowed to mix. This was, of course, a nonsense. The rich simply flouted these simple, even barbaric, precautions.

Poorer families, sometimes without food or even water from the pump, were incarcerated and left to die or survive behind sealed doors. Lord have mercy upon us indeed!

All through those hot terrible months Richard and I survived. Every morning we looked at each other in astonishment that we were still alive. We dare not follow Lucinda and Moll and Harry to Somerton for fear that we carried the Plague with us.

By August we had heard rumours that sixty thousand were dead. The King and his Court had removed themselves to Oxford. And why not? King Charles was a popular King and little good could have come from his staying in the Capital and dying of the Plague.

Then, in early September, when the number of deaths appeared to be falling, I heard Richard sneezing. 'Atishoo! Atishoo! All fall down!' A children's rhyme but also the first symptoms of the Plague.

I knocked on the door of his bedchamber and entered.

'For God's sake, don't come near me, Jesslyn!' he said.

'Don't be ridiculous. Someone must nurse you . . . until you are better,' I added lamely.

Richard smiled at me. 'Little one, it seems you either catch the Plague or you don't. What is for sure is that you don't get better. Let us not have that pretence between us. I've had a good life. I'm past forty, Jess. And the past few years since the theatres have re-opened, I've known such happiness. Working with you. Being with you. In my own strange way, I love you very much, little one.'

'Oh, and I you, Richard.' Then I added briskly, 'But you don't want a weeping woman by your bedside. We must be practical. What can I get you?'

'Nothing! Jess, you must leave this room. Just leave me, please! You must not catch this terrible thing.'

'Richard, be sensible. No one knows how the Plague spreads. In some houses all but one dies. In others one dies and the others survive! I'm as likely to catch the Plague nursing you as I am sitting downstairs in the parlour. So, no more nonsense!'

Richard could not deny the truth of what I said. Also, although I knew him to be a brave man, if his work for the King had been known he would have been executed – but even brave men do not want to die alone. And Richard was right. He would die.

'Very well, Jesslyn. My dear Jess! I'd like a jug of ale. I've a raging thirst.'

I made my way down to the kitchen. We were very fortunate. Our larder was well stocked with bacon and salted meat. We had our own pump and the kitchen garden was well stocked with herbs and vegetables. We also had fruit trees. I can't imagine how the poor devils in the old City managed. I suppose they just didn't. They simply died.

The kitchen was strangely quiet when I entered it. Usually there was the sound of the two young maids chattering, the cook moving saucepans around. I looked out into the garden and saw the servants hurrying down the path towards the Strand. Well, who could blame them? They had heard Richard sneezing and feared the worst. I would have to paint a red cross on our door and no one would be allowed in or out. The servants were terrified that they'd be sealed in with the Black Death.

I drew a jug of ale from the huge barrel in the stillroom and took it up to Richard with a tankard.

In the short time I had been away from him, only a matter of minutes, the fever had taken hold of him. He was shivering uncontrollably and I could see on his chest the red spots starting to appear. The ring of roses.

I quickly poured some ale and helped him drink it.

Then he fell back on the pillows, exhausted.

'Jesslyn, while there's still time . . . I must talk to you.'

'No, Richard. Rest, my dear!'

He managed a wry smile. 'I'll have plenty of time to rest quite soon, little one! Please listen to what I have to say. I have done you and Lucinda and Moll a great wrong. Hear me out! I am responsible for all three of you, yes, and for young Harry . . . There's no money left! I've made a will which is with my lawyer, leaving all to you, but it was made before Killigrew started building the Theatre Royal. I lent him everything I had. He's been repaying me as he could but with the theatres closed these five months, he hasn't earned a penny. I've been such a fool! How can you ever forgive me?'

'Easily and with all my heart. You did what you did out of love. Love for the theatre. You have rightly been acclaimed as one of the greatest actors of our age. You followed your heart, Richard. And, in so doing, gave me a purpose to my life also.'

'But what will you do? Where will you live? I am months behind with the rent on this house! Bedford's agent had been dunning me since the New Year. Once the Plague is over he'll renew his demands. And with you a widow . . . Oh, my dear, I'm so sorry! But . . . but . . . I'm tired now. I must . . . must . . .'

His head fell to one side and for a terrible moment I thought that he had already gone from me. When I saw how he suffered through the following days, I wished he had died at that moment.

I sat by his side for that day and night. Pulling the

bedclothes back over his poor twitching, fevered body when he threw them off. Laying cold cloths on his brow. I didn't really know how to help him, but at least I was there.

If I survived, and I doubted that I would, I'd wait for the contagion to pass then make my way to Somerton. After that, I knew not. I could hardly foist two women, a young girl and a manservant on Harriet. Both financially and as an invasion of her privacy it was unthinkable. I had some jewellery I could sell but vowed I would keep my promise to Richard and never sell the Gloriana necklace. Then I thought wryly, when . . . if . . . this terror is ever over, who will there be left to buy?

Through the long night I let my mind wander back over the past two years. Richard had spoken of how happy they'd been. For me there had been a sense of accomplishment in learning my new trade. In the pleasure of performance. The comradeship between the players. I had become particularly friendly with a young orange seller, Nelly Gwynne, who had joined the company. She was very small and impishly pretty. A cockney through and through and with a ready wit. We were in no way rivals as I had made my mark in dramatic roles and she had a great gift for comedy.

She had come into the company via the bed of one of the leading players, Hart. But she was so honest about it, so open and giving in her ways, that no one could hold that against her. Least of all me. And she had talent. She also had many admirers. There were always a number of young gallants in the tiring-room after a performance, but once Nelly joined the company I swear the number doubled.

And I had Guy's love again. I could no longer hold out against him. And once I recognized that, my love for him consumed me. I did not return to the Court or go back to my old giddy ways. My love was for him only. I had been totally honest with Richard about my feelings and he had smiled and taken my hand.

'Little one, I've waited for you to realize this. To understand that Guy took a wife only because he could not have you. The King himself arranged the marriage. Marie-Louise is second cousin to his mother, Queen Henrietta. It was a good match and Guy must have an heir. Although so far that haughty lady hasn't given him one!'

Guy had bought a little house with gardens running down to the Thames at Chiswick. And this became our haven.

I was not in every play and on my free days would have a lighterman row me downriver. Guy would be waiting for me. At those times we left behind the real world and lived only for each other.

In the summer we would picnic in the garden watching the river make its lazy way down to the sea. Guy would hold me in his arms and we would talk and laugh as only lovers can. About nothing. About everything.

Then he would carry me to the bedroom. The windows would be open to the sweet air that came from that stretch of the river and we would make love – sometimes with passion, sometimes slowly, almost languidly. But always with joy.

Now I wondered if I would ever see him again? Marie-Louise was at last pregnant and so Guy had taken her, for safety, to his country estate until the Plague had passed. No one could have guessed that it would rage for so long.

I slept fitfully in a chair by Richard's bed. Towards dawn I heard him give a most terrible groan. I quickly crossed to him. His eyes were open but I doubt that he knew where he was. His lips were quite black and the skin beneath the ugly rash on his chest was also beginning to turn black. He groaned again and tried to move his arms.

I gently tried to help and then saw, with horror, the huge swelling under each arm. The swellings were livid and full of pus. Again it was rumour, but I had heard that if these swellings burst the poison would drain out of the body and the victim would live. I have no idea whether this was true. I simply tried to place Richard's arms so that there would be as little pressure as possible on his armpits.

Later, when I changed his bedclothes and sponged him down, I saw that there was another grotesque swelling in his groin. I started to pray then. I knelt by his bed and prayed that he would die – and die quickly. But God did not heed my prayer. It took another agonizing forty-eight hours for Richard to be eased from his pain. And I must be honest, as I watched him, I felt terror that this was the way I was going to die also.

At dawn on the fourth day he suddenly said very clearly: 'The players are coming, Father! Can I see them?' And then it was over.

I pulled the sheet up over his poor tortured body. I had no tears left. I was utterly drained. Ours had been a marriage of convenience for both of us, but we had grown close and had loved each other. I would miss him desperately. His wit. His ready laughter. His compassion.

And the Town would miss his talent. I was told that I had a certain beauty on the stage and knew I had but little talent. Richard had greatness. He could hold the audience with a whisper. Bring them to helpless laughter or move them to tears.

I made a vow to his departed soul then.

'Richard, you will not be buried namelessly in some Plague pit. Shovelled from the death-carts by poor, drunken derelicts. You will have a proper grave and a tombstone, so that in years to come people will know where one of the greatest players of this age is buried.'

But how to achieve that? Then I thought of the Rector of St Paul's, Covent Garden. The Reverend Simon Patrick, unlike most churchmen, had stayed with his parish, tirelessly comforting the bereaved and the dying. Any house with a red cross on the door would be visited by him. He also loved the theatre. And I know that he admired Richard Warwick.

I had not, as was ordered, painted a red cross on our door. This was not through lack of regard for the law, simply because all my time had been taken up with Richard. Well, how could anyone punish me further for my lack of compliance? I was going to die anyway.

That night, after dusk, I slipped from the house and made my way to St Paul's. The Reverend Patrick was celebrating Evensong. I was the only member of the congregation.

At first I had felt guilt that I might be carrying the Plague to this God-fearing man. But he had exposed himself to the disease so often he was surely either immune or had been smiled on by God. I suspected the latter.

The beautiful, little church designed by Inigo Jones, which was so familiar to me, seemed reduced to a shell that night. There was no choir. No altar boys. No vergers. Just the priest and myself.

After the Blessing Reverend Patrick started to walk towards the vestry. I softly called his name.

'Mistress Warwick, I had not realized it was you,' he said as he walked towards me.

'Please, do not come too near. I almost certainly carry the Plague.'

He came to my side and took my hand. 'My dear child, I have lived with that evil day and night for all these months. I do not understand it. I do not understand why God is testing us so. But I know that I wish to live my life in my parish as I would in happier times. If I am to be taken, so be it. Now, how can I help you?'

'Richard is dead.'

'Oh, my dear. And you had survived so long. The numbers of dead are falling daily. My dear, I am truly sorry and will say a prayer for his soul. He was a kind man and a great actor.'

'That is why I am here. He *was* a great actor. This church is already being called the Actors' Church. Richard should be buried here among his peers. He can't . . . he mustn't simply be taken away on a death-cart! Please, believe me, I know what I'm asking. Is there any way he can be buried here, in consecrated ground? And, when this is all over, can a headstone be placed over his grave?'

The Reverend Patrick shook his head. 'It is forbidden. And in God's eyes we are all one.'

'But people will remember him! Write about his performances! Not only that, he practically bankrupted himself to bring a new form of theatre to this country. Surely that counts for something?'

'And what does a small, innocent child thrown into a pit without benefit of clergy or even prayer count for?'

My thoughts went instantly to Lucinda. I felt tears come to my eyes. Oh, the grief of the families who had survived but lost little ones. But I was stubborn in my desire to plead Richard's case.

'I know what you are saying. I feel the pain of those children's deaths. But Richard Warwick is . . . was . . . a man who deserved recognition of his work. Future generations *must* know where he is buried! Please, I know you loved his talent. I have seen you time after time at the play. You must understand why I ask this?'

We sat in silence for what seemed like an hour but must in reality have been moments.

'You are right. A great man of the theatre should be buried here. Have you money to bribe the men who will come to collect his body?'

I nodded. I still had a little coin left.

'Then tonight at twelve of the clock be ready. You cannot come here for the burial, it would be too dangerous if the Searchers saw us. But I give you my word that he will have a Christian burial and I will note the spot so that in better times you can mark his grave.'

I took his hand and kissed it. 'God bless you!'

After they had taken Richard's body I sat in the silent, empty house. So many memories of Richard, of

Lucinda, of Moll. Of the time Guy had hidden from Parliament's soldiers. There was nothing left for me to do but to wait. Wait for death or for deliverance. I had no way of knowing which.

A little after midnight, when I knew they would be burying him, I prayed for Richard's soul. Then, for the first time in days, I lay down on my bed and slept.

When I awoke I found it hard to focus. But then the truth of what had happened flooded in on me. I had lost Richard and most probably would never see my daughter or my lover again. But, to my amazement, I showed no sign of fever or illness. For the first time since Richard had been stricken I allowed myself to hope that I might live.

I had slept the day and part of the night away. I was thirsty and very hungry. I pulled on a wrapper and made my way to the kitchen. I drew myself some ale and cut a slice of cheese and some nearly stale bread. I sat at the kitchen table and was suddenly overwhelmed by a sense of loneliness. Then I heard a small sound. I listened. It came again. Something or someone was outside the kitchen door.

I have returned, Jesslyn.

I crossed to the door and tentatively opened it. As I did so I thought how foolish I was to unbar a door at night in these times. Gangs of robbers had been roaming the streets looting the homes of those stricken by the Plague.

On the doorstep was a black cat. Not quite a kitten but very young. The cat totally ignored me and walked slowly and purposefully into the kitchen, then sat by the cold hearth and started to wash itself.

For the first time in I didn't know how long, I
laughed. I dropped the cat a curtsey. 'Welcome! I see
that you intend to make yourself at home.'

Your need for me is great now.

Seeing the little cat by the hearth, so contained, so
intent on his toilet, my mind instantly went back to the
happy days at Somerton with my father and Ra. The
companionship. The scholarship. And I included Harriet in that happiness. I was not always able to keep up
with my father's and Harriet's debates but always I sat
and listened and was enthralled. Always Ra sat on my
lap as if to comfort me for my lack of argument. And
yet my father and Harriet never excluded me. In the
middle of a heated conversation they would turn to me
and say, 'What do *you* think, Jesslyn?' Sometimes I
would stumble out an opinion, often I would simply
shake my head and smile. But I knew that I was loved.
Was part of something precious.

In the months that followed the cat rarely left my
side. I worried about what would happen to him if I
died but then comforted myself that, cat-like, he would
find another home as he had found mine.

I longed for news from Lucinda and Moll, from Guy.
But London was virtually a closed city and no messengers, carters or even tinkers who might have carried a
letter ventured near us.

By November the crier was calling out that no new
cases of Plague had been reported. I started to think –
and I crossed myself at the thought – that I might after
all live.

But live how? As soon as the Plague had abated, the
rent on our house would be demanded. I had always

assumed that Richard owned the elegant house in Maiden Lane. My assumption had been wrong! I gave myself another four weeks. If there were still no Plague victims I felt it would then be safe to travel to Somerton. I had to see my beloved daughter and dear Moll. I also longed to see Harriet again. I felt no such longing for Somerton.

At the end of the second week in December I was just lighting the candles: only two as we had so few left. The black cat whom I had named Pitch and I lived between the kitchen and my bedchamber. I thanked God for my cat's company. Apart from an occasional visit from the Reverend Patrick, I had seen not a living soul since Richard had died. I think that small creature helped me keep my sanity. Suddenly I heard a banging at the bolted kitchen door.

'Mistress! Mistress!' a familiar voice called out. 'It's me! Harry! Is anyone bleeding alive in there?'

I pulled back the bolts and flung open the door.

'Oh, Harry! Harry!' Mistress and servant, we clung to each other.

'Even in that dead and alive hole we heard it was over. No one could understand why you and the Guvnor hadn't come for us.'

'Harry, I was terrified that I might bring the Black Death to Somerton. To those I love.'

'Jesus! It could do with something to liven it up. It ain't even got a tavern! I ask you! Where's the Guvnor?' he asked eagerly.

Then he saw my expression.

'He's been and gone and died on us, 'asn't he? Oh, Christ! And I wasn't here!' He walked abruptly to the door and out into the night. I knew that Harry, being Harry, wanted to shed his tears in private. In the solitude of the moonlit garden.

Our fuel and food were running low but I put a vegetable broth over the fire to heat through and some newly baked bread on the kitchen table.

After about an hour Harry bustled in, his arms full of logs.

'Right, the Guvnor would 'ave wanted me to take care of you! Hang on. Where did this mog come from?'

He nodded towards Pitch who had settled himself by the recently lit fire.

'I don't know, Harry. He just arrived.'

'Trust a bloody cat! One family drops down dead. Off he goes to next-door.'

I picked up Pitch and stroked him.

'I don't think of it like that. I feel instead that he chose me.'

Many thousands of years ago, Jesslyn. As I did Catherine.

Harry and I shared the simple meal at the kitchen table. I had to tell him about there being no money with which to pay him. No money even to pay the rent on the house or to put food on the table.

'I have some jewellery that I'll try to sell.'

'You won't get much of a price for it, Mistress. I should think half of London is trying to sell their bits and pieces to get themselves on their feet again. But I'll take it to a fence I know.' He winked. 'From my bad old days! He'll give me as much as you'd get anywhere else. He owes me, see?'

'Thank you, Harry.'

'Then we'd better get you out of here, fast. Once word is out that the Guvnor's snuffed it, they'll be round 'ere quicker than you can say Jack Rabbit. Don't want you in the Debtors, do we?'

I shuddered at the thought. The Fleet prison was a notoriously evil place. I wondered if I could get word to Guy who would surely help me? But how long would it take to get a message through to him? Too long. Harry was right. I must leave London as soon as possible. And the only place for me to go was Somerton.

As if reading my thoughts he said, 'Get your jewels together, Lady, and first light I'll seek out my mate. If he's still alive! You pack what you can, and as soon as I've got the money I'll get round to the livery stables . . . hire a coach. But I'll bring it round to the Strand, see? That way you slip through the gardens and no one knows you've gone, or where. I rode back on Old Nick, he should be rested by the morning. Don't you worry, we'll pull it off!'

I hated the thought of fleeing from our debts but I had no choice. I promised myself that when . . . if ever . . . I had the money, I would pay Richard's debts. I didn't even know how much was owing but imagined that the Earl of Bedford's agent would seize the fine furniture in the house and that would help pay off some of the back rent.

That night I packed my finest clothes into a trunk. If I was going to return to Somerton as a pauper, at least I would return in style. For Lucinda's sake and for my own.

At first light Harry slipped out of the house with all my jewels except the Gloriana necklace. I waited an agonizing two or three hours before he quietly entered the kitchen.

'It's all laid on, Mistress. Fortunately the old bugger survived. I only got half of what your jewels were worth but that's better than nothing, ain't it? Enough to pay for the coach and horses and a bit left over. We'll need the extra money. It'll take us three days to do the sixty miles to Somerton.'

At last the hired coach was driven on to the green at Somerton. My bones felt as if they'd never recover from the shaking and rattling as the wooden wheels had dragged over the badly rutted roads. Pitch was sleeping in the basket I had carried him in and I wondered at his composure. Harry had ridden Old Nick and was in better shape than me, having said stoutly, 'The only way you'd get me in one of them things is in me bleeding coffin!'

It had been eight months since I had seen my daughter and we flew into each other's arms, Beau and Fletch, now fully grown dogs, yapping around us. Pitch arched his back and hissed.

Over Lucinda's head, Moll's eyes asked the question: 'Richard?' I shook my head and she turned away, fighting back the tears for Lucinda's sake. For now I would simply tell my daughter that Papa was performing at the playhouse and could not join us. I needed time to renew my relationship with her and then would tell her of Richard's death. I already knew that she loved him dearly.

Harriet gave me a warm welcome but she was older and greyer and, I thought, a little frail. I couldn't let her bear the burden of my family problems for long.

On the first Sunday that I was at Somerton I determined to show the village that the girl they had driven out had returned as a successful woman.

I brushed down my most elegant winter gown and took from my trunk an absurdly dashing hat. I held my head high as I walked into the church.

Lucinda's little hand clasped in mine, Moll following.

If a dancing bear had entered the church the effect could not have been more sensational. I had to bite my lip to stop myself laughing. I swear I heard a stifled sound from Moll.

I led my companions to a pew and sat as meekly as my London dress would allow.

The only person in the church who had not turned to see us enter was Sir Thomas Kelsey. He sat alone in the family pew. Harriet had told me that he was now a widower which, given the number of dead children poor Lady Kelsey had borne, did not surprise me.

We rose as the priest and the choir walked down the aisle towards the altar. It was then that I felt Sir Thomas's eyes upon me.

In that moment I knew how to save us: I would marry Sir Thomas Kelsey.

CHAPTER FIFTEEN

THE CAT

'. . . Time in hours, days, years,
Driven by the spheres.
Like a vast shadow moved: in which the world
And all her train were hurled'

— Henry Vaughan

CATHERINE: 1992

'The wind blows out of the gates of the day,
The wind blows over the lonely of heart'
                                    – W.B. Yeats

'You look as if you could do with a drink,' he said. 'And I could certainly use one.'

I crossed silently to the drinks tray and poured us both a stiff whisky.

'I hope you don't expect me to fall into your arms,' I said coldly as I handed him his glass.

He smiled and shook his head. 'But you haven't asked me who I am, you know!'

'I don't need to. It's like looking into a mirror. How could you?' I said, suddenly very angry. 'How could you leave me without a father for nearly thirty years? How could you have abandoned Fran to bring me up by herself? You can't imagine how I've wanted . . . wanted . . .' I bit my lip and turned away.

The room was silent as he gave me the chance to compose myself. Then: 'I'm so sorry about Francesca. I read about her death in *Variety*. I wanted to come to you then but I was playing on Broadway. The play closed a couple of days ago. It somehow didn't seem appropriate to write.'

I turned and stared at him. I knew by his accent that he was an American but now I realized who he was: Greg Anderson, Hollywood legend and

Broadway star. He was up there with Lancaster, Stewart, Douglas, Peck. But unlike them he had constantly returned to the stage. His reputation was formidable.

I smiled for the first time. 'You may not be my favourite father, but you're one of my favourite actors!'

'Catherine, I have no right to ask anything of you. But will you sit down in your splendid – what was it that nice, dumpy little lady called it? – your splendid parlour, and let me tell you how it was?'

I hesitated.

'Catherine, I've flown thousands of miles and driven well over a hundred to see you. Please listen to what I have to say.'

'Very well.' I sat opposite him and tried to counterfeit a composure I did not feel. Inwardly my mind was in turmoil. I'd desperately wanted for as long as I could remember to have a father. Know my father. But Fran would never discuss him with me and finally I'd stopped asking.

'Francesca was the love of my life. I was twenty years older than her when we met. She had a featured part in a movie I was making over here. She was like no one I'd ever met: confident, crazy, funny. We had one wonderful summer together. I never wanted to lose her. But my wife was . . . is . . . a devout Roman Catholic. She would never have given me a divorce. Even so, I would have done anything to keep Fran! God, I loved her.' He stopped speaking for a moment and drained his whisky.

'Do you mind if I help myself to another one of these?'

'I'll get it for you.' I rose and took his glass. I was starting to feel sorry for him. To like him even. And I wanted to hate him.

'Were you close to your mother?' he asked as I handed him the whisky.

'Very! I was devastated when she died. But . . . and this must sound strange . . . she really didn't seem to mind about death.'

My father smiled. 'Yes. That sounds like the young woman I loved. I wanted to leave my wife and set up home with her. It would have been the end of my film career, of course. My contract with the studio had a morality clause and if I'd left my wife there's no way they could have kept that from the gutter press.'

He rose and started to pace the room.

'Oh, Catherine, I didn't care about my career! God forgive me, I didn't care about the hurt I'd cause my wife. I was mad with love for Fran.' Then he turned to me. 'It wasn't I who abandoned her. She tired of me.' He sat by my side. 'You loved her but you know how she was. Like a butterfly! She was so captivating, then she'd grow bored and want a new experience. Something . . . someone more exciting. I'm not ashamed to say that I begged her to stay with me. She wouldn't listen.'

'Yes,' I said slowly. 'She was like that.' How many times, I thought, did she tell me that she was madly in love but within weeks that lover was replaced by another? How many times had she promised to be at a school Sports Day, a Prize Giving, a concert . . . only to say airily afterwards, 'Sweetheart, sorry! I forgot.' And I could always forgive her, even though my eyes had searched in vain for her among the arriving parents.

'It was months before I discovered, quite by chance, that Fran was pregnant. I knew you must be mine but every letter I sent her was returned unopened. I sent her money but that was also returned. Well, look at this place!' His arms embraced the beautiful, panelled sixteenth-century room.

'I grew up in the Lower East Side. I've always known just what a buck meant. But Fran . . .' He shrugged. 'If money didn't exactly grow on trees, it sure as hell wasn't an important part of life!'

'You're doing her something of an injustice there. Once my grandfather found out she was pregnant, they had a terrible argument. She never saw him again. He never, as far as I know, offered her a penny. Or perhaps he did and the terms were not acceptable. We . . . how shall I put it? We had our ups and downs.'

'And all the time I could've taken care of you both! As time went on I started to wonder if Fran had been two-timing me. I mean, why shouldn't she admit that you were my daughter? But she never would! It would've meant so much to me. You see, my wife and I have no children.'

How sad and how incredibly ironic, I thought. A daughter who longed for a father. A father who longed for a child.

Greg Anderson tentatively reached out and touched my hand.

'Once I saw you, there wasn't the shadow of a doubt that you were mine.'

I knew that what he said was true.

We talked long into the night. Mrs Jessop had given my father's chauffeur a meal and I had offered him a bed but he had a Londoner's distrust of the country and drove off to Baildon.

For once I didn't find class distinctions awkward. My father and I ate exactly the same meal as the chauffeur was eating in the kitchen. But I didn't want to share Greg with anyone else.

I was too shy to reach out and take his hand but reached out with my heart.

After dinner we went into the Little Parlour, the room I liked most in the house but that in many ways overwhelmed me.

We sat by the fire. Cat joined us but studiously ignored Greg – I assumed because he was new in our lives. We drank some of my grandfather's V.S.O.P. brandy and started to become easy with each other.

He told me of his plans to start his own production company. Of the classical parts he wanted to play but, until now, had been scared to try.

I hesitantly told him a little of my life with Fran. Then, more positively, how I'd been studying the history and the manufacture of English glass.

At two o'clock in the morning we both laughed and recognized that it was time for bed.

At the foot of the stairs my father reached out and touched my arm.

'Honey, I have to get back to the States. My agent has lined up a big three-picture deal with Allied and we've got to meet with the Top Brass! I so want to get to know you better. Would you consider coming out to L.A. to stay with us? I'd pay all expenses, of course. I just . . . just want you, Catherine.'

I laughed. 'Expenses aren't a problem, Greg. But I have some business I need to see to. I can't leave my cat unless someone can care for him. That may seem strange to you,' I said hastily, 'but he means a great deal to me. And, well, I couldn't just put him in a cattery.'

'Whatever you say, honey. Just remember, I want you!'

My God, I'd longed to hear those words. But then another thought: 'You spoke earlier as if you're still married? How can your wife possibly cope with a grown-up, illegitimate daughter? It just isn't fair.'

My father smiled. 'Shhh! Don't tell the Press but we're both well into our sixties. We're comfortable with each other. She understands my need for you.'

Oh, Catherine . . . My Catherine.

Four weeks later my plane was landing at the third biggest airport in the world – Los Angeles. I'd been here many times with Fran, of course. And even when we should have flown Economy we flew First Class. No, that wasn't quite true, I thought, and smiled to myself, sometimes Fran flew First Class and I flew Economy.

When will they ever finish the damned thing? I thought as I claimed baggage and went through Customs. Or how awful if they thought they had and the sprawling plastic mess was part of some great design.

I came into the main body of the airport, searching for my father or for someone who had come to meet me. I waited for a while then went to look outside.

Almost immediately a young man came up to me. 'Cab, Miss?'

Before I could reply he was lifting up my luggage from the airport trolley. Almost immediately a broad-shouldered, good-looking, young black man was by my side. He was wearing plain clothes but showed a badge. As soon as it was shown the cab driver dropped my bags and made a run for it.

'Lot of illegal drivers about, Miss. Get in a licensed cab or nothing!'

I was about to explain that I'd thought I was being met when a metallic silver stretch limo glided into the pick-up area by us. A uniformed Vietnamese chauffeur jumped from the driving seat.

'Miss Kelsey?'

'Yes! How on earth did you know?'

He smiled. 'Oh, Miss, one has only to look at Mr Anderson.'

The cop smiled. 'Does all that make sense to you, Miss?'

'Yes! Yes, thank you, it does. And I'll remember what you said about licensed cabs.'

His eyes raked the silver limo. 'Don't let it give you a headache, sister!'

I had forgotten how heavy the air was with gasoline fumes until coming out of the air-conditioned airport. To step from that stinking, oppressive atmosphere into the air-conditioning of the limo was an enormous relief.

We drove in silence for a while as the chauffeur guided the sumptuous car through the airport traffic. When we were on Route 405 heading towards Beverly Hills and then Bel Air he touched the electric switch that wound down the window that separated us.

'There's a cocktail cabinet in front of you if you require anything, Miss Kelsey. Also splits of champagne on ice.'

'Any mineral water? I'm sorry, I don't know your name?'

'Kim Chow, Miss.' He smiled. 'Any mineral water? This is Hollywood, Miss! We've got ten different types, all on ice!'

As we drew nearer the city the traffic on the freeway became heavier and heavier. But why should I care? I relaxed on the leather upholstery, sipped an Evian water and listened to Britten's 'Courtly Dances from Gloriana' played on quadrophonic sound.

At last we turned on to Carolwood Drive, north of Sunset. The limo stopped for a moment outside huge security gates. The chauffeur identified himself on the mobile car phone and the gates slipped quietly open.

The window slid down between us again. 'A lot of nutty fans, Miss. Can't be too careful.'

Gardeners were at work watering the well-tended lawns and flowerbeds as we drove up the gravel drive where it seemed not one weed dared to grow. Yes, I thought ironically, if Fran had accepted, my father could well have taken care of us.

The limo stopped in front of some impressive stone steps leading to a massive mock-Tudor door. The house, I guessed, had been built sometime in the twenties and was a Tinseltown version of something resembling Kelsey Hall. Except that there was too much of everything. Too many exterior beams, too many leaded windows, too many gables. At some point an owner without a sense of humour had added a turret! Well, I was fortunate enough to have the real thing but I imagined that this Bel Air estate was worth many millions more than my inheritance.

The chauffeur hurried around and opened the door for me.

'I'll bring your luggage in, Miss.'

'Thank you.'

As if by magic, but of course the call from the chauffeur would have alerted the house, the front door was being opened by a uniformed Mexican houseman.

I hurried up the steps.

'Mrs Anderson will receive you in the blue drawing room, Miss Kelsey. Follow me. Your maid will unpack your luggage.'

I followed the houseman across an entrance hall that could only be described as baronial. I wondered what this household would make of Mrs Jessop and Margaret Garner and, most especially, Celeste!

The room the houseman ushered me into seemed to dwarf the tiny, exquisitely pretty woman who rose to meet me. Although she wore very high heels my father's wife barely reached my shoulder as she came and took me by the hands.

'My dear Catherine, at last. Welcome!'

'It's very good of you to invite me into your home . . . in the circumstances.'

'Oh, nonsense! I've wanted to meet you nearly as much as Greg has. By the way, he won't be long, he just phoned from his car. Another meeting at the studio. He was so upset he wasn't here to greet you.

Now, please sit down. What shall I ring for? Tea? A jug of martinis?'

I sat down on a sofa so big and so deeply upholstered that I thought it might swallow me.

'Can I be boringly British and say tea?'

She pressed a bell by the ornately carved fireplace. She might well have been, as Greg had told me, in her sixties, but you would never for a moment have thought it. Her hair was a soft blonde and arranged in a sophisticated but flattering style. Her face was unlined and expertly made up. How much this owed to natural beauty or to a deep pocket book didn't seem to matter. The whole effect was charming and very feminine. Once again I wished I'd inherited my mother's looks. Or, perhaps more practically, had had time for Cherry to design me a summer wardrobe to bring out here. Instead I was wearing my well-washed Liberty print.

A few minutes later Mrs Anderson was pouring tea from a beautiful Wedgwood pot. Was it to match the blue drawing room? I wondered. And how many other drawing rooms were there?

The blue drawing room had been impeccably styled. The walls had been papered with a Chinese-style wallpaper, blue figures on a white background. The curtains were white but lined with a fabric to match the paper and then draped back softly over heavy brass curtain furnishings. There were delicate watercolours hanging on the walls, and over the mantelpiece what I thought might be an early Edward Seago.

'You have a beautiful drawing room,' I said as she handed me a cup of tea.

'Oh, I'm so glad you like it. I chose all the furnishings myself.'

'Am I right in thinking that that's a Seago?' I indicated the painting.

'Yes! Greg bought it when he was filming in East Anglia.' She smiled wryly at me. 'A little over thirty years ago.'

I felt myself blushing and cursed myself for it. She wasn't being unkind, just facing facts. Suddenly, even though I'd longed all my life to know my father, I wanted to be back in the gatehouse, reading one of my grandfather's books with Cat curled up on my lap.

I wait for you.

I had been very fortunate about the care of Cat. Mrs Jessop's husband Reg had just retired and they were quite happy to move into the Hall as caretakers whilst I was on holiday.

'Don't worry your head about a thing,' Mrs Jessop had said. 'That animal may steal the odd bit of best saddle of venison, but I like cats. He won't want for a thing or come to any harm, I promise you, Miss.'

After that all there was to do was to drive into Baildon with Brett and sign the papers giving him my proxy votes. He'd asked me to have lunch with him after the appointment with Mr Fortescue but I'd replied that I had too much to do preparing for my trip.

We drove back to Somerton in virtual silence. When he stopped the car in the courtyard he reached out and lightly touched my arm.

'We should talk, Catherine.'

'What is there to talk about? I'm a lousy lay, that's all! Sorry I ruined your evening,' I added, and then quickly got out of the car and practically ran into the Hall.

I had nearly finished my second cup of tea when I heard doors slamming and dogs barking. The door to the drawing room was thrown open and my father entered, followed by two delighted, prancing Great Danes.

The man's personality filled the room. He crossed to me and hugged me to him. 'You finally came to me, Catherine! You're finally here!'

It seemed to me wondrous that my father couldn't get enough of my company. We walked his dogs across the estate together, we swam together, and he started to teach me to ride.

At the weekend we drove to Malibu to Greg and Raine's beach house. I'd found it difficult at first to use Raine's Christian name but she made me so welcome that after she asked me a couple of times to stop calling her Mrs Anderson, I felt it would be rude to deny her her request.

Even when Fran had had money we had never lived like this. I had money, of course, an enormous amount of money, but it had never occurred to me to live this grandly. It had occurred to Jonas and Annabel, of course. Fortunately for me, but not for them, my grandfather's will had put paid to that ambition. If I live to have children, a small voice in my head reminded me.

At the end of the first fortnight, my father and Raine threw a black tie party.

As I dressed for it, I thought that, quite frankly, I looked less than my best. Raine had taken me shopping on Rodeo Drive. We'd ended up with a chic little dress that I really didn't like but that she had urged me to buy. It was the kind of neat, understated outfit that she looked terrific in but as I looked in the mirror I thought it emphasized my broad shoulders and my height. At least I had the Kelsey pearls to wear with it.

I put on the thinly strapped high-heeled sandals which again Raine had urged me to buy, then discarded them for low-heeled pumps. It was one thing to look uncomfortable but I was damned if I was going to actually *feel* uncomfortable, tottering around on thin heels for a long evening.

A huge reception room ran along the back of the house with french windows which opened out on to a paved terrace leading to the lawns and beyond that the hard tennis courts, poolhouse and pool.

The reception room had been dressed with bank after bank of flower arrangements and the terrace was lit by hundreds of small lights strung across from the house to the pergola. For the past four days the house had been humming with caterers, florists and Raine's secretary, dashing about with lists of who had accepted and who hadn't. It seemed that very few people in Hollywood turned down an invitation to an Anderson party unless they were genuinely out of town.

The party was ostensibly to announce the launch of Greg's production company and his three-picture deal with Allied though he'd put his arm around my shoulders and whispered, 'But it's really to let the town know what a beautiful daughter I have. I'll simply introduce you as Catherine Kelsey but everyone will know!'

As I entered the reception room Greg and Raine were already welcoming a stream of guests. Greg excused himself and came over to me. 'You look lovely, Catherine.'

'Thanks. Raine helped me choose the dress.'

She was wearing a little dove grey dress by the same designer and looked gorgeous. She'd shown me such kindness that I'd found it impossible to say, 'Look, you have impeccable taste when it comes to dressing yourself but this looks awful on me!' Anyway, what the hell, I wasn't here to audition for a part in the movies!

Greg beckoned to a tall, good-looking young man in a white tuxedo. 'Come and meet Catherine Kelsey, Sammy. You may not believe it of one so young, Catherine, but this is one of the toughest, hottest agents in Tinseltown. I'm also happy to say he's *my* agent. Sammy, look after Catherine, will you? While I get back on that damned line. Why we have to say "Hello" to everyone we've invited, I'll never know!'

Sammy smiled at me. 'Well, hi there! I gather the prodigal daughter returns?'

'We're not exactly announcing it with trumpet and drums! It would be rather unkind to Raine.'

'Oh, don't let that fragile little girl act fool you, baby! Raine's as tough as old boots. I like her for it. Now, how about a glass of champagne?' He clicked his fingers at a passing Mexican waitress. 'Over here, and make it snappy!'

I decided that I would find it easy to dislike Sammy.

The evening passed pleasantly but I was introduced to so many well-groomed, stunning-looking women that I hated my dress more and more with every hand-shake.

Finally I could bear it no longer and slipped out on to the terrace. I chose a dark corner and sat on the stone balustrade. A cool breeze was coming over the lawns and the night air was heavy with scent.

I suppose I sat there for about fifteen minutes, struggling to find the courage to go back into that elegant room.

Suddenly a beautifully modulated voice spoke from behind me.

'All alone, Fair Maid?'

I started, then remembered the old nursery rhyme.

' "Oh, no, fine, sir!" ' I replied, turning. ' "I've apples to eat. Nuts to crack. A little bow-wow and a pussy cat!" '

'Then why so sad?'

'I'm not sad,' I said defensively. 'Just wanted some cool air.'

'That place –' he indicated the reception room through the open windows '– has enough air conditioning to freeze a ton of peas! So what's the problem? Fallen out with your boyfriend?'

'And what's your interest?' I asked, a little tartly. But this unknown man had sensed my feelings a little too accurately for comfort.

He moved out of the shadows and I recognized him then: Sir Robert Ashley, one time great Shakespearian actor, now a Hollywood actor. Very successful, but I'd always thought he'd thrown away a great career for a lot of money and a swimming pool.

He paused for a moment, then smiled at me. His face

showed a liking for alcohol but his eyes were beautiful, brown and expressive, and when he smiled his whole face smiled with his eyes.

'I knew your mother. She was a wicked little thing but I loved her! Oh, not literally. We never went to bed unfortunately. But I loved her company. Her wit. I was very sad when I read that she'd died. And, on a lighter note, I hate to see a lovely girl looking sad!'

'Lovely girl?' I actually laughed at him.

'Well, not in that dress! Who on earth chose it for you? The Wicked Witch of the North?'

I laughed again. 'Not quite! Actually it was someone who's been very kind to me. I didn't like to hurt her feelings!'

'She has no feelings, dearest!'

He took my hand and stepped back, holding me at arm's length. 'Hmm! Ralph Lauren would look good on you. Something dramatic. You could carry it off.'

I immediately thought of the green velvet ball gown that Cherry had designed for me.

'You haven't a clue about make up.'

'Thank you!'

'Surely Fran taught you something about that?'

'No. It somehow never came up.'

'Astonishing! With those big, gorgeous eyes you need shader and just a little liner. Then some blusher to show those cheek bones up. And your hair . . . Have you never heard of highlights? Or has that never come up either? You've got lovely hair but no one should be mousy nowadays. Never mind, we'll see to all that. Have you got money?' I nodded.

'Good, because I've got style!' He handed me a card.

'Call me tomorrow and we'll have lunch. Now come on, Cinderella.' He offered me his arm. 'Back to the ball!'

As we stepped back into the noise and glamour of the party, I whispered to him, 'I don't understand why you would do that for me?'

'Oh,' he replied airily, 'I love good-looking women. Fran was a lovely friend. And . . . I love causing trouble!'

I saw that he was glancing across the room at Raine.

I spent the rest of the evening with Sir Robert. I could see how he and Fran would have got on. He was very theatrical, almost camp, but I was sure he wasn't gay. He had a fund of stories, all of which he told well and which always made me laugh.

'A huge phallic symbol taking up the whole of the National's stage . . . Coral turned to Johnny Gielgud and said: "No one we know, dear!" '

'My dear, I went to see Sondheim's *Sweeny Todd*. I took one look at that set . . . it looked like a condemned building site . . . darling, I left even before the overture! It was a wonderful excuse to go to Sardi's and get drunk!'

I went to bed feeling happier than I would ever have thought possible at the start of the party.

I put Sir Robert's card on my dressing table and knew without doubt that I would call him in the morning. I rather liked the idea of being turned from a pumpkin into a glittering glass coach!

I awoke in the early hours of the morning, shivering slightly. I got up and turned down the controls of the air conditioning. I could see through a chink in the curtains that it was a beautiful moonlit night. I moved to the windows and opened them and walked out on to my bedroom's balcony.

Almost immediately I could hear angry voices.

'Don't be so dammed ridiculous!' my father was shouting. I heard the sound of something smashing, then Raine's raised voice. She sounded drunk.

'Ridiculous? Do you think I can't see through you? We've no children! Tonight you've shown the world that that's not *your* fault. It'll be in every scandal sheet in town tomorrow! Wonderful publicity for the new deal with Allied, eh? Even if your precious daughter is built like a broomstick and plain as a pikestaff!'

I turned into my bedroom and closed the french windows. I didn't want to hear any more, it was too painful. Perhaps after all Raine had chosen that dress out of malice?

Well, with Sir Robert's help, I'd damned well show her!

CHAPTER
SIXTEEN

THE CAT

'Touch not the cat'

– Sir Walter Scott

JESSLYN: 1667

'Dearer was the mother for the child'
— Samuel Taylor Coleridge

I had made conditions before I accepted Sir Thomas's proposal of marriage. Moll was to live with us as my dear friend and not a servant. She was to be paid an allowance that would continue for the rest of her life.

I knew that Thomas loved his son Luke, but I never wanted to see him again. I therefore suggested that he leave the Hall and meet with his father only by arrangement so that I need not be there when he called. I still thought of him with hatred but would not deny father and son's right to be together.

I told Thomas the truth: that Lucinda was his grandchild. But to the world she was the daughter of my late husband. Fortunately she was small for her age and so could easily pass for a year younger than she actually was. Harriet saw to it, through her devoted maid, that the village learned that the child I was carrying when I had been driven from Somerton had subsequently died. Thomas readily agreed to these conditions. He was madly in love with me and, to my surprise, was a caring, kindly husband. Mainly because I gave him what he wanted most in the world: a legitimate son.

Call it a woman's foolishness but as I held my baby in my arms I was instantly reminded of my father. I asked

Thomas if we could call him Edward. He kissed my brow, still damp from the rigours of my labour.

'My dearest wife, choose any name. Choose any gift for yourself, and for Moll who has helped you through these long hours.' He picked up his baby son with touching pride. 'For you have given me the greatest gift of all . . . the name of Kelsey will continue. Rest now, my precious.'

He was not a demonstrative man but there were tears in his eyes. 'Thank you, Jesslyn.'

Moll, fussing and clucking like a mother hen, took my baby from his father and ushered him from the bedchamber. After I'd fed him, she laid him gently in the cradle by the side of the bed.

'I'm going to give you some poppy syrup, my sweet. For once a man is right. And, as Sir Thomas said, you need a good rest.'

I drank down the heavy syrup, the honey blended into it not quite able to mask its bitter taste.

I smiled at Moll. 'You know, you said once I wasn't destined to spend my life having babies and tending to the stillroom. Well, I've just had my first son and we made this syrup last summer in our own stillroom!'

'Well, life has a funny way of not heeding what I say! Sleep now, my dear. You need to be strong to feed that lusty young son of yours.'

'Get some sleep yourself, Moll. You must be very tired.'

'I'll rest a while on the truckle bed in the dressing chamber. Call if you need me.'

I did need her but could not call out. Sometime in the early hours of the morning I woke to hear a floorboard creak. I was still too drugged by the syrup to focus my mind. Perhaps it was Moll or even Thomas coming to peek at the baby?

Is there such a thing as a sixth sense? I think so. Because I suddenly knew that whoever was in the room wished to harm me. To harm my baby. Still I was unable to cry out. I know not whether it was the effect of the drug or whether I was made dumb by terror.

The heavy curtains were drawn but a little moonlight had crept into the room. Or was it the dawn? I heard the creeping footsteps nearing the bed. And then I saw it: a pillow was held before the person moving with such stealth. I was going to be suffocated. I had to find the strength to cry out. Because after I died, so would my baby. There was only one person who would hate me and my child, the legitimate heir, enough to take our lives. Luke!

He was nearly at the bed now. I saw his face. It was a mask of hatred. At that moment Pitch sprang. I hadn't even known he was in my bedchamber. The little black cat looked terrifying. His hair was raised, his ears were back, his eyes large, his mouth drawn back across angry fangs. His unsheathed claws scratched at Luke's eyes. His teeth were in his face. Pitch was hissing, growling.

Luke dropped the pillow and shouted in pain. His hands were clawing at the demented cat. At last, I screamed.

Within seconds the room was in turmoil. Moll came running in as did Thomas.

'Jesslyn! What is it?'

Both Moll and Thomas stopped and stared at Luke in astonishment. Moll quickly lit a candle. Luke had his hands to his face. Blood from the wounds Pitch had inflicted was running through his fingers.

'Moll! Moll!' I cried. 'See to the baby! He was going to kill us!'

At that moment, I suppose indignant about all the noise, Edward started to cry. Moll lifted him gently in her arms.

'There, little one. You're safe with old Moll.'

Luke pointed a finger at me. 'She's a witch! She should be hanged as one. Look what her cat has done. He's her familiar.'

'Don't be ridiculous!' Thomas shouted at him. 'What the hell are you doing here?'

'Before she came, this used to be my home!'

'Thomas, he was holding a pillow. He was going to suffocate me . . . me and the baby. Pitch saved us.'

'You bitch! You've taken everything from me!'

Luke lunged at the bed, his hands towards my throat. Thomas knocked him to the ground with one blow.

'Get out of my sight! Get out of Somerton. Out of the county or you'll swing! Do I make myself clear?'

Luke started to cry, to plead, to grovel. All those years ago I'd somehow felt pity for him. But now he had tried to harm my child, I felt only disgust.

Thomas had flung open the bedchamber door and was calling for his servants. Within moments two partly dressed, sleepy-looking footmen and the steward came running.

'Escort my . . .' He stopped himself from saying 'son'. 'Escort this man from my property. He is never to be allowed near me or my family again.'

Luke struggled as the two burly footmen grabbed his

arms and started to drag him from the room.

'Bitch! Bitch! Don't think I won't repay you in the end!'

He was still shouting as they pulled him down the stairs. I put my hands over my ears to drown out his cries.

I had hoped that was the last I would ever hear of Luke. But the next morning I was lying on a day couch by the window, Edward sleeping by my side, Pitch at my feet. Through the gatehouse and into the courtyard came a sad procession. Four farm labourers were carrying a gate on which was stretched Luke's body. Or perhaps he was just injured? But from the way his neck was twisted, I knew that could not be true.

After a couple of minutes Moll bustled in.

'Well, nothing to fear from that one any more!' she said briskly.

A stray . . . the kind he liked to torture as a boy . . . ran across his path. Horses are easily frightened. Had he lived, you would never have been safe, Jesslyn.

'Poor Thomas. In spite of everything, he loved him. Do they know what happened?'

Moll shook her head. 'Just found him on the road with his neck broken, his horse grazing nearby. Something must've spooked it. Good riddance! Don't you worry your pretty head about it. You've your milk to think of. I've told the same to Sir Thomas. Nothing must upset my Lady, I said.'

Moll's expression was so fierce that, in spite of Luke's death, I laughed out loud. I held out my hand to her.

'It was a lucky day for me when I sought refuge in that barn.'

I watched my son grow and was in many ways happy. Sometimes a whole day would pass when I didn't think about Guy. When Harry had returned to London – there was no way we could persuade him to live in the country – he had taken letters for me to Guy and to Thomas Killigrew.

I dared do no more than write formally to Guy to inform him that his cousin Richard had died and that, for the time being, I was staying with my dear friend Harriet at her house, Knight's Croft, in Somerton Magna.

To Killigrew I wrote telling of Richard's death and asking him to visit the vicar of St Paul's, Covent Garden to locate Richard's grave. I expressed a hope that the playhouses of both the King and the Duke's company would re-open soon and asked that, as soon as he was in funds, he would use some of the money owing to Richard to mark suitably a great actor's grave. I also asked that he would gradually discharge Richard's debts.

I had been sad to see Harry ride away on Old Nick. I'd insisted that he accept the horse as a gift and asked where I could send any back wages when I had some money.

'Lord love you, Mistress! The bleeding 'orse is plenty. I've got a bit put by and there's no way 'Arry Buckett's going to starve in London town!'

'Harry,' I'd said anxiously, 'you won't . . . you're not going to . . .'

'Go back to me old ways? Not bloody likely! You won't see me dancing on the end of a rope at Tyburn! No, it's a new life for yours truly. And a new love.'

'Harry! Who?

'Well,' he said reluctantly. 'Don't tell Moll. I'll get a scribe to write and break the news gentle like. See, I've taken Moll over to 'er sister's tavern a few times – and we kind of clicked, know what I mean?' He winked.

'But she's . . .' I started. Then stopped myself.

'Fifteen years older than me? True! But who's to know when the candle's blown out? She needs a man. About the inn and in 'er bed. I . . . well . . . it's a funny thing, Mistress, I need '*er*! Rum old go, in'it? But there we are.'

'Harry! Dear Harry! I wish you every happiness, and my thanks for everything you've done in caring for me.'

He blew his nose on a none too clean handkerchief. 'I'd do anything for you, Mistress. As I would've for the Guvnor, God bless him!' Then he grinned. 'Anything except live in the bleeding country, that is!'

Three months later a carter brought a letter from Guy. He too recognized the need for formality. His letter simply offered his condolences on the death of my husband and his kinsman, Richard. It informed me that Marie-Louise had died in childbirth and that her son had been stillborn. He had recently married the Duke of Buckhurst's daughter. The Duke's lands adjoined his and the families were old friends.

The country had been decimated by the Plague. I was to discover later that there had been over one hundred thousand deaths in London alone. There had been no way for family, friends or even lovers to communicate. But a small voice inside me said that Guy had not sought me out. I had written to him. Now he had married again, and at the time I was about to re-marry. In my heart I felt that with a love such as ours, he should have come to find me.

If life was a little dull after London and the theatre, at least Moll, Lucinda and I had a roof over our heads. I was not in love with my husband but grew fond of him. And, the greatest gift of all, I had Edward who daily grew more and more like his grandfather.

Just before the King's Restoration, Thomas had established a glassworks. It wasn't a rich man's hobby, it was a passion with him. He talked endlessly about the need to establish an English tradition of glassmaking. How, for the time being, they had to content themselves with importing Venetian glass marbles and melting them down before re-working them.

How he was trying to find English craftsmen he could have taught by the master glass-blowers he'd brought in from Normandy.

In pride of place in the Great Parlour was an exquisite glass goblet blown and engraved to commemorate the King's Restoration. Thomas had shown it me with something akin to love for its workmanship.

'Hold it, Jesslyn! This was blown by our master glass-blower, Jean-Pierre Marchant. If I had even one more man like him, I would conquer England's trade. Feel it! Hold it! Feel the weight. Feel how perfectly balanced it is. Look at the intricate engraving.'

I took the goblet in my hand and for a brief moment the world spun. I had a sense of timelessness. Almost of eternity.

You have reached Catherine.

'Jesslyn! What is the matter, my dear? You look so pale! Come.' Thomas took the glass from my hands. 'Come sit down. Rest.'

It was at that moment that was I sure I was pregnant with Edward.

I did not meet Jean-Pierre until my son was a little over a year old. Lucinda was ten then and Thomas had been teaching her to ride from the moment we had come to the Hall. For a little girl she was a superb horsewoman and Thomas took such pride in her. In many ways her free, undaunted spirit reflected all the good that could have been in Luke if his nature hadn't been twisted by the knowledge he was a bastard.

They rode for long hours together and I had taken to walking over to see Harriet at Knight's Croft for a few hours in the afternoon.

I was surprised to be told that she was visiting Gifford's. I had found it amusing, not upsetting, that the cottage we had rented was now called after my father. We had been such outcasts when we had lived there! Harriet had left word asking me to join her.

I might have stepped back in time when Jean-Pierre Marchant showed me into the cottage. Harriet was seated on a settle by the hearth, a number of books by her side. By the high-backed chair that had been my father's was a low oak table upon which rested a clay pipe and a goblet of Canary. But what totally astonished me was the fact that Pitch was curled up on the rag rug placed before the hearth, for all the world as if this was his home. I remembered and regretted the passing of Ra.

'Lady Kelsey.' Jean-Pierre's English was virtually perfect. 'Welcome! The furnaces have been shut down so that new kilns can be installed. I therefore asked my old friend to join me for a glass of wine and an argument.' He smiled across at Harriet. 'Will you be seated, my Lady?'

'Thank you. And, please . . . not my Lady. My name is Jesslyn.'

'I'm honoured. Will you join us in taking wine?'

'Thank you. We haven't met before but I've seen your work. It's utterly beautiful.'

'Always I strive for the next piece to be better. I have to believe that, you see. It is the difficult nature of the artist.' He handed me wine in a glass that I knew from its beauty he must have blown.

'Thank you. By the way, I apologize for my cat! He should have better manners than to ask himself into your home uninvited.'

'Uninvited but most welcome. I had a cat at home in Normandy when I was a boy.' He bent down and stroked Pitch. 'I loved her very much. One should always be flattered when a cat seeks one's company.'

'Oh, don't be so mystical,' Harriet chided. 'One should always be flattered when a cat turns up for the fish I know you buy for him!'

'Touché!' Jean-Pierre bowed to me. 'Lady Kelsey . . . Jesslyn . . . forgive me. I am a cat thief.'

The following hour flew as I listened to Harriet and Jean-Pierre argue, make up, laugh then argue again. Their subjects were wide-ranging, from the poems of Milton to the Divine Right of Kings.

I sat happily, as I had with Harriet and my father and Ra, enjoying their wit, knowing I could not really contribute but still feeling a part of things.

I pulled myself away reluctantly. I realized after many years with Richard, how much I missed the stimulation of good conversation. Unless he was talking about glass, Thomas's main interests were horses and hounds. But now I wanted to be at home when Lucinda returned from her ride. She had shown no jealousy of her baby brother, indeed loved him, but I never wanted her to feel that she had been displaced by his arrival.

Jean-Pierre saw me to the cottage door. 'I would be greatly honoured if you would join Harriet and me here when you are free from your duties with your children and your great house. You have a sharp wit, my Lady, and great beauty. Both things are very rare in Somerton,' he added with a smile.

And occasionally I did join them. It was an escape from domesticity. From the kind of life that Moll had predicted I would never have. Though now I was deeply grateful for that life. Not many men would have taken on a widow without a dowry, with a daughter and dependent friend. I suppose Moll could have gone, like Harry, to her sister, but we had become so close the thought of being parted was unbearable.

My other escape was to the gatehouse. I spent long hours there with Pitch and Edward, who was growing into a studious little boy. He not only resembled my gentle father in temperament but grew to look like him also.

I would sit on the window seat, sometimes looking out over the estuary, sometimes reading, Pitch by my side. Then I would glance across at Edward, whose head would be low over his books, and my heart would lurch at the likeness.

I'd had a library table and chair brought from the Hall for him. He could study his books in peace here. Already the village priest was tutoring him and was amazed that such a small boy thirsted so much for scholarship.

This was the only cause of dissent in my life with Thomas. He wanted a son who would be fearless over hurdles in the way that Lucinda was. He wanted a son who enjoyed killing animals for sport. In short, he wanted a son like himself. He was bewildered by the boy's desire for scholarship.

'But, Thomas,' I'd protested. 'Look how you love the glassworks. Look at the knowledge you have. How you are always striving to learn more. He's simply like you!'

'Yes, I am dedicated to the glassworks. But I am also a country gentleman. I expect a son who does not pale and hold back tears when the hounds are at a fox. Good God, Lucinda is more of a man than Edward!'

'He's only a little boy, Thomas. He's only six.'

'When I was six I had nearly as good a seat on a horse as I do now. Yes, yes, that is an exaggeration. But I didn't spend my time mooning over Plato and Aristotle and Shakespeare in a room removed from the Hall. I want it to stop, Jesslyn. That is an order!'

I was furious. 'An order? An order, sir? I am not one of your country mice, at the beck and call of their husband.'

'Then, by God, Lady Kelsey, you had better learn to be.'

'Never! And if you had spent a little more time at your studies there might be a little more wit, a little more levity, in this household! If it weren't for your care of the glassworks, I would think you as uncouth as your son Luke!'

It was a cruel thing, said only in the heat of the moment, but I was deeply shocked when Thomas struck me across the face.

'Keep a civil tongue in your head, madam! It's bad enough that the whole county knows I took a London actress as my wife. You will never defy me again! Do you understand?'

I simply turned my back on him and left the room. But, as I sat in my refuge, the gatehouse, Pitch clasped to me, I knew I was trapped. Thomas would never let me take my son away. I had no money and needed protection for Lucinda and Moll.

As a woman, I had virtually no rights under the law. As a wife, I had even fewer. Tears rolled down my face and on to Pitch's black fur.

The following days passed in misery for me. Moll looked askance at my bruised cheek but I told her I had tripped and hurt my face. I don't think she believed me but she too was a realist.

At night I submitted to Thomas's unsubtle love making. He eased his desire then rolled off me with a grunt. In the past I had tried to be loving towards him out of gratitude. Now I felt like stone when he touched me. The chilling thing was that he seemed not to notice the difference in my behaviour. I tried not to remember the days, the nights, with Guy.

I started to wonder how long I could endure this. But always the answer came back: For as long as you have to. I think, at that time, it was only the occasional meeting with Harriet and Jean-Pierre, and the time I spent in the gatehouse with Edward and Pitch, that kept me sane.

The air was frosty and crisp for the first meet of the season. I did not ride to hounds but was ready to offer hospitality to those who did.

The courtyard was full of excited dogs. Lucinda, looking quite exquisite, was already mounted. Various neighbours were beginning to ride their horses into the courtyard. Thomas had not yet mounted and a groom held the head of his lively stallion.

He crossed to me. 'Where's Edward?'

'Edward? I don't know. Was he to ride with you today?'

'Of course he's to ride with us. I told him yesterday that he's going to be blooded.'

Oh, God, I thought. My gentle, animal-loving son to have to watch a fox being torn to pieces, then have its bloody brush smeared across his face.

'Where is he?' Thomas demanded.

'Truly, Thomas, I don't know. I'll ask Moll. It's so early, I thought to let him sleep. I'd no idea you wanted him to ride out with you today.' Play for time. Play for time. The Hunt might well ride out without him. 'I'll try to find him.'

'He's in the gatehouse, isn't he? With his damned books!' He struck his crop against his riding boots. 'I'll teach him to defy me!' He started to walk across the courtyard towards the gatehouse. I caught his arm.

'Please! Please, Thomas, I don't know where he is. But if he's with his books, it's because he loves studying.' I was nearly hysterical. 'Don't hurt him, Thomas. Don't hurt him. He's only a little boy!'

But my son had challenged some strange, ridiculous masculine pride in Thomas. He could love a brutish son like Luke more easily than he could a gentle soul like Edward.

He brushed me aside and I fell, crying out as the gravel in the courtyard broke my skin. Thomas strode on towards the gatehouse. I had started to rise when he suddenly stopped. He let out a terrible cry and clutched at his throat.

I pulled myself to my feet and ran towards him as he fell like one already dead. Except that he was not dead. His face was livid, his body rigid, but his hands clutched still at his throat. I knelt by him and put my arms around him. He was clearly in the threws of some kind of stroke.

'Take it away, Jesslyn! Please! Please! Take it away.'

By now he was literally clawing at his throat. I loosened his riding stock. As I did so he let out a terrible scream which chilled my blood. Servants and guests were running towards us.

'For Christ's sake, take it away!' he screamed.

'Thomas, help is coming! There's nothing there! Nothing there!'

His eyes started to glaze over. But still his hands clawed at his throat. His voice was now a whisper.

'Take . . . away . . . the . . . cat.'

Who touches you touches me, Jesslyn.

CHAPTER
SEVENTEEN

THE CAT

'Follow a shadow'

— *Ben Jonson*

CATHERINE: 1992

'Full of tumultuous life and great repose'
                    – Coventry Patmore

We met the next day at noon at the Beverly Hills Hotel. Sir Robert was waiting for me on the terrace and was already on to his second or third very dry martini.

In spite of overhearing an argument that distressed me deeply, I awoke refreshed and ready to do battle: more with myself than anyone else. I'd dressed simply in my Liberty print blouse and matching skirt, and the only jewellery I wore was a simple gold chain I'd bought in Baildon. But it was such a relief to feel like myself instead of an unsuitably dressed Raine clone.

Sir Robert rose to his feet the moment that he saw me being led to his table by the maître d'.

'My dear, how good to see you. You look delightful! Thank you, Pierre. Can you send the barman to us?'

Sir Robert pulled out a chair for me and I sat by him to look out over the lush acres of gardens and lawns.

'I thought it would be fun to lunch in the Polo Lounge and watch the world and his wife trying to outdo and outdeal each other! How did you sleep?'

I liked and trusted this man, and obviously so had my mother. She was a bad judge of lovers but a good judge of friends. I decided to confide in him.

'Well, Sir Robert . . .'

'Oh, for God's sake, child. Everyone calls me Bob.'

I smiled. 'Very well, Bob. I discovered something last night that makes me think you were right and that ghastly dress I was wearing *was* chosen by the Wicked Witch of the North! Well, I suppose, to be fair, if she was really opposed to my coming here and my father insisted, I can see how she would resent me . . .'

We were interrupted by the barman arriving to take an order for pre-lunch drinks.

'Now, what will you have? Don't be Californian and say something non-alcoholic. Ugh! Water! Just think what fish do in it! How about a champagne cocktail? They make a mean one here.'

'Right, thanks, a champagne cocktail it is.'

'A champagne cocktail for the lady and another martini for me, please. Just let the vermouth *glance* at the gin. You know how I like them.'

'Sure do, Sir Robert,' the barman grinned.

Sir Robert turned his brown eyes on me.

'I rather take it from the spring in your step as you walked towards me, that you've thought about what I've said and are taking up the gauntlet?'

'Well, I've always been a little short on confidence but when I heard myself described as a "broomstick" and "plain as a pikestaff", I resolved to end up looking so good she'll seem like one of those dolls people put over their telephone!'

'Good for you! By God, I'm going to enjoy this!'

Two more martinis and one champagne cocktail later we were shown to a very good table in the Polo Lounge. In spite of the martinis, Sir Robert's step was as steady and graceful as someone who had only been sipping Perrier water for the past hour.

As we were seated at the table he must have read my thoughts.

'Practice, dear child! Practice! Don't touch it when I'm working, of course.'

I laughed then. 'That's what Fran always said. It wasn't true!'

'Well, acting isn't for grown ups, is it? Did you know that after the first night of Sir Henry Irving's great Hamlet, on the way home from a standing ovation, his wife said to him, "Are you going to give up this ridiculous way of life, now?" He stopped the carriage, got out and never saw her again! Brilliant!'

His shout of laughter turned the heads of several grey-suited men, but when they saw it was Sir Robert they smiled and waved.

The meal was delicious but I'd never seen so much table hopping, so many embraces. The air was heavy with 'Darling, we must lunch' 'Call me, you hear, feller, call me!' 'Hear you've got a great deal at Paramount! Great, Buddy, great!'

'Delightful, isn't it?' said Sir Robert with malicious pleasure. 'Feeding time at the shark tank! Now, let's make plans. Clothes first, I think, then a trip to an old friend of mine. A top, top make up man! Liz Taylor won't go near a camera until he's done her face.' He smiled. 'Even the most beautiful women in the world need a little help.'

'I still can't get over your taking an interest in me like this! I know you've said you'll enjoy it, but there must be a deeper reason than that?'

Sir Robert sipped at the excellent Chablis we were

drinking with our Goujons of Sole. Then he sighed.

'I'm getting old, child. I've been married three times and every wife took me to the cleaners.' He raised his hands. 'Oh, I'm not saying they didn't have every right to! I'm an impossible bastard to live with sometimes. Now I live – well, if not always alone, in an unmarried state, and intend to keep things that way. With the alimony I pay, I can't afford to go back to the theatre. I'm trapped! Trapped by sunshine, a swimming pool and too much money into lending my prestigious name to crap movies! In the circumstances, one needs diversions. Apart from loving Fran,' he put his hand over mine, 'I suppose you're this month's diversion!'

A limo was waiting for us as we left the Beverly Hills Hotel.

'With compliments of the studio. They want me to play the C. Aubrey Smith part in a remake of a Shirley Temple movie. It's rumoured that some child who made a movie about getting lost at Christmas is to star opposite me. Funny! I always thought it was Jesus who got lost at Christmas!'

We settled into the rear seats and the limo slid away from the hotel, heading towards Rodeo Drive.

'I told my agent,' Sir Robert said reaching for the drinks cabinet, 'that if I was going to suffer such a fate it would take a lot of money, a lot of perks, and a sound sense of humour!'

We shopped for two days. On the second day Sir Robert stopped advising me.

'It's time for you to make your own decisions, Catherine. What the hell? A mistake isn't the end of the world. Be bold! Choose!'

And I did. I'd not only had Sir Robert's guidance, I'd had Cherry's. Sir Robert had been right: I felt good in Ralph Lauren, ridiculous in Ungaro or Dior. I therefore went for designer casual, a sophisticated but slightly preppy look.

Then we drove down to The Gap on Melrose Avenue and I bought some really well-cut jeans. Try wearing jeans with stiletto heels, Raine, I rather maliciously thought. And some simply terrific, loose knit sweaters imported from Morocco.

As we got back into the studio limo I said to Sir Robert, 'I'm having the greatest time!'

'So am I, dear child! So am I! Now, where shall we lunch – Grand at L'Ermitage or steak and eggs at The Pantry?'

'Oh, Bob, I feel so good. But I don't want to be grand! Isn't there anywhere we can go where . . . I don't know . . . there's just, well, people?'

Half an hour later we were sitting at a table outside the Sidewalk Cafe in Venice Beach. We ate outsized hamburgers with crisp french fries.

The Pacific surf rolled in as we watched the sideshow that was Venice.

Young and not so young people whizzed by on skate-boards to which had been attached sails. There were jugglers, Elvis Presley impersonators, unicyclists and, of course, the weightlifters after whom Muscle Beach was named.

'Now, child, I have a plan. I want you to leave all your new clothes at my house. It's at Malibu, not far from Greg's place, but mine isn't a resort house, it's where I live. I'm giving a party on Saturday. Nothing grand but Greg and Raine are coming. We'll see to your hair and make up in the morning. You, young one,' he added sternly, 'will choose what you are to wear. You're hardly a "deb" but this will be the launch of the new Catherine. I can't wait to see Raine's face!'

'You really don't like her, do you?'

'No, I suppose I don't! I admire powerful women who want to make it to the top. Not many in this industry do but we must never forget Dorothy Parker, Anita Loos, Peggy Webster. But I think I despise strong women who cloak their ambition, who smile sweetly and pretend that they're doing it all for their husband.' He smiled. 'Perhaps I'm becoming a feminist in my old age!'

Sir Robert drove me back to the Anderson estate. Greg was very tied up with his business affairs, and beyond politely enquiring if I was having a good time, Raine was busy with her charities and her lunches.

'I don't know if you would enjoy this but a group of us get together on a Thursday evening to . . . what shall I say? Argue? Debate? Anyway, it's good-natured and there's wine and music. I'd be so pleased if you'd join us. I'd send the car,' Sir Robert offered.

'I'd like that very much but Greg has lent me a convertible. I can drive.'

'California isn't all it seems, dear child. I'd rather you didn't drive by yourself at night. All right?'

I reached across and touched his face. 'You pretend to be a bear but you're an old dear really, aren't you?'

'Shhh! If my agent discovers that, my fees will be halved! Good night.' He blew me a kiss. ' "Our revels now are ended." '

Sir Robert's Thursday evening reminded me of Marcus's evenings in his studio. Very informal, a good mix of people. But the personality of the host and, yes perhaps, his ego, the dominant factor.

The house was one of the oldest on the privately owned Malibu Beach Colony, pleasantly ramshackle and dominated by views of the ocean. There was nothing grand about the decor but the ambience was individual and creative.

There was a huge living area with french windows that opened out on to a wooden terrace made rickety by too much salt air and too little maintenance. White walls, some splendid Mexican tapestries, an apparently haphazard arrangement of comfortable sofas and floor cushions, dhurri rugs on bleached oak flooring. Some good and not so good modern paintings – bought, knowing Bob, I was sure, to encourage the artists. All mixed strangely with Richard Warwick's sword over the Art Deco fireplace. It had been handed down from generation to generation. Warwick was supposed to have carried it when he played Hamlet. Tradition had it that when the holder of the sword recognized a performer greater than he, he passed it on.

A young drama student from U.C.L.A. laughingly told me that when he'd asked Sir Robert who he was going to pass it on to, Bob had laughed and said, 'Sod it, it's mine!'

I had a wonderful evening, the happiest I'd had since coming to California. I was growing to love my father and longed for any moments he could spend with me, but life at the Bel Air mansion was so formal I felt stifled by it.

Nothing could have been in greater contrast than Bob's get together. Once a month, apparently, he gave a seminar for the drama students of U.C.L.A. The whole class was invited. The great thing was that for all his formidable reputation they were not in awe of him. They respected him, yes, but felt secure enough to challenge him in conversation. To confide in him. To be angry with him. But always to sit at his feet. Perhaps, I thought quizzically, he's really the Pied Piper!

But not only students were there. A few musicians who, late into the night, started to extemporize jazz. A famous actress whose last two movies had been panned and was now being healed by Bob's common sense: 'One, two, three! The script, the director, the camera! Get that combination wrong and we've had it!' He kissed her forehead. 'Don't let your agent push you into anything until those ingredients are there. You're too good for them to fuck you up.'

I mentally shook my head, watching him give so much that evening as he had to me. And yet this man had his own demons. He was, to put it baldly, a drunk.

The next morning I felt like a naughty child slipping away from the house, this time driving the car Greg had lent me. I was meeting Bob at a house in Laurel Canyon.

When his limo had driven me home in the early hours of Friday morning, I'd doubted that my host would be able to beat his hangover in time to meet me at 8 am on Saturday as we'd arranged.

But, as I turned into the drive of a mock log cabin

halfway up the canyon, his limo was already parked. The chauffeur grinned and waved at me, then went back to reading his comic book.

There was no reply when I rang the doorbell and so I made my way around to the back of the cabin.

This wasn't nearly so rustic. Part of what I suppose you would call a mountain had been reclaimed and levelled. There was a gazebo, a pool, and a beautifully arranged terrace. There was also a very aggressive-looking Doberman. We eyed each other. I had a nasty feeling he was considering me for breakfast.

Then a cheerful voice called from the gazebo: 'Don't take any notice of him, doll! He's an old pouf . . . just like me!'

As if reassured by these words and thankful not to be required to be a guard dog, the Doberman rolled on its back and put its paws in the air. I tickled his tummy and his tongue lolled happily.

From the gazebo emerged a strange-looking little man, almost a gnome. He was wrapped in an oversized towelling robe and wore a brightly coloured flowered shower cap on his head.

'Can't bear anyone to see me without my rug!' he confided, pointing to the cap. 'You must be Catherine.' He studied me for a moment. 'Oh, yes. You'll do. Come on, Bob's inside brewing up some Buck's Fizz. All that Vitimin C, you know. It's good for you!'

I declined the Buck's Fizz but an hour later was seated in Barney Cabrillo's studio . . . for this was his unlikely name . . . looking into a mirror and watching him expertly cut my hair. Sir Robert was jauntily perched on a stool, a jug of freshly pressed orange juice and a bottle of vintage champagne by his side.

'I'm layering the top, doll. It'll emphasize those gorgeous cheekbones and big, big eyes. But your hair is thick and lush so we'll cut the rest to shoulder-length.' He turned to Sir Robert. 'You're quite wrong about the highlights! Blonde would be desecration with her white skin. No, we're going for a tortoise shell effect.' He now took me into the conversation. 'Differing shades of gold and red highlights. Believe me, kiddo, it'll be sensational.'

And it was! Two hours later, having had strands of my hair twisted up into foil then baked under a dryer then blow dried, I couldn't believe the difference in my appearance.

Bob thrust a glass of champagne into my hand.

'I'm not leading you astray. But from your expression, you need it!'

'Let's not go raving mad,' Barney said. 'I've got the make up to do yet.'

His expert hands ranged over my face: tweezing eyebrows, lightly applying foundation then a little blusher on my cheekbones, two tones of shadow on my eyelids, a lighter one under my newly plucked brows. Then the lightest dusting of a neutral powder and an understated lipstick, and I was finished.

Barney looked into the mirror and smiled.

'Oh, yes! The old queen hasn't lost his touch, has he, Bob?'

'I can't thank you enough! Bob says you do Liz Taylor's make up?'

'Used to, honey. I'm retired now. All I want is my

pool, my dog, and a good glass of plonk on a Saturday night.'

'Which you'll certainly get this Saturday night!' Bob said.

'Not only that, from what I gather. Not only that.' Barney scooped the make up he'd used into a plastic bag and handed it to me.

'Practise! You've seen the difference it can make. So practise!'

I felt very humble about the kindness offered me by these two very disparate men.

'Barney,' I said tentatively, 'I'm astonished by what you've done. Please, what is your fee? I must pay you.'

He snorted loudly and Bob intervened. 'Raine was a not very successful starlet when Barney was starting out. However, where she was successful was in the bed of the Head of the Studio. We won't say which one! One day she didn't like the way Barney had done her hair . . .'

'And so the bitch got me fired!' he interrupted, then lightly dropped a kiss on top of my head. 'This one's on the house, kid!'

I'd told Greg and Raine that I was spending the day with new friends and would meet them at Sir Robert's in the evening.

On the afternoon of the party, whilst Bob slept off breakfast and lunch, I walked by myself along the beach. The wind tousled my newly cut hair but I knew that Barney had styled it so well that wouldn't be a problem. I needed to ask myself whether or not I had really found confidence in myself at last. Not because of some new clothes, a new hairstyle and a lesson in how best to put blusher on my cheeks. But Bob's friendship, although originating from his love for Fran, seemed to me to be the first time I'd stood on my own two feet in a relationship.

When Fran had been alive, I'd been in her shadow. With the Kelseys I was family, friend or foe, depending on their feelings. With Brett . . . Ah, yes! With Brett I had been willing to give, but my cursed shyness had held me back from truly sharing in our love making.

Bob's party was not organized by a smart firm of caterers, it was simply a barbecue on the beach in front of his house, some really good salads and good company.

I'd stood in the guest bedroom for a long time, choosing what I would wear. Then I had it! That morning I'd been wearing the cotton sweater that Cherry had made for me with a design that incorporated several pictures of Cat. It was highly individual and I felt good in it. I added well-cut shorts from The Gap, chunky socks and trainers.

I threw back my head and laughed with sheer pleasure. I'd suddenly realized that I'd gone through some kind of barrier. I no longer wanted to 'show' anyone. I simply wanted to find myself. And I had.

And, although I felt great pleasure when Greg looked at me with admiration, I knew only sadness when I saw Raine's astonished reaction to my new appearance.

To Barney it had been a score to settle. To Sir Robert it had been a 'diversion'. But I felt a little ashamed that I'd wanted to prove something to a woman well over thirty years older than me, who had had to come to terms with her husband's infidelity with my mother.

I couldn't see how I could really build bridges with Raine but neither did I want to hurt her. Then I remembered how she'd had Barney fired simply because she didn't like the way he'd done her hair one day, and wondered how many other people in this town had scores to settle with her? As to hurting her – well, I thought ruefully, Raine could probably chew me up and spit me out and *still* keep a smile on her face and not a lacquered hair out of place!

My father came over to me just as Bob was handing me a glass of champagne.

'So! This is what you two have been plotting.' He bent down and kissed my cheek. 'It seems I have a beautiful daughter.'

'You always have had!' Bob said lightly. 'You just hadn't noticed.'

Greg smiled. 'Well, Svengali was never a role that appealed to me.'

Bob slipped his arm around my waist. 'You miss the point, old chap, Catherine's no Trilby. I didn't invent her – I just took the trouble to give her a little of my time. And, by God, what fun we've had!'

I saw a flash of anger in Greg's eyes as Bob's implied reproof sunk in. This is interesting, I thought. These two men don't really like each other. But they were both good actors, in Bob's case a great actor, and falsehood hidden by charm was their stock in trade.

Grateful as I was to Bob, I sprang to my father's defence. 'Greg's been incredibly busy since I've been here. The deal with Allied seems really big. Greg and his agent have been working on it night and day!'

'Speaking of agents,' he said, looking around, 'I don't see mine here. Isn't Sammy coming?'

'I doubt it,' Bob said smoothly. 'You see, I didn't invite him.'

Greg looked genuinely amazed. 'But he's the hottest agent in this town right now! Why on earth risk offending him? He's bound to know you're giving a party. Sammy knows everything! Why not invite him?'

Bob smiled at my father then said languidly, 'Because he's an arsehole. Excuse me, must mingle. See you later, Catherine.'

Greg looked after Bob, frowning, then turned to me.

'You're not having an affair with him, are you?'

'With Bob?' I replied, absolutely astonished. 'Of course not! Why do you ask that?'

'Don't be fooled by the gentleman actor bit, honey! He's quite a ladies' man . . . and he treats women appallingly.'

'I just don't believe that, Greg. He's too . . . too intrinsically kind.'

Greg shrugged, put his arm around my shoulders.

'Just remember you heard it from your old man first!' His hand squeezed my shoulder affectionately. 'I guess I'm just a jealous devil who doesn't want to have found a daughter only to lose . . . Come on, honey, let's eat steak!'

My father took my hand and started leading me towards the beach where a huge barbecue had been set up.

'No, wait, Greg. Let's ask Raine if she wants to join us.'

Without waiting for his answer, but still holding his hand, I led the way across the room to where Raine stood at the centre of an admiring circle. She turned to us. Her eyes assessed my new appearance but all she said was: 'Catherine – well, well!'

She put out a beautifully manicured hand and touched Greg's arm.

'I was coming to find you, darling. I've the most splitting headache. Sorry to be a party pooper but will you see me home?'

'Surely the chauffeur can drive you?'

'I'm feeling unwell, Greg,' Raine interrupted, tight-lipped. 'In the circumstances I think the very least I can expect from my husband is to take me home. It could be a migraine coming on. It would be rather nice if my beloved paid a little attention to *me* for a change!'

'I'm sorry you're not well, Raine,' I said, trying to pour oil on troubled waters. 'I'm sure Greg will . . .'

'There you are, darling, you have your daughter's permission to take your wife home. Good night, Catherine. Give my apologies to Bob, will you, Greg? I'll wait for you in the car.'

He watched her leave, then sighed. 'I'm sorry, honey. This kind of party isn't really her scene. And she does suffer from the most blindingly awful migraines at times. Shall I send the car back for you?'

Before I could answer Bob, who had just joined us, spoke.

'Sorry Raine had to leave so early, Greg. But don't worry about Catherine, I'll see she gets home safely.

Oh! Don't look so worried. I wouldn't dream of driving
her. My studio has laid on a limo service. Twenty-four
hours a day.'

'Really? What it is to be an Oscar winner, Bob!'

He smiled. 'One thing I've learnt out here, Greg. If
you're going to do crap, make 'em pay! Surely Mr
Sammy Wald lives by that dictum?'

'I don't really know. You see, I never do crap!'

Bob shouted with laughter. 'Game, set and match,
old son! Frankly, when I sit down to write the alimony
cheques, I always reflect that I'd play an organ grind-
er's monkey if they paid me enough money!' He held
out his hand to my father. 'Glad you could come,
Greg.' Then he added sincerely, 'You're a fine actor.
Don't wait too long before you give us your Lear.'

My father kissed me good night and followed Raine
to the car. As Bob had been one of the greatest Lears
of the past two decades, I thought how generous it had
been of him to say that to Greg, and I told him so.

'Well, dear girl, to admire another's talent doesn't
diminish your own! Now, come with me. I know you
haven't eaten yet. Let's get some steaks and sit on the
beach under the stars.'

'How about your other guests?'

'Oh, they can take care of themselves,' he said airily.
'Most of them are awash with champagne and no doubt
a few are slinking off into broom cupboards to snort
coke. Ghastly habit! Imagine getting high on something
you can't taste!'

The steaks were huge and delicious. After we'd
eaten Bob took my hand and we walked down to the
water's edge. He looked up at the sky and softly

quoted, ' "We are all in the gutter, but some of us are looking at the stars." '

'Some gutter!' I said, turning and looking at his Beach Colony house.

'Yes, some gutter,' he replied sadly, almost wistfully. Then his mood changed and he started to dance on the sand, singing from *My Fair Lady*.

' "She did it! She did! We said that she would do it! And she damned well did! . . ." I'm pissed enough to give you some advice, Catherine. Something I rarely do. What you've found, don't lose!'

I smiled. 'That sounds very profound!'

'But you know what I mean?' he said seriously.

'Yes! Yes, I do. And it's thanks to you!'

That famous voice roared out across the ocean.

'Bullshit!'

On Sunday Greg was having lunch with his agent and Raine was entertaining a group of Hollywood wives dedicated to the enhancement of life for underprivileged children.

It was a buffet lunch around the pool and I immediately turned myself into a social pariah by suggesting that the ladies' tennis courts and pools could be opened to the kids of the Los Angeles ghettoes. As I met their horrified stares I was reminded of the Sondheim song, 'Here's to the Ladies Who Lunch'.

Greg's dogs were sleeping on the terrace and I excused myself, saying I felt the need of a little exercise.

I called the two Great Danes who, in spite of the heat, bounded up to me. I fussed them and fondled their silky ears. Then we set off for a walk across Greg and Raine's green acres.

I knew in my heart that the time to return home had come. Greg was engrossed in his work. Raine, quite understandably, didn't really want me around. I longed for Cat. For my Knight's Croft cousins. Funnily enough, for bad weather and . . . Yes, I longed to see Brett again and perhaps . . . I briskly shook my head and quickened my stride. Perhaps nothing!

Brett Fitzgerald was not the marrying kind. But then, a little voice said to me, perhaps you aren't either, Catherine.

The light fades early in California. No twilight. No long still evenings when the smoke from the bonfire rises above a dim but still visible garden.

The dogs and I returned from our long walk, all of us pretty exhausted. But it was clear that the 'Ladies Who Lunch' were not exhausted! They were around the pool now. Cocktails being served. No doubt they were toasting orphans, I thought, pretty unfairly.

I knew I couldn't face joining them and so decided to drive to Bob's place in Malibu and pick up all the clothes I'd bought. In spite of his warnings I didn't really think I'd be set upon by thieves and looked forward to the drive blowing the cobwebs away.

The light had totally faded when I pulled off the freeway and on to the road that led to the Beach Colony. Lights were on as I parked behind Bob's house but the house was in silence. It occurred to me that I'd been very naive, driving out without phoning him first. He'd told me that he didn't always live alone and I'd no idea whether or not he was involved with someone at the moment.

I hesitated, wondering if I should simply drive away? But I was worried that the house was so silent. I walked quietly around to the terrace and looked into the living room. The windows were open and Bob was sprawled on the floor. I ran to him, thinking the worst.

'Bob! Bob! Oh, my God . . . what's happened?'

I reached him and turned him over. His eyelids flickered, and a tired smile came momentarily to his lips.

'The chimes of midnight, Cathy. I . . . I hear them often now.'

'Oh God, Bob! Oh, my God!'

I raced up to the first floor and grabbed a comforter from the first bedroom I came to. Ran downstairs and threw it over him. I started chafing his hands.

'Bob, Bob! Don't die on me! I'll get help!'

He opened those astonishing brown eyes. Then: 'Die on you? Don't be bloody ridiculous! Warwick's sword would pass on to another actor.' His eyelids flickered. 'Must've been something fishy about that last martini.'

He fell into a deep sleep then. I put a cushion behind his head. Tucked the comforter around him. I sat with him for at least an hour to make sure it was only a 'fishy' martini.

Soon his breathing was easy and he was gently snoring. I looked down at him with affection and wondered that such a kind, infinitely understanding man felt such a desperate need to escape. But, perhaps, there lay the answer: understand too much about the world's pain and it is unbearable to live with.

I felt I could leave him for a while although I'd decided to stay the night. I needed sea air, needed to stretch my legs, needed to dissolve the sadness I felt for Bob.

I hadn't really noticed in which direction I was walking, I was so preoccupied by my own thoughts. I was nearing my father's beach house before I actually took in my location. To my surprise, lights were on there. I hurried forward with a sense of joy that we might have a little time together.

I walked from the dark of the deserted beach towards the wooden staircase which led to a raised deck on which the main living area of the house was built.

As I started to climb the staircase I heard an argument in progress. I thought I recognized Sammy Wald's voice.

'For Christ's sake, Greg, how do you think I got the deal at Allied? Your last three movies have been dogs. I promised your production company would bring in funds.'

Then my father's voice: 'And I thought it would! My God, with my reputation . . .'

'Oh, sure, you're Tom Cruise! Don't give me the reputation crap – I gave my *word*! I staked a lot when I said you'd got finance! Do you honestly believe Allied would have done the deal if not?'

'Thanks for the vote of confidence, Sammy!'

I was about to rush up that staircase and tell Sammy Wald to go to hell. Then I heard my father's tone change. It was almost wheedling.

'Come on, Sammy. Let's not fall out. You're new on

the block and so are Allied. They can do with a little class.'

'Only if it comes with money, Big Shot! Mortgage that fancy estate in Bel Air, for Christ's sake!'

I heard someone throw a glass which shattered.

'Do you think I haven't already? There's nothing left to mortgage. This deal meant . . .' Greg's voice nearly broke and my heart went out to him.

'Sammy, put the deal on hold for a week or so. I'm sure I can get to her. The damned girl's sitting on a fortune.'

'Your daughter?'

'Of course, my daughter! I'm hardly talking about my latest screw! She's kind of vulnerable, and if I can make her believe I love her . . .' He laughed. 'I can fake anything.'

My legs gave way beneath me and I sat down on the sand.

To give Sammy Wald his due, he sounded embarrassed.

'She seems a nice enough girl.'

'Of course she is, thank God! How else would I persuade her to invest in Anderson Productions?'

Again I felt the pain of his need. To be a great star whose career was fading but had a chance to be back at the top. His next words killed my feelings for him.

'Her mother was a great lay but I needed a wife like Raine. Someone who could entertain. Stay in the background.'

'Not compete,' Sammy Wald added cynically.

'Well, maybe that. When Fran told me she was pregnant and asked what we were going to do about it,

I nearly laughed in her face. "Get an abortion, doll!" Now the kid's inherited millions. Thank God I didn't get Fran set up in one of those fancy Swiss clinics. Well, to tell you the truth, she refused. Told me in good old Anglo-Saxon English where I could put my cock and my person!'

I felt the tears starting to run down my face. Oh, Fran! You had such guts!

But as I sat on that beach in Malibu with the tide turning, I was at last my own woman. The next day I would buy a ticket to take me home.

I wait, Catherine. Beware.

I had to return to the house in Bel Air to collect a few of my things, but would then return to Bob's beach house for the remaining hours before my flight left.

I checked that he was all right before driving back to collect my belongings from my father's house. He was sleeping peacefully and I stroked his forehead before driving away.

It came as no surprise to me that my father wasn't home as I knew him to be at Malibu. The quiet Mexican who opened the door to me simply nodded a good evening. There was no sign of Raine. No doubt she was exhausted by her good works!

To my surprise there was a flashing light on the telephone in my bedroom, indicating a message. I checked with the staff. A Mr Brett Fitzgerald had called me from the UK urgently. I was to return his call whatever the time of day or night.

I looked at my watch as I dialled the Somerton number. It was three o'clock in the afternoon there. Would he be home?

After five rings the telephone was answered.

'Brett?'

'Catherine, thank God I've got you! We've a crisis on our hands here. Jonas has announced that the glassworks are reducing the lead content by four per cent! Cost saving etc. The bastard!'

'But ever since the end of the seventeenth century we've been known for . . .'

'Yes, yes! I've had argument after argument with him. He obviously timed this for when you were away.' I could hear the distress in his voice; knew how much this man loved glass and what Jonas's down grading of our product would do to him. Suddenly he chuckled. 'If you could've seen his face when I told him I held your proxy votes and was calling an extraordinary general shareholders' meeting . . . Well! Serious as it is, I think it would've made even Cat laugh! The thing is, Catherine, it's in four days' time. Can you get back for it? And if not, how do I vote?

'Don't worry, Brett. I'll be back! In fact, I've a flight booked for tomorrow.'

'Thank God for that! I don't exactly see myself as a power broker.'

'It's a funny thing, Brett, but maybe I do. Goodbye!'

CHAPTER
EIGHTEEN

THE CAT

'For some must watch'
                    – William Shakespeare

JESSLYN: 1675

'To have loved, to have thought, to have done'
                                    – Matthew Arnold

My daughter looked so beautiful. We had come to London to present her to His Majesty a little after her seventeenth birthday.

I'd talked long and hard with Moll about this but could see no path for a young woman except marriage or, God forbid, for Lucinda to become some rich man's mistress. She was not like my dear Harriet, content to live quietly in the country, studying and tending her herbs. She was a vigorous, almost wayward young woman. Moll and I had schooled her a little in housewifery but she was not remotely interested. Well, I could hardly blame her for that. Neither was I. And although she loved riding and was a superb – I feared sometimes reckless – horsewoman, she also loved pretty clothes, and to dance and play upon her lute.

The local young men were attracted to her like moths to a flame but they were so unsophisticated, such country gentlemen, that I couldn't see Lucinda being fulfilled by marriage to any of them.

At the same time I was terrified that, once we were in London and at the Court, she would be sucked into the decadent style of life that I had briefly thrown myself into.

But Moll reassured me. 'She'll have you to chaperone her.' She suddenly chuckled. 'And I've seen how you protect your young. God help any young gallant who tries to lift Lucinda's skirts!'

I hadn't travelled to London since becoming Sir Thomas's wife. I had therefore never seen the new City that had emerged after the destruction of the Great Fire.

Lucinda, Edward, Moll and I had driven through to the east of Covent Garden. Building works were everywhere, but in such a contrast to the old timber-framed houses that had so easily been destroyed.

The new buildings were of stone, the streets much wider, and, under the supervision of the King's surveyor, Christopher Wren, a magnificent new St Paul's was arising from the ashes.

But it wasn't only in the old City that re-building was taking place. New squares and crescents were being built, very much influenced by Inigo Jones' work in Covent Garden.

It was to one of these new squares, Soho Square, that I brought my family and dear friend. The houses were tall and graceful with mews for coach and horses at the rear. My lawyer had arranged the rental, which I thought astronomical. But I was a wealthy woman and wanted to introduce Lucinda to Society in a style befitting her.

The bulk of Thomas's estate had, naturally, gone to Edward. But Lucinda had been well provided for with a handsome dowry. I too received a large legacy which had surprised me. But the main source of my fortune was from my dearest Harriet.

She had died quite suddenly and, it would appear, peacefully in her beloved garden. I had suspected that all was not well with her but, for all our friendship, she was a fiercely independent woman and I respected that. All I could do was to watch and hope.

I was amazed that, apart from some very generous bequests to her servants and a number of books left to Jean-Pierre, her considerable fortune had been left to me. There was also a letter.

My Jesslyn,

I always think of you as that. For yourself and because of the love I felt for your father. Your path has not been easy child. But I have watched you grow from a brave young girl to a thoughtful, caring woman and I have loved you for it.

Use this bequest for your happiness. I want you never to marry again from necessity. I have left some books to Jean-Pierre in thanks to a spirited opponent and friend. My books and your father's which are in my library I know Edward will enjoy.

God Bless you.

Your friend,

Harriet

On the day that I was to present my children to His Majesty, I looked at them both with such love and such pride.

Edward looked small and grave but wore his velvet doublet and breeches and lace-edged shirt with assurance. As if, for all the world, this was how he usually dressed – instead of the comfortable broadcloth clothes he always wore in the country.

Lucinda was wearing a gown of palest blue satin, the sleeves ruched and slit to reveal a cream taffeta lining. Her petticoat was also of cream taffeta with tiny blue satin rosebuds trimming it.

Her hair was auburn like mine and curled naturally. As she was so young, she wore it simply, falling over her shoulders and with a fringe of kiss curls across her forehead.

I felt such pride as I fastened the Gloriana necklace around her throat.

'Your father gave me this. One day it must go to Edward's bride, but wear it now with my love.'

The sapphires glinted in the light from the window. Lucinda looked truly beautiful.

We went by coach to the Palace of Whitehall. It had been arranged with the Lord Chamberlain that Lucinda and Edward would be presented when His Majesty returned from the Playhouse. I knew from my own experience that that could be anything from five to seven o'clock, depending on whether or not a pretty young actress had caught the King's eye.

But there was much to divert my children as we waited. As a little girl, of course, Lucinda had been to the Palace. But after the quietness of Somerton, the noise, hustle and bustle of courtiers coming and going, members of the Government pacing through the long corridors, the endless chiming of His Majesty's clocks and yapping of his twenty or so dogs, seemed little short of Bedlam.

Then I heard a dear remembered voice at my side.

'Lady Kelsey? And can this be little Lucinda?'

I turned and looked into my love's eyes. Guy was there. He took my hand and bowed low over it. I curtsied, as did Lucinda.

'Edward,' I said, trying to keep my voice steady, 'this is a kinsman of my first husband. My Lord, this is my son, Sir Edward Kelsey.'

Edward made a good stab at a courtly bow but it was a little wobbly and I loved him for it. I saw the amusement in Guy's eyes. And something else – yes, envy. Moll, who always seemed to know all the latest gossip, had told me that Guy's second wife, after ten years of marriage, still had not provided a son and heir to the Earldom.

'May I call on you, Lady Kelsey?'

'Yes, that would be delightful. We would all like that.'

I had laid slight emphasis on the word 'all' because I had no intention of compromising my reputation, not only for my own sake but for that of my children.

Then the babble around us grew louder and from the renewed barking of the dogs I knew that King Charles had returned to his Palace.

Lucinda and I curtsied low as did all the ladies as His Majesty entered the Banqueting Hall. All the gentlemen doffed their hats and bowed. Once again,

Edward made his much practised but none too successful bow.

As I straightened up I saw His Majesty for the first time in eleven years – and was shocked by what I saw. His build was still slim but the lines of debauchery were deep on his face. I had heard that he had a new nickname, 'Old Rowley' after one of the Royal stallions. I wondered how such a clever man could be such a fool where women were concerned. Certainly one would not expect a King to be faithful to his Queen, the marriage being one of State necessity not love. But to have so many mistresses and, it was rumoured, still visit brothels in London, Newmarket, Oxford, wherever the Court went, was surely likely to endanger his health? The clap made no distinction between King and commoner.

I was brought out of my thoughts by a loud shriek and a raucous cockney voice shouting, 'Gawd, love us, it's our Jess!'

The next thing I knew I was being hugged and kissed by little Nelly Gwynne. Even in far off Somerton we had heard tell that the orange girl turned actress I had known at Drury Lane was now the King's favourite mistress, but I had expected her to be changed. To have become grand. After all, her son by His Majesty had been created Duke of St Albans. But here she was, and in the presence of the King, as buoyant and delightfully vulgar as ever. Nelly might be vulgar but she would never be common. There was an honesty and robustness about her that was irresistible.

The only thing that puzzled me was why she was wearing black.

'Nelly! It's wonderful to see you. But why are you in mourning?'

'Oh!' she cried in a voice that could carry to the back of the Theatre Royal and so would easily reach the King. 'His other whore, Louise de Keroualle . . .' she mimicked a high-born lady as she said the name '. . . is in mourning for one of her relatives. A French duke, no less! I am therefore in mourning for the Cham of Tartary, don't yer know?'

His Majesty threw back his head and roared with laughter. He turned and moved quickly towards us. I could see that he was still sprightly of step and that the eyes in his well-worn face were still bright and merry. He pulled Nell to him and kissed her heartily. Then he slapped her bottom.

'Nelly, you're a devil! But what would I do without you?'

'Find another whore, no doubt, Sire! Your Majesty, you know Jesslyn Warwick?'

The King's eyes were upon me. 'Mistress Warwick . . . Now Lady Kelsey, I understand? I was sorry to hear of your husband's death. And sorry too that when the playhouses opened again, you were not amongst our company.'

'Thank you, Your Majesty,' I said, curtseying and kissing his hand. 'May I present my daughter, Lucinda Warwick, and my son, Edward Kelsey?'

This time Edward made his low bow perfectly. The King patted him on the head affectionately. I remembered how kind he'd been to Lucinda when she was a little girl. And I thought how ironic it was that, like Guy, His Majesty lacked a legitimate heir, although he had enough illegitimate children to fill a team to play the game of football.

'Your daughter is as beautiful as you are, Lady Kelsey. You are all welcome to my Court. I hope you will grace us with your presence for some time to come.'

Then he moved on, his dogs at his heels and Nelly hanging on his arm. He might be a roué but he was surely the most intelligent and charming monarch the kingdom had ever known.

Lucinda made a beautiful bride. She had made, I was sure, a love-match. The youngest son of the Duke of Charwell, Lord Howard Beauchamp, had courted her with charm and restraint. All that summer we had picnicked, danced and dined at Court. Lucinda had many suitors. Some came to me and sought her hand. Some merely wanted her to take to bed. I did not leave my daughter alone at that increasingly depraved palace.

And yet, in spite of the unrest in the country about the King's mistresses and the lack of a Prince of Wales, His Majesty remained well loved.

My Lady Castlemaine had at last been eclipsed by Nelly and the King's newest mistress, Louise de Keroualle. Even so she had hardly gone away empty-handed. She had been created Duchess of Cleveland and given the Royal Palace of Nonsuch. Upon receiving the gift she promptly proceeded to dismantle the ancient palace and sell off both the contents and building. I doubt anyone was sorry to see her star wane.

Neither was Louise popular. This was on two counts. Firstly, she was a Roman Catholic, and secondly it was suspected she was in the pay of the French government.

Nelly had told me how a mob had surrounded her coach, swearing and threatening, thinking Louise was inside. As always my friend was nothing if not full of Cockney cheek. She told me she had put her head out of the coach's window and cried out, 'Good people, desist! I am the *Protestant* whore!'

As I watched my lovely daughter at the altar of St Margaret's I felt she was safe now. I knew that Howard loved her deeply. He had told me so with the utmost sincerity. My darling girl would never fall into the abyss of corruption and despair that had claimed me all those years ago.

Moll and Pitch and I spent our time between Somerton and the house in Soho Square. During Edward's holidays from Eton I was always at Kelsey Hall. He was such a gentle, caring boy. Edward and I would often walk across the green to Gifford's. Often we would find Pitch there before us, comfortable with Jean-Pierre Marchant. And I felt that the ghosts of my father and Harriet must smile as I heard my son take up the role of advocate. I was happy to sit, Pitch on my lap, listening to them right the wrongs of the world, past and present – and often the future also!

Soon I had a new child to love. I became a grandmother. I was thirty-four when I held Lucinda's baby boy in my arms. Surely too young to be a grandmother. But many women had grandchildren at an even younger age.

Moll and I returned to Soho Square happy but tired

for we had stayed with Lucinda throughout her labour. To know that she and the child were safe was such a relief. Such a joy.

I sat opposite Moll by the hearth in the elegant, light and spacious parlour. I was amused to note that we had both kicked off our shoes. Is this to be my life now? I thought. Mother to my children. Grandmother. Growing old in Moll's dear company. I closed my eyes and leant my head back against the chair.

'And what of you, Jesslyn?' I had thought my friend asleep.

'What of me? I'm a grandmother!'

'And still a great beauty! Many men want you. But you desire only one. Am I right?'

I sighed. 'Oh, Moll! I've never stopped loving him. But he has a wife. He is one of His Majesty's Ministers now. I must resign myself to the fact that all my feelings for Guy have to be buried in the past.'

'Why?' she asked bluntly.

'Please! I have only so much fortitude. If I felt I could, I would go to him tomorrow. But I cannot.'

'You know that he and his wife are estranged? She lives in the country hunting, haring, hawking. Killing any creature large or small that crosses her path. I gather they can hardly bear to be under the same roof with each other.'

I laughed but it was without humour. 'No wonder Guy does not have his longed for heir! But truly, Moll, how on earth can you know all this?'

'I gossip with servants!' she said smugly. 'We have only one life, Jesslyn,' she added seriously. 'The Earl entered into yet another arranged marriage. Is that any reason for you to deny your love for each other?'

'I don't want to be . . .' My voice was low. 'I don't want to be as I was.'

Moll moved to me and put her arms around my tired body.

'Lovey, you were so young! You changed. Do you not think that I know why you married Sir Thomas? To take care of Lucinda and, yes, of me too! Now you have a life to live for yourself.'

I was still so fearful of the Court's wantonness that I would not let Guy close to me. We were friendly and formal when we met but I saw the longing in his eyes as he must in mine. I had loved him since I was a girl. There had never been another man for me. I doubted there ever would be. But still I held out.

There was a masked ball and masque at the Palace in the early summer of the following year. I attended with Lucinda and my son-in-law, Howard.

Moll and I had been at Somerton for many weeks and I was longing to see my beloved daughter again. When I heard the coach stop outside the house in Soho Square I ran down the stairs to greet them myself. Just as their postillion was raising the heavy, brass door-knocker, I flung open the door and opened my arms to them.

Howard was just handing Lucinda down from the coach and I almost gasped at his appearance. The fresh faced country lad – albeit the son of a duke – that I had known had changed, in a few short weeks, into a fashionable gallant. Almost a fop. His doublet and breeches were of midnight blue satin, the sleeves slashed and lined with crimson silk. There was lace at his knees, his wrists and throat. His stockings and heeled shoes had been dyed the same crimson as the inserts to his sleeves. His plumed hat was decorated with two large ostrich feathers that had been singed and curled and dyed crimson also. It would have been a good costume for Malvolio in Will Shakespeare's *Twelfth Night*. What on earth could have possessed the dear boy? I wondered.

But then my daughter was in my arms, hugging me. I led them both up to the first-floor parlour where Moll was waiting with Rhenish and sweetmeats.

Lucinda and Howard had been to the Theatre Royal that afternoon. Then, after the performance, to the Mermaid Inn for dinner. I soon realized that they were both a little drunk, but not unattractively so. Just two young, privileged children embracing the heady life that London had to offer, with a little too much enthusiasm. Or so I told myself.

'Beaumont and Fletcher, Mama!' Lucinda said. 'How I miss Beau and Fletch! But His Majesty has promised me two pups from his favourite bitch's new litter!'

She smiled wickedly. 'Perhaps I should choose two bitches this time. I could name them Nelly and Louise!'

'Lucinda, I have no love for the Duchess of Portsmouth but Nelly is an old friend of mine and the only one of the King's mistresses who hasn't held him to ransom! By all means have two new puppies but do not do anything to hurt Nelly Gwynne.'

Lucinda pouted prettily and then shrugged.

'As you wish, Mama.'

She sipped at her wine for a moment then turned her attention to her husband.

'What do you make of Howard, Mama? Doesn't he look fine?'

Her tone was mocking but Howard, nice boy that he was, did not understand that and preened. I looked across at my daughter and wondered if she was being deliberately cruel to this kind, none too intelligent, but loving young man? For a moment, and only a moment, I saw an expression in Lucinda's eyes that I had seen in Luke's: A desire to hurt. To be dominant through pain. But I couldn't believe that Luke's soul inhabited my darling girl. Then she smiled and ran to Howard's side. She kissed him playfully and so lovingly, I pushed all thoughts of her natural father from my mind and remembered only Richard. He had loved my daughter so much and had passed on to her a feeling that life was to be lived to its fullest, but always with compassion.

There was a headiness in the air on that May evening. The war with the Dutch was in abeyance. Parliament had voted the King further funds, overlooking the fact that much of the Royal purse was spent on His Majesty's illegitimate children and avaricious mistresses, past and present. All but Nelly.

The masque itself was spectacular and devised by Richard and Killigrew's old rival, Sir William Davenant.

Afterwards there were fireworks and dancing on the lawns in St James' Park.

The park was like something from a fairy tale.

Lanterns were strung among the trees and reflected in the water on the canals that King Charles had designed to flow through the park.

Lit only by the moon and flickering torches, pavilions had been erected in the park. The beautifully draped cloth-of-gold tents could have been there simply for decoration but the Court knew they were there for seduction.

In spite of our masks there were no secrets at the Palace of Whitehall that night. I was briefly concerned to see Lucinda on the arm of the Earl of Rochester, a well-known rake only recently allowed to return to Court, having been in disgrace over a witty and pertinent rhyme found pinned to the door of His Majesty's bedchamber:

> Here lies a great and mighty King
> Whose promise none relies on;
> He never said a foolish thing,
> Nor never did a wise one.

Although His Majesty had banished Rochester for a few months it seemed the King could not deny himself for long the company of such a hedonistic and witty courtier.

This then was the mood at Court. Diversion was everything. I marvelled at how I had changed. That I longed for the simple pleasures of love and loathed the ritual of sexual dalliance.

I had danced a galliard with my son-in-law and then had wished to walk quietly through the scented gardens. As I passed a pavilion I could not help but over hear His Majesty's voice and then Nelly's, softly teasing.

I became aware of a figure standing by the opening of the pavilion. Even masked, I could not mistake Louise, Duchess of Portsmouth.

I stood for a moment in the shadows. My wish was not to pry. I simply paused, filled with sudden concern for Nelly.

The King, for all to see, pulled Nelly's breast from her dress and bent to suckle it. His other mistress moved towards the pavilion. Oh, no, Nelly! No, I thought. I'd heard rumours that the King could now only function if there were three in his bed but I hated to think that Nelly . . . Dear, honest Nelly.

Then, ringing across the night air, a cockney voice: Nelly's.

'Bugger off!'

A shout of laughter from the King and the deeply unpopular duchess pulled her cloak around her and slipped away into the shadows. Perhaps, I thought, she took comfort from the fact that, for all King Charles's love, she and Castlemaine were Duchesses while Nelly had nothing.

I walked slowly back to the dancing. A tall, heavily masked man asked for my hand to dance a pavan. I knew instantly it was Guy. I could hear the water running through the canals. I could smell the heavy night scent of flowers from the privy garden. I was Titania walking through an enchanted wood.

I danced and danced. Always with the same man. If that caused comment, for that night only, I did not care.

A cloud passed across the moon and, in that moment of darkness, Guy pulled me to him and kissed me passionately. The years melted away. He was my only love. I was his.

Lit by moonlight we danced again. But as the dance drew us close, Guy whispered to me, 'I still have that little house by the river at Chiswick. Slip away. Come with me there.'

How was I to know that Lucinda had seen me run down to the river's edge and into the waiting boat?

We could be together rarely. Partly because I was always at Somerton for Edward when he returned for the holidays, partly because of affairs of State, but mainly because of the agreed need for discretion.

But, oh, our joy in each other! I look back on that time as wondrous. At my age to have rediscovered love, both physical and spiritual. I still shivered at my lover's touch. Was still moist for him when he entered me. My life seemed complete. But there was more happiness to come, something I could not believe to be true. A little before my fortieth birthday, I knew for sure that I would bear Guy a child.

I suppose it was naive of me to hurry to my lover's apartment in Whitehall instead of waiting for our next meeting at Chiswick. But, even though my child could not inherit, I knew how Guy longed for a son or daughter.

My many petticoats and long cloak must have muffled my footsteps as I approached his rooms near the King's Privy Chamber. I briefly knocked at the door and entered. The withdrawing room was empty and I sat down to wait for Guy to give him my glad news.

Then I heard the sound of laughter from his bed-chamber. Still I did not hold back. If only I had . . .

'Guy?' I pushed open the bedchamber door – and froze. Guy was not alone in bed. He was with my daughter, Lucinda.

I felt such pain that I thought I would die from it. Lucinda looked at me coolly.

'He likes the younger version, Mama!' she giggled.

Through the mist that was blurring my eyes I realized she was a little drunk.

Guy leapt from the bed, not bothering to cover his nakedness.

'Darling!' He put his arms around me. 'This means nothing! Nothing!'

Then I felt the rage hit me. 'Nothing?..Nothing!' I shouted. 'With Edward you are the people I love most in the world! NOTHING?!!'

'Oh, for Christ's sake, Mama! Let's not have a scene! You're not exactly as pure as the driven snow, are you?' my daughter sneered. It was as if she was someone I had never met before.

'Get out!' Guy said to her coldly.

'I think not,' Lucinda replied, totally in control of her emotions.

I walked slowly to a chair and sat in it as if I was an old woman.

'Why? . . . Why? . . . Both of you . . . I don't understand. Why?'

Guy put his hand on my shoulder. 'Don't touch me!' I screamed at him. I turned on Lucinda. 'And you! What of Howard? What of your baby boy?'

'Oh, really, Mama. Howard goes his way and I go mine. Surely you understand the way of the world? I've been given to believe that you were something of a courtesan in the past.' Her beautiful eyes flickered towards Guy. 'If not indeed the present! It struck me as . . . exciting to take away my mother's lover.'

'And you, Guy? Did it strike you as exciting to betray our love?'

'She was available. Christ, Jesslyn!' he added angrily. 'Don't you know about your daughter? She's been in every bed at Whitehall. Including that old lecher the King's!'

'I'll never stop loving you, Lucinda. But I doubt I can ever forgive either of you.' I turned to Guy. 'I came here with such joy in my heart. I am to have your child.' I turned on my heel and walked from the room.

He caught my arm as I moved towards the outer door of the apartment. 'She means nothing to me, Jesslyn. Please, please forgive me! A child oh, my love. I'll divorce Annabel. She's barren. We'll marry. Please!'

But I walked away.

There was only one place for me to go. I turned my back on Guy and Lucinda. I still loved them so much, but the pain of their betrayal was more than I could bear.

Quiet days followed. I walked in the gardens of Kelsey Hall. Moll and I walked across the green to Gifford's and spent the occasional evening with Jean-Pierre. I cared not a jot that my pregnancy was increasingly obvious and I was unmarried. The village could not drive me out this time. My son was Lord of the Manor and owned it.

I tried not to be bitter about Guy and Lucinda but to calm myself for the coming of my child. At forty I was worryingly old to be bearing another. But I cast such thoughts from me.

Walking back at dusk from Gifford's, Moll suddenly chuckled and said, 'Another conquest, Jesslyn. Another man in love with you.'

I was about to say 'Nonsense' but recognized there was some truth in what she said. 'Not *in* love with me. He loves me as a friend. Yes, and as a woman. But it is a mature love. Something without passion that could last. I could love Jean-Pierre in return like that.'

Messengers came with letters from Guy – begging, pleading, finally threatening. I wondered how I had given my love to him for so many years without realizing his selfishness. His ruthlessness.

His final letter simply stated that he had petitioned Parliament for a divorce. He would ask the King to intercede. To demand that his child be handed over to him.

I wept as I held my baby son in my arms for I had no doubt that Guy would carry out his threat. He was an immensely powerful nobleman, a Minister of the Crown.

I could only wait and pray.

On the day after the birth of my baby boy, Jean-Pierre came to me.

'Jesslyn, at this time I will not talk of my feelings for you. But Moll has told me of your fears for your son and I have a plan. I have talked this through with your young but, oh so wise, son, Edward.'

'Yes?' I replied, not believing that anything could

stop Guy when backed by the King's command.

'I have a small estate in Normandy. Not grand, but the land is gentle and from the upper windows of my farmhouse you can see the sea. I could make you happy there, Jesslyn.'

'But the King's men would follow.'

'Not if you were dead.'

I stared at him in astonishment. 'Dead?'

'You will have a birth-fever. Your baby son will not survive either. A coffin will be brought to your bedchamber.' Jean-Pierre smiled. 'You are small, Jesslyn. It will not take many books to weigh it. Edward and Moll will grieve and see you buried. The Earl of Colne, with all his money and power, will also grieve and no doubt erect an elaborate tomb. But you and your son . . . and, yes, old Pitch . . . will be with me in Normandy. Under cover of darkness a clipper run by the Gentlemen will see us across the Channel. What do you say?'

'Moll, you would follow on?'

'Do you doubt it, lovey? And Edward, as a young gentleman, would need to make the Grand Tour. To travel often.'

'Lucinda?'

Moll shook her head sadly. 'Perhaps one day, lovey. Perhaps one day.'

I knew she was lying.

Some pain has to be borne, Jesslyn. For the joy of life.

CHAPTER
NINETEEN

THE CAT

'Come away, come away, death –'
                    – William Shakespeare

CATHERINE: 1992

'Not to destroy but to fulfil'
— St Matthew

I dressed carefully for the shareholders' meeting. Power dressing wasn't exactly my style but I knew it was important that I looked like a confident, wealthy woman. I decided on a cream linen trouser suit, which I wore with a white silk blouse and the Kelsey pearls. Cat watched from my bed as I dressed and made up. I'd been a little hurt when I returned home to find that he totally ignored me for about twelve hours. Then, as if deciding that I'd been punished enough for leaving him, he jumped on to my lap and rubbed his head against my face, purring loudly.

The couple of days before the meeting had been busy. I'd had a long meeting with Mr Fortescue, checking every aspect of what I intended to do.

I'd seen Brett briefly. He laughed delightedly when he first saw me as I opened the door of the Hall to him.

'My God, girl! I see what you mean. You *have* grown up. How was your trip?'

'I was shown great kindness by one or two people, and I was given a very important lesson – a hard lesson – but I've learnt from it.'

'And that is?'

'The meek *don't* inherit the earth! Can I get you a

442

drink? I'm about to open a bottle of Chardonnay if that appeals.'

'It appeals!'

We sat in the Little Parlour and sipped our wine. The glasses were, of course, Kelsey glass. I touched their loveliness.

'What on earth does Jonas think he's playing at?'

'I can't see there's any villainy in it. Just stupidity.'

'Not a very useful attribute in a managing director,' I said tartly.

Brett looked at me penetratingly. 'You have learnt some lessons while you've been away, haven't you? Have you . . . have you been hurt, mavourneen?' he added gently.

'A little,' I replied lightly. This was no time to tell Brett about my father nearly breaking my heart. Or that in doing so he'd given me the impetus to govern my own life.

'You were saying, about Jonas . . .?'

'His argument is that with the recession we must find ways to cut costs. The man's mad! Glass is a luxury item. Of course sales are hit in a recession, but if we lose our reputation through making an inferior product, where will we be when people start buying again? And they will. Humans can only live without beauty for so long.'

'There's another thing. There are magnificent shops in Beverly Hills. There's a lot of incredibly wealthy people there. People who like and appreciate good things. I couldn't find one shop that sold Kelsey glass. Waterford, yes! Caithness, yes! Why haven't we gone after that market?'

Brett shrugged, then smiled at me. 'I told you a long time ago you should be running the glassworks.'

'I'm not ready for that yet,' I replied seriously. 'But I'm ready to take care of my inheritance.'

Kelsey Glass being a privately owned company, there were very few of us seated in the boardroom for the meeting. Sir James and Marcus representing their thirty per cent holding, Jonas as managing director, the company secretary and myself.

Sir James had kissed me lightly on the cheek when we met. Marcus had hugged me to him and whispered, 'By God, Catherine, California agreed with you!'

Jonas was the last to arrive, huffing in importantly, a number of files under one arm, a bulging briefcase in his other hand.

After the formalities had been completed, he looked at me and said, 'Well, Catherine, your lackey called this meeting. What have you to say?'

'Firstly, that I will vote you off the board if you do not immediately apologize for calling one of the most brilliant glassmakers of his generation, my lackey!'

If a pin had dropped it would have been too loud. My Uncles James and Marcus were suddenly very engrossed in the papers in front of them.

I suddenly realized I was beginning to enjoy this! I looked across at Jonas and waited.

After a few moments, he smiled.

'Silly to fall out when we all have one thing in common . . . an interest in the success of Kelsey Glass. Didn't mean to offend you, old girl. Or Fitzgerald. Er, take it back, all right?'

I nodded, but it wasn't all right. His attitude had set

the tone of the meeting. Mainly patronizing. Definitely hostile.

'Would you like me to come straight to the point, Jonas? Uncle James? Uncle Marcus?' I didn't wait for their assent. 'I've been given to understand that our managing director is about to put into action plans to reduce the lead content of Kelsey crystal by four per cent. Is that correct?' I looked askance at Jonas.

'I intend to do that, yes!' he replied curtly.

'Without consulting the shareholders?' I asked. 'Uncle James, Uncle Marcus, I don't know your feelings about this but from the latter part of the seventeenth century we've been making crystal to the original Ravenscroft formula we bought under patent. I care about that! Yes, yes, Jonas, I can see from your expression you're questioning that from a johnny-come-lately who entered your lives a little more than a year ago! I surprised myself with the passion I felt. But I've struggled to learn. To teach myself about the "Art of Fire". And I've grown to love it!' I took a deep breath.

'I won't allow you to destroy my inheritance, Jonas.'

'Your inheritance? YOUR INHERITANCE!' He banged his hand angrily on the table.

'I think you're out of line, old son,' Marcus said quietly. But Marcus being quiet was rather like a grizzly bear snoozing.

Jonas was too angry to heed the warning tone.

'It should have been *my* inheritance! If I'd had my way, I'd have contested the old fool's sanity in leaving everything to you. My father . . .' he indicated Sir James '. . . wouldn't hear of it! Family honour and all

445

that. And where has it got us? I've a load of debts because I borrowed against my future income. My father Sir James, holder of a proud title, is living in a gamekeeper's cottage instead of the Hall. While you . . .'

'Shut up, Jonas!' Sir James spoke softly but with great authority. 'You're my only child and I love you. But, by God, a lot of the time, I don't like you!'

I saw the hurt in Jonas's eyes then and realized that this bombastic, in my view unlikeable, man needed the approval of his father. Was perhaps in his own way as insecure as I was. He was part of my family and I knew I must reach out to him. I also knew that nothing I could offer, except the Kelsey inheritance, would be enough for him. Or, indeed for Annabel.

There was silence whilst we all addressed our own thoughts. Our own attitudes. Finally I broke that silence.

'Jonas, I hope you can work with me. I hope you can understand the admiration I feel for Kelsey glass and for the craftsmen who, for over three hundred years, have dedicated themselves to it. Yes, for reward, but also for a sense of achievement. I sincerely hope that before I call for a vote you'll drop the idea of – how shall I put it? – dishonouring our glass.'

Jonas simply stared at me.

'Very well,' I said with as much authority as I could muster. 'As a family company, I'm very sad that it has come to this. I'm so sorry, Uncle James, Marcus, but as a matter of record I'm going to ask you to vote on this issue.'

'If you vote against me, I'll resign!' Jonas interrupted.

Marcus sat back in his chair. 'Well, old son, that could be the making of you. Then you'd have to hold down a job instead of a sinecure. I vote against Jonas's policy, Catherine.'

I looked at Sir James. There was a pause as he looked at Jonas, his only son.

'Oh, I'm so sorry!' I said. 'Look, it won't make any difference. We have eighty per cent of the shares against the managing director's policy. Uncle James, vote your shares for Jonas.'

I saw him clench his hands, sadly twisted at the joints by arthritis. He looked down at the table for a moment then raised his head.

'I vote against the managing director,' he said with a clear voice.

Jonas sat for a moment, stunned. He had gambled on my being an insignificant woman. Someone who'd be easy to control. He had gambled and lost.

As I walked across the green to Gifford's that evening, I knew that after we had dined Brett and I would make love. But this time as equals.

Not because I'd won in the boardroom. Not because my hair had been re-styled, my make up expertly designed. But because a dear man, Robert Ashley, had given me what I needed most in the world: a sense of myself.

It amazed me that I felt so complete at Gifford's. I sat with Brett and told him about the meeting.

'So Jonas is out? No turning back?'

'I can't see how that could possibly happen. His pride . . . But also, if I'm going to hold faith with all the master craftsmen, all the families whose lives have been linked with the glassworks, and perhaps with my grandfather – how can I compromise?'

'Someone's got to run the glassworks,' Brett said as he lifted me into his arms.

'Mmm,' I replied, kissing him. 'I thought perhaps Rupert . . .'

His lips were on my mouth. His tongue seeking. Finding.

'Rupert . . . Shrewd lady! I told you a long time ago . . .'

We never finished our conversation.

I was in Brett's arms in the bedroom under the eaves. The tiny windows were open and the smell of early summer drifted over us. An ancient gnarled apple tree stood by the window and at one point in the night I stirred when an owl hooted and noisily blundered from it.

Oh, the joy of being in my love's arms again. He'd lowered me gently onto the bed and slowly undressed me, at every stage kissing, and caressing.

Then I responded, helping him to undress. Our need became urgent but there was so much tenderness. Anything, everything I had known before, every unhappy experience, was cast aside in the beauty of those moments.

Brett made me feel precious. And, even if he didn't love me, I felt he had need of me. Perhaps even a longing for me.

I moaned as his tongue flicked over my breasts. Instinctively my hand reached out for him. I felt how hard he was. How ready for me. But still he made love to me.

Then he was inside me. I instinctively thrust my body to his rhythm, experiencing such joy.

Such beauty. Love me or not, when I fell asleep in Brett's arms, I knew he was the only man I would ever want.

Early the next morning I slipped across the green to the Hall to bathe and change my clothes. Cat was sitting on the bridge which crossed the moat, for all the world as if he was waiting for me. And perhaps he was.

I picked him up and he clambered on to my shoulder, leaning his silky body against the side of my head. I whispered my apologies for having left him alone all night. Then, suddenly, I had a sharp image of Cat curled up in front of the fire at Gifford's. Totally at home.

I was, Catherine, with my Lady.

I drove to the glassworks, going over in my mind things I'd been considering since Brett's call to me in California. I knew I had learnt a great deal about glass. I certainly wanted to return to California to sell Kelsey Glass and then try New York. Brett's work deserved recognition in the States. But I knew I wasn't ready for the day-to-day running of the business.

I'd thought long and hard about Rupert. For all his lightweight manner I remembered the authority with which he'd introduced me to the making of our glass. His knowledge and dedication went far beyond what was required of a Public Relations man.

Briefly I remembered my fears that my life had been in danger. But again I came back to a point of sanity that told me that only Uncle James or Jonas had a motive for killing me. And I couldn't believe it of either of them, although Jonas must be hating my guts now. And I knew I could trust my Knight's Croft cousins.

After the shareholders' meeting the day before I'd sounded out both of my uncles on the idea of offering Jonas's position to Rupert. I'd assured my Uncle James that I'd try to change Jonas's mind about resigning. I'd felt so much admiration for the old man when he'd said simply, 'Don't, Catherine. It pains me to say it but I should never have made way for him.' He briefly indicated the gnarled joints of his hands. 'The enemy within defeated me, I'm afraid. And we're talking business here, not family. I've watched young Rupert, he's a good choice. But he needs the support of you and Joe.' He looked across at Marcus.

'My brother and I have had our differences in the past. In a strange way, Catherine, you've made me see what a strong thing a family is. We squabble and feud, but at the end of the day we cling together. Marcus.' He took his brother's hand between his two crippled hands. 'There's been a lot of rivalry and resentment between us in the past. I'm too old for that now! I want my brother back . . . and I think your son can succeed where mine failed.'

I met with Joe and Rupert at the glassworks and told them of the decisions that had been made: Rupert to be appointed managing director, Joe and I to join the board. They were both stunned. I thought wryly that this was the only time since I'd known him that Rupert had been lost for words. I admired him for what he said next.

'And what about Jonas? I can't pretend I think he's been good news for Kelsey Glass . . . but he's always been pushed to try too hard, you know. By Uncle James, to follow in his footsteps. By Annabel, to be a great social success. On the one hand he's been handed everything on a plate. On the other he's been trying to please everyone but himself.'

I thought of the moment when Jonas had looked at his father, longing for approval, and my realization of how alike we were. But I couldn't allow him to ruin Kelsey Glass.

'I've written reassuring him that he'll receive a handsome golden handshake. Oh, don't worry. Not from Kelsey Glass. From my own funds. After that, it's up to him what he makes of his life'.

I was so pleased when Sophie telephoned me that evening and asked me over to Knight's Croft for supper. I'd telephoned to say Hello on my return from California but had not had a chance to see her. I'd missed her.

'I telephoned Brett to ask him over but his answer phone is on. Apparently he's gone to some meeting.'

'Yes,' I replied. 'The gallery that mounted his exhibition last year want to do another. It's very exciting for him, I think. Especially in these hard times.'

'Too warm for stew but there's quiche in the freezer and I'll dig some potatoes and there's salad from the garden. Is that all right?'

'All right? Sophie, when did you ever ask me that before? Of course it's all right. I can't wait.'

'It's just that . . . from what I hear . . . you've changed. I hope you still like me?' she said in her breathy, almost child-like voice.

'Oh, come on, Sophie! I grew up a little, that's all. Please never think I'm anything but your dear friend.'

'Whatever happens?'

'Whatever happens!'

As I walked across the green in the golden, early evening light, I was struck again by the timelessness of the village. How many stories had these old houses to tell? I wondered.

A child's pony on a long rope was grazing on the green. From the rear of one of the cottages a mower could be heard. The widow who ran the Post Office and General Stores was working in her garden and waved to me. It was an incredible contrast to the excitement and bustle of Los Angeles but, much as I had enjoyed that, in spite of my father's betrayal, I felt very much at peace as I walked towards the kitchen door of Knight's Croft.

Everything was as I had remembered it. Untidy, welcoming, lived in. I'd decided to walk across a little earlier as I had often done in the past, to help Sophie with the supper.

There was no sign of either Sophie or Marcus. Salad herbs and a Cos lettuce had been washed and were on the draining board. Also a bowl of small, thick-skinned outdoor tomatoes. I picked one up. It smelt of summer.

I turned as I heard the kitchen door open and Sophie was there, carrying a trug full of freshly dug potatoes. Even wearing a floppy old cotton tee-shirt, an apparently unironed linen skirt and grubby plimsolls, her beauty shone. Once again I wondered that such a creature seemed to be content to stay in Somerton, keeping house for her father and brothers.

She put down the trug and then ran across the room to hug me.

'Oh, Catherine, I've missed you so.'

'And I you. I really have, Sophie.'

She caught hold of my hands and stepped back, holding me at arm's length.

'Wow! So you've finally discovered you're good-looking. About time too! Seriously, Catherine, you look marvellous. Your hair. Your make up. But it's more than that. You know who you are now, don't you?'

I smiled at her perception. 'Sort of! Look, I came a bit early so that I could help. Shall I make a start on scrubbing the potatoes?'

'Thanks. If you would, I can make the salad dressing. This isn't nearly grand enough for your homecoming.'

'I don't want anything grand. I just want to eat your delicious food and sit around the kitchen table with the family again.'

Sophie was pouring wine for us. She frowned. 'Might be just Marcus and me, although I *think* Rupert will be back in time for supper. Here.' She handed me a glass of wine.

'Marcus will be back in a moment. He's looking forward to seeing you but he's taken Lottie for her walk. Honestly! Everyone walks that dog except Rupert and she's *his* dog!'

We started to get the supper ready, companionably chatting of this and that. Suddenly Sophie said, 'I am sorry I couldn't get Brett to come over.' She grinned mischievously. 'He's very good in bed, you know.'

Fortunately she was busy chopping garlic for the salad dressing or I know my face would have betrayed me. I turned back to the sink and started scrubbing at the potatoes fiercely. Sophie chattered on but I had no idea what she was saying. Although I'd suspected all along that she was having an affair with Brett, facing the reality of it was practically unbearable.

The bastard! I thought. The two-timing bastard! And he knew how close I was to Sophie. Try as I might I couldn't erase from my mind images of them together. Their bodies naked and entwined. Brett's lips on hers.

Marcus came in with Lottie. The silly old dog made a great fuss of me, Marcus hugged me and then poured Sophie and me more wine. Rupert dashed in just as we had given him up. We stayed a little longer in the studio, Rupert and Sophie laughing and teasing each other. Nothing had changed. Everything had.

I wanted it to be like old times. I wanted to enjoy sitting in Marcus's studio, the familiar smell of size and turps and oil paints wrestling with the scent of honeysuckle, jasmine and Sophie's herb garden. But all I could think about was Brett and Sophie.

A little after ten I rose to leave.

'Forgive me, but I haven't quite caught up with jet lag, I think. It's been a lovely evening. Thank you.'

Sophie pulled an old jacket from a peg by the kitchen door.

'I'll walk part of the way with you. It's a lovely evening.'

When we were away from the house she slipped her arm through mine.

'Actually, I'm meeting someone. None of Marcus's or Rupert's business but they do pry so!' She kissed my cheek. 'Good night, Catherine. Sweet dreams.'

She slipped away into the shadows. Don't think about it! Don't think about it! She seemed to be walking towards Gifford's. No lights were on there, but maybe that was by arrangement.

I found it hard to get to sleep that night. I'd left the door to my grandfather's bedroom, the room where my dreams had troubled me so, open. Cat had not turned up when I let myself into the Hall which was unusual. I wanted him to climb the mulberry tree and keep me company.

The grandfather clock in the hall chimed midnight and then one o'clock. Grimly I resolved to have it moved to where it could not be heard in any of the bedrooms.

At last I fell into a fitful sleep only to be awakened by the insistent ringing of the telephone. I put on the bedside light and glanced at my watch. Two o'clock.

Kelsey Hall had not joined the twentieth century enough to have telephones in the bedrooms. I ran down the hall and stairs to the library. I could only think that it was Robert Ashley phoning from California. The note I had left my father would've denied him further contact.

'Yes?' I answered breathlessly.

'Catherine, I need you! I need help!' To my

astonishment it was Sophie. 'Please, please, help me! I'll be at my favourite place.'

Then the line was dead. I was half asleep. Totally bewildered. Her favourite place? Of course! Jesslyn's tomb. She'd told me she always went there when she was troubled.

I raced back up the stairs, my mind in turmoil. What the hell was going on? Had she been with Brett then had some terrible argument about his involvement with me?

I pulled on jeans and a sweater. I'd no idea what was troubling Sophie but I cared so much for her I had to help.

I briefly looked around the kitchen for a torch but, looking through the windows, the moonlight was now so bright, I decided not to waste any more time.

An empty church in darkness is eerie. Why is that so? We should feel reassured by the silence. By the presence of those who have gone before us. But as I pushed open the heavily studded oak door, I felt overwhelmed by the silence.

'Sophie?' I whispered. Then more loudly: 'Sophie!'

The moonlight was streaming through the stained glass windows, casting strange shadows on the floor of the aisle. Her favourite place was Jesslyn's tomb but as I drew near there was no sign of her.

'Sophie!' I called again softly.

I looked around the body of the church, fearful for some reason that harm had come to her.

Then I saw it: candlelight flickering from the open entrance to the Kelsey crypt.

'Who's there? Sophie? It's me, Catherine!' I called out as I moved towards the crypt.

She was sitting on the floor of the crypt, her arms wrapped tightly around herself. She was rocking to and fro, sobbing. The word 'keening' came to mind.

I ran to her and knelt down by her. I put my arms around her and hugged her to me.

'Sophie! Sophie! Tell me what's happened. Oh, my dear!' I held her as close as I could. 'You're safe now! Tell me. I'll do anything to help you.'

She struggled to control the rasping sobs that wracked her slight body.

'I . . . I met Jonas tonight. There's an old boathouse on the estuary. Very isolated. We always meet there . . .'

'I don't understand! Why do you meet Jonas?'

She didn't answer me, just stared. Her large eyes swam with tears and the flickering candlelight threw strange shadows over her beautiful face. She looked ethereal . . . eternal . . . crouched amongst the remains of our long dead ancestors.

'You're giving Jonas money, aren't you?'

'Is that what's worrying you, Sophie? Of course I am. He resigned as managing director but I pushed him into it. It's only fair that he should have the means to start a new life for himself.'

'Yes, a new life!' she said bitterly. 'Thanks to you, a new life – and without me! He . . . he told me that he and Annabel are going to sell the house, settle their debts and try to find each other again. But he doesn't love that old crone. He loves me! Me! And so I told him what I'd tried to do for him. What I would do for him. Then we could both have the Hall . . . the Kelsey inheritance. You see, Catherine, I've always known it would be mine one day.'

'Sophie, it's freezing in here. Let me take you home. I honestly don't understand any of this but we can talk in the morning. Or I'll stay with you tonight, if you wish.'

She gripped my arm so tightly that I gasped as her nails sank into my flesh.

'I love them so, Catherine,' she whispered. 'My favourite is Jesslyn but I love them all. And I saw a way to get what I'd always wanted. Get Jonas away from Annabel and everything he inherited would also be mine. It was so simple. The best plans are, you know.'

I suddenly shivered. Not only from the intense cold but because I saw opening up before me Sophie's poor tortured soul.

'It was so easy, Catherine.' She smiled then added slowly, 'I'm very, very good in bed.'

She suddenly pulled away from me and rose to her feet, running her hands down her body sensuously. 'Look at me. Do you honestly think Annabel could compete with me? Jonas was mad for me! He would have divorced her and made me Lady Kelsey, I know he would.'

She turned and looked at me and for the first time I felt frightened of her.

'He would have married me . . . but for you!'

I stared at her. Everything fell into place. Her strange obsession with the Kelseys. With the crypt. With the dead. After I had nearly drowned, I'd suspected Annabel. But another woman in Jonas's life . . . a woman who believed he would marry her . . . a woman who wanted the Kelsey inheritance more than anything else on earth, had just as strong a motive.

'It was you,' I whispered. 'You tried to drown me!'

'Oh, yes! Yes!' She caught my wrist again and I was amazed at her strength. 'I was so clever! I walked Lottie up there in the morning and hid my diving things in the reeds. I slipped back there at dusk and waited. Waited for you! When I heard your car arrive I slipped into the water and undid the jubilee clips. I knew it would only take minutes for the water to rush in. A yacht had gone down on the Blackwater like that only months before. Once you were on the barge I climbed on board and jammed the door.

'You should have drowned, you should! Then Jonas would have got what you'd taken from him! From me!'

I tried to force myself to be calm but I was truly frightened. 'Sophie, that's all in the past. I'll do everything I can to help you . . .'

She shook her head with infinite sadness.

'I'm sorry, Catherine. It's too late. I wanted so to hate you yet I started to love you. You were the sister I should have had. But you have everything and I have nothing . . .'

She smiled at me, truly sweetly, and I knew terror then.

'I want us to be even, Catherine. If I can't have the Kelsey legacy, neither can you!'

Too late I remembered her telling me about Rupert shutting her and Joe into the crypt as a childish prank. I leapt to my feet but she was too quick for me.

The heavy, marble door slammed shut before I could get to the steps from the crypt. From my tomb.

I shouted, I pleaded, I screamed. My fingers bled from my desperate clawing at the crypt's door. But the Kelseys who had entered here would have had no thought of an exit. I was literally entombed.

I looked at the candle. It would tell me when the end was near. Lack of oxygen would snuff it out.

I weighed options in my mind. Whether to shout and use up air or not? How foolish! At least make a noise in the faint hope that someone would hear rather than prolong my death by a few hours.

I had a purpose. To live! I made myself be methodical, believe that I could survive. I held my watch in my hands and timed the intervals before I would cry – no, scream – for help.

The candle flickered. I willed it to stay alive, as I was willing myself. It spluttered and died. How to tell of the terror that engulfed me then? I started to fight for breath.

Think of the good things. Think of Fran, think of Robert, think of Cat. But most of all, think of my love for Brett.

As I slipped into what I knew to be my final sleep, I was sure that Cat was with me. Not in the spiritual sense but nudging my face, patting me with his paws, walking over my body. Anything to keep me awake.

The next thing I remember is Brett holding me in his arms. I think I was lying in the churchyard. I was alive!

'Catherine! How on earth . . .? Dear God!' He was rubbing my hands. Then I felt him wrap his coat around me. I opened my eyes. 'Catherine. Oh, my dear one!'

I clung to him and started to sob. From relief that I had survived and from a sense of great sorrow for what my inheritance had done to Sophie.

He took me back to Gifford's, I couldn't face going back to the Hall.

Brett wrapped me in a blanket and I lay on the sofa sipping brandy as he lit a fire in the hearth. I found that I couldn't stop shaking, both from shock and from the cold of the crypt. Once the fire was lit Brett took me in his arms and held me close. After a while I started to feel warmth spreading through my body. But still I clung to him.

Brett stroked my face. 'Can you tell me about it, Catherine? Can you tell me what happened?'

How to tell him that his lover had tried to kill me? I hesitated for a moment then took a deep breath.

'I wish I didn't have to tell you this . . . I know about you and Sophie, you see.'

'Know?' he interrupted. 'What is there to know? We had a brief affair a few years ago and then drifted apart. We stayed friends but were never really suited to each other. Sophie likes to be the centre of attention and I think she didn't like that I . . . well . . . that I loved my work more than her.'

'I thought that you were still seeing her,' I said slowly. 'At first I thought you were the man in Sophie's life who was making her unhappy . . . I know differently now but I imagined you still cared for her.'

'Why, Catherine? Why?'

'Because you never said . . . This is hard for me, Brett. You've never said that you . . .'

'Loved you? No! I've never said I loved you. But I

do, Catherine.' He held me close. 'I've been frightened to admit it, even to myself. I saw what love did to my mother and father. I suppose that's why I've shied away from commitment. From truly giving myself.' He kissed me very gently. 'I've never told anyone that I loved them before. I'm saying it to you, Catherine. In a strange way that's how I came to find you . . . I got home too late to call on you so I just had a nightcap and went to bed.'

His arms tightened around me. 'I had a most terrible dream. I dreamt that you'd died and I'd never had the chance to tell you I loved you. The person I cared about most in the world was gone from me. I awoke with a start and found that there were tears on my face. I knew it was only a dream but I couldn't rest until I knew you were safe . . . had told you what you meant to me.'

'Oh, Brett.' I reached out and touched his face. 'I love you so much. But I don't understand. If you were going to the Hall, why come to the church?'

'I don't think I had any choice in the matter! I was halfway across the green when I saw Cat. He was sitting quite still as if waiting for me. I walked on towards the Hall but he kept walking in front of my feet, almost tripping me. I decided to pick him up and carry him to the Hall, it seemed the easiest thing to do, but he ran off in the direction of the church. Then sat down again, looking at me. Every time I got near he repeated this until I was virtually at the church gate.'

I remembered how Cat had led me to the church on my first day at Somerton. How strange.

'I could probably be certified for saying this but I

462

knew that that little animal wanted me to follow him. So, I did. He led me straight to the Kelsey tomb. I would've turned and left the church but Cat kept pawing at the entrance to the tomb. I thought I heard a slight moan. And, thank Christ, I opened the tomb and found you . . . What happened, Catherine? Did someone lock you in there? And if so, why, for God's sake?'

'For the Kelsey inheritance! Under the terms of my grandfather's will, if I die without having a child the whole estate goes to Uncle James and then to Jonas.'

'Jonas? He locked you in there? I've never liked the man but I wouldn't have thought him capable of doing something so terrible!'

'No, not Jonas, I'm sorry to tell you this, Brett . . . It was Sophie. She and Jonas have been having an affair. She expected him to marry her. In time she would have become Lady Kelsey . . . Lived at the Hall. She's obsessed with the Kelseys. I used to think it strange the way she cared so much for the family and its history. I just didn't realize her obsession was making her sick. Unbalanced. She convinced herself that I was her enemy.' I covered my face with my hands. 'God, but it was terrifying!'

'You're safe now, darling. No one will harm you again.'

Brett rocked me in his arms then carried me up to bed. I lay in his arms that night, not making love just being close. At some point in the night I heard a rustle in the apple tree outside the bedroom window and Cat leapt on to the end of the bed and settled down, for all the world as if he lived at Gifford's.

I slept fitfully. Just before dawn, we heard the sirens.

Brett ran to the front windows and looked out.

'Christ, Catherine! It's the Hall. The Hall's ablaze.'

I leapt from the bed. 'Sophie! It must be her. If she can't have it then neither can anyone else. Oh, my God, Brett. Supposing she's still in there?'

We pulled on our clothes and raced across the green. People were coming from cottages and houses and running towards the Hall.

Three fire crews were in the courtyard but it was hopeless. The Hall was timber-framed and the fire was engulfing it at a terrible speed.

The heat was incredible but even so I had only one thought: that Sophie might be in there.

I ran towards the Hall calling out her name. I was aware of being pulled back, first by a fireman, then by Brett.

'Let me go! I've got to get to her! I know she's in there!' I shouted as I struggled in Brett's arms.

He shook me. 'Stop it! Stop it, Catherine! No one could survive in there. No one can go in there. And think . . . think! If she's in there, that is what Sophie chose. Oh, Catherine, my Catherine, I know you care for her in spite of everything. She chose this!'

He held me close. 'Can you imagine her locked away? Who would wish to cage a nightingale? Let her go, Catherine, with love.'

At that moment, I don't know why, I looked up to the first floor of the house. To the room that had been my grandfather's. The room which, by tradition, had always been the bedchamber of the owner of Kelsey Hall. The room I had slept in when first I came to Somerton. The room where I'd dreamt such terrible dreams. Where I thought I'd heard Jesslyn's name being called.

Just before the roof collapsed I saw her. I saw Sophie. And the terrible thing was . . . she was smiling.

Finally it was evening. I sat in the garden at Gifford's waiting for Brett to come home. Apart from him not another living soul would ever know that Sophie had tried to kill me. Marcus, Rupert, Dickon and Joseph had enough to bear already. I grieved for the loss of my family home, but most of all I grieved for Sophie. She was right: we could have been to each other the sisters we'd never had. Instead, not because of greed or ambition but because of a warped need to belong, there was this tragedy.

Eventually I would rebuild the Hall, but life was more important than a building. I felt secure in Brett's love but knew that, although I had longed for it, I had changed. I had become my own woman.

My life would always be linked with his but I hadn't stepped out of Fran's shadow to disappear into another shade. I knew that sometimes I would come second to Brett's love of his craft. Well, sometimes he would come second to the role I now saw for myself. I had found an identity and that identity was inextricably tied to my family's fortune and its great love: the art of fire.

Cat was dozing on my lap in the early evening sun. It suddenly occurred to me that, because he was a stray, I didn't know how old he was.

I instinctively held him close. In that moment it seemed impossible to me that I would one day lose him.

I will always be with you, Catherine, as I am with my Lady. I do not heed Time, nor Place, nor Death. Wait for me.

ACKNOWLEDGEMENTS

My thanks to:
Theatre Museum, Covent Garden;
Caithness Glass, Kings Lynn;
Robert Blakeborough, not only for his knowledge but for his infinite patience in answering my questions about company law.

SELECT BIBLIOGRAPHY

Cathcart Borer, Mary: *The Story of Covent Garden*
Falkus, Charles: *The Life and Times of Charles II*
Fraser, Antonia: *King Charles II*
Harwood, Ronald: *All The World's a Stage*
Honey, W.B.: *English Glass*
Hutton, Ronald: *Charles II*
Kenyon, J.P.: *Stuart England*
Nagler, A.M.: *A Source Book of Theatrical History*
Pepys, Samuel: *His Diary* (ed. Richard Latham)

More Enthralling Fiction from Headline:

Wychwood

E V THOMPSON

His magnificent new saga

Dolly Quilter leaps at the chance to take her son Sebastian out of the festering London slums to the household of Sir Nelson Fettiplace. The baronet's large estate on the edge of the Wychwood Forest, in the Cotswolds, seems the ideal place for Seb to regain his failing health.

But Swinbrook Manor proves a false haven, and – with the help of the Manor's head groom and his daughter, Carrie – the pair eventually find a home with the kindly farmer, Christian Timms. Here Seb grows strong and sturdy, and discovers he has a natural skill with horses. But a fateful encounter with a beautiful woman has already thrown the young man's emotions into turmoil. For Anna is a gypsy and her way of life is completely alien to Seb's own.

Torn between his romantic inclinations and pressure from his mother – who hopes he and Carrie will make a match – Seb finds himself caught up in an upheaval that goes beyond the merely personal: for the ancient forest of Wychwood is as doomed as the way of life of the gypsies who inhabit it, and Seb must take on the might of the Establishment before he can follow the dictates of his heart.

'Well researched and appealingly done...a slice of English history that is of perennial interest' *The Sunday Times*

Praise for E.V. Thompson's previous novels
'A vigorous and fascinating piece of storytelling from the pen of a first-class professional' *Sunday Telegraph*
'Romantic adventure unfolds in masterly style' *Today*
'An engrossing read' *Best*
'Excellent characters enhance a fine tale' *Liverpool Daily Post*

FICTION/SAGA   0 7472 3918 5

PETER LING

HIGH WATER

A girl grows to womanhood
in London's East End docklands

When seventeen-year-old Ruth Judge finally rejects the harsh values of her stern, authoritarian father, she leaves home, finding refuge at The Three Jolly Watermen, a docklands pub run by the O'Dells and their two sons, Sean and Connor.

Ruth is attracted – and not a little frightened – by Connor's fierce masculinity, but it is Sean's easy charm that seduces her, and she marries him; even though this means an inevitable rift with her family.

Marriage does not solve all Ruth's problems. Sean's fecklessness and Connor's brooding presence have an unsettling effect on her, and while the close-knit East End community provides warmth and humour, the sinister influence of the Brotherhood – a secret society of dock-workers, controlled by the Judge family – casts a dark shadow over the Isle of Dogs, and a shocking punishment results in violent death.

1914 brings many changes to the Island; with their menfolk away at war, the women face hardship and poverty with cheerful stoicism. When her son Daniel is born during an air-raid, Ruth resolves to put the past behind her and make a fresh start with Sean... But there are many surprises still in store for Ruth before she discovers the truth about herself, and begins a new and happy life.

FICTION/SAGA   0 7472 3761 1

A selection of bestsellers from Headline

THE GIRL FROM COTTON LANE	Harry Bowling	£5.99 ☐
MAYFIELD	Joy Chambers	£5.99 ☐
DANGEROUS LADY	Martina Cole	£4.99 ☐
DON'T CRY ALONE	Josephine Cox	£5.99 ☐
DIAMONDS IN DANBY WALK	Pamela Evans	£4.99 ☐
STARS	Kathryn Harvey	£5.99 ☐
THIS TIME NEXT YEAR	Evelyn Hood	£4.99 ☐
LOVE, COME NO MORE	Adam Kennedy	£5.99 ☐
AN IMPOSSIBLE WOMAN	James Mitchell	£5.99 ☐
FORBIDDEN FEELINGS	Una-Mary Parker	£5.99 ☐
A WOMAN POSSESSED	Malcolm Ross	£5.99 ☐
THE FEATHER AND THE STONE	Patricia Shaw	£4.99 ☐
WYCHWOOD	E V Thompson	£4.99 ☐
ADAM'S DAUGHTERS	Elizabeth Villars	£4.99 ☐

All Headline books are available at your local bookshop or newsagent, or can be ordered direct from the publisher. Just tick the titles you want and fill in the form below. Prices and availability subject to change without notice.

Headline Book Publishing PLC, Cash Sales Department, Bookpoint, 39 Milton Park, Abingdon, OXON, OX14 4TD, UK. If you have a credit card you may order by telephone — 0235 831700.

Please enclose a cheque or postal order made payable to Bookpoint Ltd to the value of the cover price and allow the following for postage and packing:

UK & BFPO: £1.00 for the first book, 50p for the second book and 30p for each additional book ordered up to a maximum charge of £3.00.

OVERSEAS & EIRE: £2.00 for the first book, £1.00 for the second book and 50p for each additional book.

Name ....

Address ....

....

....

If you would prefer to pay by credit card, please complete:
Please debit my Visa/Access/Diner's Card/American Express (delete as applicable) card no:

Signature ....Expiry Date ....